I0593162

The Long Road into Hell

Beverley Young

Historical Fiction

Sunshine Coast, Queensland, Australia

First Published – 2023
This edition published by Beverley Young
Sunshine Coast, Qld Australia

Copyright © Beverley Young 2023

The National Library of Australia Cataloguing-in-Publication

Creator: Young, Beverley, author.

Title: The Long Road into Hell / Bevelery Young.

ISBN: 978-0-6457061-0-9 (paperback)

Subjects: Historical fiction.
Australian fiction writer.
Argentinian fiction.
South American history

Typeset in Times New Roman 12pt by Donna Munro Graphic Design.
Cover artwork by Donna Munro.
Printed and bound in Australia by Ingram Spark.

Dedication

To my son Anthony, the light of my life.
You make me laugh and keep me grounded. You hide your 'light under a bushel', but I know how beautiful your soul is; the greatest gift God ever gave me was you, my son.
Mum

Acknowlegements

☼

Many people have shaped my life, and no doubt, others will continue to do so. While the words on the pages are mine, they may never have seen the light of day without the encouragement, wisdom, guidance, and patience of others,

At the top of the list of helping angels is Michelle Geissel, my son's classmate, a fellow nursing student, and my much-loved friend. Her belief in my writing ability was a driving force that kept me moving forward.

A close second was Gary Crew, who attempted to turn a sow's ear into a silk purse. This coveted author, scholar, and word genius helped me understand so much more than just punctuation and grammar, inspiring in me a love of words and how they can change your life. My gratitude for his wisdom and knowledge is boundless.

To Warwick Halse Hill, thank you for lighting the spark of encouragement in my first writing group. Also, my fellow students in both Gary and Warwick's classes for their ready support, especially my friend, mentor and writing colleague Graeme Smith; his insight greatly appreciated on many occasions. I must also acknowledge invaluable information gained from reading 'Guidelines on Writing' by Jerry Jenkins, another well-published author.

To all these people, friends and family, I am deeply indebted and humbled by your generosity and love. I give you my eternal thanks.

Bev

Public Domain, https://commons.wikimedia.org/w/index.php?curid=32805

Genealogy

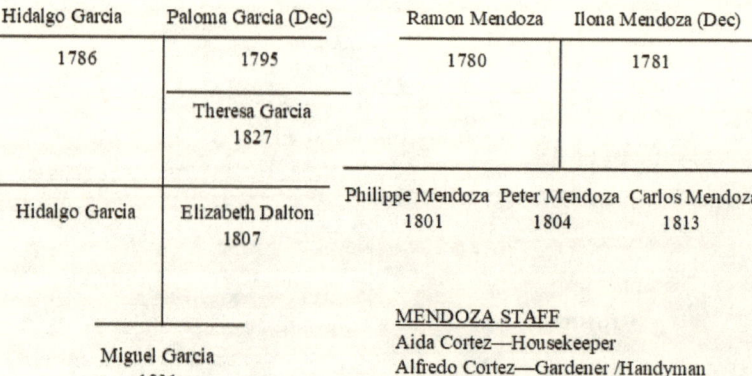

Hidalgo Garcia	Paloma Garcia (Dec)		Ramon Mendoza	Ilona Mendoza (Dec)
1786	1795		1780	1781

Theresa Garcia
1827

Hidalgo Garcia	Elizabeth Dalton	Philippe Mendoza	Peter Mendoza	Carlos Mendoza
	1807	1801	1804	1813

MENDOZA STAFF
Aida Cortez—Housekeeper
Alfredo Cortez—Gardener /Handyman

Miguel Garcia
1831

GARCIA STAFF
Elena Ruiz—Housekeeper
Josè Ruiz—Gardener /Handyman

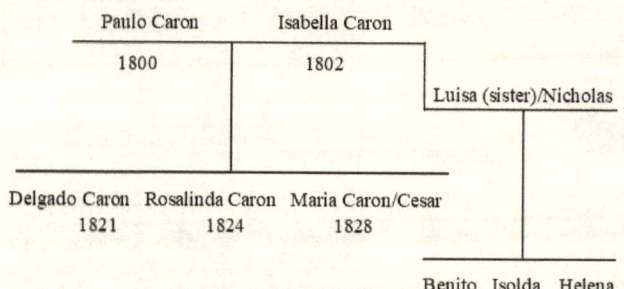

Paulo Caron	Isabella Caron
1800	1802

Luisa (sister)/Nicholas

Delgado Caron	Rosalinda Caron	Maria Caron/Cesar
1821	1824	1828

Benito   Isolda   Helena

REBEL CAMP
Pedro—Leader
Carmelita—Would-be lover of Miguel
Ernesto—Partner pf Carmelita   Alberto Diaz—Cattle Breeder. Santa Fe
Omar & Felix—Rosa's kindnappers
Arturo—Blacksmith
Thomas—Wounded team leader

Introduction

☼

Atrocities have existed throughout human history. Man's inhumanity to man is well documented. Beatings, intimidation, rape, torture and even murder were common in the quest to control nations.

Human habitation in Argentina can be traced back to the Pre-Columbian era, 11,000 years before Christ. Autonomous Indigenous tribes inhabited much of South America when the Conquistadors arrived in 1516 AD. This one event would change their lives irrevocably. A new history of Argentina was about to be written.

A nation of immense beauty and rich in natural resources, Argentina was a land of treasures yet to be discovered. Stark desert plains, volcanoes, soaring mountain ranges, deep valleys and vast forests. Eighteen hundred and sixty miles south of its capital Buenos Aires, the southernmost tip spilt into the great Southern Ocean.

This account, although fiction, fits comfortably into almost every era of an evolving Argentina. The graphic portrayal of violence, corruption, and manipulation of political power, highlights the atrocities and turmoil that dogged Argentina's early history. From the beginning, two victims' lives are inextricably entwined in their quest for justice and freedom.

Many other stories remain untold, their relevance and details hidden or lost to time. It is hoped this novel, in some small way, honours those who never had the opportunity to tell their stories or receive justifiable retribution.

The story commences in 1854 in the Pampas, the vast expanse of grassy plain spread across central Argentina. Miguel Garcia, aged twenty-four, and three travelling companions make a shocking discovery. Miguel's already shattered psyche comes one step closer to complete mental collapse.

A Date with The Devil
☼
Late Summer 1854

They'd been riding for several hours. Miguel was unwell; he winced with pain from the stab wound in his left side; it was troubling him once more. He tried not to think about it. Finally able to reflect on events of the past two months, he acknowledged he was physically and mentally exhausted.

There was little conversation exchanged within the group. Miguel had no idea about the relationship between his newly acquired riding companions, Mateo and Jamie; neither displayed any sign of camaraderie. Emilio, their guide, made it clear he had no affinity with any of them. He was none too happy playing nursemaid, saddled with the task of guiding them to the rebel camp. Suspicious of them all, his mood remained belligerent.

Emilio studied the half-gringo Miguel riding alongside. Something about him held his attention; he was not just any cowboy. It had nothing to do with the fancy boots or how he talked. There was a power about him. Emilio hadn't decided yet, whether this was a good thing or a bad thing; time would tell. He suspected the other two were opportunists, guessing they had strayed onto the wrong side of the law more than once!

Fearing detection with these greenhorns in tow, as a precaution, Emilio detoured further west than usual. The terrain was unfamiliar and hard going for the horses as they struggled through an area of dense vegetation. Razor-sharp edges of the purple tussocks reached up to the riders' stirrups, punishing the horses.

Riding through the night, the men could see city lights; Miguel suspected it was Cordoba; they gave it a wide berth. By the time the sun was high, they were well to the north—the Andean mountains in the west, little more than a blue haze.

The terrain began changing to low scrub, a welcome relief for both horses and men; you could never be sure what might be lurking in the tall grass. They were some distance from any township and might easily disturb a sleeping wildcat. Should that happen, the riders could only hope the puma's hunger was satisfied by the many red deer roaming the open plains.

The sun was relentless; the only relief the swirling *Pampero,* a cold wind blowing most of the year across this seemingly endless grassland.

Miguel wasn't faring as well as his three riding companions. He couldn't call them friends, far from it, but at present, he knew there was no choice but to depend on them.

His wound ceased weeping long ago, but under the pressure bandage, he could feel the constant throbbing and wondered if it was infected. Not that he could do anything about it. Miguel was pondering this when a putrid smell filled his nostrils. They all reacted at once.

"What the hell is that?" Jamie's screwed-up features said it all.

All four men were familiar with the smell of dead livestock, an occasional native animal, or even a wild horse. This smell was like nothing any of them had ever experienced.

Mateo winced, "Dios Mio, my God, I have never smelt carrion like that before." He could feel his stomach churning.

The horses mounted the slope of a grassy outcrop. An overpowering stench engulfed them as they reached the top; Jamie was the first to gag, then Emilio. The sound of violent retching echoed across the valley, deep, guttural. Acrid bile spewed out as they tried to purge the assault on their senses.

They looked down on the grim discovery; there was no mistaking the source; human remains protruded from the ashen earth. The patch of uneven ground was extensive, leading to the stark realisation this was the final resting place of many bodies.

Miguel stared in disbelief, fixated on the skeletal remains of an outstretched hand jutting out of the ground, one last gesture of a victim pleading to be spared. Grizzly remains to identify where a barbaric act had taken place.

Stunned by what they saw, Miguel tried to assimilate the horror into his consciousness. Mateo drew his attention to the sun striking a metal object nearby, unearthed by some scavenging animal. It was a *Facon,* a knife widely used by Gauchos for fighting, usually silver with an elaborately decorated sheath.

Despite wanting to escape from the scene, something compelled Miguel to investigate. Dismounting, he placed a bandana firmly against his mouth and nose, quickly bending to take a closer look.

Miguel's shock was profound; he had seen this knife before and held it in his hands. He remembered admiring the beautiful craftsmanship and the distinctive decoration, the way the florid engraving of the leaf motif captured the initials T.G. The knife was unique; it belonged to Tony Gonzales, a share farmer working the property adjoining one of his father Hidalgo's holdings, south-east of Cordoba. Their paths crossed several times at Agricultural Shows and livestock sales. Tony was a good man, a hard worker with a wife and three children. Miguel admired and respected him.

The government had made a paltry offer to buy his share, which he refused. Harassed and intimidated by threats to his family, like many others, it was assumed he fled without warning in an attempt to protect his wife and children. Miguel recoiled in horror, staring at the silver knife. He made the sign of the cross. The implication was all too clear.

Emilio was the first to break the stunned silence, "Let's leave this evil place; there's nothing to be done here." Overcome with fear, he broke into a trot, leaving the others to follow.

The numbing shock of the grim discovery finally permeated Miguel's senses. Mounting quickly, he jerked the horse's head roughly, the bit cutting cruelly into the side of its flaring mouth. Miguel spurred his steed hard to catch up to Jamie and Mateo, a short distance behind Emilio. Anything to get away from this place of death. The galloping horses carved a path through the sea of pampas, ironically bathed in sunlight as if this was like any other beautiful summer's day.

No distance could erase the images imprinted in Miguel's mind; terrified men and women preparing to meet their death. He could hear their screams, voices pleading to be spared, children crying. God, he had not wanted to think about children…Miguel felt the bile rise in his throat once more.

Things made more sense now. The unexplained 'departure' of neighbours and friends was no longer a mystery. It was assumed they would return when things quietened down. My God, he thought, the Alvarez family…Santos Mendio…Jose Barbados and so many others sprang to mind. From this day forward, nothing would ever be the same.

Once more, fury ignited in Miguel's heart. He remembered the horror of finding his own family brutally murdered. The weeks following were a blur of hate and bitterness, overwhelming him with the need for revenge.

Beyond any shadow of a doubt, this was the work of the ruling autocracy. They had to be stopped. The very fabric of the nation was under threat. The treachery had to end. What began as a personal vendetta was now of far greater significance; someone had to deal with the murdering swine.

With stark clarity, Miguel realised - he was that someone!

To understand how it had come to this… one needs to go back to where it all began, before Argentina found itself on the brink of anarchy…

The Garcia Dynasty

☼

1829

Hidalgo Garcia solemnly placed the flowers on the white marble slab as he did almost every week since laying his beautiful Paloma Estella Garcia to rest. After four years, his wife's passing still felt surreal, the memory as painful as when she left him.

Hidalgo placed both hands on the headstone, almost like a caress, the marble icy cold to his touch, despite the hot summer's day. A strong breeze dislodged a shower of mauve blossoms from a Jacaranda tree, brushing against him fleetingly as they fell. He took this to be a heavenly blessing. Abundant with blossom, the trees framed the hillside, edging their way along the gentle slope almost to the entrance of Our lady Of the Rosary Church, its pristine whitewashed walls gleaming in the sunlight.

Hidalgo and Paloma had been so happy awaiting the birth of their first child. He often wondered if his frequent absence had left Paloma vulnerable. If so, she never complained. Descended from a proud Castillion family near Madrid in central Spain, he was the fifth generation of Garcias born in Argentina. His earliest ancestors were traders of animal hides and tallow with Mapuche, one of the several nomadic Indian tribes northwest, near Cordoba.

Hidalgo's ancestral grandfather married an indigenous woman, which was not uncommon in those days. Few refined ladies arrived from Spain in the early days of settlement. Argentina was a vast wilderness—inhabited mainly by scattered nomadic tribes, members of the Spanish Army and early traders coming to those wild shores.

It wasn't long before they realised there was far greater potential for wealth in ranching and agriculture than in trading. Hidalgo's ancestors aimed to become landowners at the first opportunity. Since the early eighteenth century, vast herds of wild cattle and horses had roamed the Pampas unhindered.

The Garcia family were proud of their lineage. They built a small empire through good management and hard work. Hidalgo followed suit.

Kneeling before Paloma's grave, Hidalgo wondered whether life without Paloma was worth living. He had lost the thing most precious to him. He could still recall meeting his shy bride for the first time— a formal dinner arranged by their families, both sets of parents hoping for an acceptable match. There was an instant rapport.

From the moment they took their wedding vows and pledged their love for each other, they had been inseparable—ardent lovers and best friends. Hidalgo was twenty-seven at the time, Paloma an innocent eighteen. He could still remember his first glimpse of her bathed in white satin as she entered the Cathedral of The Holy Trinity in Buenos Aires. Her beauty left him breathless.

They shared a passion from the outset, hoping to start a family as quickly as possible. It was not to be. After almost fifteen years, they were still without a child. Hidalgo remembered returning from their estancia in Santa Fe to Ataliva Roca. The house was quiet when he entered, which was most unusual. Usually, it was a hive of activity; Paloma always made it a special occasion, welcoming him home after being away on business.

The housekeeper informed him, "The mistress, she is not well; she is resting."

Alarmed, Hidalgo quickly went to Paloma to find her beaming, not unwell in the true sense but experiencing the first signs of pregnancy. At last, there was to be an heir to the Garcia family.

On the 5th of April 1827, Theresa Paloma Garcia entered the world with lusty cries. She was adorable. From the moment Hidalgo held her in his arms, she lay claim to his heart.

Labour had been long and complicated; Paloma was exhausted. There was so much blood, and it would not stop. She was only thirty-three, but her body's resilience was poor. Hidalgo was beside himself; they were a long way from help. Paloma lay there so calmly;

perhaps she knew she would not see her beautiful daughter Theresa grow to womanhood. Her ghostly face turned upwards, smiling sweetly at Hidalgo as tears ran down his cheeks. Baby Theresa slept peacefully in a crib nearby, blissfully unaware of the drama unfolding. Paloma's sighed gently, closed her eyes and left this mortal world.

After Paloma's death, Hidalgo was often absent from Ataliva Roca due to multiple business holdings, the furthest near Cordoba. The new Telegraphic Service allowed him to send and receive messages or pass on instructions without requiring him to attend in person. He was fortunate to have good managers and tenant farmers, ensuring the estancias and smaller holdings prospered, although occasional supervision was still necessary.

Being away from his daughter, Theresa, was difficult at any time. She was the image of her deceased mother and a joy to be around. Even at four, she was an exceptionally bright child. Walking and talking at twelve months, wanting to get on a horse by age two, there was no stopping her, but there was a dilemma. As Hidalgo watched Theresa grow, he realised he would not always be around to guide her, and one day she would be a wealthy young lady of some significance. Equipping her to manage their many investments independently was paramount.

Education was not a high priority for girls in his culture, but Hidalgo disagreed, and besides, Theresa was the heir to the Garcia Estate. She must have the best education possible. Elena and Jose Ruiz, his housekeeper and her gardener husband, had done their best until now, but they were not equipped to educate a child or teach her the finer things of life as she grew. Despite their well-meaning protests, Hidalgo knew Theresa's future demanded a comprehensive education. With this in mind, Hidalgo arranged for his manager in Buenos Aries to place an advertisement in several prominent journals seeking an English Governess.

Elizabeth Dalton

☼

Elizabeth was a linguistics teacher at the prestigious Gough House Private Girls School, Paradise Road, Chelsea; her future was assured. Her free days she spent wandering the lush, misty countryside in the midlands of England, safe, secure, respectable. Therein lay part of the problem. Elizabeth's foreseeable future was too predictable. While it was certainly comfortable, it had little potential for excitement. She had a passion for the unknown. The idea of teaching upper-class teenage girls for the next thirty or forty years was mortifying. Elizabeth knew, without doubt, that she could not settle for a mundane existence.

While looking through international magazines gathering ideas for curriculum development, a small section in an American periodical, 'Youth's Companion', drew Elizabeth's attention. Among the educational advertisements, the magazine listed employment opportunities in South America. Most enticements were seeking skilled workers in cattle ranching or sheep herding. One specific advertisement, however, made Elizabeth catch her breath

In urgent need of a female Governess with appropriate educational qualifications. Multilingual capability essential (Spanish / English), to assist with the care and education of a small child. The position offers an extended tenure for the suitable applicant. A generous salary, to be re-negotiated annually to the satisfaction of each party. Be aware, the geographical location of the Estancia (Ranch), Ataliva Roca, is 380 miles south of Buenos Aires, in the La Pampa Province of Argentina. Provision for

9

annual paid leave, including transportation to and from the capital city, if desired, is inclusive. See contact details below:

The words captured Elizabeth's imagination immediately, almost as much as the name listed at the end, 'Hidalgo Raphael Garcia - Esquire'. Elizabeth knew her qualifications were impeccable. Teaching Greek and Latin was her speciality, but she was also more than competent in Spanish. A long-held dream had been to visit the leading art galleries of Europe one day and view the works of Spanish masters El Greco, Goya and Velasquez. For that reason, while at College, Elizabeth had decided to take Spanish as an elective.

She had so much to ponder. Where was the child's mother? Were there no other family members who might help raise the child? Education, it seemed, was of some significance to Senor Garcia, which led Elizabeth to assume the child was a boy, presupposing education for a female offspring would not be a high priority in remote areas of Argentina. The child, she guessed, must be around five or six. She knew nothing about little boys, except they were boisterous and prone to mischief; Elizabeth had only ever dealt with female boarders.

The isolation might be difficult, but Elizabeth was no shrinking violet. The position offered a long-term tenure. The idea of returning to England following a great adventure, financially secure, and perhaps able to start her own school, was a desirable proposition.

Hastily heading to the school's extensive library, Elizabeth sought out the gigantic Atlas, a heavy leather-bound volume with elaborately embossed gold lettering. She knew it well, having spent many hours gleaning information from its pages. She placed the heavy Atlas on the burnished oak desk. Elizabeth dreamt of visiting far-away places, completely in awe of the courageous men who ventured into the unknown, exploring the sea and the land.

Turning the pages to the 'Americas', she studied the southern continent with its Spanish place names. Buenos Aires, the capital of

Argentina, meaning 'fair winds', was quickly located. With the map scale noted, Elizabeth took a ruler and estimated the approximate location of the ranch Ataliva Roca, somewhere in the central La Pampa Province. The only discernible town near Elizabeth's calculation was Santa Rosa, a tiny dot on the map. Elizabeth stared at that name for the longest time. She wondered why this opportunity should arise now—having questioned her future recently and her desire for change. She didn't believe in coincidences. Slowly closing the Atlas, an enigmatic smile on her face, her decision was made.

Elizabeth telegraphed a carefully worded application; the return acceptance was startlingly rapid. It would take several weeks to arrange passage on one of the infrequent ships transporting cargo, machinery, and immigrant workers to South America. The delay suited her perfectly; it would allow her time to give appropriate notice to the school, pack, finalise any affairs, and arrange a caretaker to look after her cottage.

Elizabeth had meagre savings but splurged on ensuring passage on a merchant ship accommodating steerage passengers, having heard disturbing accounts of 'below deck' sea voyages. Her excitement outweighed any immediate doubts, although nearer to departure, she gave a lot more thought to the impact of her decision. Elizabeth wasn't overly troubled about leaving family, friends or possessions. Not even the possible isolation vexed her. She was more concerned about the unpredictability of the journey and the potential dangers for a young single woman travelling alone.

Neither had Elizabeth given much thought to a prolonged sea voyage. The relentless Great Southern Ocean produced gale-force winds and massive seas. Such seas had taken many ships and crew to the bottom of the ocean. Changing her mind was not an option. Elizabeth had given her word, and that was sacrosanct.

Late Summer 1829, Elizabeth stepped ashore from the ghastly vessel, having been ill with motion sickness for six weeks. She swore she would never set foot on another ship; she would rather die first. Her initial steps on solid ground were grossly unsteady. It would be days before she would not automatically sway whenever she closed her eyes.

Buenos Aires harbour was a surprise. Many vessels lay at anchor, from tiny fishing boats to several luggers and a Merchant navy Ship proudly flying the Argentine Flag. The city itself was much more advanced than Elizabeth anticipated, there were almost seven hundred thousand permanent residents throughout Argentina, and a significant portion lived in the province of Buenos Aires.

Still, there was a raw feel to the place. Elizabeth learned brawls were common, usually fuelled by too much alcohol. Most disputes usually involved men arguing about gambling or some woman. Buenos Aires was becoming a central hub for trade of all descriptions. Cattle ranching and agriculture primarily, but many sought to make their fortune looking for gold. When men have too much money, alcohol, and time on their hands, trouble is not too far behind.

Elizabeth relished the comfort of the hotel for a few days' rest, finally able to catch her breath. Her room was beautiful; organza drapes fluttered at the window. Several colourful woven native rugs graced a gleaming polished timber floor. Looking down from the first-floor landing to the street below, Elizabeth watched the flow of traffic. Many covered wagons piled high with goods pulled by cumbersome oxen. The burdened beasts, focused on the road ahead, were not about to change direction for anyone.

Elizabeth's coach was due to leave in the morning, accompanied by several wagons carrying goods to outlying forts and rural villages. There was only limited room for personal luggage. She was fortunate to have her extra crate of books and other teaching paraphernalia loaded onto a wagon which followed. The excitement of what lay ahead began to erase the memory of the six weeks spent at sea.

Not much after sunrise, Elizabeth's carriage, one of three, headed southwest away from Buenos Aires, followed by four wagons. The wide dirt trail snaked off into the distance; each gust of wind sent spirals of dust dancing across the landscape. The first change of horses would be at a *Posada*, an overnight resting place

12

approximately forty miles down the road, one of many dispersed across the countryside. Elizabeth enquired from the wagon master how long that might be,

"Maybe six or seven hours, ma'am, if we don't strike any trouble."

Elizabeth experienced her first pang of misgiving; what might 'trouble' mean?

The plan was to stop every hour, stretch their legs, and take some water. It was easy to become dehydrated in the debilitating summer heat. At each stop, the wagons and carriages would rotate their position. Everyone would eventually share the burden of dust stirred up by the other wagons. Elizabeth innocently asked why they didn't space the wagons far enough apart to avoid the dust. The other passengers on the coach turned in unison to stare at her. There was a tall gent with a squint sitting opposite. He screwed his eyes up even more and drawled,

"Well, ma'am, if the Indians pay us a visit, we'd probably stand a better chance if we all huddle together rather than spread out and let them pick us off one by one."

Elizabeth thought he was joking. Silence followed; nobody was smiling or laughing. Suddenly she realised what 'trouble' meant, and began wondering what she had been thinking, taking a job as Governess in the middle of nowhere. The coach lapsed into silence, everyone lost in their thoughts, considering what they might do should an attack occur. Elizabeth shuddered, unable to control her growing doubts and fear.

The native horses of the Pampas had incredible stamina, coping with temperature extremes, poor feed and little water. They were known for their endurance; a single rider could cover eighty to one hundred miles a day, but travel would be slow with loaded wagons and coaches carrying passengers. Elizabeth could only pray that they would still be alive at the journey's end.

After an hour-and-a-half, the wagon train stopped beside a creek to water the horses and allow the drivers to take a break. Elizabeth's body was already affected by the swaying motion of the coach hitting ruts in the road, throwing the coach roughly from side to side. She was dismayed; it was as bad as being at sea. The action also threatened to split the rails on the wheels as the drivers tried desperately to steer the wagons straight and maintain traction without tipping the coach over. The heavier wagons fared better; the oxen were able to choose their footing more carefully, which made their passage safer but slowed them down even more. Inquiring if it was any easier returning empty on the trip back to Buenos Aires, her travelling companion with the squint obliged her once more, or perhaps he just felt sorry for her ignorance,

"Well, ma'am, they return laden with bales of beef hides, pelts from wild animals, barrels of tallow, dried meat, and sometimes logs."

Of course, how stupid. Elizabeth had a lot to learn. The rest of the journey passed in silence.

Someone noticed smoke on the horizon. At first alarmed, Elizabeth's travelling companions reassured her it was their first night's camp. They arrived at the Posada late afternoon after several unscheduled stops. A pregnant woman in one of the other coaches had been ill. Elizabeth imagined attempting this trip pregnant – she decided she would never complain about anything again.

Everyone was covered in a powdery film of dust and sand on arrival. Despite a handkerchief held firmly over her face, Elizabeth could feel the grit in her mouth. There was a cauldron of boiling tea to welcome them, not what she was used to, and bitter, but better than nothing—anything to parch her thirst and rinse her mouth. There were racks of beef roasting alongside a platter piled with slabs of bread cooked in the ashes. Much to Elizabeth's surprise, everything was delicious.

Looking at the misshapen clay hut, Elizabeth wondered how it would accommodate so many people. There were fifteen passengers, among them six women, the coachmen, and the wagon drivers. Having lived roughly at some stage, most men headed to the barn for shelter or slept in the coaches. There was no room to spare, but each woman found a spot to bed for the night. The old fellow running the

14

coach house kindly gave up the only real bed to the pregnant woman. The toileting and wash areas were primitive but adequate; everyone was respectful of each other's privacy.

Elizabeth decided that bundles of straw tightly wrapped and covered with an old army blanket did not produce the most comfortable bed, but they served the purpose. She tried to ignore the sharp barbs of straw poking into several bruises acquired on the journey. Drifting off to sleep, she dreamed of soaking in a tub of hot soapy water before sinking into her soft bed in Chelsea.

The smell of eggs frying wafted through the hut's open door and helped rouse her. Walking out into the daylight, dishevelled but none the worse for wear, Elizabeth could already see the heat haze rising off the ground. The day would be a scorcher. She refused to think about her aching bones and spoil breakfast. Not having noticed any chickens wandering about, Elizabeth wondered where the eggs appeared from, then learnt they were courtesy of partridges nesting in the long pampas grass.

The plains were beyond anything Elizabeth might have imagined. It was difficult to comprehend such a vast body of land; many thousands of square miles could be almost devoid of trees. The few thus growing there were unique, having a strange configuration with multiple trunks and an umbrella-shaped canopy. Informed they were Ombu trees, resistant to burning. They were one of the few trees to survive the many fires that swept the plains in summer. Fierce storms were common, sheet lightning illuminating the skies and sparking firestorms. A variety of trees grew along the banks of most creeks, wherever there was sufficient water. Elizabeth recognised some familiar species, Acacia, Pine, and Eucalypts.

The travellers encountered salt pans and passed flood plains, crossing many shallow rivers. Elizabeth speculated that heavy seasonal rains, common to the area, most likely flooded a vast portion of the pampas. There was abundant birdlife; she recognised storks, waterfowl and several varieties of finches.

On one of the detours delivering cargo to a fort, a wagon lost a wheel in a dry creek bed, but other than that, the trip was uneventful. Thankfully they didn't encounter any Indians, although they found

15

freshly slaughtered cattle near one watering hole; perhaps it was fortunate the wheel replacement caused a delay. Elizabeth doubted the forts were much of a deterrent to the natives. These small establishments were grossly undermanned should a serious attack occur. Elizabeth felt their presence probably gave comfort to the settlements. At each stop, the men offloaded goods as quickly as possible. The locals assisted, going about their work methodically. They nodded and smiled but had little to say.

The following week passed similarly, each day seeming longer than the last. The only thing that sometimes broke the monotony was a brief glimpse of wildlife. They witnessed many deer wandering the plains in small groups, and late one afternoon, a couple of scrawny foxes out on a hunt, most likely. Early on their final day, the wagon train spotted a giant bird about to run into the front wagon before suddenly veering off into the scrub. One of the passengers identified it as a Rhea, a large flightless bird native to South America. Elizabeth thought it was extraordinary.

On the afternoon of the ninth day, the outline of Santa Rosa came into view. Elizabeth had noticed the countryside slowly changing over the last forty miles. The land was now carpeted in lush grass, thick trees, and gently rolling hills stretched to the horizon. The wagon train meandered through the town centre, stopping in front of the local grocery store. A pretty little village, Elizabeth decided. One of the drivers unhitched a single wagon, which two men began to unload.

Herders led the rest of the wagons to the edge of town to settle the animals for the night—removing the yolks from the oxen, unsaddling the horses, pumping water into the troughs and scattering bales of hay for the animals to graze.

An elderly priest stood on the sidewalk in front of the store. He smiled and nodded as Elizabeth stepped down from the coach, then looked past her as if waiting for another passenger to alight. The driver flicked the horse's reins, and the coach moved off to join the rest of the wagon train on the edge of town. The priest turned slowly to address Elizabeth, looking somewhat baffled.

"Senorita Dalton? Elizabeth Dalton? The new Governess joining Senor Garcia's household?" The priest, visibly flustered, added, "Forgive me for staring, Senorita; I was expecting someone much older."

Elizabeth was amused. People often had the preconceived idea that all governesses were middle-aged spinsters. When thinking back, Elizabeth realised that nobody had inquired about her age; she hadn't considered that detail relevant. Elizabeth smiled, acknowledging she was indeed the Governess.

The priest stepped forward, extending his hand, "Excuse me, please; I didn't mean to be rude. I am Father Augustus; Senor Garcia sent me to meet you in his absence, for which he apologises. I hope you will do me the honour of being my guest overnight in one of the church cottages. Senor Garcia comes to town every Saturday to visit the grave of his beloved wife, Paloma, and he will escort you home following this."

Elizabeth now understood why a Governess was necessary; obviously, the child's mother was deceased. The priest picked up her two cases and headed towards a nearby buggy. She suddenly remembered her remaining property. The wagon carrying her goods had already been unloaded, and they were piled high in front of the store. Fr Augustus quickly identified Elizabeth's belongings and arranged for the shop owner, Senor Torella, a friend, to store the crate overnight.

It was late afternoon when the priest steered the buggy to the rear of the church. Elizabeth noticed the rows of white crosses dotted on the adjoining slope. She thought of the child without a mother.

The priest's voice cut across her thoughts, "You will surely fall in love with Theresa; she is a wonderful child and very smart."

That was the next surprise for Elizabeth. She had wrongly assumed the child in question was a boy. Immediately she felt more confident, girls she understood.

Awake early, Elizabeth explored her surroundings, spending time in the beautiful chapel. Entranced, she watched the sunlight spread a rainbow of colour across the whitewashed walls and stone floor as it streamed through the stained-glass windows. Doves

17

fluttered in the arched beams overhead, cooing at the stranger disturbing their peace. Fr Augustus appeared from a side entrance and briefly knelt at the altar before joining Elizabeth.

"I'm afraid, Senorita Dalton, I must apologise once more on behalf of Senor Garcia. One of his ranch hands has delivered a message, then departed to attend to some business. Senor Garcia cannot personally escort you to his estancia; you will return to Ataliva Roca with the ranch hand later in the day."

Elizbeth, quite happy for the opportunity to rest, reassured the elderly priest. "Fr Augustus, that's fine. I am happy to explore Santa Rosa a little."

Fr Augustus was relieved this young lady was so amenable. "We will be joined shortly by one of my parishioners, Isabella Caron, who kindly assists each Saturday in cleaning and preparing the church for Sunday Mass. You will enjoy her company, I'm sure. Isabella and her husband Paolo are among the many share farmers working for Senor Garcia." The priest excused himself, leaving Elizabeth to her own devices.

Wandering around the grounds of the church and admiring the gardens was relaxing. There was a lagoon a short distance from the rear of the church; a tributary ran parallel to the road heading south. Trees hugged the banks, providing welcome shade. It was mid-summer, and even this early in the day, Elizabeth was affected by the heat. She wondered if anyone accustomed to a mild English climate ever really adjusted to living through an Argentine Summer! Tempted to kick off her shoes and stand in the cool water, she decided that might be unbecoming for a young lady, especially one currently a guest of the priest.

Returning to her quarters to await pickup, Elizabeth encountered a woman she judged not much older than herself, whom she assumed was Isabella Caron. "Buenos Dios, you must be Senora Caron? My name is Elizabeth Dalton; I am the new Governess employed by Senor Garcia. Fr Augustus told me to expect you; I am pleased to meet you."

18

A little startled at first by the unexpected presence of this young foreign woman speaking fluent Spanish, Isabella quickly regained her composure, "I am pleased to meet you also, Senorita; please call me Isabella."

It was clear Isabella was in the latter part of pregnancy; Elizabeth happily offered to help in any way. A young girl came barrelling into the church from the vestibule, calling out to her mother. She stopped abruptly, staring wide-eyed at this beautiful lady with golden hair and blue eyes; she was struck dumb.

"Senorita Dalton, I would like to introduce my second child Rosalinda, aged seven, who is very energetic, as you can see, and quite a handful." Both ladies laughed. "She prefers to be called Rosa," Isabella offered as Rosa hid behind her mother's skirt, overcome with shyness. "I also have an older boy, Delgado, ten, helping his father on our farm."

Elizabeth had a way with children and quickly won Rosa over, who then chatted incessantly, asking countless questions. Isabella apologised, chiding Rosa to be quiet, scolding her once for touching Elizabeth's hair; rather than being offended, Elizabeth found it amusing.

The time passed quickly until Elizabeth was due to depart. It had been fun helping Isabella. Fr Augustus was right; she had enjoyed her company and hoped they might meet each other again. She thanked Fr Augustus for his hospitality and waved farewell as the buggy headed out of town. Rosa was nowhere to be seen, probably getting into mischief somewhere.

Ataliva Roca

☼

Elizabeth caught frequent glimpses of water throughout the twenty-five-mile journey to Ataliva Roca. The surrounding countryside was lush. Cattle grazed freely as far as the eye could see. Landholdings in this area appeared extensive. Curious where the boundary to Ataliva Roca might commence, she asked the ranch hand. He was respectful but reluctant to enter into conversation. Elizabeth finally settled into a comfortable silence, letting her thoughts wander, looking forward with anticipation to meeting Senor Garcia and Theresa.

Throughout the day, they passed villages, Toay, Cachirulo, and Naico. Elizabeth was surprised to see *Tolderias,* Indian camps, scattered across the plains. Fr Augustus explained earlier to Elizabeth how much of southern Argentina was blessed with artesian springs, one of the reasons the nomadic Indians thrived long before they acquired horses. The free-range cattle and the existing wildlife continued to sustain the indigenous population. Frequent skirmishes occurred during the acquisition of native lands by the Spanish. Father explained there were few instances of conflict in southern Argentina now, primarily due to intermarriage between the Spanish and native inhabitants, decreasing hostilities in most provinces. Sadly, savage encounters still happened in the north and occasionally in the west.

It was almost dark before the lights of the homestead came into view. Elizabeth wasn't sure what she had expected, but the spacious dwellings surrounded by manicured lawns and extensive gardens were a surprise. An avenue of trees guided visitors to a central courtyard. A shallow pond held the statue of an angel. In the fading light, her benign smile welcoming. Elizabeth experienced an eerie feeling like she was coming home.

The buggy halted outside enormous arched doors fastened with brass brackets and hinges. Spread along each side of the veranda were ornately carved benches, their length adorned with colourful cushions. An old spinning wheel leaned against the wall among rows of clay pots filled with herbs. The effect was charming. The ranch hand quickly tethered the horses and attended to Elizabeth's luggage while she sat quietly, taking in her surroundings. Oil lamps lighting the adobe residence cast shadows of muted red. The hacienda, not built this century, had been beautifully maintained, like a precious heirloom.

The heavy oak door swung open, and a man in his mid-forties stood framed by the light. His posture said this was someone who commanded authority. Elizabeth felt daunted, yet when he finally stepped where she could see his expression, a kind, weathered face smiled back at her. He greeted her warmly.

Hidalgo extended his hand, "Senor Garcia - welcome to my hacienda Senorita Dalton; let me help you," he grasped Elizabeth by the arm as she stepped from the buggy. I hope you had a pleasant journey. I apologise once again for being unable to meet you personally. I hope Diego took good care of you?"

"Yes, thank you, Senor Garcia; the hospitality of Fr Augustus and Senor Diego was exceptional. You have a lovely home, Senor." Hidalgo was frowning slightly; Elizabeth, unable to discern why decided to say nothing further. The silence seemed to go on forever. Eventually, Hidalgo spoke, contrite.

"Forgive me, Senorita Dalton; you must be weary from your journey. My housekeeper, Senora Ruiz, will see to your comfort, then bring supper to your room. There is no need to rise early in the morning; rest well, and take your time joining us." Speaking almost apologetically, he continued, "I'm afraid we have little formality here. I now take my meals in the kitchen with my housekeeper and her husband, Jose`. My daughter Theresa spends most of her time under Elena's feet, so it seemed only natural to join them."

Elizabeth could hear the amusement in his voice. When speaking of Theresa, Hidalgo's words were filled with love. Moving to one side, he ushered Elizabeth into the hacienda. There was a fire

21

smouldering in a stone hearth. Elizabeth failed to notice how the temperature had dropped.

It was difficult to know where to look first. Elizabeth felt as though she had stepped back in time. Many family portraits adorned the walls, some clothed as if from a bygone era. Glass-fronted cabinets held an amazing array of porcelain and other personal treasures. Still, other cabinets were laden with books.

A portly woman in her sixties entered the room; a bright scarf wrapped tightly around her head. Embarrassingly, she curtsied to Elizabeth.

"Welcome, Senorita Dalton; I am Elena Ruiz, the housekeeper. I apologise, my husband Jose' would generally be present to greet a new household member, but he is unwell this evening. Come, I will show you to your room Senorita, so you may rest while I prepare your supper."

"Thank you, please call me Elizabeth; Senorita Dalton is too formal."

Elena beamed, unexpectedly warming to this very pretty English lady. When first told a governess had been employed, she had many misgivings, not convinced anyone else should raise *her* beautiful Theresa. Elena hoped Senor Garcia might change his mind. He was adamant Theresa must be fluent in both English and Spanish. She imagined the Governess would be old and set in her ways, perhaps picky; instead, this attractive young woman seemed very nice.

Elena stole a look in Senor Garcia's direction as she left the room, curious to gauge his reaction to the new Governess. She decided he looked like a prairie deer about to be hit by a wagon. Chuckling to herself, the housekeeper indicated for Elizabeth to follow her.

Elizabeth excused herself to Senor Garcia. With everything happening so quickly, she hadn't had a real chance to study her employer, although she acknowledged feeling awkward in his presence for some reason. The housekeeper's lantern illuminated more treasures as they walked through the hacienda. Elizabeth jumped, startled by a grandfather clock nearby chiming the hour.

Something was amusing the housekeeper, who continued to chuckle as she led the way down the corridor. For a moment, Elizabeth thought Elena had addressed a question to her when she heard her mutter, 'I wonder if the rooster will crow', but realised the housekeeper was talking to herself about nothing that made any sense.

On entering her room, Elizabeth could see everything was immaculate. Sparsely furnished, the beauty was in its simplicity. A woman's touch was in evidence everywhere. Lace doilies on the furniture, an exquisite crocheted cover adorned the single bed, and white sheer organza curtains graced the windows. An oak washstand with a floral pitcher sat perched in a matching washbasin by the window. Elizabeth's luggage had been placed neatly alongside a mirrored wardrobe. On one side of this, a single chair and a writing desk. The housekeeper informed Elizabeth her husband had safely stored her crate of books in a room next to the hacienda. This room was where Elizabeth would school Theresa.

In Summer, the temperature on the plains plummeted in the evening, at times dropping below zero. Hidalgo stood transfixed, staring into the glowing embers of the dying fire, the cold the least of his concerns. He was struggling to maintain his composure. It had never occurred to him to stipulate an age range for the governess position. Elizabeth's appearance had completely taken him by surprise.

Hidalgo never looked at another woman once he gave his heart to Paloma. Now he was shocked at how much Elizabeth's presence had shaken him. It wasn't anything that she said or did. From the moment of her arrival, helping her from the buggy, he was unsettled; he kept pointing out trivial things, aiming to deflect her attention and give him a valid reason to avoid eye contact. This situation was not good.

Hidalgo decided to rise early and join the ranch hands mustering out on the plains. There was a holding bay a few miles from the main homestead. After calving, the men rounded up the young livestock for branding and then culled heifers chosen to be sold at the market. The horses and wagons had to be well prepared; it was a long cattle drive to Buenos Aires; he knew his men were more than capable of handling it without him. His sudden presence would raise a few eyebrows. If asked, Hidalgo would have vehemently denied he was running away.

Well before daybreak, still tired after a restless night's sleep, he dragged himself out of bed, shaken by the vivid images now imprinted on his mind. He couldn't remember when he last dreamt of making love to a woman - he'd felt the surge of passion as his body responded to the woman's intimate touch - shocked awake to roaring thunder. Lightning lit up the room...in the dream, the woman caressing his body had been Elizabeth.

Meeting Theresa
☼

Elizabeth awoke gently. She lay watching the sun stream through the sheer curtains. It was strangely quiet for a working ranch, although she thought she could hear children's voices in the distance. Various birds competed for attention, the occasional squawk indicating a possible dispute.

Elizabeth looked around, smiling to herself. Few would have imagined a young English woman of twenty-four embarking on such an adventure and having the courage to relocate halfway around the world. There was a gentle tap at the door.

"Miss Elizabeth, when you are ready, you may wish to join Theresa and me. We have the whole hacienda to ourselves; the men have all gone, even Senor Garcia."

"Thank you; I will join you shortly, Elena." Elizabeth rose quickly, washed and dressed in under ten minutes, excited to begin her new life and meet Theresa.

In daylight, the hacienda was even more beautiful than first imagined. Many rooms led off the main corridor; each had a different décor. There would be ample time to explore them later, but now Elizabeth headed across the ochre tiles that led into the kitchen from the formal dining room. She could hear the sound of a child giggling. Elizabeth was smitten from the moment she set eyes on the four-year-old toddler. Theresa was wearing a buttercup yellow pinafore over a checked blouse. A shock of black curls framed a sweet face. She was sitting on the floor cross-legged, her feet bare.

Theresa swung around as Elizabeth entered the room, her laughter cut short. Unsure of this stranger, she quickly looked towards the housekeeper, wide-eyed, seeking reassurance.

25

Elizabeth smiled, introducing herself. "Hola Theresa, mi nombre es Elizabeth, espero que semos buenos amigos."

Theresa's expression did not alter; her bottom lip trembled as though she might cry. Elizabeth frowned, sure her Spanish greeting had been accurate. When the housekeeper drew Elizabeth's attention for a few seconds, Theresa took the opportunity to study her.

"I am sorry, Miss Elizabeth, but Senor Garcia requested we converse in English if you please. He wishes to ensure Theresa is fluent in both Spanish and English."

Theresa interrupted, a twinkle in her eye, suddenly stood and curtsied, then, in perfect English, said, "I am pleased to meet you, Miss."

Elizabeth couldn't help but laugh. Soon the two women were chatting away agreeably. Theresa sat nearby, hands cupped under her chin, head turning from side to side, trying to follow their conversation.

Hidalgo had allowed for a few days' grace before Theresa's lessons commenced. He wanted Elizabeth to be well-rested and take time to settle into her new surroundings. She was grateful. It was an opportunity to become familiar with the layout of the hacienda and the household routine.

Elizabeth was more than a little surprised to learn Hidalgo had gone on the cattle drive to Buenos Aires; she was positive he indicated business would be conducted from Ataliva Roca. Owning one of the first Estancias to establish the new telegraphic link allowed him to access his properties throughout Argentina. The cost was high but worth it. The housekeeper confirmed his departure was most definitely unexpected; Elizabeth was puzzled by her look of amusement.

A bond quickly developed between teacher and pupil; a bright child, incredibly advanced for her age. Showing Theresa how to do something once was enough.

Elena had to acknowledge being wrong about Senor Garcia employing a governess for Theresa. Miss Elizabeth was an excellent

26

teacher. Theresa was learning etiquette, deportment, and many other things, along with her regular lessons. Much of what the Governess was teaching was way beyond Elena's capability. The only sadness for the housekeeper; Theresa no longer turned to her first when seeking comfort. It was hard not to be jealous or resentful. It took a while for those feelings to lessen. As the weeks passed, admiration for the Governess grew, and Elena accepted her as a good friend.

The cattle drive had been underway for five weeks when a solitary rider appeared. Hidalgo, on horseback, came trotting down the avenue of trees. The ranch hands who remained to look after and protect the property were surprised. They greeted him warmly. Elizabeth, seated on the veranda reading, witnessed the arrival. She liked the camaraderie he had with the men. They treated him respectfully, but it was apparent that he was much more than just their employer. Elizabeth reflected on his easy interactions with everyone…except when he was in her presence. Hidalgo would find every excuse to make his exit as quickly as possible. She realised, since her arrival, he had done his very best to avoid her company.

The household gathered in the kitchen for the evening meal. The men talked about plans for the following day and the repairs Hidalgo required. They discussed how the cattle drive had gone so far. Hidalgo did not mention why he went in the first place or returned when he had. It would have been considered improper for an employee to ask such questions, even though Elena and Jose` had a closer relationship than most. Elizabeth learned the housekeeper and her husband had taken care of Paloma as a child; when she died giving birth to Theresa, they arrived to care for Hidalgo and the new baby and stayed.

The sound of high-pitched squeals dragged Elizabeth from the edge of sleep. At first, she was alarmed until Theresa's bubbling laughter followed the squealing. Elizabeth went to the window to investigate. She remained out of sight, amused as Hidalgo and Theresa played hide and seek in the extensive front garden. Having just been 'found' by Theresa, Hidalgo, displaying mock indignation, picked up a garden ornament, scooped water from the pond and was now chasing his daughter, threatening to douse her. Almost hysterical with laughter, Theresa ran as fast as her little legs could carry her, weaving her way through the shrubbery with Hidalgo in hot pursuit. Here was the master of the household, commander of hundreds, acting like a small schoolboy to amuse his daughter.

Feigning exhaustion, Hidalgo collapsed onto an open grassed area. Theresa stopped immediately, turned on her heel and ran back towards him, throwing herself into his arms. They both lay on the ground laughing, looking at the clear blue sky. Theresa started chattering non-stop, neither of them in any hurry to get up. Elizabeth was mesmerised watching this heart-warming interaction unfold. Hidalgo stroked his daughter's hair, his expression one of complete adoration; anyone could see she was his reason for living.

Elizabeth stepped away from the window. There was so much she was yet to know about this man. Her admiration for her employer continued to grow over the weeks since her arrival. Hidalgo was a kind man, always considerate of others. Elena and Jose` he treated not as employees but as equals. They, in turn, adored him.

Elena presented the meal and then commenced cleaning up, declining Elizabeth's offer to help. That was strictly her domain; Elizabeth kept Theresa amused by playing games, drawing pictures with crayons, or telling stories about when she was a little girl. Every once in a while, she could feel Hidalgo's eyes on her, which he quickly averted if she looked in his direction. Occasionally, Theresa would interrupt the men and insist on gaining her father's undivided attention, which he gave readily. Elizabeth enjoyed watching them together. The love flowing between them was palpable. More and more, her admiration for Hidalgo was growing. She always addressed him directly as 'Senor Garcia', but she thought of him as Hidalgo in her musings.

One morning during lessons, Theresa suggested rather than taking their morning break, they go for a walk to the stables instead. Theresa loved spending time with her horse. Elizabeth, amused by the pleading expression on Theresa's face, agreed, her expression quickly turning to one of delight.

Running ahead of Elizabeth, Theresa kept turning frequently to tell her snippets of information about how to look after horses. Elizabeth was taken aback at the level of understanding this small child possessed.

They entered the stables cautiously, careful not to get in the way of ranch hands going about their business. They all greeted Theresa affectionately. The temperature inside was stifling, the humidity almost overwhelming. Elizabeth wondered if she would ever get used to the climate of Argentina.

Theresa ran to where her horse *Plata* was stabled. 'Silver' was an appropriate name for the white stallion. He arrived during the night, wet and shining in the moonlight, the name a perfect fit. On hearing Theresa's voice, he quickly leaned over the stall, nuzzling his head into her upstretched arms; Theresa was entirely at ease with the enormous animal towering over her. Elizabeth was entranced.

Without warning, Hidalgo stepped out of the adjacent stall. He and a ranch hand had been attending to another animal; both men were shirtless.

Elizabeth's breath caught in her throat as she looked at Hidalgo with a woman's eyes rather than as his employee. He was tall, his dark wavy hair showing the first hint of silver at the sides. Clean-shaven, olive skin darkened even more from time spent in the sun. Broad shoulders framed over a narrow waist. Elizabeth had never seen Hidalgo without a shirt. Silently admiring his physique, she wondered what it would be like being held by those strong arms, blushing at the thought.

Startled seeing Elizabeth standing before him, Hidalgo and the ranch hand hurriedly donned their shirts.

"I apologise for our lack of attire Senorita. We were not expecting company. After all, it is a working area and a hot day."

Elizabeth wasn't sure if she was being rebuked for being somewhere she shouldn't have been. "I am sorry, Senor Garcia; Theresa and I shall head back to the classroom. We were taking a small break." Elizabeth felt Theresa slip her tiny hand into hers. Looking down, she appeared close to tears. It seemed she, too, thought they were in trouble.

Hidalgo looked at Theresa, seeing her expression suddenly contrite at his harsh tone.

"Do not concern yourself, Senorita Dalton," Hidalgo said pleasantly, "my men and I are finished here, for now, please, look around."

With that, the men headed out of the stables discussing their next plan of action. Hidalgo glanced briefly in Elizabeth's direction, her expression masked by the shadows.

Elizabeth stood unmoving, lost in thought. She had enjoyed the unexpected, though brief, encounter with Hidalgo. Images of him shirtless came readily to mind; oddly, she had little opportunity to observe his face.

Gathering for dinner, Elizabeth found herself studying Hidalgo. He looked tired. Managing a ranch the size of Ataliva Roca was no small task. Whenever he grinned, the skin puckered at the corners of his eyes. Laughing aloud at something Jose` had said, he looked in Elizabeth's direction. Such a beautiful smile. For the briefest moment, their eyes locked before Hidalgo turned his attention back to Jose`.

Elizabeth was becoming dismayed by her growing attraction to Hidalgo. It did not sit well with her professionalism.

A few weeks later, Elizabeth asked if she might accompany him to town, remembering Fr Augustus saying Hidalgo went into Santa Rosa every Saturday to visit Paloma's grave. It was her day off, a change of scenery would be welcome, and she wished to purchase some personal items from the store.

He had no good reason to refuse, although she sensed his reluctance to agree, seeing his discomfort at her request. She was genuinely flattered when it finally dawned on her that his awkwardness may be because of a possible attraction. He was a handsome man, decent, hard-working, a considerate employer, and devoted to Theresa. Elizabeth had no doubt many women would be delighted to attract his attention.

Hidalgo and Elizabeth left the ranch early to avoid travelling in the midday heat, intent on arriving in town late morning. On the way, Elizabeth made small talk about her life before coming to Argentina, hoping it would put Hidalgo at ease. He kept his eyes firmly focused on the trail ahead. Never rude, responding to any direct questions, but keeping answers abrupt. The buggy's swaying gait caused their bodies to brush against each other several times during the journey. Whenever this happened, Hidalgo flinched.

As the buggy stopped in front of the store, Fr Augustus appeared carrying his purchases. Greeting them warmly, he stepped forward to assist Elizabeth onto the sidewalk. The look of relief on Hidalgo's face did not go unnoticed by the priest. After arranging a pickup time with Elizabeth, Hidalgo departed in haste. Fr Augustus asked if she had settled into her new surroundings, his tone casual but his questions shrewd. He scrutinised every response.

Elizabeth happily shared the news of Theresa's progress, how welcome Elena and Jose had made her feel, and the workings of the ranch. Composed and relaxed up until the priest casually inquired about Hidalgo. She became flushed and hesitant, lowering her gaze. Elizabeth responded he had been kind and welcoming also, adding how infrequently she saw him, Hidalgo being so heavily involved in overseeing the running of the ranch. Fr Augustus said farewell to Elizabeth, inviting her to visit anytime she might be in town.

Fr Augustus hurried off, needing to speak with Hidalgo at the first opportunity, unsure how to discuss the gossip around town. And then there were his observations of Hidalgo and Elizabeth's reactions to each other. After visiting Paloma's grave, Hidalgo would drop into the vestry and share a cup of matte` with the elderly priest. Approaching the church, the priest could still see him sitting at the graveside, his back against a jacaranda tree, elbows on knees, head cradled in both hands. Hidalgo's buggy was tethered in the shade at the side of the church. Out of respect, Fr Augustus would bide his time and wait quietly in the vestry.

This week for the first time, Hidalgo had no words for Paloma. Every week for nearly four years, he sat at her graveside and shared the

31

previous week's happenings, mostly talking about Theresa and how proud Paloma would be to see her growing into such a spirited little girl. He would boast of their daughter's achievements and how beautiful she was, just like her mother. Today the words wouldn't come. Instead, Hidalgo was slumped against a tree, weighed down by guilt. He was ashamed to acknowledge the feelings building inside for Elizabeth.

Hidalgo headed for the buggy, his head bowed. The priest approached him. Looking up, he was not surprised to see Fr Augustus standing there. At first, neither man spoke. They stood, eyes fixed on each other, the topic of conversation known to both.

Fr Augustus spoke first, choosing his words carefully. "Hidalgo, I have known you for a very long time. I know without a doubt you are a man of honour. I do not question your integrity. At first, I ignored the gossip around Santa Rosa as scurrilous mischief, although I suspected Senorita Dalton living under your roof would raise many eyebrows." The priest waited for Hidalgo to respond.

"I don't know what to say, Father. I didn't expect a governess to be so young and..." Hidalgo never finished the sentence; he raised both arms and shrugged as if that explained everything. He felt defeated. "What would you have me do, Father? In the quest for a Governess, I promised a long-term contract. This young lady has come halfway around the world?"

"There is a simple solution, my son, and one I would not even suggest…had I not witnessed how you are with each other."

Hidalgo protested, "I swear, Father, I have never said one improper word to Senorita Dalton!"

The priest held up his hand, halting any further conversation, "I believe you, but I watched you with her, and there is no doubt in my mind; that your heart desires to be with her. Hidalgo, there is nothing wrong with this; you are still a young man. I know you may deny the need for a woman in your life. Perhaps you fail to acknowledge how lonely you are, and Senorita Dalton is a beautiful woman." The priest could see Hidalgo about to shake his head in protest. "Let me finish, please." the priest continued, "You are a widower Hidalgo, may your

32

beloved Paloma rest in eternal peace, but she would not have wanted you to be alone forever, and Theresa needs a mother."

Hidalgo looked like a wounded animal, his face now ashen, tears welling in his eyes, his shoulders hunched over.

"You must ask her to marry you, and soon. I can post the Banns this Sunday in church and perform the ceremony in the chapel at Ataliva Roca at the first opportunity. You look shocked that I would make such a suggestion, nor would I...except I believe Senorita Dalton has similar feelings for you."

Hidalgo's head shot up; he looked at the priest incredulous. Since Elizabeth's arrival, he had studiously avoided her. How could she possibly have feelings for him? "No, this cannot be possible," he protested. But the priest knew better. He believed Hidalgo's words were filled with hope.

Elizabeth waited patiently; seeing the buggy approach, she braced herself for the silent trip home. Immediately she knew something had changed. At first, thinking perhaps Hidalgo was upset from the time spent at Paloma's grave. He took a long time getting down from the buggy. He quickly took Elizabeth's parcels from her and placed them on the seat; his hands shook. Concerned, she instinctively put her hand on his arm.

"Whatever's wrong, Senor Garcia?" He didn't respond at first, then slowly, he placed his other hand over hers and looked into her eyes. Now it was Elizabeth's turn to be unsettled.

"It seems *you* are my problem, Senorita Dalton." For the first time in weeks, Hidalgo knew what he must do. "I am ashamed that I may have inadvertently compromised your good name with our living arrangements. I want to amend that transgression, so I am asking for your hand in marriage."

Elizabeth stood transfixed, her mouth open, eyes wide with shock, unsure whether she'd heard Hidalgo correctly. Her heart was beating erratically, and she felt faint. The word *marriage* swam in her head because he wanted to protect her good name? Inexplicably, Elizabeth wanted to cry...

33

"Thank you for the noble gesture, Senor, but if that had been a concern for me, I would not have come here in the first place. Thank you for the offer, but I free you from that obligation."

Hidalgo protested, "No, Senorita Dalton...Elizabeth, you misunderstand. That may have been my reasoning initially, but that is because I was in denial of my true feelings." He quickly continued, "It was not by choice, I assure you. I fought these feelings from the moment of our first meeting. When I lost Paloma almost five years ago, I believed it was my destiny to remain alone." Hidalgo continued, afraid Elizabeth might stop him before he dared to finish. "I know; I have no good reason to hope you might harbour similar feelings." He stood looking helpless, not knowing what to do next.

Elizabeth studied his kind face. She could only imagine how difficult it must have been to summon the courage to make such a declaration. Quite a few things made more sense now. She was still processing everything Hidalgo had said. She felt her heart lift, realising he was trying to tell her he loved her.

Hidalgo saw the tears on her cheeks and felt desolate. "I am so sorry, Elizabeth, to upset you; it was not my wish to do so." To Hidalgo's shock, Elizabeth gently touched his cheek.

"On the contrary, Senor Garcia...Hidalgo, you do me a great honour. Over these past months, watching you with Theresa, my admiration for you has grown. I'm not sure when it started to become something else, but if I am candid, I must also acknowledge my feelings for you. I accept your proposal of marriage."

For a moment, neither moved, disbelieving what had happened. Hidalgo briefly encircled Elizabeth awkwardly with his broad arms before quickly releasing her.

"I swear Elizabeth, on my honour, to cherish you all my days."

Elizabeth's tears were now replaced with a gentle smile. In her heart, she knew this was a good decision. Ataliva Roca already felt like home. She had come to love Theresa, doubting she could love her more had she been her child. "Theresa! We must ask her permission."

Hidalgo had already considered this and loved Elizabeth even more for her understanding.

They left town in haste, silent at first, then immersed in the revelation they were to be husband and wife. Just before the hacienda came into view, Hidalgo slowed the horses, bringing them to a halt. He turned to Elizabeth, taking her into his arms, lowering his mouth to hers. There was no resistance. Abruptly he sat back. For an instant, Elizabeth thought she may have done something wrong. She had almost no experience of physical contact with a male; only a few fumbled stolen kisses long ago with the twelve-year-old boy next door. Hidalgo held her briefly at arms-length, then let her go with a wry grin. The realisation came to Elizabeth; she had done nothing wrong; instead, Hidalgo was having difficulty controlling his desire for her. She was suddenly shy, a little embarrassed, and more than a little flustered, knowing her limited knowledge about men.

Hidalgo found it challenging to speak. "As soon as we have talked with Theresa, I will send word to Fr Augustus to post the Banns and arrange for him to marry us in the chapel."

By the time they came to a standstill at the front entrance of the hacienda, Elizabeth felt as though she were floating on air. The housekeeper welcomed them at the front door, a fire blazing in the hearth behind her, the cool night air closing in. One look at their faces told Elena all she needed to know. She sent silent thanks heavenward; her prayers had been answered. She quickly left to prepare a late supper, beaming broadly.

Their late arrival meant Theresa was already asleep. They would speak to her in the morning.

Leaving Elizabeth at her door was difficult, but Hidalgo was an honourable man. He wanted to start their life together in the right way. Kissing Elizabeth's hand, he felt overwhelmed; those same feelings reflected in Elizabeth's eyes. Hidalgo wondered why God had blessed him, allowing such a love twice in his lifetime.

Theresa ran squealing into the kitchen, knowing her father and Miss Elizabeth would be there. Jumping up on her father's lap, she threw her arms around his neck like he had been gone for a month rather than just one day.

"Theresa," Hidalgo's voice was serious; she sat back, a little startled. "I have something I wish to discuss with you. It is of great importance to me, and I must also have your approval for it to happen."

Theresa looked at her father wide-eyed. She could tell it was not a bad thing because he did not look sad, just worried. It must be very important; she had not seen him like this before.

"Since your beloved mother left us, I have been very lonely. We have had our wonderful Elena and Jose` to help us, but I would like us to have a real family, with a mother, father and a *princess*." At this, Theresa smiled; she knew he meant her. She looked at her father, trying to understand what he was trying to tell her. Hidalgo continued, "So I have asked Miss Elizabeth to marry me…with your approval."

Hidalgo and Elizabeth held their breath; Theresa suddenly burst into tears, burying her head in her father's shoulder. He looked at Elizabeth helplessly, and she sat wondering what she should do next. Hidalgo patted Theresa's back, trying to comfort her until the sobs ceased. Without warning, Theresa turned around, throwing her arms around Elizabeth's neck, as the tears started again.

Elizabeth held Theresa slightly away from her and asked, "Why are you crying, Theresa?"

"I thought papa was telling me we were going away somewhere to start a new life, and I would never see you again." Both Elizabeth and Hidalgo, relieved, dared to hope this was Theresa's way of accepting their sudden announcement.

"So, do I have your blessing to help look after your papa and love you as my little girl?"

Theresa was now smiling like it was Christmas. This was the best thing she could remember happening, ever. It was easy to love Miss Elizabeth. No longer scared she might go away one day, happy she would have her here forever. Looking puzzled, she asked, "Do I have to keep calling you Miss Elizabeth? Can I call you mama instead?"

With that, it was Elizabeth's turn to cry. She clutched the toddler to her chest as if she would never let her go.

Elena, the housekeeper, walked into the kitchen at that moment and was soon caught up in the excitement.

Hidalgo decided it was time to go, now amused at the prospect of dealing with three emotional females. He was laughing, feeling like he had just been granted a miracle. He was sure Paloma would have approved.

Ataliva Roca had a beautiful chapel, commissioned almost fifty years earlier for Hidalgo's devout Great Grandmother; there was seating for about fifteen people. Paloma had maintained it studiously. It was especially significant because it also contained many portraits of earlier generations of the Garcia family. It was a private family chapel available to those employed at Ataliva Roca. Also welcome, were close neighbours who wished to attend when the priest came to celebrate mass or communion. Fr Augustus was aware large estancias required constant attention, understanding the difficulty for ranch hands to attend mass regularly; it wasn't possible. He was committed to serving his parish personally whenever he could manage trips to the rural community.

From the moment the pending marriage of Hidalgo and Elizabeth became common knowledge, things moved quickly. Elena gathered wives of the ranch hands and other household workers. Together, they transformed the chapel and organised a sewing party to fashion one of Elizabeth's dresses into a wedding gown. Elena provided 'something borrowed', a beautiful white Chantilly lace Mantilla that had belonged to her mother. Elizabeth found the gesture incredibly moving. Theresa was beside herself with excitement. She was going to be a flower girl. Jose` would stand up for Hidalgo, and Elena would accompany Elizabeth as her maid of honour.

Fr Augustus arrived the evening before the wedding, spending time hearing their confession and giving communion, later advising them on the sanctity of marriage. He was delighted, having played a significant part in bringing these two fine people together. The elderly priest kept Hidalgo company in one of the outer buildings; the nervous groom determined not to see the bride before arriving at the ceremony the next day.

Too excited to sleep the night before the wedding, Elizabeth watched the sun creep above the horizon; it would be a perfect day, but she was apprehensive about the wedding night. Lack of experience filled her with doubt. Elizabeth tried not to think about it...

The chapel was resplendent with the scent of jasmine. Theresa entered the chapel first in a pretty pink floor-length dress, a halo of flowers on her head. Solemnly she walked the short distance to the altar, sprinkling petals; Elena followed one step behind. Everyone stood as Elizabeth appeared at the entrance. Hidalgo's eyes never left her. Looking radiant, her skin like alabaster, golden locks piled high under the Mantilla, eyes sparkling blue. Theresa stood with Elena and Jose` as Elizabeth joined Hidalgo at the altar.

Fr Augustus' booming voice filled the tiny space as he recited the matrimonial litany and prayers. All too soon, the ceremony was over. They were husband and wife. Hidalgo briefly touched Elizabeth's lips with his. Taking her by the hand, they walked out into the sunlight, where he introduced the newlywed Senora Elizabeth Garcia to the ranch hands, their families, and other guests. A cheer went up.

Hidalgo shouted, "Let the celebrations begin."

Everyone helped make it a day to remember—so much food, music, and dancing fuelled by more than a little Tequila. The party continued well into the night.

At last, they were alone. Hidalgo retired briefly to the washroom to allow Elizabeth some privacy to change into her nightwear.

Elizabeth lay deathly still, almost too frightened to breathe. Never had she felt so vulnerable, the thin silken nightgown highlighting every curve of her body. She could hear her rapid heartbeat and feel the blood pounding in her ears. It was that terrifying moment before surrendering yourself to someone completely, letting them take control of your body. Elizabeth had no idea of Hidalgo's expectations but knew in her heart she could trust him.

The door opened quietly; Hidalgo stood framed in the candlelight, naked to the waist, a towel wrapped around his lower body; Elizabeth was trembling. She also supposed he was naked beneath the towel; she had never seen a naked man before. She closed her eyes. The bed creaked as Hidalgo lowered his body beside her; he gently stroked her arm.

"Don't be afraid, Elizabeth; I will be gentle." Opening her eyes, she saw the concern etched on Hidalgo's face. Ever so slowly, he undid the lace ties at the neckline of her gown, peeling away the flimsy material until she lay naked beside him. His lower body was now like hers, fully naked, his manhood erect.

He covered her mouth with a long, lingering kiss. Fully aroused, Hidalgo knew it was too soon for Elizabeth. His hand moved rhythmically down her body, resting on her inner thigh. Slipping fingers gently between her legs, he began stroking her softly. Elizabeth moaned, letting herself embrace the feeling slowly building inside. The throbbing was no longer in her ears but between her legs, growing with every stroke of his fingers. The feeling was hard to describe; it was like no other sensation Elizabeth had ever known. Hidalgo's mouth was more urgent, his tongue seeking hers as his hand moved faster. Suddenly he stopped. Elizabeth almost cried out; she didn't want him to stop.

Hidalgo knew she was ready. He was sure she was a virgin without having to ask. He moved across her body, entering her, feeling the resistance. Each gentle thrust was a little more vigorous than the last. Finally, unable to control the need to climax, he thrust deeply, exploding inside her. Elizabeth cried out briefly, clinging onto Hidalgo tightly until his rhythmic movements ceased. Lifting himself carefully off her body, he lay beside her.

Hidalgo brushed a wisp of golden hair from Elizabeth's face, gazing at her in wonder, still intrigued at how quickly he had grown to love this woman.

"I am sorry I hurt you, my love; I promise it will be better for you next time."

39

She smiled at him shyly, remembering her growing desire as he stroked her intimately, shocked at the intensity. He wrapped his arms around her, cradling her to him, rocking her gently until sleep claimed them both.

It would not be long before Hidalgo and Elizabeth realised they would need to call upon Fr Augustus again, this time to christen a new member of the Garcia dynasty.

Word of Hidalgo Garcia's marriage met with mixed reactions throughout the colony and eventually the other provinces. Hiring a British governess was one thing; marrying her was another. Strong resentment still lingered amongst native Argentinians towards the British. Elizabeth remained unaware of such sentiment, too busy learning to manage the Garcia household and preparing for the birth of their first child.

In late November of 1830, she gave birth to their son and heir, Miguel Raphael Garcia, just short of eight months from the day of their marriage, a legitimate premature birth but one that drew unkind presumptions. At Ataliva Roca, they lived in a kind of protective cocoon. It wasn't until they ventured further did Elizabeth experience any negativity. She paid little heed, too busy running her household, schooling Theresa, and caring for a newborn baby.

Miguel

1838

When Elizabeth Dalton arrived at Ataliva Roca as Governess, Theresa embraced her presence wholeheartedly. This shy, quiet little girl revelled in the attention given by this young woman, who quickly became so much more than her teacher. Elizabeth opened her heart to the child.

Theresa was in awe of Elizabeth. Elizabeth's lips were bright red and always framed in a smile. In the same year of their marriage, Theresa held her baby brother for the first time. He had slightly darker hair than Elizabeth but the same bright blue eyes. Tentatively touching the little outstretched hand, tiny fingers curled around hers. Tears spilt down Theresa's cheeks; in that instant, she became a devoted slave to all of Miguel's whims. A big sister who would love and protect him forever.

From his first unsteady steps, there was never any doubt Miguel was born to life on the land. The horse stables housed animals impatient to be out on the grasslands. If not restrained, Miguel would wriggle under the lower fence and move amongst the magnificent animals towering above him without fear. There was little risk of Miguel being in danger; big sister Theresa was never far behind.

Observing them grow was a joy. Elizabeth delighted in watching Theresa and Miguel charge around the grounds. It was difficult to rein in Theresa's exuberance. Enthusiasm was an excellent catalyst for achievement, but Elizabeth knew succeeding in a man's world required her to be better equipped. It was common for men to complete business deals over a bottle or two of tequila. Such a proposition would never do for Senorina Garcia!

Theresa had a natural affinity with horses. She was passionate about riding and showed great skill. By the time Miguel was seven, he also displayed the same aptitude. From the outset, Hidalgo insisted they experience as much as possible about the running of the property, training that would eventually extend to all the Garcia holdings throughout the country. He encouraged both children to ask questions and spend time amongst the herders and their families. He wanted them to learn the finer points about raising and caring for cattle and horses but also teach them humility and gratitude by understanding how hard farm hands worked

The hacienda nestled beneath a gently sloping hill, providing shelter from violent storms that swept in from the north. Early morning was Miguels' favourite time of day. Before sunrise, he would head out onto the veranda to watch the morning mist swirl above the warming earth. Daybreak seemed to unleash all of mother nature's wonders. Birds fluttered amongst the damp grass, seeking insects, hurriedly returning to nesting chicks squawking in hungry protest. Nearby, cattle grazed contentedly. A gentle breeze carried the scent of smoke. Glowing coals, re-stoked by ranch hands hurrying to devour breakfast and get on with the long day ahead.

The cloudless sky turned from dusky grey to bright blue as the sun rose. Miguel loved this land almost as much as his father. He chuckled, remembering mornings like this as he and Theresa wolfed down great slices of freshly baked bread smothered in butter and honey. The housekeeper was encouraged by the 'oohs' and 'ahs' coming from the children, signifying that breakfast was to their satisfaction.

"Elena, you spoil those children something shamefully," the kindly voice of Hidalgo would call from the entry hall.

"I am sorry, Senor," Elena would reply with feigned remorse, then wink at both the children, who would burst into laughter. Theirs was a good childhood.

Ataliva Roca was a fine property, well cared for and thriving, thanks to generations of good management. Many landowners with extensive holdings chose to divide their properties into smaller farms.

The Garcia family had withstood hardships to survive, resisting the same temptation and prospering. Their land remained intact; several thousand square kilometres spread across the plains into a shallow valley, framed to the west by a low mountain range. An impressive number of cattle and horses grazed as far as the eye could see. Several fields were ripe with rye and barley, shimmering in the early sunlight. Miguel reflected on the words his father Hidalgo often repeated: "You must treat the land with respect. Never take anything for granted. You must work hard to achieve your goals and remember to take care of those less fortunate. If you do this, God will bless your efforts."

Miguel never tired of hearing how his father had toiled to build up their many properties spread over Argentina. From the time he could comprehend, he embraced the responsibility of his future position.

Santa Rosa
☼
1838

Hidalgo introduced many new initiatives with his share farmers. He recognised the necessity for the local community to thrive and grow. Looking after their interests was of prime concern; they helped him become a wealthy man.

During the reduced rainfall caused by El Nino, smaller share farmers struggled to access enough water to irrigate crops and produce feed for livestock. Some failed to survive.

Elizabeth maintained a close friendship with Fr Augustus over the years, and it was during one of their social visits she learned that many were struggling. By incorporating the priest's help, they formulated a plan to supply and distribute goods to those in need. As the priest in residence, Fr Augustus had a legitimate reason to visit his parishioners, subtly enabling him to deliver supplies. He recognised these people had great pride and were not used to accepting charity, never seeking help even when the need was dire. Although Elizabeth had sworn the priest to secrecy regarding her part in the scheme, the considerable increase in Elizabeth's purchases from Senor Torella's store quickly raised speculation that the true benefactor was Senora Garcia. Whatever antipathy remained toward the British mistress of Ataliva Roca promptly vanished, replaced by overwhelming gratitude for her kindness. Hidalgo could not have been prouder of Elizabeth. He never questioned the purchases, no matter how large. He and his family had such abundance. It was only fitting to share.

As 1838 came to a close, reluctantly, Fr Augustus announced his retirement. He was returning to the Monastery of San Lorenzo in

Santa Fe to live out his days. He would be close to several family members to help support him as he aged. The new priest, Father Peter Anuncio Mendoza, was due to arrive any day.

Elizabeth decided she should make a special effort to attend Fr Augustus's farewell. She had become very fond of the elderly priest and was going to miss him. Hoping the children might attend also was wishful thinking. Elizabeth had little success persuading them on previous occasions. They always preferred staying at home to help out on the ranch. The Garcias rarely attended services in Santa Rosa, more frequently using their private chapel.

Elizabeth would arrange for one of the ranch hands to take her to town for the farewell. Sadly, she had only encountered Isabella Caron a few times over the years; their visits to town rarely coincided. Happy to see the whole family attending the farewell mass, Elizabeth was pleased to meet Isabella's husband, Paulo, for the first time, son Delgado, and their youngest, Maria. Isabella had been heavily pregnant with Maria when they first met. Sitting alongside her mother was Rosa, whom she remembered well, marvelling at what a beauty she was becoming at fourteen. Was it only seven years ago…it seemed much longer.

Another source of pride and joy for the Garcias was their cattle stud in Cordoba, the envy of many wealthy graziers in the surrounding provinces. The original breeding program commenced three years earlier at Ataliva Roca. An extensive dry spell significantly reduced the natural spring water with the potential to affect the herds; their ranch was less affected than most. Most of their cattle survived well. Eventually, the pampas grassland, on which the stock depended, was affected; when feed became sparse, Hidalgo let the herd graze unchecked.

The breeding program began with prime Criollo steers, descendants of Andalusian cattle first introduced into the Americas by Christopher Columbus. They were sturdy beasts with a gentle nature, easily worked with horses, and had good longevity. Later he imported several prime Shorthorn stud bulls from northern England.

Hidalgo was fast developing a reputation as one of the finest breeders in Argentina; his livestock was highly prized, known for producing the most significant yield of flesh per beast, and accredited as having excellent quality.

Invited to join the Stockman's Association in Buenos Aires, Hidalgo was jubilant, although determined never to get caught up in a competitive way like many other breeders. His focus was that of a businessman; to maintain quality, increase sales, and ultimately lead to greater prosperity. Argentina had both the highest consumption and export of meat worldwide. Still, he was honoured.

Ranching was big business. As the nation's wealth grew, so did the hunger for power. One of Hidalgo's rivals amongst the top breeders was Ramon Mendoza, owner of multiple large Estancias from north-western Cordoba to Santa Fe and beyond. Ramon, previously Mayor of Cordoba, had just been elected governor of Buenos Aires Province. Rumours quickly surfaced there had been voting anomalies, but when the only opponent withdrew his candidacy, reportedly due to ill health, there was no further investigation of the claims. Ramon was elected unopposed.

Hidalgo met the Governor only once. Coincidentally, Ramon Mendoza had been president of the Cattle Breeders Association of Buenos Aires before running for office. As governor, he attended the awards dinner to present the Breeder of the Year trophy for 1839, the stud of note, Ataliva Roca.

Though usually never one to judge in haste, meeting him for the first time, Hidalgo disliked the man instantly. There was an air of arrogance about him. He had a prestigious reputation, but the way he ignored those he judged less worthy of his attention raised Hidalgo's ire.

While Ramon had been animated and effusive in praising Ataliva's achievements during the ceremony, Hidalgo knew there would be no further social exchange between the two following the award, which he didn't find displeasing. Hidalgo was also aware they were in direct competition as breeders. With this win, he usurped the Governor's entry from Reinado Stud in Santa Fe.

Buenos Aires
☼
1839

Elizabeth remembered when she first arrived in Buenos Aires almost eight years earlier. Back then, life was comparable to what she read of wild west towns in America. Over time, the level of sophistication emerging was evident. Most activities centred around the port, Rio de la Plata, the hub of the river trade, once the Capital of Argentina.

Trade was stifled under the Spanish Viceroyalty, rendering Buenos Aires a backwater. Many generations of Argentinians, descended from the Spanish, no longer considered their allegiance to Spain, and actively sought self-governance. Left to their own devices, the portenos, *people of the port*, thrived on contraband traded with Brazil. A growing number of settlements spread along the northwest banks of the Riachuelo River, a fertile area easily navigated by boats exporting cereals, cattle hides and dried beef.

The British briefly ruled the country in 1806 before being overthrown. Despite establishing strong trade links with South America, the foreigners remained potential enemies, not having given up hope entirely of regaining control. An undercurrent of unrest remained, with skirmishes between the two prevalent.

The visit north had been a pleasant change from their insular existence on the ranch. Elizabeth had a wonderful time purchasing gifts for the children and the household staff. Hidalgo's planned visit to his northern properties coincided with Ataliva Roca winning the Best Breeder's Trophy that year. The holiday also served as a belated honeymoon.

After the trophy presentation, they returned to their lodgings, both in high spirits. Elizabeth had made acquaintance with people she only previously knew by name. She thoroughly enjoyed sitting down to fine food, locally produced wines, and dancing. Both she and Hidalgo had a wonderful night.

They retired to bed, Elizabeth seeking the warmth of Hidalgo. He was amused, remembering how shy and naive she had been when first married. Now well-practised in the art of making love, she often initiated the foreplay. Hidalgo rose to the occasion, literally. Elizabeth's hands deftly cradled his genital area, and he moaned. Instinctively, she knew when to stop. She was fully aroused from their mutual foreplay. Boldly, Elizabeth lay her body across Hidalgo. She could see his salacious grin in the moonlight, anticipating her next move. They had become skilled at synchronising their climax. Lowering her body slowly over his, she guided his erect manhood, letting out a gasp, embracing the sensation of him entering her fully. Their bodies moved in unison, simultaneously enjoying the pleasure.

Too soon, it would be over. The overwhelming sensation of orgasm never ceased to amaze Elizabeth; she reflected on how such a powerful urge was beyond human control. When carnal desire took over, any reason seemed to vanish, dispelled by a craving to experience the explosive sensations flowing through her body.

They shared a lingering kiss before separating. Hidalgo's love for Elizabeth was mirrored in her face as she lay beside him, in awe at this man who had completely changed the trajectory of her life.

Visiting the Garcia holdings in Cordoba, Santa Fe, and Rosario had taken its toll; Elizabeth and Hidalgo were eager to head home. Receiving regular telegraphic updates was sufficient to still any concerns, but they missed Theresa and Miguel terribly. They agreed two months away from home was too long.

The positive outcome of their journey was to find their outlying properties thriving, doing far better than Hidalgo expected, and weathering the El Nino exceptionally well. He had good managers and experienced ranch hands. Selective in his choices, he paid them well. It was rare for anyone to leave the employment of Hidalgo Garcia.

There were other compensations from the trip. While in Cordoba, there was gossip about one of the top breeders amassing a large gambling debt and needing to liquidate some assets to settle it. Speculation was rife; The rancher was forced to consider relinquishing several of his prize stud bulls. Luck was on Hidalgo's side; he approached the man discreetly, offering him a price he couldn't refuse—a tremendous coup.

When Ramon Mendoza received this news, he was beyond furious. Usually, he would be the first to have the opportunity of acquiring such livestock. In his role as Governor, much of the running of his estancias fell to the managers. Their communication was not as astute; they failed to ensure Ramon knew of the pending sale. Someone would pay for that blunder. Hidalgo Garcia was becoming more than a minor irritation. He was now presenting a serious challenge to Ramone's reputation as a breeder of the best prime livestock and threatened his reputation as the best exporter Argentina had to offer.

Santa Rosa – The Caron Family

☼

1839

Santa Rosa was home to almost two hundred people, primarily farmers and their families. Most of the residents lived close to the township. Many were share farmers for the Garcia family, like Paulo and Isabella Caron. Some leased farms and others worked as labourers, maintaining big estancias while owners lived 'the good life' far away in Buenos Aires, Santa Fe or Cordoba. They produced mainly grain and beef, headed for Buenos Aire's markets 385 miles to the northeast. Transportation of goods took place on wooden carts, hauled by teams of oxen. Santa Rosa was a happy community of hardworking people.

The town hosted less than a dozen buildings. One was a general store incorporating a haberdashery, produce section, and farm supplies. Next door, passenger coaches dropped off visitors. The blacksmith's shop stood alongside the coach terminal, with a large corral outback holding fifty oxen, exchange animals for travelling wagon teams, while half a dozen sizeable carts, also belonging to the blacksmith, sat abandoned in a paddock nearby.

A laneway separated two buildings: a temporary vegetable stall and the baker's shop. If you ventured down the laneway to the back of the hardware store, you would find a *pulperia*, a rough-hewn shelter where they dispensed alcohol from a makeshift bar—frowned upon by the decent citizens of the town, although tolerated for travellers passing through. A few locals were inclined to indulge, happily out of sight from those opposed to dispensing alcohol.

There were two other buildings some distance from the town centre, the school, a single timber dwelling marked the southern perimeter and the Church. Every town had a church. Perched on a plateau midway between the school and the town centre stood Our Lady of The Rosary Church, its stark whitewashed adobe walls blinding in the sunlight. A bronze bell in the left tower chimed loudly, echoing across the valley, calling the faithful. Sunday, the school was silent, but each day, Monday through Friday, the raucous sound of children at play carried to the township.

On the north side of the church was an avenue of Jacaranda trees. Scattered along the slope shaded by the trees stood several elaborate marble graves, along with twenty or thirty white crosses, all marking the final resting place of Santa Rosa's citizens.

Late for School

☼

For Rosa and her family, life outside their little village was good. Three miles south of Santa Rosa, the farm on which they lived was thriving; her father, Paulo, and mother, Isabella, studiously worked their holding twelve hours a day. Isabella also supplemented their income as a seamstress. Rosa idolised her parents.

Being the middle child was not always easy. Quiet, studious and deeply religious, sometimes Rosa felt overlooked. Younger sister Maria was the opposite, a bundle of energy, always running, never walking, full of laughter and joy. She chattered non-stop. Rosa's elder brother Delgado also worked on their farm, receiving high praise from their parents. He was very protective of his sisters but knew little about the workings of young female minds, so he kept mainly to himself in his spare time.

Rosa loved the simplicity of her life and the order this presented. She would rise early, take a simple breakfast, help with the chores, go to school each weekday, enjoy an occasional treat on Saturday, and attend church on Sundays, without exception.

Like most young girls, Rosa had a fertile imagination. With little access to the world outside the village and beyond, she could only dream of what life might be like in a big city. Rosa pored through any book or newspaper that came into her possession, gripped by a passion for seeing the wondrous places on display. She imagined herself in delicate gowns of lustrous silk or organza, glittering jewels at her throat.

"Rosa, hurry up, or you will be late for school!" her mother's voice chided.

Rosa grumbled to herself; unusual for her, she was always respectful and obedient to her parents. Grabbing her school satchel, she headed to the front door, where her mother waited with a packed lunch.

"Thank you, Mumma," Rosa responded politely but with little evident gratitude.

Isabella had a look of scorn on her face but thought better of rebuking Rosa. At fourteen and in her final year at school, she was uncharacteristically moody. Isabella understood what to expect when teenagers transitioned into young adults, especially girls with bodies approaching womanhood. "Hurry along now," she said more gently.

Maria, her sister, was long gone, so Rosa had no one to grumble with on the almost two-mile walk ahead. Disgruntled, without a further word, she headed off down the dirt road, dragging her feet, every step sending up a spray of dust until both feet and shoes looked like they had always been putrid. She couldn't have cared less.

Trudging along, her head down, Rosa was oblivious to the clear blue sky and surrounding beauty. In this unique part of the southern pampas, the valley was lush with vegetation—the cattle, sheep and goats roaming the paddocks nearby were in robust condition. Trees of a wide variety dotted the landscape, primarily natives like the Ceibo. In contrast, Italian and German immigrants introduced others, following the Spanish in their elusive search for Eldorado. The expectation of wealth, mainly gold, proved futile. Skirmishes with indigenous Indians caused most to flee the area. Those remaining reaped the rewards of rich pastures as they wholeheartedly embraced the Argentinian way of life.

Sadly, in Rosa's state of mind, she could only think about today being Friday and the weekend ahead. She might be lucky enough to go shopping in Santa Rosa for a store-bought dress, a promised present for her upcoming fifteenth birthday. Rosa contemplated the prospect as she dawdled along, daydreaming of a pale lilac dress with voluminous petticoats.

Jolted from her reverie by the clanging of the school bell sounding a final warning, Rosa began to run, knowing regardless, she was going to be late, dismal at the thought of the detention she would incur. Trouble at school meant there would be no trip to town tomorrow. Her mood descended once again. It was going to be a long day.

Late for Church – Welcoming the New Priest
☼

Rosa lay gazing up at the sky, the sunlight almost blinding as it slipped out from behind billowing clouds. Since early morning, she had been out in the fields. Isabella sent her to gather wildflowers to adorn the church altar for Sunday mass; she was easily distracted by her surroundings. Daydreaming was Rosa's full-time hobby, much to her parent's dismay.

She watched, enthralled, as Cardoon Thistles, almost three metres tall, swayed with each gust of wind, sporadically releasing a puff of white transparent spheres into the atmosphere. They would travel long distances before their journey's end, gently fall to earth to start the cycle of renewal. Cradled within the comfort of long grass, soaking up the sun's warmth, she fell asleep.

Rosa sat upright, aware of someone calling out, hearing her name carried on the wind. Grabbing the pitifully small posy of flowers gathered, she bolted for home, brushing the tell-tale twigs and grass from her clothing. Rosa could envision her mother, Isabella, long before she came into view. Standing legs askew, hands-on-hips, a scowl covering her face, ready to give Rosa a tongue lashing. She was in so much trouble.

Charged with the responsibility and honour of keeping the church in immaculate order today, of all days, Isabella wanted things to go smoothly. It was an auspicious day. The elderly priest, Father Augustus, was retiring to Santa Fe. Today, the town would welcome the new priest, Father Peter Anuncio Mendoza, into the close-knit community of Santa Rosa. Everyone was curious to know and engage with the person who would hear their dark secrets in the confessional.

Hopefully, the new priest would be an effective intermediary with God when seeking absolution for their sins.

Flustered and out of breath, Rosa came charging down the dirt road. The simple adobe hacienda came into view, her mother Isabel livid, standing just as Rosa had imagined. Clutching the small offering of wildflowers in a vice-like grip, she squared her shoulders, bowing her head as Isabella vented her anger and, worse, her disappointment at once more being let down by Rosa.

The three miles to the church passed in silence, the usual banter non-existent. Even Rosa's brother and sister, absolved of any part in their mother's mood, maintained their silence. They did not want to risk drawing attention to themselves, fearing they, too, may become the focus of their mother's simmering anger.

The gentle clip, clop of the horse's hooves, and the creaking rhythm of the buggy wheels on the uneven dirt road eventually seemed to have a soothing effect on Isabella's mood. Along the route, there were many carriages headed for the church. The anticipation and excitement finally worked a little magic. Everyone sighed with relief when Isabella finally spoke.

"What a beautiful day God has given us to celebrate all we have; to give thanks for his new servant sent to administer our needs."

The effect was instantaneous; excited chatter was now exchanged between Delgado and Maria as the façade of the Church came into view. Even Paulo, Rosa's father, who could not profess to be as devout as Isabella, was caught up in the excitement. The church was overflowing.

Fr Augustus Farewell

☼

Welcome to Fr Peter

Father Peter Mendoza, the new priest, stood looking at the sea of smiling faces. Good folk, curious about this stranger taking the place of their beloved priest and friend, Fr Augustus.

The dedication liturgy over, Peter took a few minutes respite in the vestry, ostensibly to change his ceremonial robes, but really to take time reflecting on his life. Closing his eyes, he thought back over his thirty-five years, wondering about this little town in southwestern Argentina, far from his roots. Even as a young child, he had never doubted the presence of God in his life. Ilona, his devout mother, instilled an unshakeable faith in her two eldest sons. There must be a reason his journey had led him to Santa Rosa.

Born in Cordoba in 1804, Peter's earliest memories before age six were few. With little warning, he and his older brother Philippe aged ten, were sent off to All Saints Boarding School in Santa Fe, two hundred and ten miles away. Both boys possessed the same gentle nature as their mother, a trait their father Ramon likened to weakness, something he couldn't abide, hoping the austere life would toughen the boys up.

Peter sighed; reflecting on his family history only filled him with sadness. He had been separated from them for a long time, happily dedicated to serving the church for many years. Smiling, he joined the farewell celebrations now in full swing. Some names would escape him for the present, but he would come to know their weaknesses and strengths intimately. He hoped many would become good friends.

Fr Peter learned Senora Caron and her daughter Rosa came each week to clean the church and the surrounding outer buildings as volunteers. They brought flowers for the church altar in readiness for mass on Sunday; he was grateful for their assistance and looked forward to getting to know them.

The Mendoza Family

Ramon Artigas Mendoza

Ramon was a statesman, charismatic, clever, and very ambitious. Distantly related to the sixteenth-century governor of Chile, Don Garcia Mendoza. His 'allies' were usually in debt to him for something. Likewise, his many enemies, jealous of his success, were happy to spread rumours his wealth was built on gambling and rustling other people's cattle. He gained power through shrewd manoeuvring, acquiring many properties through shady dealings. Ramon was reputedly also a womaniser; worse still, he lacked discretion.

Over the years, his two eldest sons, Philippe and Peter, had little contact with their father. He was absent even when they went home for the end-of-year holidays. Being Mayor of Cordoba meant Ramon spent a good portion of his time in town rather than at his ranch; at least, that was the explanation given to the boys by their mother. There were Gauchos to manage the estate in his absence. As Peter grew older, he realised his father treated his mother, Ilona, with disdain. He never witnessed physical violence towards her, although he suspected it had occurred. She never complained.

Ramon returned home from a failed business meeting in Santa Fe in late March. In a foul mood and drunk, he started an argument. Usually, Ilona would avoid him at such times, having felt the sting of his hand more than once. For some perverse reason, she stood her ground; perhaps it was enjoying seeing him so upset or knowing someone had gotten the better of him. The one mistake she made was to mock him.

59

Without a word, Ramon turned, snarling, his face filled with rage; with the back of his hand, he knocked her over the settee. Shocked and shaken, Ilona lay sprawled across the seat, trying to clear her head before attempting to get up. Suddenly Ramon was on top of her, tearing at her clothing.

"It's time I taught you a lesson" She would not laugh at him again in a hurry!

Ilona cried out as he abused her. Afterwards, he staggered off to his room without a backward glance.

Ilona lay whimpering, regretting her stupidity. Even she had underestimated Ramon's capacity for brutality. Bruised and bleeding, she slowly gathered up the remnants of clothing, shakily managing to get to the washroom, desperate to cleanse every vestige of him from her body. Soon the sobbing started.

When Ilona surfaced from her room the next day, bruised and shaken, Ramon was long gone, telling Aida, the housekeeper, he was going to Cordoba and didn't know when he'd return. Ilona prayed he would never return. Aida could see the state of her mistress, but there was nothing to be done. No one challenged Ramon.

Ilona was horrified when she realised she was pregnant. Despite her devotion to God, she prayed he would cause her to abort the baby. It wasn't to be. As the months passed, Ilona felt she was losing her mind; she struggled writing to her precious boys, unable to tell them she was with child. The only good thing to come out of this horrific situation, Ramon had not come near her again, staying in town most of the time.

Appalled to find out Ilona was pregnant, Ramon cursed her vehemently, not once considering his accountability in the matter.

Christmas 1813, a ranch hand collected the boys from the coach depot in Cordoba. It had been a three-day journey; they were tired but excited to head home for the holidays. Receiving only an occasional letter from their mother over the previous months was unusual; they were worried. Ilona's letters were always full of love and encouragement, with lots of news, anecdotes, and updates about

60

their pet horses and other farm favourites. Without fail, they usually expected letters to arrive every second week.

Loading their cases onto the wagon, they headed off. Travelling through the centre of town they passed by the impressive council chambers. Peter looked up to the top floor balcony; in clear view, his father was laughing loudly, his arm around the waist of a pretty young woman.

Shocked was hardly sufficient to express how Peter and Philippe felt greeting their mother, not only because she was obviously in her final months of pregnancy but because she also looked ghastly. Both boys were filled with concern. Philippe inquired after their father. The look on Ilona's face was immediately fearful; she stammered,

He was "Very busy, away in Buenos Aires."

Peter had been standing with his head down. He couldn't bear looking at his mother, seeing her like this. At her response, he looked up abruptly; he knew what she said wasn't true but decided not to say anything. Whatever was behind her statement, confessing to seeing his father in town with another woman would not help the situation.

As always, the housekeeper Aida and her husband, Alfredo, made a great fuss about the boy's arrival, making them feel pleased to be home.

Over the holidays, both boys insisted their mother rest. They completed many jobs around the homestead that needed doing in their father's absence. Ramon never did make an appearance. Some expensive gifts and a note arrived Christmas morning wishing them all season's greetings. Ilona did not comment, but Peter noted the look of loathing on her face as she turned away. New Year came and went as they prepared to go back to school. Less than a week after returning to school, they were summoned to the priory office and informed their mother had produced another son, to be christened Carlos, a child dedicated to the Glory of God.

Carlos Mendoza entered the world crying incessantly, demanding attention from his first breath. Ilona could barely look at him. Deeply depressed, she withdrew, spending most days on her

61

knees in prayer before the shrine in her room. Aida became a surrogate mother to Carlos, spoiling him in Ilona's absence.

In November of that same year, El Nina struck, flooding the northern part of the continent and cutting off all roads to Cordoba. Sadly, the boys realised there was no going home for the upcoming Christmas break. The rains finally eased by the end of January. At the beginning of March, they were again summoned by the head Prior, informing them their mother had taken her own life.

The Cathedral of the Immaculate Conception in Cordoba was overflowing. Many were present out of curiosity. There was little sympathy for Ramon; disliked by those who knew him and greatly feared by others. He was a powerful, dangerous man. Colleagues who failed to attend the funeral would pay for such disrespect. On the other hand, many in the community attended, feeling great sorrow for Ilona's sons and a desire to show respect to the deceased, Senora Mendoza.

Standing at the front of the church, with his head bowed, Ramon looked suitably distraught. Truthfully, he was angry more than anything else, humiliated by Ilona taking her life and how this might reflect on him. No one dared to hint such an act showed how overwhelmed she was. Ilona was devout; this was well known. She was aware the Catholic Church considered suicide a mortal sin, which only emphasised how desperate she was to be free of her husband.

Philippe and Peter stood beside him, ashen-faced, desolate, grieving openly. Ramon squirmed uncomfortably, unable to comfort them. He had nothing in common with either boy.

Carlos Mendoza

☼

Carlos proved to be the opposite of his older brothers. To Ramon's amusement, even from an early age, he ordered ranch hands around, quickly becoming the apple of his father's eye. Sadly, he also showed early signs of having a cruel streak. When upset, it was not unusual for him to kick his pet dog, even as it approached to comfort him. He was sly and adept at lying. When expedient, Carlos had no trouble blaming others for things he'd perpetrated. Aida spoiled him terribly, pandering to his every whim and letting him cheat without offering a rebuke, even when they played a friendly game of cards.

Ramon had given up on the idea of Peter or Philippe carrying on the ranching business, but he did hold out hope for Carlos. Deciding to have him home-schooled, he hired a Governess. Not one but three Governess quit within a short period due to Carlos's unruly behaviour. He was rude and arrogant, refusing to comply with directions. Finally fed up, Ramon had little patience with anything disrupting his routine; he acted swiftly.

Carlos was furious when told his father was sending him to the same boarding school his older brothers had attended. Philippe, now graduated, was studying accountancy. Peter entered the priesthood despite his father's opposition, much to Ramon's disgust.

Carlos was barely one when his mother, Ilona, thirty-three, committed suicide; he grew up with a sense of abandonment, disbelieving anyone who expressed affection for him. Another legacy was his obsession with possessing anything forbidden to him. Once in his grasp, he hated letting anything go.

In Carlos's formative years, Ramon was away campaigning for long periods. Neither did he benefit from the company or guidance of his older siblings, both away at boarding school. He was a loner.

63

Carlos idolised his father and was always eager to please him, but he had already decided he would never be a rancher as Ramon planned. From an early age, Carlos realised ranching entailed hard work. Instead, he aimed to emulate his father's political career, preferring to use his brains to achieve financial success rather than the heavy physical effort required for ranching.

Philippe Mendoza
☼

Philippe Mendoza was almost fourteen when his mother died. Quiet by nature, he became even more withdrawn. Though Ilona's death was not directly due to Ramon's abuse, Philippe suspected there was a connection. He didn't dare explore this theory. If candid, he had to admit he was terrified of his father, having witnessed his violent temper more than once.

In 1826, after completing studies at the Seminary, Philippe joined the other graduate Dominican and Franciscan Brothers at the Monastery of The Incarnation in Buenos Aires. Life in the seminary was orderly and predictable. Both he and his younger brother Peter embraced the monastic life, loving the sense of peace and serenity. There was never any discord. Still three years from ordination, Peter looked forward to serving the general community.

For Philippe, it wasn't quite that simple. His fellow graduates had already chosen their missions. He strongly desired to join a Franciscan order involved in any charitable enterprise and missionary work. Expressing this desire with his father, Ramon flew into a vile rage. He recognised Philippe did not have what it took to be a rancher but determined he would get something worthwhile out of his eldest son.

The question of Philippe's future wasn't up for negotiation. Ramon had already gifted a sizeable library to the University of Buenos Aires, anticipating Philippe's entry for training to become an accountant following graduation. Philippe, proficient in all subjects, excelled in maths and science. Ramon needed someone trustworthy to manage his business affairs and not ask too many questions. He didn't want outsiders asking where the money came from or where it went.

Well-trained in obedience, Philippe always accepted the will of his superiors. Piety and servitude were the backbones of the seminary; he saw his father's demands as no different, his personal goals no longer considered.

Bitterly opposed initially to Philippe undertaking theological studies, Ramon reconsidered when realising how he might use this to his advantage, as long as Philippe agreed to complete a Degree in Business Management simultaneously. If his plans succeeded, they would completely corrupt his son's integrity and honesty, which was of little consequence to Ramon.

It would be strange spending time at their property, Negro Garza, named after the black Herron that frequented the lagoon nearby. Philippe and Peter played there often as small children, fascinated by watching the birds work in tandem to catch fish. It hadn't felt like home since his mother's death. He had little enthusiasm to return. His father *summoned* him home to celebrate the completion of his studies. Philippe was more than a little surprised by the 'invitation'. It was the first time his father ever sought his company. He hoped his younger brother Peter might join them; it would be just like when the boys arrived home together from boarding school.

Ramon sat gazing out over the lagoon, enjoying a cigar in the late afternoon. He rarely took a break during campaigning, but he had a good reason. Besides, his youngest son, Carlos, would also be home for Easter. Ramon smiled, watching the smoke rings curl above his head, slowly dissolving in the breeze. He sat thinking about Philippe's future.

He reflected on his success in imposing a loading on many goods produced in the area. Villa Maria, run by the Franciscan Brothers, registered as a not-for-profit organisation, qualified as a charity and was therefore exempt from the levy, adding many extra thousands of dollars to their coffers. Ramon visited Brother Bernado on several occasions over the previous couple of years. As the church's holding grew, he was happy to make generous donations to support that growth, eventually boldly suggesting they could use a good business

66

manager. He just so happened to have someone in mind, amply qualified and with a heart dedicated to the Franciscan Order. Who could be more fitting than his son Philippe?

Rosa's Dream

☼

After joining the Santa Rosa parish, Fr Peter regularly visited parishioners outside the church precincts. On his return trip, he always dropped by the Caron farm to be greeted warmly. Peter had become particularly fond of the whole family. The priest was an average cook at best. Isabella had the reputation of being one of the finest cooks in the district, and Peter was not about to pass up any opportunity to savour her wares.

Rosa and Fr Peter quickly became firm friends. Like the rest of the parish, Rosa recognised the priest's outstanding qualities to their community. A sort of hero worship was developing in her young mind, a situation he would have discouraged had he been aware.

Outstanding in his studies, the Theological Hierarchy at ordination bestowed on him the consecrated name of Father Peter Anuncio, meaning someone exceptional.

Years later, when he arrived in Santa Rosa, the priest encouraged the congregation to call him by the less formal name of Fr Peter. This gesture was very popular. The parishioners felt like they were already friends with the new priest. He was kind and compassionate, even to those who might curse or speak ill of the church. The humblest of men, he did not abide the sin of pride, his good deeds coming from someone pure of heart, with no expectation of reward or praise.

For Rosa, the most challenging part of her faith had always been the act of confession. Whenever she did anything wrong, she was remorseful and quick to apologise. There was little to confess, perhaps cursing her teasing siblings on occasion. Rosa was a hardworking and obedient daughter, honest and diligent with her school lessons. Everyone who knew her spoke highly of this quiet, gentle lass. Completing her schooling, Rosa proved scholastically outstanding, something that surprised her friends and neighbours, most of whom attended the same local church.

Upon hearing her confession, Rosa was shocked when Fr Peter asked if she had any 'impure' thoughts to confess. Rosa was not sure just what an impure thought was. Somehow guessing it might be like when the silly young men pointed to her chest and encouraged her to wiggle her shoulders. They hooted with laughter at her discomfort, whispering amongst themselves. Rosa didn't know what they were saying, but she was sure it had to do with her changing body. Rosa was self-conscious of her developing breasts, their outline and fullness now clearly evident against the soft fabric of her blouse. Rosa blushed when she thought about the boys chiding her.

"No, Father, I don't believe so…" she answered indignantly.

Rosa could almost see the smile on his face as he blessed her and commended her to say a Novena and three Hail Marys' and to go and sin no more.

Hurrying from the confessional, Rosa considered the awkward question put by Fr Peter, blushing again, wondering what impure thoughts might be, yet knowing by instinct that they were immoral and something God would consider a sin. At nearly fifteen, Rosa decided she should know these things. How else to guard against making such a mistake through ignorance? Perhaps she could ask her mother, Isabella, to explain.

Caught unawares by Rosa's question, Isabella, outraged, threw up her hands in horror at having to explain such a thing. Frantically making the sign of the cross, exclaiming, "Almighty Father, who puts such questions into the mouth of my innocent child? God forgive them, and you, Rosa, we will not speak of this again!"

Rosa dared not disclose that Fr Peter had asked the question. She felt ashamed without even knowing why, which left her more curious than ever, but none the wiser.

It was late Spring, and the atmosphere was ripe for change. The air was charged; there was a restless mood amongst the town folk, as though everyone was …waiting, for what... Balmy nights caused many to have disturbed, broken sleep. The rains would come soon, the land would be washed clean, the pastures would flourish, and those that went a little loco at this time would calm down and get back to normal.

Rosa drifted in and out of sleep. Lately, she was more unsettled than usual, with no logical explanation. Sudden mood changes, uncommon for her, would find her yelling at her brother and sister over minor things that didn't warrant such anger. Isabella and Paulo exchanged glances at such times, a slight nod and faint smile passing between them; they knew Rosa's rite of passage to becoming a woman was near, so they tolerated her infrequent outbursts without rancour or reprimand. Rosa's siblings did as they usually did most of the time…ignored her as if she wasn't even there.

The dream began innocently enough. Rosa was in the magnificent hacienda, *her* hacienda lying on a bed of the softest feather down. Fine cotton sheets covered her young, lithe body, outlining the curves of her burgeoning womanhood. It was almost like watching a small insignificant moth turn into a beautiful butterfly. It was the dead of night; the soft silver moonlight spilled through the elaborately arched windows, caressing the restless form. Shadows danced across the room as swirling clouds raced westward, hinting at the approaching storm.

The door slid open without making a sound…her 'mystery man' stood silent, unmoving, taking in the vision before him. Rosa's breath caught in her throat, but surprisingly she felt unafraid. Instead, if anything, she was aware she was more excited than scared. If only she could see his face, even for a second. The enveloping darkness and the sombrero guarded his identity, something she had never been quite able to imagine clearly; she just knew he would be handsome.

The stranger slowly crossed the room and lay down gently beside her. Feeling lightheaded, she realised she was holding her breath. Deep gasps shook her body as she sucked air into her lungs. The stranger gently stroked her body, first her arm

70

and then her face. Finally slipping his hands under the fine cotton sheet, he began stroking her body. Finding no resistance to his touch, his hands gently moved down the length of her body to her upper thigh.

The moan was audible; Rosa was shocked to realise it came from her. The stranger's fingers began to explore more intimately, and as much as Rosa knew she should protest vehemently, a new sensation awakened deep inside her being. She felt helpless to fight it, wanting more, as a deep throbbing took hold of her lower body.

The stranger removed the sheet slowly; her naked body was now fully exposed; there was nowhere to hide. Sweet, gentle kisses took the place of the stranger's probing fingers. When he bent to kiss her most private parts, Rosa cried out as unfamiliar spasms wracked her body, intense, uncomfortable, filling her with sensations she had no words for, like dying and being born all at the same time.

Rosa, still moaning, awakened from her dream. Without needing further clarification, Rosa knew what impure thoughts were. The following confession she would make was going to now be torture. There was a good chance she would die of shame or, at the very least, be doomed to burn in hell. The sun had barely risen when Rosa could hear her mother,

"Rosa, get out of bed." Mortally ashamed of her dream during the night, she was reluctant to face the day; instead, Rosa wanted to stay curled up in bed and try to make sense of what happened in the dream, realising she couldn't block it out of her mind.

Isabella's voice called more impatiently this time. Groaning, Rosa forced herself to get out of bed, becoming aware the bedding underneath her felt damp. With further investigation, she was shocked to see blood on the sheet. Now a woman in every sense, Rosa wanted to climb into bed, pull the covers over her head, and will the world to go away, wishing she could go back to being a little girl again and not have to deal with these strange feelings she didn't understand or, worse still, couldn't control.

71

Now sounding very angry, Isabella's demanded, "Rosa, get up - immediately!" With a final agonising groan, Rosa realised why her mother had woken her up so early. Today was Sunday. It was time to get ready for church.

The Winds of Change
☼
1843

Cities far to the north continued undergoing rapid population growth. There was news of political turmoil and corruption by government officials throughout much of Argentina. Hidalgo's wisdom was born from knowledge and experience. The Bible said, 'For the love of money was the root of all evil', but he believed that such problems seemed unlikely to disrupt the Garcia way of life so far south.

One troubling rumour persisted. There was talk amongst the land barons of some being coerced into relinquishing significant land holdings. The government planned to run 'Communes' *for the greater good of the people!* This prospect, proposed by Ramon Mendoza and some of his lackeys, galled Hidalgo. He trusted none of them. Over the years, there had been several incidents affecting his northern properties. Hidalgo suspected Mendoza's mob were involved, but he lacked proof. For the time being, Hidalgo introduced greater security and extra men to guard his herds. This show of power had stemmed further incidents at the Garcia holdings.

So far, Santa Rosa was unaffected by the country's volatile politics, a situation most locals embraced. They went about their daily business contented, far removed from the government machinations, but slowly things were changing. Since the advent of the Telegraph, outside news came more readily. There were disturbing rumours of unrest to the north and west almost daily. One significant item of interest was a proposal to build a rail network across Argentina sometime in the future, starting with Buenos Aires and eventually extending throughout the continent; this would change Argentina and South America forever. The plan was to import steam engines from far-off Britain. It would also bring an influx of those hoping to get rich.

Immigration in Buenos Aires was increasing rapidly. Newcomers, once predominantly from Spain and Portugal, now flocked to South America from many nations. The population in Argentina was close to a million people, and the Capital, Buenos Aires, was thriving. They were initially hampered by *Malones*, ferocious attacks by indigenous natives. Despite these incidences, the growth continued. Several vast estancias were established throughout Argentina by the Catholic Church under the powerful patronage of the Spanish Monarchy.

Carlos Mendoza and a small contingent of rough-looking horsemen travelled southwest from Buenos Aires over several days; they were weary, happy to be approaching their journey's end. Carlos was more than a little amazed, having discovered many desirable properties from Buenos Aires to Santa Rosa. There was only one skirmish between his troupe and a hunting party of Quechua natives, who, having rounded up several cattle, chose to flee with their bounty. Carlos was happy not to engage in confronting them, which was unusual for him. He rather enjoyed killing things.

Carlos had a more sinister agenda in the region than ostensibly campaigning for his father. He realised building a power base required lots of money. At present, land, cattle and horses were the new gold. Investors were flocking to Argentina, cashing in on its burgeoning growth, and he didn't intend to miss out.

Landholdings provided diverse options for expeditiously increasing wealth. The Argentinian pampas had massive potential for harnessing thousands of cattle and horses which roamed free. The advent of wire fencing introduced in the north could aid this. Also, sheep were brought to north-western Argentina from America in 1814 as an additional source of wealth. Talk of a rail network continued. The rapid transporting of goods would see fortunes made, although the proposal was still a long way off.

The large landowners would control the balance of power and wealth, and Carlos intended to be one of them. Achieving this required him to persuade reluctant landholders to sell. Of course, he needed like-minded people to make this happen. Carlos was capable of dictating his terms; he just needed to find enough people who held no allegiance to anyone, had no strong moral or ethical compass and were willing to do anything for money. Gauchos were a perfect choice.

Gauchos were the native horsemen of Argentina. Displaced from their nomadic lifestyle with the advent of boundary fencing, their freedom to wander the open plains no longer existed. They needed to find new ways to survive. Easily identified by their distinctive dress, long pleated trousers called *Bombaches*, a woollen poncho slung over their shoulders, and a wide strip of woven fabric called a *Faja* wrapped around their waist, which served as a belt. At the back of their costume was a *Falcone*, a long silver-handled knife tucked into the waistband. Their horses, just as distinctive, had elaborate silver trappings on faceplates, halters, and bridles.

Fiercely proud and unmatched as trackers, the Gauchos lived as single men, outdoors, ignoring the elements, eating nothing but meat slaughtered from any stray beast or wild animal in the area.

Having roamed the Pampas for many decades, they answered to no one. They carried all their worldly possessions, on their person. Rough by nature, few settled to take a partner, acknowledging only a connection to the land and their steed.

When not droving for absentee Ranch owners of large estancias, they gathered in small groups, drinking, gambling, playing the guitar, hunting or fighting. They were outstanding horsemen who could bring down a charging wild beast with a *Bolas*, a twine weapon of native origin. Made of several woven strands of twine with tightly bound balls of yarn at each end, when thrown with accuracy, they wrapped around the animals' legs, entangling them.

Many Gauchos were *Mestizos*, descendants of Spanish and Indigenous natives. They inherited diverse skills from the Indians, known for their ability to locate water in a desert plain. They also inherited many of their superstitions.

Carlos quickly seized the opportunity of hiring men like these, fighting for survival. A group of faceless thugs soon followed Carlos all over the countryside, *visiting* properties he had an eye on owning. First appearing unannounced, a threatening presence intimidating small landholders, *persuading* them that selling their properties was a desirable option. Prices offered, of course, were well below the land's actual value, but far more acceptable than the casual suggestion of some insidious alternatives.

The Vestments: Isabella
☼

The sun was streaming through the window as Isabella washed the breakfast dishes. It was going to be a lovely day. Both girls grumbled about such an early start but knew their father well. As a farmer, Paulo was up at first light most mornings. Today was no exception; their plans had to fit in with his. Paulo agreed to drop Isabella and the girls off at the church even though it would delay the start of his day. He assisted his family onto the wagon in good humour, quickly heading the three miles into town, wanting to return home as soon as possible.

Isabella, Rosa and Maria were the first to arrive at Our Lady of The Rosary Church, which wasn't surprising due to the early hour. Isabella was honoured to have a key to the entrance door of the Vestry. A regular amongst the volunteers, she held a unique position of trust.

Isabella's dedication to her faith was instilled by her parents. Even as a small child, she was devout. There was a beautiful shrine in her home where she and the children said prayers every day. Isabella had given up imploring Paulo to join them. He was not so committed to the daily ritual of thanksgiving but a good man nevertheless.

It was fun setting up the sewing tables for the other ladies. Rosa and Maria chatted happily together. Isabella looked at them with pride, Rosa almost eighteen, and Maria fourteen, such good girls, never giving her a minute's bother. She sighed, thinking about Delgado, their brother, now twenty-one, a good lad but restless. Since he was a little boy, he'd helped Paulo on the farm before and after school. Of late, he was unruly, almost belligerent, most unlike him. He was keen to explore the world outside their farm. Isabella sensed

77

he would leave home soon to seek his fortune. It was easy to forget he was no longer a boy but a young man. Isabella sighed deeply, more than a little sad at the thought. It was hard to accept that soon; all her children would eventually leave home to start a new future.

The girl's laughter broke into her reverie. Together they were winding different coloured pieces of cotton onto wooden spools in preparation for at least a half dozen ladies. Isabella had taken the necessary measurements from the old vestments and started cutting some patterns. Today was the first of several sewing days planned over the next few weeks; the group of ladies joining Isabella would arrive soon, all eager to complete the garments.

The life of a farmer's wife was never easy, and raising three very individual children was challenging— Isabella was looking forward to taking time out to mix with other womenfolk; it would be a welcome change.

Fr Peter appeared at the side door. "Good morning, Isabella – girls, thank you for leading the ladies' sewing group. I greatly appreciate it and look forward to blessing my new robes on completion. Please excuse me, I have morning prayers to attend, and then I am off into town for a while."

"Certainly, Father, I will see you before we leave; I pray The Holy Father blesses our work."

Fr Peter nodded, smiled, and disappeared out the side door. Since arriving four years earlier, he had led the congregation in Santa Rosa, quickly endearing himself to the whole community. Once a month, he would load up a wagon and head out into the countryside for several days, administering the sacraments to faithful parishioners unable to attend mass in Santa Rosa.

These were simple, hardworking, kind and generous folk who recognised the innate goodness in Fr Peter and embraced him into their community. Few knew he was the Governor's son and were often shocked when they learned this. In some ways, it endeared him even further to the community. No doubt he could be living far more comfortably in a luxurious mansion in Buenos Aires instead of choosing to live modestly in a tiny town in the middle of nowhere. He exemplified a pious man of good faith.

The ladies arrived, greeting each other warmly and sharing titbits of friendly local gossip. Everyone settled into their appointed tasks. They all displayed fine needlework skills taking great pride in producing beautiful garments. The quiet chatter slowly ebbed as they concentrated on the task at hand. Rosa and Maria amused themselves by practising sewing scraps of material left over on the cutting board.

Fr Peter was not expecting the arrival of his younger brother. Carlos swept into town with a flourish, his entourage in tow. He was on the campaign trail for their father. Although it was no secret to those close to him, Ramon Artigas Mendoza greatly relished being the Governor, but his ultimate aim was to become the President of Argentina.

It was late afternoon when Carlos strode through the open doors of Our Lady of The Rosary Church, seeking his brother Peter. He walked in, amused, trying to remember the last time he entered a church, probably during school days? Compulsory, no doubt, the only way he would have been there. Carlos used to scoff when the religious Brothers implored, "The meek shall inherit the earth." He begged to differ!

Tidying up after the ladies had departed, Isabella was startled by the sudden appearance of this unannounced powerful-looking stranger in the church Vestry. She instinctively stepped in front of Rosa, like a lioness guarding her cub. Carlos barely paid her any attention, demanding arrogantly,

"Where's the priest?"

Isabella was unsettled by this man, though not sure why. She couldn't imagine a man such as him seeking a priest. He certainly didn't look like someone who followed the teachings of the Lord.

"I'm sorry, Senor, Fr Peter is in town but due back. May I assist you until he returns?"

Carlos studied Isabella, obviously a woman well below his station but pleasant looking, maybe ten years his senior. He let his eyes survey her body. She was shapely. Carlos had no objection to enjoying an older woman, as long as they weren't unattractive and served his purpose.

Isabella, eager to escape Carlos's unsettling scrutiny, offered to guide him to Fr Peter's quarters, "Would you care to wait in Father's sitting room, and I could fetch you a tea?" Isabella led the way, exposing Rosa to Carlos's view for the first time; she heard his indrawn breath. In that instant, Isabella felt a chill of alarm; she quickly made the sign of the cross; her rapidly beating heart told her something evil had just entered her world.

"Carlos, is it really you?" Fr Peter's voice boomed as he entered the Vestry. The stranger's face now bathed in a smile, full of charm, as they turned to look in unison at the priest. Fr Peter walked rapidly to the younger man, embracing him awkwardly. "I see you have met my friends and able assistants, Isabella and Rosa Caron. They help prepare the church every Saturday for the mass on Sunday." Fr Peter spoke with genuine warmth in his voice. "Isabella, Rosa, I'd like to introduce my younger brother, Carlos."

Carlos responded pleasantly to his brother's introduction, but his eyes did not leave Rosa for a second, now standing awkwardly beside her mother.

"My first visit. Long overdue, brother; I would have come sooner had I known the treasures hidden here." Before Fr Peter could respond, Carlos stepped forward, took Rosa's hand and placed a wet kiss on her palm. She tasted of lavender. He wondered how the rest of her body would taste?

Isabella was aghast. The look on Carlos's face said it all, his eyes devouring Rosa's body. Isabella shuddered, feeling physically ill. Rosa stood frozen, not knowing how to respond to this man who had made a very personal gesture without even knowing her. There was shock and anger on her mother's face after she pulled Rosa aside. Why was her mother also looking so fearful? Rosa didn't understand. Blissfully ignorant of the undercurrent, Peter invited Carlos to join him in his quarters.

"Come, brother, we have much to catch up on. What of our father? Busy as always, no doubt. What brings you here, and to what do I owe the pleasure of your company?"

Excusing themselves, the two men chatted amicably, heading to Fr Peter's quarters. Carlos glanced back fleetingly, with a look that drove a knife through Isabella's heart. This was a man used to getting everything he desired, and at this moment in time, that was her beloved daughter Rosa. Isabella quickly knelt before the statue of the Holy Mother and began praying. Rosa was startled to see her mother so distressed; she had no idea why.

"Mother, what is wrong? Why are you so upset?

Isabella made the sign of the cross once more; rising, she propelled Rosa out of the church and started walking rapidly down the dirt road towards home several miles away, something they had never done before. They always waited for her father, Paulo or brother Delgado to collect them with the wagon. Rosa could see her mother was distraught, unable to comfort her without knowing the source of her distress.

As a charitable man, Fr Peter welcomed Carlos and his assistants, providing sparse but comfortable accommodation for their stay in several small rooms attached to the church proper.

Peter, and his elder brother Phillipe, had little in common with Carlos. If truthful, neither claimed to know much about their youngest sibling, spending no significant time in his company. Carlos had only ventured home from boarding school during semester breaks.

Peter's most vivid memories of Carlos were of his being incredibly spoilt and always getting his way. Once, when ten, despite advice to the contrary, Carlos was determined to ride one of the wild horses just brought in from the plains. Nobody told him what he could or couldn't do, even at a young age. He was unceremoniously bucked off, breaking his forearm. Over the next several weeks, everyone paid for this folly with his frequent tantrums and belligerent behaviour. Not even Aida, the housekeeper who spoiled him rotten, escaped. She was probably the only person he ever showed affection to, other than their father. The beating Carlos ordered for the horse was brutal.

81

Later, several helpers allowed the animal to *escape* from the corral, convinced Carlos would not be satisfied until the horse was dead.

Carlos had never ventured this far south from the capital before. The idea of seeing his brother Peter was a secondary consideration, not much more than a curiosity. It was some time since he'd been re-acquainted with either of his brothers, fleeing boarding school in Buenos Aires at age sixteen, quickly outgrowing the restrictions of the Colegio del Salvador, a prestigious school run by the Jesuits.

Hitching a ride with a group transporting supplies north to Santa Fe, Carlos was determined to join his father, Ramon, on the political trail hoping to secure a second term. He was upset with Carlos's appearance in the middle of campaigning but secretly admired his tenacity. Charmed by his youngest son since he was a baby, he rarely said no to anything Carlos wanted.

Rosa awoke early Sunday morning to gather flowers and herbs from the fields. The previous day's rain had delayed her from creating the usual posies for the church. During the mass, it was often possible to detect the faint aroma of rosemary, lavender or sage, or whatever Rosa had gathered, according to the season.

Rosa was stunned when her mother tried to persuade her not to go to mass for the first time in her eighteen years.

"I want you to stay home and say your mass here. I will deliver the flowers to the church with your father." Isabella was not requesting that Rosa stay at home; she was demanding this was how it must be.

Rosa was visibly upset. "Have I done something wrong, mother? You are angry with me." Rosa was more shocked still when her mother began to weep; holding her head in her hands and imploring God,

"Dios Mio, what do I do?"

Rosa stared at Paulo, urgently seeking some response from her father. Instead, he looked on awkwardly, shrugging his shoulders, hands raised, indicating he had no idea why Isabella was so adamant that Rosa should miss mass.

Raised to believe in the innate goodness of man, Isabella instinctively knew Carlos was someone to fear the moment she met him. She could not explain her concerns to her family without any valid grounds to go on and in direct conflict with her faith. Isabella was in crisis. He was the brother of a man she admired beyond all others for his sanctity and goodness; surely Carlos could not be so very different?

Isabella, troubled since their meeting, had thought of little else, arguing with herself, doubting her instincts. Feeling defeated, she finally relented, agreeing to let Rosa attend mass, unable to give any reasonable explanation for why she should not go.

It was a silent journey to Santa Rosa that morning. None of the usual chit-chat or arguing between Delgado and Maria. They wisely stayed silent, sensing all was not right. Rosa, also silent, sat wondering what she had done wrong, even though her mother assured her she was not in trouble.

Most of the townsfolk attended church. For many in this small community, it would be the only outing of the week, so it was as much a social occasion as it was to pay homage to God. Isabella never left Rosa's side for a second. It was unusual that Fr Peter had not yet appeared to cast his eyes over the altar and greet the congregation. He always did this before the mass, even though he knew it wasn't necessary. Isabella prepared the sacraments meticulously, presenting them according to the ritual of the Holy Church. He trusted her implicitly.

There was a hush as Fr Peter finally entered from the Vestry, an unfamiliar guest beside him. He introduced his brother to the congregation and invited them to welcome him accordingly. Everyone obliged by clapping their hands - except Isabella, her head bowed, eyes closed, her lips moving in silent prayer. Paulo, Rosa, Delgado and Maria looked at each other with dismay, at a loss to know what was troubling her or how they might help.

The Proposal
☼

Paulo was becoming concerned about Isabella. She was always devout, and he respected her commitment to her faith and church, but he had never seen her so rigorous in dedicating every spare minute to devotions and prayer. This behaviour coincided with meeting Fr Peter's brother for the first time. When questioned about the meeting, Isabella refused to talk about it.

Invited to several community functions to celebrate Carlos's arrival, the Caron family attended out of respect for the priest. As usual, Carlos, full of charm, was busy extolling the virtues of Santa Rosa, his admiration for the community, and his fine brother Peter, whom it was apparent the people loved. Carlos ultimately steered most of the conversation towards support for his father becoming Governor Mendoza for a second term, hinting that this support would ensure improvements to aid the community.

To Paulo, somehow, his words lacked sincerity, although judging by the locals' reception, they seemed happy to embrace Carlos. Paulo found any time spent in the company of Fr Peter's brother awkward. Not a man astute at judging character, Paulo never needed this skill before.

Carlos took every opportunity to place himself where he could observe Rosa. Rarely had Carlos been so enchanted or intrigued by a female. Perhaps it was her innocence or because she was *forbidden fruit*. No one ever denied Carlos anything. He watched as Rosa approached the older citizens with a platter, offering them food and refreshments. She was astoundingly beautiful, unaffected, without guile; her long dark locks fell over full breasts, and her hair glistened as she moved, framing a blemish-free complexion and rosebud lips.

Carlos longed to crush those lips and slowly peel all the petals from the little rose. Rosa's movements were lithe like a panther as she crossed the compound. Carlos imagined himself the hunter in pursuit, intent on possessing her.

It became clear Carlos wasn't going to have the opportunity to get Rosa alone. When they were in his presence, her mother, Isabella, never left her side, always politely responding to Carlos when he spoke. He was amused; she never once raised her eyes to his. Isabella had understood him only too well from their first meeting in the church three weeks earlier.

He should have been long gone from this non-descript village with its peasant population. Carlos sensed even his brother Peter was wondering when he might leave. After spending time together, he realised they still had little in common. The intention had been to spend only a few days campaigning for their father, check out what landholdings might be to his liking while there, and be on his way…that was until he met Rosa.

Carlos had never contemplated marriage; it wasn't necessary. After joining his father, he had access to as many whores as he wished. There were also plenty of others ambitious to become 'Senora Mendoza'. He used this to his advantage, often leaving them shattered when he shamelessly abandoned them, his lust satisfied. A less powerful man might have been murdered in revenge, but Carlos always had a strong bevvy of thugs watching his back.

If necessary, and only if it were in his best interests, Carlos might *buy off* the family with concessions or money. Men, after all, were pragmatic, including the fathers of the society daughters he bedded, especially when they were well compensated, at times even happy to overlook his indiscretions when he was exceptionally generous. Often, they would quickly marry the girl off to someone seeking favours from the family. Everyone ended up satisfied, well, anyone that mattered. What the girl might think was of little consequence!

Recently Carlos had given some thought to his lack of an heir. Not so much as leaving a fortune but producing a legitimate child to carry on the Mendoza name. Carlos adored his father and tried to emulate him in every way. The idea of creating an heir was interesting to contemplate. It never dawned on him that he might have a daughter; such was his ego.

When Carlos approached Peter proposing marriage to Rosa Caron, his brother was shocked; he didn't quite know how to respond. While having many apprehensions about the possible union, it wasn't up to him. The decision would rest with the head of the Caron family and eventually Rosa. Fr Peter didn't believe Carlos did anything on the spur of the moment, so believing it to be a genuine proposal, he agreed to Carlos's request to approach Rosa's family on his behalf.

Surprised by the priest's unscheduled visit that Monday, Paulo and Isabella welcomed him with great delight. It was early afternoon, but Paulo was happy to delay getting back out into the field, enjoying the company of their special guest. Fr Peter chatted to Paulo while Isabella laid out the beautiful hand-embroidered table cover, set the best China, and then hurried off to prepare freshly made corn cakes, one of Isabella's well-known culinary delights. The delicious odour wafted throughout the house, filling everyone with anticipation.

When Fr Peter introduced the reason for his visit, it was as if time froze. Paulo stopped mid-rise, about to stand to help Isabella place the food tray onto the table. Isabella stood stock still with a horrified expression; the colour drained from her face. Fr Peter had been a little apprehensive about presenting Carlos's offer of marriage, but he never expected such an extreme reaction. Indeed!

Paulo was the first to recover, not wishing to seem rude. Isabella, on the other hand, had not moved. Lost for words, Fr Peter arose and took the tray from her shaking hands while Paulo helped her be seated. The priest apologised for delivering what appeared to be an unsettling prospect. Isabella finally found her voice, choosing her words carefully, hoping not to offend the priest. Speaking ever so quietly,

"Thank you, Fr Peter, and thank your brother Carlos for his most generous offer, but I'm afraid it is impossible."

Fr Peter, to his credit, smoothed over the awkward moment, reassuring them both.

"Isabella and Paulo, it will be fine. I will explain to Carlos the barrier was Rosa's youth. I know he will respect your decision; of course, he must; you are her parents."

Isabella was not sure about anything concerning Carlos; she was filled with an overwhelming sense of dread. Paulo abandoned the idea of returning to the field; he needed to talk to Isabella to try to calm her down and find out why she was so distressed.

In her innocent youth, at their first meeting, Rosa had viewed the thirty-something Carlos Mendoza as old and had not given him a second thought. After the proposal, when Isabella almost fainted, Paulo began understanding the source of her anxiety over the previous three weeks.

When Fr Peter left the farm, the wind had picked up considerably. Storm clouds rolled across the heavens threatening a deluge. Peter prayed it wasn't a bad omen for his breaking the news to Carlos.

Carlos took a long time before responding to his brothers' news; he could still hear Peter's words informing him there would be no marriage because of her young age. The very generous offer graciously declined, Peter had added tactfully.

"A pity indeed; perhaps they'll change their mind when they realise what a great offer it was. One a simple country girl could never hope to better." It was said flippantly, but inside, Carlos was seething. How dare this petty little farmer and his peasant wife reject such an outstanding offer, denying their daughter the chance to become his wife, and First Lady to the Governor one day, no doubt! "Or perhaps they just haven't had an offer they couldn't refuse before?"

Peter was initially surprised Carlos was taking the rejection so well but was alarmed by this final statement. Peter knew his brother's determination well. If he set his mind to having something, there was no dissuading him. Peter was filled with unease.

"Well, dear brother, it seems like I'll be moving on, though I will return in a month or so." Carlos's mood shifted, unexpectedly now relaxed, untroubled.

Peter's surprise was evident, and then shocked at Carlos's following words. "I have been greatly impressed with this part of the country and the surrounding area. I failed to mention earlier, but I purchased a large landholding twelve-odd miles southeast of here. Father decided we should diversify and establish a base of some description in the southern part of Argentina. There is a magnificent hacienda being constructed on the property as we speak. In the future, Hierro Castillo will be my home base when campaigning this far south."

Peter was speechless. What was there to say? He realised this was not just a random visit or secondary to campaigning. It was an orchestrated plan to put down permanent roots in the area. With growing unease, Peter feared for the Caron family. What was it that Carlos wasn't telling him? With little enthusiasm in his voice, Peter responded, "Congratulations, Carlos, I had no idea; I hope you will find contentment in your regular visits to the area. I'm sure you will have much to contribute to the community's welfare." In truth, Peter wasn't sure about anything anymore.

The hesitancy and insincerity in his brother's voice were apparent to Carlos. Not that anything his brother or anyone else might say or do would impede his plans for the future – including his plans for Rosa Caron.

At first light, Carlos and his entourage were gone, a brief note of thanks perched on the stark wooden table scrubbed bare over the years. Somehow Carlos's message made it feel soiled all over again.

Peter had an overwhelming need to pray for God's guidance and the protection of his flock, especially the Caron family.

Fr Peter regretted delaying the news that Carlos planned to return and that he was building a mansion no more than twelve miles away from Santa Rosa. Intuitively he knew this information would be a constant source of worry for Paulo and Isabella Caron. He also knew he must not put off telling them any longer. The priest would raise the subject tomorrow after mass when Paulo called to pick up the family.

Paulo Caron

☼

It was Saturday, a glorious sunny day; a gentle breeze stirred the wild salvia, the masses of blue and purple blossoms filling the air with the smell of Liquorice. Paulo loved tilling the land, never tiring of the aroma of freshly turned soil. Planting each new crop was like a reaffirmation of life. Today he would clear the back paddock in preparation for planting corn. He might not even stop for lunch, a habit he'd developed of late.

Isabella prepared an abundance of food for him and Delgado before her departure. Along with Rosa and Maria, she intended to spend the day with the local ladies on this final sewing day to complete the new vestments for Fr Peter. Later, along with her sister Luisa, they planned to join a pre-wedding celebration for a friend's daughter.

It would be quite late after the wedding shower; it was unpleasant and sometimes risky to travel in a wagon after dark. Paulo discussed it with Isabella; they decided she and the girls should stay overnight in Santa Rosa with her sister. The prospect was exciting. Paulo would bring the wagon and collect them in the morning following mass. No doubt he would apologise profusely to Fr Peter for being too late to attend, and Fr Peter would smile wryly and give his usual response - having heard these exact words many times before.

"Perhaps we might discuss this at your next confession, Paulo?"

Paulo didn't see or hear them coming; suddenly, they were just there behind him, slipping a hood over his head, taking him by surprise. Two men pinned his arms back roughly. He couldn't tell how many there were, but he was sure at least three or four. He felt the presence of someone step closer to his face. Paulo recoiled at the reek of stale tobacco and rancid body odour. The gravelly voice was harsh, the words slurred. Waves of fetid breath, pungent with alcohol, assailed Paulo.

"Buenos Dios Senor, it is a fine day to welcome visitors, is it not?" The menacing tone overshadowed the seemingly friendly greeting.

Paulo had heard stories of intimidation beginning to circulate from districts to the north, dreading that such evil might one day reach this far south and affect this peaceful, hardworking community. Very afraid now, Paulo knew it was pointless shouting out for help; there was no one to hear his pleas. His closest neighbour, Juan Petto, called in with his wagon on the way to town. A good man, he was checking to see if Paulo needed anything. Delgado went along to assist Juan in town. Paulo suggested he could lend Juan a hand and, in return, pick up a small order he placed last week. They would not return for some hours. Paulo thanked God Isabella and the girls were safe in Santa Rosa.

Suddenly, his legs were knocked out from under him, sending him sprawling face-first onto the ground. He could smell the damp earth and sour odour of the pig swill nearby. One of the assailants lashed out with his boot; Paulo yelped in agony, gasping as he tried to catch his breath. A further blow to the stomach sent searing pain across his abdomen, making him gag.

"What do you want, Senor? I have no money; I am just a poor farmer!"

Another swift kick, this time to the head, left his senses reeling, the sickly-sweet taste of blood suddenly filling his mouth.

The leader screamed at him, "Shut your mouth, filthy pig, until I tell you to speak."

Paulo could hear others ransacking or maybe destroying the barn. It made little difference; he was in no position to protest.

The leader spoke once more, sneering, an amused tone in his voice this time, "We don't want your money; we've come to do you a favour. You have worked hard; now you should rest, take a long holiday, retire maybe?"

Paulo felt sick to his stomach, which wasn't just from the beating. They wanted his farm. He knew they weren't military. Mounted soldiers had a unique smell. The scent of woollen tunics and waxed leather boots. No, these were ruffians or vagabonds, employed for a few pesos to do the dirty work of others - the faceless evil. Behind closed doors, many whispered one name, 'Carlos Mendoza', the son of the Governor, Ramon Artigas Mendoza. On hearing the rumour, Paulo was stunned, recalling his brief acquaintance with Carlos and instant dislike. God help them if this proved to be true. The country would be doomed if someone this close to their leader orchestrated such evil.

"Listen carefully to me, old man," the menacing voice was back. "You have two choices. You can sell this miserable piece of property for whatever you are offered, or your family are likely to suffer some serious accidents."

Paulo winced in pain as the thugs dragged him roughly off the ground and positioned him on the back of the empty horse cart. The same slimy voice suggested, "Perhaps we might entertain your lovely wife, Isabella and your two daughters to help you decide?"

Paulo thought his heart would stop at the mention of Isabella's name. Any hope that this was some terrible mistake was gone. They knew who he was; this had been carefully planned.

Weeping softly, completely desolate, his voice barely above a whisper, Paulo responded forlornly, "Whatever you wish, Senor, just leave my family alone, I beg you."

The leader's demeanour changed immediately. "Well done! See, we understand each other perfectly. We will leave you now, but know we are never far away if you think of changing your mind."

Paulo sensed they were preparing to leave; His head throbbed ceaselessly; he ached all over. At least he was no longer swallowing blood. He wished they would finish whatever they were planning to do and go.

"I'll leave you with one final thought, Senor." It was the leader again, his stench unmistakable. "If I have to come back, I might just take the time to initiate your youngest daughter to the pleasures of the flesh, a delicious thought."

Raucous laughter was the last sound Paulo registered before suffering a final blow to the head, then darkness.

It was mid-afternoon when Paulo looked up to see his son hovering above him. Why was Delgado screaming? And why was Juan yelling at him? Paulo tried to open his eyes properly, attempting to get up. One eye remained closed, swollen shut. Delgado stopped screaming, grabbed his father's arms to steady him, and then started weeping, pulling his father close to his chest, relieved he was alive.

Juan was standing a short distance away, his head in his hands. "My God, what happened here? What have they done to you, man?" There was horror in his voice, disbelief.

Paulo answered slowly, his voice devoid of emotion, "They want my farm, or they will destroy my family. I have no choice, none at all."

Juan felt helpless to comfort his friend, the finality in Paulo's words leaving him dumbfounded.

Paulo was still trying to comfort Delgado, who continued to cling to him, sobbing quietly, in shock. Looking around, he could see chaos and debris strewn everywhere, the least of his concerns now. Every part of his body ached. Finally, standing upright on unsteady legs, he tested his injuries by determining where he hurt most. Taking a deep breath was impossible, the pain excruciating when attempted. Paulo suspected he had broken ribs. The many swollen areas over his abdomen and torso were turning various shades of purple. He could feel a broken tooth with his tongue, the probable cause of blood in his mouth.

Paulo watched, detached, as Juan and Delgado cleaned up the mess to the best of their ability, trying to make the area safe to negotiate. He suspected Juan was also in shock; he was an awful colour and muttering quietly to himself. Finally, Paulo stopped them. "Juan, you should go home, my friend; get your house in order. I think this evil has only begun; God help us all."

Paulo trying to take Delgado's mind off events, sent him out to round up the farm animals, two horses, some pigs, several goats, and a milking cow named 'Luna', born on the full moon. Paulo smiled at the memory, causing him to wince with pain. The damage to his face must be severe when it hurt even to smile. He hated to imagine how he must look. Paulo dreaded the thought of Isabella seeing him like this. He had no idea what he would say to make her understand what they must do. The farm had been their life's dream, a way to secure their family's future.

The pain started in his right arm. At first, Paulo thought maybe he also had a broken bone. Knowing how much damage he'd sustained from the savage beating was difficult. His throat felt tight, and his jaw was becoming rigid. A vice-like grip was crushing his chest. Paulo stared at Juan, desperation on his face. He opened his mouth to speak but couldn't form words.

Juan's face was concerned as he stretched out his arm to Paulo. Gripping Juan's arm, his eyes pleading, terror on his face, Paulo lurched forward, his legs buckling without warning. Crumbling, he fell to the ground clutching his chest; Paulo was sure he could hear Isabella calling his name when the darkness claimed him.

The Final Fitting

☼

Isabella kept all the ladies busy assembling the new vestments. The embroidered silk brocade, heavily embossed with gold, shimmered in the light. They handled every item with the utmost care—the material had been ordered by Fr Peter from the Holy Priory Church, La Mancha - Castille, Spain. The seamstresses of Santa Rosa were in awe of their designated task. There was no room for error.

Rosa and Maria prepared lunch while the ladies concentrated on putting the finishing touches on the garments. Such intricate work required meticulous attention to produce the best results. Isabella's thoughts drifted to the last few weeks. The departure of Fr Peter's younger brother was a great relief. Full of apprehension at the decline of Carlos's marriage proposal to Rosa, Isabella was surprised that he left town graciously. He did not seem the type to take 'no' for an answer. Life settled back into a comfortable pattern.

The day passed swiftly. By mid-afternoon, the *Chasuble* and *Stole* hung magnificently in all their glory. Fr Peter would be pleased, without a doubt. The quality of the finished garments was a credit to them all. The group were beaming with well-deserved pride.

There was a commotion outside the church—they could hear raised voices heading towards the vestibule. Suddenly the door swung wide; Fr Peter, face deathly pale, entered, visibly shaken. Close behind him, Juan Petto, their neighbour, and beside him Delgado, white-faced and trembling, his face tear-stained, his clothes dishevelled and bloody, but where was Paulo?

Isabella jumped to her feet, her heart racing, addressing Delgado, panic in her voice,

"Where is your father?" she shouted - then to Juan, "Why are you here? Where is Paulo?"

Fr Peter stepped forward to steady Isabella, grasping her hand, "I have some terrible news; you should sit down."

Isabella heard the words, shaking her head in utter disbelief. Her beloved Paulo was no more, suffering a massive heart attack after being savagely beaten. How was this possible? Why would anyone want to hurt this kind, gentle man who had never wronged anyone in his whole life? Isabella started to sob quietly. The other ladies were also crying, trying to comfort her; they, too, were shocked. Her sister Luisa was desperate to help. Isabella and the girls were to stay with Luisa as an overnight treat. There was a piercing scream, and then another – the girls! Oh my God, Isabella thought, this can't be happening.

Rosa and Maria charged into the room, crying hysterically, throwing themselves into their mother's arms. In the kitchenette cleaning up, they heard the commotion coming from the church. Parishioners gathering there informed them of Paulo's beating; the sisters were shattered to learn their father was deceased.

"Why? Why? Why? Isabella repeatedly said, rocking back and forth like a wounded animal, her arms wrapped tightly around her girls. Isabella looked at Juan imploringly, shaking her head, seeking an explanation without forming words.

"He said they wanted to take the farm." Juan was a broken man. He didn't think he would ever recover from holding Paulo in his arms, seeing his eyes filled with terror, unable to speak, and then watching the life ebb out of his dear friend until his eyes no longer focused on anything. That was when he knew Paulo was dead.

Delgado was in shock and barely coherent at the time. Juan wasn't sure how they made it to town; Paulo's lifeless body lay outside the church in the back of the wagon, an old horse blanket covering his still form.

The Farewell

☼

Fr Peter tried desperately to convince Isabella to let others attend to Paulo's body, but she was adamant. With the help of her sister Luisa, they washed and dressed his broken body. There was hardly any part of him that wasn't hideously bruised. Swollen and bloodied, his face almost unrecognisable as the man she had loved and nurtured for twenty-one years. He was forty-three years of age, too young to die.

In his Sunday best, Paulo lay as if asleep, arms folded across his body, a golden crucifix over his heart, her beloved rosary beads wrapped around his right hand. He was ready to go *home*. Luisa placed a flower in his lapel as Isabella kissed him farewell on the forehead. Both women wrapped their arms around each other, sobbing in despair, shocked, trying to comfort each other and comprehend how this could happen.

Isabella, a solemn lone figure shrouded in black, sat deathly still, staring at the simple pine coffin surrounded with flowers as it rested in the nave of Our Lady of The Rosary Church. Numb from the events of the last forty-eight hours and desperately tired. Isabella had been keeping vigil since before dawn.

Today would be the last day Isabella and Paulo Caron would spend together in this life. She refused to share this time with anyone. It belonged to them alone. Soon, Fr Peter and others would come to pay their respects to this fine man; before committing him to God and laying him to rest on the hillside above the church. He would wait until Isabella joined him, and together they would remain under the jacaranda trees for eternity.

Paulo wasn't just her husband; he was her life. Everything sprang from him: their children, home, farm, and future. Isabella tried to imagine life without him. Bone-weary, she wished it were all over, allowing her to crawl into a corner somewhere and not have to think. The logical part of her mind told Isabella this wasn't possible. She was the mother of three distraught and terrified children. The children were safe at the moment, with Luisa's family supporting them, but this could only be temporary. Isabella couldn't gather her thoughts and contemplate the end of this day, let alone their future.

She began to weep when she thought of the children; racking sobs echoed throughout the empty church. Isabella needed to be with Delgado, Rosa and Maria to comfort them before the service; she must go to Luisa's house, even for a little while.

The church was overflowing when Isabella, the children and Luisa's family returned for the funeral service, many with heads bowed, other familiar faces etched with sorrow, weeping. Fr Peter met them at the main entrance, his face contorted in pain; words were unnecessary. He clasped Isabella's hands in his, visibly fighting back the tears. Isabella nodded, mirroring his grief. Fr Peter spoke briefly to the Caron children offering comfort, trying to ease their distress, and then guided them to their seats at the front of the church.

Isabella remembered little of the service, a requiem mass. The voices of the choir, the prayers and hymns all became a blur. It seemed no time before she was standing on the grassy verge, watching the coffin lowered into its final resting place. The sound of Fr Peter's voice barely registered as he delivered the committal prayers. Once completed, the service was over.

One by one, the townsfolk filed past, some shaking her hand, others just nodding, too sad to speak, knowing words were futile. Fr Peter guided Isabella back into the vestry, away from men waiting to fill the grave. The children went home with Luisa's family for the time being. Isabella assured them she would join them soon.

Father Peter had spent much of the previous night contemplating the conversation he intended to have with Isabella. He would offer her and the children sanctuary in the small apartments attached to the

97

church proper, where Carlos and his men had stayed. They were simple but adequate. He would encourage Isabella to add anything she liked to make them feel at home.

Fr Peter knew Isabella was devoted to her faith, and God would guide her through this terrible time. More importantly, he wanted her to be able to grieve freely, hopefully finding solace in prayer and believing that living in the confines of the church would aid this. He spoke briefly with Luisa about his plan. While happy to help, Luisa was relieved; her family cottage with three children and a husband had little room to spare.

Fr Peter knew Isabella would never accept charity; he planned to offer Isabella a job as his housekeeper. It would be a paid position, a small amount, but enough to get by. When a new share farmer purchased the Caron portion of the lease, there would likely be ample funds to provide for Isabella's future needs.

The parish was multiplying, requiring more time visiting congregation members unable to attend mass. Peter had been contemplating hiring a housekeeper for some time. Someone he could trust to open the church up daily in his absence and take care of the body of the church. Isabella was a perfect choice. Groundsmen took care of any maintenance; they would assist Isabella should she need help in his absence. He never imagined offering her this position under such circumstances, but he believed it provided a solution for them both.

At first, Isabella was taken aback by Fr Peter's proposal. It was too soon to think about anything, much less talk about what she might do. It was impossible to stay with Luisa; there wasn't room. Having decided she could never return to the farm, Isabella couldn't think of any alternative. There was no other choice. She accepted the offer with a heavy heart but one filled with gratitude.

In anticipation, Fr Peter had organised some church committee ladies to prepare the rooms in advance. He took Isabella's arm and walked her across the portico to the entrance, suggesting she may wish to lay down and rest awhile. He would fetch the children from Luisa's a little later. The ladies from the church had prepared enough food for several days. Isabella put her face in her hands and wept, grateful for such kindness. Fr Peter was finding it hard to speak,

"May God bless you, my child, and give you peace." After blessing Isabella, Fr Peter left her to grieve alone while fetching Delgado, Rosa and Maria. When he was on the buggy heading down the road, it was only then he gave in to his grief, letting the tears fall. Despite only knowing the Carons' for five years, they had become like family. He would miss his friend Paulo. Peter whispered a silent prayer, promising Paulo that he would always be there for his family.

Less than a week following the funeral, Isabella had taken to her bed, partly out of exhaustion, barely able to sleep, overcome with grief and loss. Maria and Rosa did what they could to comfort her, not an easy task when they were also grieving. Rosa left her younger sister to keep their mother company while she attended to cleaning the church and Fr Peter's apartments. Delgado had already gone to return their neighbour's cart, the one used to transport their father's body to the church. Several friends offered to take his place, but he felt it was his duty.

Delgado felt an unusual bond with Juan, having experienced the terrible circumstances of his father's death. When he arrived, Delgado could see his neighbour was still visibly upset. Neither would be at peace for a long time. Delgado struggled with the thought of returning to their farm to gather things for his family. When Juan offered to accompany him, his relief was profound. Even though he was almost twenty-one, Delgado felt like a lost little boy; he was incredibly grateful for the offer.

Returning to where his father had been murdered was far harder than imagined. Delgado avoided the area where Paulo had died, hurrying past the barn. He was shaking as he entered the house. Was it only a week or so? It felt like a lifetime. While he put together personal items, Juan busied himself gathering eggs, cleaning the horse stalls, anything to keep himself occupied and not focusing on why they were there. Having attended to the property and taken care of the animals in the family's absence, he was familiar with the farm's layout.

Juan managed to harness the horses to the Carons' cart unaided, bringing it up to the house, ready to load. He helped Delgado quickly pack furniture and anything else they thought Isabella and the girls might need to settle into the apartments. Both were relieved when they completed the task, glad to be departing. Juan agreed to remove the remaining animals from the farm and keep an eye on the Caron property until someone took over Paulo's leased share-farmers agreement. Juan was concerned about who that might be. The whole community was alarmed by what happened at the Carons. There had been no other incidents, but the district remained unsettled, fearing this was just the beginning.

Return of The Prodigal Son

☼

Rosa didn't hear him enter, concentrating on trying to lift one end of the heavy oak table on which the devotional candles stood.

"Here, let me help you do that."

Startled, Rosa swung around, unsure if her fear emanated from being suddenly surprised or seeing the offer of help come from Fr Peters' brother Carlos.

"Fr Peter is not here, Senor; he has been visiting parishioners in the district for two days; he is due this evening."

Carlos took his time before answering, his tone and appearance very different from the last time they met. He even looked a little sad, Rosa thought.

"A pity; I will call again later this evening." Turning as if to go, he continued, "I was deeply sorry to hear of your father's passing; my condolences to you and your family. Is your mother here? If so, I would convey them to her in person?"

Rosa was struggling to hold back tears at the mention of her father. "I'm sorry, Senor, my mother is indisposed and is resting. Fr Peter offered us sanctuary here for as long as we wished. It was not possible to return to the farm." Rosa lowered her head, not wishing to be reminded why, and she certainly didn't want to discuss it with this man she hardly knew. Suddenly she blushed.

Watching her like a hawk, Carlos noticed the sudden change in her demeanour as her cheeks flushed and guessed she remembered his marriage proposal. He casually sat down on one of the pews, indicating an invitation for Rosa to join him. Rosa slowly took a seat. Carlos was amused; she looked like a deer about to be eaten alive. He mustn't let himself be distracted by such a delicious thought.

"I'm sorry to hear your mother is unwell, it is understandable under the circumstances, and then there is the worry about you children. Undoubtedly, the burden of how she will feed and care for you must be of great concern to her."

Rosa hadn't considered this. She knew Delgado raised the subject of leaving Santa Rosa soon, wanting to go as far from here as possible to escape the memories. Isabella, upset at first by the idea, relented, fearing for his safety though not expressing this, finally agreeing to the proposal. At the moment, she was incapable of caring for herself, let alone her three children.

Carlos's smooth voice cut across her thoughts; his words were soothing and sympathetic to her family's dilemma. "What if you could provide everything your family might ever need? A home, food, clothes, trips to the city, anything they might desire?"

Rosa looked at Carlos wide-eyed. What was he saying? She didn't understand.

"I have spoken to the property owner who issued the share farm lease, Mr Garcia. He says no one will buy your father's share out of fear. Therefore, there will be no payout to your mother; he said there may well be a debt owing, a penalty seeing your father's obligations will not be fulfilled."

Rosa was horrified, suddenly alarmed that her father's untimely death through tragic circumstances might leave her mother saddled with a debt she couldn't pay. No one would be left to earn money for such debt with Delgado gone.

Carlos watched Rosa process the information. Such a plausible lie. He knew she was too innocent even to contemplate he might not be telling the truth. She was looking distraught. He waited some time before speaking.

"As I said, you could solve all such problems and provide the best possible future for your mother, brother and sister and pay off your father's debt." His voice was gentle, coaxing her compliance before delivering his poison. "You could simply accept my proposal of marriage. I would be honoured to have you as my wife, and one day you may even be the wife of the Governor."

Rosa, unsettled by the suggestion, was glad she was sitting down. Her mother would sacrifice everything for her family without hesitation. Isabella had suffered enough with the loss of her father; she couldn't stand to see her mother or Maria suffer even more. It was difficult for her to think straight, but she realised the future for her family looked bleak. Rosa could change that. It was something she would never have considered under different circumstances, but it seemed a simple answer to all their problems.

Carlos sat, looking down at his feet. He didn't look up until Rosa started to speak.

Rosa jumped up as if bolstering her courage, "I will do it, Senor. I accept your proposal of marriage."

Carlos stood and bowed, careful not to touch her. He didn't want to frighten her. "I will make all the arrangements. Of course, my wonderful brother will officiate; no doubt he will be overjoyed for us both."

Rosa could barely manage a smile as Carlos turned, leaving in great haste, calling back over his shoulder. "I will spare no expense. You must invite everyone in the village."

Carlos wearing a victorious grin, strode out of the church without looking back.

Rosa lowered herself to the pew, wondering about the commitment she had just made. She was still sitting there an hour later when Fr Peter walked in. Rosa became agitated.

"My child, are you alright?" It was apparent something of great importance had unsettled Rosa. "Has something happened to your mother?" he was alarmed by Rosa's expression.

"No, Fr Peter, my mother is okay, well, no worse than before you left. She is in her *happy place* by the lake. I have some important news to tell her, and I'm unsure how to go about it."

Fr Peter, frowning, sat down on the pew opposite, taking Rosa's hands in his. "What is it that troubles you, my child?"

Suddenly shy, Rosa didn't know how to tell Fr Peter about her marriage plans and ask for his blessing. The words came tumbling out, "Your brother Carlos has asked for my hand in marriage once more, and I have accepted his offer."

Little shocked him these days, but Rosa's words had that effect.

"Rosa, I am lost for words; when did this happen? Why have you decided such a thing now? Are you sure about such an important decision?" Peter remembered Isabella and Paulo's reaction when he raised Carlos's proposal earlier. He couldn't imagine how Isabella might react to such an announcement. He was filled with dread.

Rosa's face flushed. It was evident Fr Peter was shocked. She hoped he might help her break the news to her mother and family. "Of course, we want you to officiate at our wedding, Fr Peter." How strange it was to talk of her and Carlos as a couple.

Peter recovered quickly, "Of course, Rosa, it would be an honour. Where is my brother? I would like to offer him my congratulations."

Rosa frowned. She wasn't entirely sure where Carlos was. "He left to start the necessary arrangements; he mentioned Hierro Castillo del Lago."

Peter smiled wryly. There was nothing humble about his brother Carlos, naming his new hacienda 'Iron Castle by the lake'.

The enormity of the situation began to sink in…and what being a wife entailed. She had never so much as felt a man's lips on hers, except in her dreams. Contemplating and consummating their marriage filled Rosa with terror.

Fr Peter was still recovering his wits. He would post the bans tomorrow and announce them to the congregation at Mass on Sunday morning. He prayed God might create a miracle and make Carlos worthy of being Rosa's husband.

The Wedding Announcement
☼

Isabella spent most days visiting the lake at the back of the church. Fr Peter observing this had a wooden bench placed under the trees. At times she appeared to doze. The priest often wondered what disturbed thoughts invaded Isabella's mind. After Paulo's tragic death, he found it difficult to broach the subject in her troubled state. She had escaped into a world of denial, behaving as if it was all a bad nightmare that would pass. Peter was a priest, not a doctor of the mind; he dealt with troubled souls, leaving God to mend broken hearts.

Isabella sat mesmerized, watching the shadows play over the flowing water. It was so peaceful sitting here, the Autumn sun warming her weary bones. Soon Maria would come with refreshments and inquire about her comfort, perhaps join her for a little while. Isabella was unsure where Rosa was, but no doubt she was busy looking after the church, seeing the surroundings were in good order. Fleetingly, Isabella felt a pang of guilt. She felt she had neglected the girls. In future, she vowed to do more to help.

Where was Delgado? Perhaps he was staying with her sister Luisa, although Isabella didn't think so. She vaguely recalled being told he went to seek work in the city. Isabella smiled. He was a good son but eager for some adventure, and he had wanted to leave Santa Rosa and seek his fortune for a while. Suddenly a shadow played across Isabella's face, and she frowned. But who was helping Paulo with the farm if Delgado had gone to the city?

Reality came flooding back, like a dam bursting its banks, drowning everything else out of Isabella's mind, except the realisation Paulo was dead, gone from her forever. The only audible sound was the water gently lapping the shoreline. No one could hear the piercing screams tearing through Isabella's mind, trying to expel her worst nightmare.

Maria arrived with drinks. Her Aunt Luisa was paying Isabella a surprise visit also. Both were suddenly concerned when they saw Isabella's ashen face. "Mama, is everything okay?"

When Isabella turned smiling, they were reassured once more. Isabella had already slipped into that other world where nothing painful could reach her, safe in the knowledge God would take care of it all. Maria and Luisa kept their visit short, not wanting to tire Isabella too much.

Rosa stood in the shadows, staring at where her mother was seated, contemplating how to break the news of her impending wedding. It all happened so suddenly; she could barely grasp the reality herself.

With Delgado gone, Rosa had to step up and be the head of the family. She wanted to take care of her mother and sister. By marrying Carlos, she could accomplish this. Her dilemma was not burdening Isabella by thinking the marriage was for the benefit of her and Maria. Rosa remembered her mother's intense dislike of Carlos from their first meeting, still unsure why this was so.

Rosa sat on the grass, facing her mother on the bench.

"Hello, mama."

Isabella looked down at her beautiful daughter. She could see glimpses of herself when she was a girl. Rosa was such a sweet-natured child, obedient and kind. God blessed her with three wonderful children. The fog in her head, which seemed to be there most of the time, cleared briefly. Isabella tried to concentrate on what Rosa had said, something about a wedding soon. It was to be Rosa's wedding.

Isabella was desperately trying to process her thoughts into a logical response. She couldn't possibly make a wedding dress in a week, decorate a cake, or make the other hundred necessary arrangements. Isabella's head began to hurt. She tried to concentrate even harder...It was Fr Peters' brother. Anyone related to such an outstanding man as the beloved priest would undoubtedly possess

106

great qualities. Rosa's voice continued talking about the groom. The name struck a chord. Deep inside, Isabella's heart contracted violently as if squeezed in a vice. She was not equipped to deal with this; it was better to let it go to that other dark place. Isabella blocked out anything that made her fearful, unaware of how closely insanity hovered.

"Mama, did you hear what I said? I'm going to marry Fr Peter's brother, Carlos Mendoza."

Up North

☼

The last time Hidalgo visited, Cordoba was such a pretty town, although he never got to spend much time there, except for an occasional cattle breeder's sale. His ranch, El Dorado, he named after the Silver Trumpet trees. He loved being there in Autumn, the whole countryside awash in burnished gold just before they shed their leaves.

It was a couple of years since he'd been this far north. Cordoba was well on the way to becoming a city, rivalling the Agriculture of Buenos Aires with the harvesting of salt and other rich mineral discoveries.

Hidalgo had been on the range with his men mustering cattle for nearly a week. It was a welcome change arriving back at the hacienda, anticipating a hot bath, a hearty meal, and a good night's sleep in a real bed.

Antero, his manager, greeted him on arrival, concern on his face.

"Senor Garcia, I have disturbing news from Ataliva Roca. One of your share farmers, Paulo Caron, near Santa Rosa, was attacked and beaten, later dying from a heart attack."

Hidalgo was shocked, "When did this happen?"

"Nearly two weeks ago, Senor."

Paulo Caron was a good man. A hard worker with a wife and three children. For some time, there had been rumours trouble was brewing further south, but in all honesty, Hidalgo couldn't imagine Santa Rosa becoming a target.

The Carons were the ancestors of one of six families in Mendoza with Mestizos links. Those families had been instrumental in helping his great-great-grandfather live harmoniously with the Mapuche

Indians. The family received numerous land grants from the Government of the Province. The decision to share that wealth by sharecropping with the families who helped establish the Garcia dynasty was easy. When Hidalgo's grandfather decided to expand to Southern Argentina and open up new land, several families went with him. Paulo's Grandfather was one of them.

Hidalgo's first thoughts were for Isabella Caron and her children. He knew they were close associates of Fr Peter, the local priest in Santa Rosa. He would contact the priest to assist the family and assure them there was no financial burden. Hidalgo planned to make a settlement with Isabella on his return. The lease could lapse. Hidalgo would arrange for some of his men from Ataliva Roca to manage the property until his return, which was several weeks away.

Hidalgo contacted Elizabeth urgently to pass on their condolences. He knew she made friends with Isabella on arrival in Santa Rosa on her way to Ataliva Roca as a governess. Elizabeth often expressed her regret at not being able to spend more time catching up with Isabella, the last time being the departure of Fr Augustus and the arrival to the parish of Fr Peter.

The Wedding
☼

The day dawned clear and bright, heralding a promising start for this special day. Crisp mountain air swept down the valley, sweet and pure, bearing a faint hint of honeysuckle. Excitement rippled throughout the village of Santa Rosa. A wedding provided a valid excuse for a measure of pomp and ceremony; special occasions were rare. This wedding promised to surpass any other event in recent memory. The groom was the son of the Governor-elect. Nothing would be left to chance to mar the day.

Carlos ensured the most lavish preparations were in place. The wedding gown alone, rumoured to have cost a small fortune, arrived with great pomp and ceremony, kept under wraps until the big day. A steady stream of wagons rolled in and out of town, delivering produce and delicacies for the wedding breakfast. Carlos had invited every resident in Santa Rosa and the surrounding area.

The church looked resplendent; floral displays surrounded the altar and Nave. At the back of the church, trestle tables were laden with Glasses, crockery, and gleaming cutlery. Abundant alcohol sat in readiness. Fire pits loaded with urns bubbled away with all manner of food as a specialist team prepared the feast, The air filled with marvellous aromas.

Rosa studied her reflection in the gilded mirror. What should have been the happiest of days was clouded with doubt. She thought of her childhood dream, the magnificent hacienda and handsome mystery man. To many, it might seem as though she had achieved her desires. Rosa knew her life ahead would have all the trappings of wealth, and her family would never face the fear of being plunged into poverty. Despite knowing this, she felt empty.

There was no joy on this day, no matter how hard she tried to be positive. Her mother, Isabella, was almost catatonic, barely aware of where she was, slipping a little more into the abyss each day. Since Rosa shared the news of her impending wedding, Isabella hadn't uttered a single word. With her beloved father Paulo gone, her brother Delgado would generally be the one to stand beside her and walk her down the aisle; but he was somewhere far away in Buenos Aires. Rosa felt tears spill down her cheeks.

Maria, her younger sister and maid of honour, would lead the way down the aisle where Fr Peter waited to deliver the sacrament of marriage. Their old neighbour, Juan Petto, was emotionally overcome when asked to give Rosa away. He was honoured to do this on behalf of his dear friend Paulo.

Of course, the groom, Carlos, would be waiting at the altar. Well known to everyone, a political superstar in the making—wealthy, charming, and very handsome.

Rosa's gaze rested on the voluminous white tulle wedding dress hanging beside the bed. It was the most magnificent thing she had ever seen. Seed pearls adorned the bodice in their thousands, hand-sewn, forming intricate circular patterns. Looking at the veil and headpiece decorated with tear-shaped crystals, Rosa thought how ironic; they could easily represent the unshed tears she felt inside. At eighteen, Rosa was so young. Her long dark locks had been fashioned into a crown sitting high on her head in preparation for the headpiece. Her blemish-free skin was deathly pale. Almond-shaped eyes looked back from the mirror, full of fear. Maria's voice cut across her thoughts,

"Rosa, it is almost time."

The faint strains of music from the church organ reached Rosa. She felt ill, afraid her legs would give way. Closing her eyes, she prayed to the Holy Mother, asking for her blessing and the strength and courage to fulfil her promise. In a few short minutes, Rosalinda Caron would be no more.

Familiar faces swam in Rosa's vision as she made her way to the church entrance. She could hear the indrawn gasps and sighs of approval. The church was packed; those unable to find seating spilt outside into the blazing sunshine. The heady scent of roses and jasmine in the church was almost overpowering. Maria handed her a small bouquet of orange blossoms; as a shrill chord drew the congregation's attention, they hushed. Bridal music followed. Juan Petto stepped to her side, solemnly taking Rosa's shaking arm. Smiling faces looked back at her from every direction. She had no idea of her expression, but inside she had the crushing sensation of slowly dying.

Rosa stood facing Fr Peter, his benevolent smile like a lifeline. She tried to focus on his face and what he was saying. Carlos took her shaking hand in his as the priest commenced the vows.

"Do you, Carlos Ramon Mendoza, take this woman Rosalinda Caron as your lawful wedded wife…"

The words hit home. From this moment, Rosa was joined to Carlos for life. The rest of the ceremony passed in a blur. Carlos placed a brief kiss on her lips, then they moved down the aisle to the clapping and cheering of friends and neighbours, stepping out into the sunshine to be greeted by more applause and whistles. The church bells shattered the air, loudly proclaiming the union between Rosalinda Caron and Carlos Mendoza.

Carlos was lapping up the attention despite the bride by his side looking stricken. Rosa was a good choice, Carlos reasoned, beautiful, innocent, untainted and easily malleable. He could enjoy all she had to offer without the burden of any real commitment. There was no intention of changing his behaviour or propensity for a variety of female companionship. Carlos didn't suppose Rosa would be tiresome, but if so, he would banish her to one of his many provincial homes. Out of sight and out of mind. Carlos knew that having a wife was advantageous for a politician and essential if he wanted to produce an heir. A partner by his side gave him an air of respectability, hopefully creating an image that might persuade constituents to see him as a future leader. Carlos was trying to form the impression he was like any other man on the street. It was all about appearances. To him, it was a marriage of convenience only.

The wedding breakfast was everything Carlos had promised. The feast was magnificent, all part of the Mendoza sideshow, hopefully garnering him some votes down the line. The speeches were few. Fr Peter spoke on behalf of Rosa as her friend and mentor and briefly as the groom's brother. There wasn't a lot he could say about Carlos. He wished them well. Peter's heart ached seeing silent tears on Rosa's face. He felt troubled.

Carlos, full of charm, responded with an effusive welcome to everyone, thanking them for being present to share his joy. Many commiserated at the absence of Carlos's father, who could not attend. Carlos thanked everyone for their concern, feigning great disappointment, but explained it was unfortunate Ramon was cut off by floodwaters while campaigning in the northeast of Argentina. Truthfully, his father's absence did not faze him in the slightest.

The rowdy mariachi music and raucous laughter went on into the early hours of the morning. After the bridal waltz, Carlos shared very little of the merriment, happily watching others dance and sing, content to raise his glass with many. He retired before midnight, more than a little intoxicated, ready to claim his prize.

In their bedroom, Rosa stood frozen like a specimen waiting to be dissected. Carlos was in no hurry studying her closely, silently congratulating himself. She was a beauty. As much as he desired it, there had been no opportunity until after the wedding to savour his booty.

Carlos felt himself harden with anticipation. He was becoming bored these days with the countless whores and their endless whinging, competing for his attention or trying to coax gifts from him in exchange for their favours. It would be nice to take hold of a body that was untouched. It had been a while since he'd initiated one of his colleagues' stupid young daughters who believed him utterly obsessed with them, silly fools.

Even more appealing was the look of abject fear on Rosa's face. Did he also detect a hint of loathing? Carlos smirked…even better!

"Take off your clothes."

Rosa stood stock still, unmoving, her eyes fixed on the floor, fighting the rising panic threatening to engulf her.

"That was not a request," Carlos's steely voice commanded, "Take off your clothes, now!"

Rosa had no choice but to obey. Slowly undoing the ribbon at the neck of her gown, the garment fell away, sliding down the length of her body to the floor.

The gasp from Carlos filled the silence; Rosa flinched hearing it, standing there exposed, vulnerable, bracing herself for what was to come. Carlos gaped in awe. Even with his jaded eye, he was impressed by what he saw. Rosa's skin was translucent, her breasts voluptuous, the well-rounded mounds of her buttocks inviting exploration. Carlos noted her long, lean legs, visibly shaking; his excitement grew.

Carlos moved across the room in one deft movement, crouched like a panther stalking his prey, his face filled with lust as he grasped Rosa's left breast. His touch was not gentle, causing Rosa to cry in shock and pain.

"Please, you are hurting me."

Carlos's grip only tightened, excited by Rosa's discomfort. She needed to learn submission, know that she was his and that he could do anything he liked to her from this day forward. Loosening his grip, he feigned remorse, noting the look of relief on Rosa's face; it was short-lived.

Without warning, Carlos pushed Rosa backwards. Her balance shifted dramatically, sending her toppling to the floor, her head making a sickening thud as her forehead made contact. No sound left her lips; she just lay there dazed. He picked her up like a rag doll and threw her onto the bed. Dropping his trousers, he mounted her like some animal, rejoicing as he felt her hymen tear, climaxing as Rosa whimpered pitifully.

"Ah, the little virgin is no more," he gloated, "now, there is a woman in her place." He boasted as if he had achieved some great victory.

With those few words, he brutally took Rosa once more, then swaggered out of the room with a bottle of tequila. Slamming the

114

door behind him, he sprawled out on the settee, satisfied to celebrate the remainder of his wedding night alone, sated.

Rosa lay there like a beaten animal. Instead of the most memorable night of her life, it had been a complete violation of her physically and mentally. She couldn't decide what she felt most, shame or disgust. If only her father Paulo had not died and left them at the mercy of the Mendoza family. The only saving grace was knowing her mother, Isabella, and sister Maria would receive the care needed. Rosa reflected on the Bible's lesson about the 'sacrificial lamb', fully understanding how it must have felt.

Finally, the tears came; Rosa's body shook as she lay there sobbing, praying this would not be the pattern of her life with Carlos. Somehow deep inside, she knew those prayers would not be answered.

Carlos – Leopards Never Change Their Spots
☼

A resounding crack shattered the silence, breaking into Peter's sleep. Not many hours had elapsed since the revellers finally headed for home, the last clatter of horses, wagons, and raised voices finally fading into the distance just before dawn. The residents of Santa Rosa had never partaken in such a celebration before; they made the most of it.

Now fully awake, Peter headed to the window to investigate the commotion below. He spent the night in the storeroom above the stables, having surrendered the comfort of his quarters to the bride and groom for their wedding night.

Peter looked down, shaking his head in disbelief as Carlos cracked the whip again, causing the silver stallion to rear up and bolt forward, propelling the carriage onto the winding dirt road heading out of Santa Rosa, his entourage in tow. Peter had no idea where Carlos was going at this ungodly hour; he was never one to share his plans.

Peter sighed, thinking back over the previous day's events, remembering Rosa's pale face as she knelt at the alter taking her vows. She looked so young and vulnerable. Knowing Rosa's innocence, Peter prayed Carlos had been gentle with his new bride. Still more than a little shocked at Carlos's marriage to Rosa, Peter hoped it might change him for the better; because of this, he did nothing to discourage it.

After a quick wash, Peter headed for the chapel to commence morning prayers. First, he would need to clean up the celebrations' aftermath and begin preparations for early mass. He chuckled to himself, expecting a much-reduced congregation, anticipating many would be the worse for wear after the lengthy festivities.

The church's nave was still decorated with wedding finery, the abundant flowers wilted but still infusing the crisp morning air with a heady perfume. The resident pigeons fluttered in the rafters welcoming Peter as he genuflected, made the sign of the cross, and then headed for the alter. It was still only half-light. Peter nearing the front row of seats, could see a figure curled in the foetal position, sheltering under the pew. Peter was startled, at first thinking it was a drunken reveller leftover from the wedding breakfast, then shocked to discover it was Rosa.

Nothing prepared Peter for the pitiful sight before him, Rosa's stark face, an ugly bruise on her right temple. Peter was lost for words. He gathered Rosa into his arms, muttering, "May God forgive Carlos and my part in allowing this to happen."

Rosa wept silently, relieved at last to feel safe, even if it was only for the present. She was in no doubt whatsoever; a life of torment had only just begun.

Later, on the table in the vestry, Peter found a brief note from Carlos thanking him for his hospitality, informing Peter of his intentions to head for Buenos Aires to reconnect with their father, Ramon. Almost as an afterthought, he added a carriage would come in a day or two and take Rosa to their new mansion Hierro Castillo.

Rosa – Santa Fe
☼
1846

Since marriage to Carlos Mendoza three years earlier, Rosa's life followed a pattern. Carlos divided most of his time campaigning for his father Ramon, re-elected as Governor, and managing their mutual ranches throughout Argentina. He also used these visits to look for other properties he might annexe. Rosa had no interest whatsoever where Carlos might be, as long as it was as far away from her as possible.

The abuse initiated on their wedding night never ceased, only the intensity. Rosa learned the more discomfort or pain she displayed fuelled Carlos's passion. She quickly became adept at feigning pain. There were also his unexpected violent outbursts to contend with. It was not unusual for Rosa to remain isolated in the hacienda, her body exhibiting tell-tale bruises, a testament to his behaviour. The servants and other employees turned a blind eye. There was nothing they could do.

Relocating two years earlier from Santa Rosa, the only sadness for Rosa was leaving her family behind. At least living at Hierro Castillo allowed her regular access to Isabella, Maria and her extended family.

Rosa was restless, wondering what she might do to add meaning to her life by contributing something to her local community— finding happiness and fulfilment in her marriage was impossible. An added sadness was her mother's declining health and the separation from her brother. Unable to face life in Santa Rosa following their father's brutal death three years previously, Delgado fled to Buenos Aires, his whereabouts remained unknown.

118

Rosa's friendship with Fr Peter also sustained her. She preferred to think of him as her religious advisor and mentor rather than her brother-in-law. It was almost impossible to believe he and Carlos were siblings. Fortunately, Carlos didn't object to Rosa maintaining contact with him. Her faith saved Rosa's sanity. Despite the ordeal of being Carlos's wife, Rosa remained devout. She did often wonder why God chose to burden her this way, but somehow, she managed to survive, blocking out Carlos's infrequent returns and what that usually meant.

Fr Peter suggested Rosa make acquaintance with the nursing nuns at the Hospital attached to the Convent of Santo Domingo. Desperately short-handed, they provided care for the rapidly increasing population of Santa Fe. There were always accidents, burns, or infections, in a district primarily involved with trade and farming. Increasingly, care was required for those falling foul of the soldiers or invisible thugs intimidating landholders.

When Rosa stepped inside the infirmary, it felt like she was coming home. Originally a pavilion used for exhibitions, the domed ceilings, at least fifteen feet high, were adorned with a faded mural of cherubs in flight. Light flooded through the multitude of glass panels stretching the length of the hall. Twenty or thirty beds were placed neatly down both sides of the ward. Above each bed was a bronze crucifix.

The ward was a hive of activity. Half a dozen figures clad in white, their hair pulled back and secured under a white veil, scurried about carrying washbowls or piles of linen. The strong scent of disinfectant filled the air and other unidentifiable substances associated with a hospital.

"May I help you, Senora?" a nun, approximately sixty, looked at Rosa curiously, wondering what this young woman was doing there.

"I'm looking for Sister Angelina, please," Rosa answered nervously.

The nun's face broke into a broad smile, "I am Sister Angelina, the Mother Superior of Santo Domingo. Are you by any chance Senora Mendoza?"

"I am," Rosa responded nervously. She could see the nun's smile quickly turn into a frown. Sister Angelina took some time before responding.

"Forgive me, Senora; I was expecting someone much older. What we do here is often very difficult, even for those experienced in dealing with such things. I do not wish to be unkind, but you are very young, Senora. I am not sure you will find what we do here to your liking."

Rosa felt a knot form in the pit of her stomach. She was desperate for change. "I beg you, Sister, please give me a chance. I am more resilient than you might expect. I have experience of things much worse than might be found here."

The nun studied Rosa, jaw set, determination on her face. Somehow Sister Angelina knew she spoke from the heart. This one had seen a lot in her young life. "Father Peter is a good man. He spoke highly of you, Senora. He was confident you would be capable of helping here; I must trust his judgement."

Rosa almost cried with relief. Instinctively, she knew this place would be her salvation. God had led her steps to the Convent of Santo Domingo for whatever reason. Six days each week, Rosa would arrive at 07.30 a.m. and leave at 3.30 p.m.

There was a great deal to learn. In the beginning, Rosa was like a Novice in training, initially given menial tasks scrubbing floors, sterilizing utensils, and cleaning urinals. Rosa found the work physically demanding, something she didn't mind. Very quickly, she realised assisting the nuns had been a blessing, her most rewarding undertaking in a long time. It was a team effort. Everyone worked equally hard; no one was exempt.

The other nuns welcomed Rosa to the convent and infirmary. Gradually given more responsibility, she attended to simple wound dressings at first and then those requiring greater skill. Over the following year, she gained permission to observe in the theatre and watch simple surgical procedures, eventually being trained by the nuns to assist when they were short-handed.

120

When Carlos was home, Rosa was not permitted to attend the hospital, expected to be on hand to meet his demands and attend any functions he graced with his presence. These days she was little more than an adornment. He still abused her physically in the bedroom, but less often. He delighted in telling her he found her dull and lifeless and unable to satisfy the sexual pleasures he sought. Carlos taunted her by boasting of his travels, saying he always managed to find some woman available to satisfy his lust, willingly or otherwise. Every time Carlos departed, Rosa rejoiced at seeing him and his entourage heading down the exit road from their hacienda.

Sister Angelina always noted the change in Rosa when she returned from one of her absences but never questioned her, accepting with gratitude the time she gave to help the nuns. Rosa never offered any explanations but did wonder what information Fr Peter may have provided in his initial letter of recommendation to the Mother Superior.

When the Sisters stopped for a siesta at 1 pm, everything came to a standstill. It was her favourite time of the day. Rosa sat quietly in the back of the Chapel, enjoying the silence. She could catch her breath and reflect on what had taken place during the morning, satisfied if things had gone smoothly, concerned about how she could perform better if not.

She admired the beautiful old church built with sandstone blocks, different from Our Lady of The Rosary in Santa Rosa. The years had flown; it seemed like another lifetime since she prepared flowers for the altar with her mother and sister. She reflected on her current life with Carlos. He and his father, Ramon, grew wealthier and greedier. Rosa realised that no amount of wealth either of them accrued would ever be enough. Both narcissists, their need for self-gratification was a bottomless pit.

Stepping out of the main chapel, Rosa wandered through the rooms attached to the adjoining pavilion. Over time the nuns had converted each one into a treatment room. The original dispensary and treatment rooms were now completely inadequate to address the volume of those seeking attention. Sparsely furnished, they held a platform for the patient, a cabinet containing instruments, bandages and medications, and a small desk with two chairs. The atmosphere was austere; there were no luxuries here. All painted the same drab off-white, the walls bare except for a Crucifix.

The violence was escalating. People presented with broken limbs and others with severe burns; many did not survive their injuries. Stab wounds were becoming commonplace. Rosa was now adept at suturing wounds and setting simple fractures. She couldn't imagine life without the Convent Hospital, nor a time when her assistance would no longer be needed. Sighing, she wondered if the brutal treatment of the landholders would ever cease. People were fleeing the country in ever-increasing numbers.

Buenos Aires – Elections

☼

1852

Carlos sat back, congratulating himself after receiving the final tally of votes confirming Ramon's re-election as Governor of the Province of Buenos Aires for a third term. For some reason, a strong lobby against Ramon in Santa Fe developed over the previous few weeks. Carlos left immediately to find the source of unrest and quell any dissenters before the vote. He had done just that.

Carlos held the telegram confirming his father's win. The small group remaining in the office in Santa Fe celebrated quietly. They had done their job well and would reap the rewards. Costing many thousands of pesos to *appease* the troublemakers didn't matter; that was common. Carlos decided it was too late to head to the hacienda. He would spend the remainder of the night in town.

In Buenos Aires' celebrations went on long into the night. It had been a great victory. Of course, there was no doubt about the outcome; Ramon left nothing to chance. Any opposition was quickly dispensed with by threats of violence to them or their family, or Ramon simply bribed them. In his opinion, everyone had a price.

The new Governor sat sprawled in the leather easy chair, sweating, naked from the waist down, a glass of brandy in one hand and a cigar in the other. Kneeling on the floor before him, a woman about twenty performing oral sex. Ramon's expression was close to ecstasy, the perfect ending to a victorious night. He put down his brandy and cigar; he was close to climaxing. Taking a fistful of the woman's hair in each hand, amused at her futile attempts to get free.

Ramon roared, laughing at her discomfort, finally letting her go. Half drunk, he pushed her away with his foot.

"You can go now whore; you've earned your money."

The young woman got up, gathering her robe off the floor. Without looking back, she headed for the door, her face expressionless. Senor Mendoza was well known to the establishment; she was just grateful this encounter was without his often perverse demands.

Revellers were still celebrating in the street, discharging guns and yelling obscenities—some of Ramon's accomplices letting off steam. Ramon laughed; dragging himself out of the chair, he fell across the bed, thinking about the day he would be celebrating an election not as Governor but as President. The smile was still on his face as he drifted off to sleep.

A small group of Ramon's gauchos had bedded down in the stable below the brothel; those very drunk settled quickly. The few remaining awake played poker, smoked and drank, telling bawdy stories of their prowess with women, eventually turning in as the candlelight dimmed.

The full moon lit up the now deserted back streets of Buenos Aires. A slight breeze cooled the night. No witnesses to see the first whisp of smoke curling out from under the door of the stable below the brothel. Too much alcohol would prove a deadly sedative for those trapped behind bolted doors. There was only one exit.

The brothel was well alight before anyone sounded the alarm. Smoke billowed from most windows of the three-story building. Other similar buildings in the area hosted an external staircase joining the landing on each floor, but not this one. Voices broke the stillness of the early morning; people were screaming. The first respondents organised a bucket brigade, using water from a horse trough nearby, but all efforts were futile.

After sunrise, it was evident the fire had destroyed most of the brothel and two other establishments. Buenos Aires had lost one of its better-known houses of pleasure…along with the newly elected Governor, Ramon Mendoza.

Retribution

☼

Carlos awoke to the smell of stale alcohol and tobacco. The office daybed was a poor substitute; his bones ached. He should go home, bathe, and get some proper rest. Still elated with the election results, he was happy to tolerate the inconvenience and discomfort.

A few carts rattled along the street below, and a donkey brayed in protest somewhere off in the distance. Santa Fe was waking up early. It was no longer a nondescript regional district north of Buenos Aires but had quickly gained importance as a crucial trade port. Major centres to the West, Cordoba, San Juan, and Mendoza, often became inaccessible during the wet season when roads flooded. Santa Fe, situated on the Salado River, had the advantage of trading regardless, using cargo boats and small luggers to move grain, cattle, hides and tallow with little interruption.

Raised voices drifted up from the street, a disturbance of some kind. Carlos paid little attention, preparing to head home. Rosa, he was sure, would be her usual dour self. Usually, thinking about her caused him to feel disgruntled. Carlos acknowledged marrying a simple farm girl was a mistake; she would never be anything else. Pretty to look at, but even her looks left him cold these days. Sex with her was barely worth the effort.

As Carlos opened the office door to leave, a barrage of men came running along the corridor towards him, all yelling at once.

"What's going on? What are you doing here this time of the morning, causing a commotion? My office is off-limits to everyone except my men!" Carlos was angry. Someone would pay for letting this rabble invade his privacy.

125

The group froze in their tracks, aware of Carlos's reputation when angered. They looked for direction; no one wanted to start the conversation. One older man in a crumpled striped suit stepped forward, turning his hat in his hands nervously; he cleared his throat,

"Senor Mendoza, I fear I have some distressing news. Might we go inside and speak privately?"

Carlos, a man of little patience, had none when hungover and tired. "Speak up, you imbecile; I have no time for whatever this is about."

"Senor Mendoza, I am on the city council. I receive all messages of significance for Santa Fe. There was a fire…in Buenos Aires; several buildings burned down before the townspeople controlled the fire." The man hesitated, afraid to continue.

Carlos's anger grew; he growled at him, "Get on with it; I don't have time for this nonsense," he spat the words, starting to push past the old man.

The words tumbled out of the man in a rush, "It is unclear how many lives were lost as yet, Senor, but one of the deceased was His Excellency, the new Governor."

Nothing ever really touched Carlos. People enraged him but never caused him any deep pain. He scoffed when people talked about having a broken heart. Fond only of his housekeeper Aida, his carer from birth, he even questioned her devotion; after all, she was paid to care for him.

Without further thought, Carlos lashed out with his right arm knocking the older man out of his way, charging through the rest of the mob, rapidly clearing a path for his exit. Taking the stairs two at a time, he burst out of the building, barely able to breathe, his chest constricted.

Carlos staggered to the telegraph office where a crowd had gathered. Everyone scattered when they saw him approach. White with shock, he stood before the operator, Benito. "Is it true? Governor Mendoza, is he dead?"

The operator handed Carlos the telegraph message. Several Buenos Aires locals had positively identified Ramon. He had died of smoke inhalation. There was no mistake.

Carlos was shattered. His legs almost gave way leaving the telegraph office. As he headed for the buggy tied to the hitching post, no one dared approach him. He didn't know to whom it belonged, and he didn't care. Whipping the horse into a frenzy, he sped out of town towards home.

The Aftermath

☼

Rosa heard Aida's cry of alarm before she heard Carlos's booming voice swearing obscenities, cursing the world. About to leave for work at the hospital, she realised gloomily that this was now impossible. She found the elderly housekeeper sitting at the bottom of the staircase weeping. The maids scurried about, not knowing what to say or do. As Rosa bent to comfort Aida, Carlos's office door slammed shut with an almighty bang.

A blood-curdling scream rang out; it was Carlos. Aida spoke up,

"Senor Mendoza's father, His Excellency the Governor, is dead, killed in a fire in Buenos Aires."

Carlos was rampaging, cursing all and sundry, smashing whatever was in reach, venting his pain and grief to the world. While Rosa was all too familiar with Carlos's cruelty at the slightest provocation, his current state was terrifying. She had never been more afraid, realising how unpredictable his behaviour might be, losing the one person he loved and respected; It was hard to know what to do next. She dismissed the household staff for the rest of the day as a precaution; it seemed like a good idea.

The remainder of Carlos's men returned from town; they settled down to drinking, their mood subdued, none sure they would escape their boss's hostility. Rosa locked herself in one of the spare rooms, intending to stay out of harm's way, hoping Carlos would eventually get so drunk he would fall asleep.

Rosa knew it was wrong to wish misfortune on another, but knowing the Governor's reputation, she couldn't help but think this was somehow God's retribution.

Ramon rarely came to their hacienda when in Santa Fe, preferring to stay at a hotel in town where he could drink unhindered and seek female company. Carlos was always happy to join him there. Over the years, Rosa often reflected on how alike they were. Her mother would have said, 'cut from the same cloth'.

Rosa's heart ached when she thought about her mother, now totally dependent on Maria and her Aunt Luisa for care. Fr Peter kept Rosa informed of her deterioration, but she felt sure he played down her actual condition, not wishing to cause her undue worry. As well as looking after Isabella, Maria continued assisting Fr Peter with the cleaning and housekeeping in the church and surrounding buildings. Rosa felt guilty being so far away. She sent money to ease the burden a little, but it wasn't the same as being there to lend a hand.

There was no further word of their brother Delgado after he left Santa Rosa. Fr Peter made many inquiries on their behalf through personal contacts in the Capital, to no avail. It seemed as though Delgado vanished after he arrived in Buenos Aires.

Rosa awoke with a start. Despite the drama, she had fallen asleep. She could hear Carlos yelling her name, his speech slurred. He was drunk. Unsure of the time, she could see it was pitch black outside. There was a full moon. Carlos's angry voice grew closer; he was cursing her. Rosa felt sick listening to him stumble into every room, searching for her. With a sinking heart, she knew he wouldn't give up until he found her. Like someone going to their execution, she got up slowly and walked to the door; unlatching it, she said a silent prayer.

Carlos stood in the doorway, his bulk almost blocking out the light; she couldn't see his face in the shadows. He reeked of alcohol, and his clothes were messy. The blood on his hands and clothing was most likely from whatever he'd smashed earlier. Suddenly his hand shot out and grabbed a fistful of her hair, yanking her towards him roughly.

"Hide from me, will you, you little bitch!" With that, he punched with his free hand. A second before losing consciousness, Rosa wondered if he'd broken her neck.

Rosa opened her eyes slowly, almost afraid to move. Sunlight spilt across the floor, highlighting the coloured rug beneath her. She moved her arms and legs gingerly; everything seemed to be intact. There didn't appear to be any broken bones; she just ached. When Rosa tried to sit up, the room started spinning, her vision blurred, and she wanted to be sick. From her experience working at the hospital, Rosa knew she was suffering from a concussion. Touching the back of her aching head, her hand came away sticky with drying blood. She guessed the wound wasn't deep. There was a sizeable lump present. Rosa's right cheek was also severely swollen. She had been unconscious for a few hours; she was probably lucky to be alive.

Aida's troubled voice hesitatingly called, "Mistress Rosa, are you there?" Fearfully Aida called her elderly husband Alfredo, "Come and help me find the mistress."

Rosa became aware she was half-naked. It was apparent Carlos's depraved sexual abuse continued regardless of her state. Reaching up, she pulled the silk cover off the bed, wrapping it around her as best she could.

Alfredo's shocked face appeared at the door, Aida close behind, now crying, holding her face in her hands, shaking her head. Ever so gently, Alfredo managed to scoop Rosa up and carry her down the hallway to her bedroom, placing her on the four-poster bed. Rosa thought her head would explode; she tried to block out the pain by closing her eyes.

Aida gently bathed Rosa and then applied a bandage to her head wound. It would be nearly a week before Rosa left her bed. When finally able to limp down the stairs, she was shocked at the legacy of Carlos's rampage.

Carlos's cronies left behind on the ranch informed Alfredo that Carlos had gone to Buenos Aires to arrange Ramon's burial. She would have to attend. Ramon's body had lain in state in Buenos Aires for a week already; she would have to leave soon. God forbid. The one saving grace, Fr Peter, would be there also.

130

The Funeral

☼

Since the night of Ramon's death and the appalling behaviour of Carlos, he had avoided Rosa. He barely acknowledged her presence at the funeral, choosing instead to leave her in the care of his brothers, Peter and Philippe. Consumed with his grief, nothing else registered with Carlos.

Despite the sad circumstances, Rosa was pleased to see Fr Peter and Br Philippe. It had been some time. Passing on her condolences, she was surprised neither appeared greatly affected by Ramon's death. The relationship with their father was unknown to Rosa; she didn't know he had been a father to them in name only. They stood at the Cathedral entrance awaiting the Archbishop's presence.

Fr Peter studied Rosa closely. He could see the toll living with Carlos was taking. She looked gaunt. Although her pleasure at seeing him was obvious, her mood remained sombre. He wondered just how much physical violence she endured. Peter abhorred violence against women, often wondering what his mother Ilona experienced. Both brothers attended the funeral out of respect. He provided for them growing up and ensured they received a good education. As followers of the faith, they embraced the concept of forgiveness.

The Archbishop of Buenos Aires met the family at the entrance to the cathedral. Making the sign of the cross, he recited, "May God our Father's grace and peace, who raised Jesus from the dead, be with you always." He turned without another word, leading the procession down the nave with several attending priests, followed by Carlos, Rosa, Fr Peter, and Br Philippe.

The cathedral was packed. In the front row to the right sat a distinguished-looking gentleman representing the President of Argentina. Government dignitaries, members of The Cattle Breeders

131

Association, Landholders Association, representatives from Councils throughout Argentina, and anyone considered important, made up the congregation. The procession moved along the nave as the choir on both sides of the chancel commenced singing the first hymn, 'Sanctus', accompanied by the pipe organ; the voices and music resonated throughout the church.

Rosa looked about in awe. The Cathedral of The Holy Trinity of Buenos Aires was something to behold. She had never been in a church of this magnitude. It wasn't just the size; the architecture was astounding. Immense, pointed arches led down each side of the central nave. She caught glimpses of side chapels dedicated to the veneration of individual saints. Columns of marble stretched skyward, leading the eye to statues above, portraying the stations of the cross, culminating in Christ's crucifixion. The surrounding walls displayed religious artworks and frescos of angels. One wall held a massive woven tapestry depicting The Last Supper. Above the chancel, a stained-glass dome flooded the stone floor with light, illuminating the high altar, behind which stood a larger-than-life bronze crucifix bearing the body of Christ.

In the centre of the chancel stood Ramon's Coffin, burnished timber draped with the flag of Argentina, almost invisible beneath the enormous wreath of white Lillies.

Having seated the family in the front left pew, the archbishop proceeded to the altar. Stepping into the pulpit, he began the requiem mass with a nod toward the Tabernacle and Eucharist, acknowledging God's presence. The requiem 'Gloria in Excelsis Deo' started playing, waiting in preparation for the final dignitaries and guests to be seated. The Latin mass began,

"Eternal rest grant them, O Lord."

Rosa tried not to judge Ramon. In all honesty, she knew little of him, but what she did know was shrouded in deception, secrecy, and fear. If Carlos were any reflection of his father, prayers asking for the absolution of Ramon's sins would be lengthy.

Those giving the eulogy were few, colleagues of either Ramon or Carlos. Men with ulterior motives. When the pomp and ceremony were completed, the family members attended a private interment at the family crypt in Recoleta Cemetery.

The wake was a subdued affair. Brothers Philippe and Peter circulated amongst the guests conveying their thanks for attending. Carlos, grief-stricken, was barely capable of interacting. Rosa found it impossible to think about what the future was likely to be. Just the thought of returning home with Carlos made her feel ill. They were due to return the day after the funeral to their hacienda in Santa Fe, Solitario Lobo, aptly named Lone Wolf.

Dreading the day ahead, Rosa was taking breakfast with Fr Peter and Br Philippe in the hotel when Carlos presented himself in a state of excitement; his mood completely altered. Carlos was not returning to Santa Fe. Elated, he had been approached by his father's close political allies to run for the vacant position of Governor. They believed Carlos was the ideal choice, having been closely aligned with Ramon throughout his election campaign and familiar with strategic plans already implemented. The election was just a *rubber stamp* on Carlos's return as Governor. The ruling party reasoned with his father's untimely death, there would be a considerable swing toward a sympathy vote for his son.

Rosa was overcome with relief Carlos wasn't returning home. Peter couldn't help but notice her reaction.

Rosario

☼

1852

Hidalgo Garcia's property Mirlo, nestled on the perimeter of the pampas thirty miles north of Rosario, the hacienda was coming to life as the distant sound of gunfire disturbed the tranquillity. Blackbirds nearby filled the sky, startled by the sound. It was faint but unmistakable. The ranch hands, instantly alarmed, mounted quickly and headed towards the outlying corral.

Lorenzo had been caught napping; it was too late to wake the other ranch hands. They would all pay dearly for his lapse of judgement. The raiding party were almost on top of the cattle herd before he saw them. There was no reason to expect any company this far out in the pampas. In the dim light, he counted maybe a dozen or so men. As they drew closer, he could see soldiers' black and red garb, but instinctively he knew they had been gauchos before becoming soldiers by the way they sat in the saddle. These men would show no mercy. It was pointless hoping for more.

Senor Garcia had instructed the property manager, Samuel, to corral the cattle ready for market in one of the outlying holding pens, which was inconvenient. Lorenzo thought it a waste of time and effort when there had been no raids on properties this far south of Santa Fe, although talk of trouble elsewhere was becoming prevalent. He should have posted sentries. There were none.

The light was still insufficient to see the gleam of metal in the rider's hand until the resounding pistol shot found its mark. Before Lorenzo's lifeless body hit the ground, another dozen shots rang out, shattering the silence of the early morn.

134

The group swung into action, throwing the corral gate wide. Spooked by the gunfire, the animals charged out of the yard, the men barely able to keep up as the herd stirred up clouds of dust. As instructed, the cattle would be driven westward to the Mendoza property some distance away. Once they crossed the boundary, no one would dare offer a challenge.

When Hidalgo's men arrived, they found the bloodied bodies of their five amigos still in their bedrolls, huddled close to the smouldering embers of the dying fire. Lorenzo, charged with rounding up the cattle at Mirlo, lay face down in the dirt, a single gunshot to his forehead still oozing blood. The riders were shocked at the brutality confronting them, and more than a little afraid whoever did this might return. They were ranchers, not prepared for such things. Samuel galloped back to Mirlo to telegraph his boss Hidalgo Garcia and alert him of the attack.

A similar event was taking place two hundred and thirty miles to the west near Rio Cuarto. The Garcia property Sangre Rio, *Blood River*, was living up to its name; it, too, was under siege.

The troupe of twenty soldiers surrounded the hacienda, calling out to those inside the building. The ranch hands were out on the plains mustering cattle; a few workers were nearby in the fields. As soon as they saw the soldiers approaching, those in the area fled, hiding amongst the tall maize, seeking any safe refuge.

Those working inside the hacienda slowly filtered out of the building, forming a line alongside the barn as instructed; they were terrified. The seven household staff included the housekeeper, two maids, a cook, and three groundsmen. They watched as five soldiers walked around the perimeter of the hacienda, lighting bundles of brush soaked in oil, throwing some on the roof through the open doorway or smashed windows. The faces of the soldiers remained expressionless as the home exploded into flames.

The Sergeant in charge cantered over to where the captives stood. The men, heads bowed, nervously clasped their hands in front. The four women were weeping; two stood with eyes closed, praying. The Sergeant's expression was pitying, looking down at these simple

135

folk for the briefest moment. They were of no immediate threat to him or any of his men…but they were all witnesses to this treachery. Without a second's hesitation, turning to exit Sangre Rio, he ordered his men to shoot them.

Argentina
☼

1852

Miguel, Elizabeth and Hidalgo's son, was a virile young man with a good head on his shoulders. Despite his youth, he was more than capable of running the Garcia holdings. However, he did lack exposure to the broader community. For that reason, over the last three years, Hidalgo insisted Miguel join him when visiting their properties and the cattle markets in the northwest. The aim was to raise his awareness and gain experience in attending to business matters unaccompanied.

Theresa, Miguel's half-sister, entered womanhood with all the grace and beauty of a fine lady, equipped with the best attributes from her parents. More than a few hopeful young men courted Theresa, but she rejected their advances; like Miguel, her focus was on caring for their land instead. A shrewd businesswoman, she had learned all aspects of ranching and the cattle industry well.

Theresa insisted on going along with the men when they attended the major cattle sales in Cordoba or Santa Fe. While her father and brother talked business with the other competing ranchers, Theresa mingled amongst the crowd, an *invisible butterfly* listening attentively to all the gossip... the suspected genetic faults of certain animals, the breeding mishaps, and the frailty of those competing against the Garcia's. Such information proved invaluable. Hidalgo and Miguel both quickly realised the advantage of having Theresa along.

Disturbing reports filtered back to Ataliva Roca of farms burnt out, wells poisoned, and cattle rustled. Uneasiness crept over the whole countryside. Some families packed up and left rather than wait to see if the trouble headed south. Many considered letting their stock

137

free to roam the plains and take some leave until the danger passed. Still, others believed the rumours to be scurrilous, ignoring what they thought was just gossip.

Surprisingly, there had been no follow-up attacks near Santa Rosa after the murder of his father's sharefarmer and friend Paulo Caron in 1843. In the north and northwest of the country, things were different; there was a significant escalation of violent incidents against those resisting the government authorities.

Hidalgo remembered the precise moment he awoke to the clatter of the morse telegraph in the early hours of the first week in May. It was his foreman Samuel, from their property Mirlo, near Rosario. The message conveyed his distraught state following the deadly attack at the corral, the killing of Lorenzo and the other ranch hands.

There were no witnesses. Hidalgo was reeling from the shock; he awakened Elizabeth to discuss what they might do. Shortly afterwards, a further telegraphic message delivered the horrific news concerning their property at Sangre Rio; the hacienda burnt to the ground, and the household staff murdered. Those who escaped by hiding in the fields identified the assailants as soldiers.

Two weeks earlier, Hidalgo had dispatched Miguel to the north of Cordoba to investigate a delay in shipping cattle and grain from their El Dorado property to Santa Fe. The last message from the market at Santa Fe stated that the delivery registered for shipping was well overdue. He had not received any reply from messages urgently dispatched to the ranch.

Hidalgo and Elizabeth were almost paralysed with fear, not knowing if Miguel had walked into an ambush. They had no direct contact with their son, only receiving a message informing them of his safe arrival in Cordoba and his intention to head to El Dorado the following day. That was two days ago.

Cordoba

A clear morning in May. Miguel looked out on the streets of Cordoba, peaceful before the day's rush began. Disturbing news reached him late the previous evening about their property, *Silver Stallion*, managed by a close friend and share farmer with the Garcias. Orlando Velez sent a desperate message while under attack, later beaten and forced to watch the farm razed.

The property near Villa Maria was almost ninety miles away. Miguel found it hard to believe this could happen in such a quiet, close-knit community. He could not offer immediate assistance. He would have to delay his planned visit to the Garcia property at El Dorado, north of Cordoba, as Villa Maria was in the opposite direction. Whatever was causing a delay in sending produce to the market in Santa Fe would have to wait; this matter was of greater urgency. He was sure Hidalgo would agree. He would notify his father at the first opportunity.

Miguel hired a wagon to carry supplies he anticipated might be needed, taking several spare horses. The trip itself was unremarkable. He heard more disturbing reports from far and wide at each posada while taking a break and changing horses. It seemed violence against the farming community was happening on a far larger scale than previously known. Well-planned and orchestrated attacks were usually carried out after dark. No perpetrators had been identified or apprehended.

Arriving at the property north of Villa Maria, Miguel halted his mount, staring aghast at the scene of destruction that confronted him.

"My God," he said out loud, shocked. The once beautiful home looked as if a bomb had hit it. The ashen ruins were still smouldering in the afternoon breeze.

The faint sound of voices carried from a hillside nearby. Miguel quickly tethered the wagon to a tree, mounted his horse and headed for the grassy outcrop a short distance away. He found Orlando lying under a tree, bruised and covered in swollen red welts, his terrified wife and three frightened children nearby. Orlando had been beaten and brutally whipped. A large strip of flesh had pulled away from his left forearm where he'd tried to prevent the hacienda fire from igniting the barn, succeeding at considerable cost. He was in danger of losing his arm. The smell of burnt flesh made Miguel's stomach churn. Bianca was ghostly pale and trembling with shock, barely capable of comforting her husband and reassuring the children.

Over the past two days, Orlando's condition deteriorated. They had been without water for half a day; Miguel quickly provided a canteen, emptied the supplies from his saddlebags, and dressed Orlando's wounds as best he could. Miguel knew the risk of infection was high; Orlando needed to be in a hospital; without one, he would, in all probability, die. While talking gently to Bianca and the children, reassuring them they were safe, Miguel formulated a plan. He would go back and unload the wagon, set up a temporary overnight shelter in the barn for them, and in the morning, head for Cordoba, the nearest major city with a hospital. If they left at first light, it would still take the better part of two days if they didn't strike any trouble. Miguel didn't want to think about what that might be. There wasn't another alternative.

Miguel threw the doors of the barn wide open, setting the frightened house animals free. Orlando and a few seasonal workers had managed the property which produced grain. He had no idea where they might be, probably too afraid to return. There was only a small amount of fire damage to the barn. The homestead was another matter. Now just a pile of ashes, wisps of smoke wafted up from the charred remains. Miguel put up a canvas sheet in one corner to afford Bianca and the children some privacy. He had brought ample food and water as a precaution.

The most challenging part was getting Orlando onto the wagon. Miguel cleaned the tray as much as possible and placed another canvas sheet over the base. There was only a small supply of blankets. They would have to make do.

Unfortunately, Miguel had nothing to ease Orlando's pain. With Bianca's help, the two managed to get him upright. Hoisting him over his shoulder, Miguel lumbered him onto the tray with force. Orlando cried out in pain. Miguel couldn't be sure what other damage Orlando might have sustained during the beating.

He couldn't tolerate much movement; it would be necessary for him to remain on the wagon until the journey's end. The dilemma for Miguel would be how fast their journey should proceed. The roads were rough, but a slow trip risked Orlando not reaching the care he desperately needed in time to save his life.

There was little sleep that night for Miguel or Bianca. Her face was etched with concern for Orlando and what would become of them all. The children slept soundly, looking as if they didn't have a care in the world. Miguel learned from Bianca the perpetrators were soldiers. They no longer feared striking in broad daylight or the risk of being recognised. There was no longer any need to hide from the law. They were the law!

Throughout the night, Orlando drifted in and out of consciousness, moaning quietly, calling out, reliving the nightmare of the past few days.

They set off before dawn; By midday, Orlando had a raging fever. Bianca sat quietly in the swaying wagon, sponging Orlando's face and neck; her tear-stained face said it all. By the time they made camp, he was no longer lucid. The moaning had stopped entirely. There was no overhead shelter for the wagon, Miguel chose to stay with Orlando. The night air was cold; Miguel hoped it might aid Orlando's comfort.

No other travellers were staying at the Posada. The man in charge was pleased to have some company. Few travellers had been on the road since the *trouble* began. Miguel learned resistance or protests from decent district Councils and prominent citizens trying to restore order, which soon dissipated in the face of overwhelming odds when they realised any form of retaliation was futile. They risked being labelled enemies of the province.

141

Before starting early, the following day, the children ate heartily. Neither Miguel nor Bianca had any appetite, partly due to the smell emanating from Orlando's left arm. Miguel saw the flesh above the bandages slowly turning black; he had gangrene. Just before the outskirts of Cordoba, late afternoon, Orlando stopped breathing.

Quest for Justice

☼

Miguel was sick to his stomach and filled with fury. With the destruction of the homestead, the family lost everything they possessed. Someone had to pay for taking Orlando's life and leaving his wife and three children destitute. Bianca's brother, a blacksmith, lived in Cordoba, her place of birth. It was a sad reunion.

They laid Orlando to rest in a quiet grove at the bottom of the property. The children were too young to grasp what was happening. Miguel was confident that Bianca would manage with the help of family and friends. Reluctantly he bid farewell. He needed to contact his father urgently to report what had happened.

When Miguel arrived at the telegraph office in Cordoba, there was a sheath of messages from his father, frantic to hear of his whereabouts and gauge his safety. Miguel learned of the raids on Mirlo and El Dorado, a situation repeated all over Argentina. Landowners were suffering everywhere; others were being targeted, not only the Garcias.

Miguel hurriedly sent off a telegraph reassuring the family of his well-being before adding the sad news concerning Orlando and the Velez family. Finally, informing them that he was abandoning plans to visit their other properties. Instead, there was no other recourse than to place a case before a General Assembly in Santa Fe. Should that fail, he would take their fight to the state capital. Miguel prayed the parliament in Buenos Aires was not so corrupt as to stand by and watch Argentina's destruction.

Miguel knew it was pointless fighting his battles in Cordoba; it was like the Governor's backyard. Carlos Mendoza grew up only a few miles outside the city; his deceased father, Ramon, was once the mayor before becoming the Governor of the Province. The Mendoza family controlled the majority of information within the district. It was unlikely the world outside Cordoba was aware the scale of corruption was staggering, bordering on anarchy.

Miguel headed to the Hotel he usually stayed at when in Cordoba. He was well known there. They greeted him warmly. The owners were decent people, appalled at what was happening around them. They were discreet; he could depend on them to keep his presence quiet. They reassured Miguel they would remain alert to anything indicating a potential threat.

Miguel arranged to have dinner in his room, then have a bath and a good night's sleep. It would be the first time in weeks since he had slept in a real bed. He needed all the rest he could muster. It was two hundred and six miles from Cordoba to Santa Fe. Even if his journey were without incident, travelling hard, it would still take him three to four days.

If there were any back roads to Santa Fe, Miguel took them, aware his distinctive fair hair and blue eyes set him apart; he aimed to be as invisible as possible. On his three-day journey, he became increasingly distressed, witnessing damaged or deserted properties and carts laden with people and belongings fleeing the area. There was no end to it.

After skirting the main entry road to the city, Miguel approached from the southern end of town. Before leaving Cordoba, he contacted several of his father's associates in Santa Fe. He had a clear idea of where he could stay with safety, with those sympathetic to his cause. The information Miguel received was heartening.

There was a groundswell of growing anger and talk of a significant protest group forming. Alberto Diaz agreed to meet Miguel, suggesting a safe rendezvous away from prying eyes. He and many others knew they were under surveillance. It was too dangerous for Miguel to approach them directly. Alberto would guide him to a *safe house* until they could meet undetected and discuss the best course of action as a group. They would need a coordinated, cohesive plan if it were to have any chance of success

144

Miguel was reasonably familiar with the inner streets of Santa Fe, especially near the waterfront. This area was always a hive of activity, popular with sailors and traders frequenting the many bars there. It would be much easier to lose himself in a crowd there. He heard the commotion well before arriving near the harbour, raised voices and the sounds of rioting. Dismounting, he tied his horse to a guardrail and sprinted down an alleyway. Stepping out from between two buildings, he was confronted with the sight of an angry mob slowly backing down the street towards where he was standing. Most of the crowd appeared to be farmers or labourers. They were wielding pitchforks, shovels, fence posts or anything else that might serve as a weapon. Despite their number, which appeared to be several hundred, they were no match for the soldiers on horseback bearing down on them, riding straight for the mob, cracking heads with batons as they trampled the helpless victims. Without warning, the soldiers started randomly shooting. Panic erupted; the crowd fanned out, frantically trying to escape the onslaught.

The crowd surged, and Miguel trying to get away, became caught up with those fleeing; he turned, intending to head back down the alleyway, but it was too late; looking up, he saw the horse bearing down on him, the blur of a red jacket and a swinging arm as the baton made contact. He tried to lunge to one side, but the animal was on top of him, trampling his legs as it passed. Miguel screamed in agony. Before he lost consciousness, the foot soldiers closely following the cavalry were upon him, kicking and beating him, and then oblivion.

Noise from the fighting lessened as the melee continued streets away. The carnage was horrific, bodies strewn as far as the eye could see. Some lay with broken bones or cuts and bruises, moaning or crying out in pain, pleading for help. Others were clearly beyond help. Slowly a wagon passed down the street, oblivious to anything in its way. Four soldiers walked alongside, looking closely at each victim. The cart stopped alongside Miguel.

"Here, this one. He is no farmer; look at his clothing and fancy boots and a gringo by his looks. One of the leaders, no doubt." The soldier in charge prodded Miguel with his boot, then bent down to look at him more closely. "He's still breathing; throw him on the wagon and get him to the hospital; if he lives, we'll question him. Leave two men on guard." The wagon moved off quickly. There were three captives on board.

Safely out of view at the end of the street, a lone observer watched the battle from beginning to end. He had a meeting to attend. He was filling in time when it all began. Not wanting to hang around his planned destination and draw too much attention, he would leave for the waterfront with little time to spare; that's when the rioting began. It was pointless to panic; there was nothing Alberto Diaz could do about the situation; he would have to wait it out.

He gasped as he saw the tall stranger step out of the alleyway. By some quirk of fate, it was Miguel Garcia. At that instant, he watched the soldier on horseback descending on Miguel.

Return to the Convent
☼

After the funeral, Carlos left Buenos Aires to pursue campaigning for the office of Governor, while Rosa returned alone to Santa Fe. He might be gone for weeks or months if she was lucky. Rosa thought about her marriage. For a long time, she had blamed the deficits on her inadequacy. Over time, she realised nobody deserved to be treated the way Carlos treated her, regardless of her innocence and naivete. He was a narcissistic bully, only able to derive pleasure at the expense of someone else's suffering. Rosa shuddered, thinking about him. She placed tremendous faith in the power of prayer but had given up praying to redeem Carlos's soul, believing it already belonged to the devil.

Sister Angelina didn't question Rosa's six weeks absence from the hospital. Previously it had never been more than four or five days at a time. There was also the funeral of her father-in-law Ramon Mendoza. Fr Peter paid the convent a surprise visit following his father's funeral. He didn't elaborate on Rosa's absence, although Sister Angelina suspected he knew much more than he was saying.

When Rosa presented for duty, Sister Angelina was shocked by her changed appearance. She was very pale and had lost a considerable amount of weight.

"My child, are you well enough to be here? You know how taxing the work can be."

"Sister Angelina, I beg you to let me stay and assist the nuns. It is everything to me. I cannot explain, but the hospital is my sanctuary and salvation."

Sister Angelina nodded her head, hearing the desperation in Rosa's voice. Against her better judgment as a nurse, she agreed to let her stay, intending to assign her only light duties. Rosa sighed with

147

relief; life could go on as normal, whatever that was; she didn't know anymore.

The infirmary was overflowing; Rosa had never seen it so crowded. Violence continued to escalate throughout the province, disrupting every facet of life. Sadly, as supplies dwindled, a lack of cohesion developed amongst the local landholders, each protecting their interests. Infighting began to occur, adding to the growing numbers at the infirmary. Rosa shook her head in disbelief. The trauma inflicted by the soldiers and accomplices of the ruling party was bad enough!

Everyone was exhausted. When Rosa had returned to work after Ramon's funeral six weeks earlier, her sense of relief at being where she felt she belonged was overwhelming, overriding any thoughts of self-preservation. The knowledge she was contributing something worthwhile was a driving force, but she quickly realised she was not up to working at the intensity required.

After completing a nasty wound dressing, Rosa felt a wave of nausea. Being used to dealing with much worse, she was surprised. Since returning to work in the hospital, it had happened a few times. Rosa decided she must be getting weak in her *old* age. They worked non-stop throughout most of the morning. The nurses run off their feet, trying to attend to everyone's needs. Rosa desperately wanted to sit down for ten minutes and have a quick cup of tea. It was not going to happen; sighing, she realised there wasn't time for a break.

Rosa heard the clatter of a wagon arriving. A commotion erupted in the courtyard outside the hospital pavilion as voices shouted commands. Glancing through the window, she saw six armed soldiers yell at some nurses crossing the square, ordering them to stop whatever they were doing and give their full attention to the wounded prisoners on the wagon; she could make out the forms of three men. Rosa hurried down the corridor to lend a hand.

Halfway to the entrance, sweat started to run down her forehead, but she was suddenly icy cold instead of hot. Rosa stopped; she wanted to throw up. She leaned against the wall, trying to steady herself. Everything started spinning as she slid to the floor.

The room came into focus. Rosa looked up into the kind face of Doctor Perez. Sister Angelina stood beside him, her face full of concern. They were in one of the treatment rooms alongside the chapel. Rosa went to sit up, but Doctor Perez restrained her; she protested.

"I am all right, Dr Perez, I promise. I was working very hard and failed to stop for a break. It was hot, and I just fainted."

Sister Angelina stood shaking her head, eyes downcast. "My dear Rosa, you must rest. I will have one of the volunteers take you home in a little while. We will see you again sometime in the future, perhaps?"

Rosa was aghast; something was not right.

"Doctor Perez, what is wrong? Why can't I return to work?"

In a gentle voice, the doctor replied, "Rosa, you're pregnant."

His words hung in the air as if someone had proclaimed a death sentence. Rosa didn't respond. The doctor looked puzzled, wondering if she had heard him.

She was shocked; she heard perfectly, clearly understanding the impact of those few words; her life was about to change forever.

Rosa fought to sit up, trying to suck air into her lungs. She felt like she was suffocating; this couldn't be happening. There must be some mistake. Her mind was racing; she couldn't even remember the last time Carlos had taken her to bed. With horror, Rosa realised the only possible time he could have impregnated her was the drunken abuse following Ramon's death. They had been married for almost nine years. She thanked God for the fact that she had never conceived a child.

Rosa began to weep. Could life be crueller? Doctor Perez, bewildered, had no idea what to say, leaving Rosa to be comforted by Sister Angelina. Usually, the news of a coming baby was a joyous event. Everything about Rosa's demeanour spelt disaster. Seeing Rosa's distress gave Sister Angelina a glimpse into what she suspected was the real life of the young woman before her.

149

One of the hospital orderlies helped Rosa into the buggy. As they drove out of the compound, the wagon Rosa had seen through the window was still there, surrounded by staff.

They headed towards the Mendoza mansion. Rosa had little recollection of the journey, too dazed to think straight. She would be forced to bear a child she could never love. She was desolate. Rosa prayed the child would not live.

The Will to Survive

☼

Sister Angelina watched as the carriage headed for the Mendoza mansion. There was little time to reflect on what Rosa might encounter; her focus was now on the men in the wagon. She watched one inert body lowered onto a pallet. Two soldiers carried the man inside while another two followed. It was impossible to judge his condition; he was unconscious, bloody and covered in mud. Sister Angelina glanced over to the wagon; the two remaining soldiers stood smoking cigarillos. Guarding the remaining fugitives was no longer necessary; the bodies of two deceased men protruded from under a canvas.

In the cloistered world of the convent, anything out of the ordinary stirred the nun's curiosity. It wasn't long before the grapevine was buzzing with rumours and speculation about the fugitive. Sister Angelina chastened the nuns for gossiping. Word filtered back from Dr Perez's initial assessment. The patient was critical and unlikely to live.

Sister Angelina left the most experienced nurses assisting the Doctor while she went to the chapel to pray for the injured man hovering between life and death.

The captive lay battered and broken, his face swollen beyond recognition. The deep laceration on his forehead was now sutured, along with several other wounds, his fair hair matted with dried blood. The fracture in his left leg was splinted and tightly bound. Sister Angelina looked down on the young man with pity, noting his deeply tanned body. Dr Perez and the nursing assistants were still attending to his body. His rugged physique indicated an active life; his calloused hands spoke of hard toil. Most of the man's torso was

151

tightly bound, immobilizing broken ribs. Ugly purple patches appeared over his exposed flesh, the bruising caused by the blow of batons or being trampled by the mounted soldier's horse.

Dr Perez looked up at Sister Angelina and slowly shook his head. It was his way of indicating he had done everything possible, but in his estimation, the young man would most likely die. Sister Angelina made the sign of the cross. Now it was up to the will of God; only by his grace would this man live or die.

Solitario Lobo

☼

The ornate iron gates swung open as Rosa's carriage headed for the front entrance of the two-story mansion. Rosa could see Carlos's carriage with the distinctive insignia on the side. Her heart sank; she would have no chance to slowly come to terms with the news that she was pregnant. Just the thought of carrying Carlos's child filled her with revulsion. Rosa prayed God would forgive her; she hadn't stopped hoping her body would expel the monster's child. Rosa knew it was unfair to blame this innocent baby, and wishing it dead was contrary to God's teachings. She wanted to throw up, unsure if it was due to the pregnancy or because she was about to face Carlos with the news.

The elderly housekeeper Aida stood at the open door, a puzzled look on her face,

"Mistress Rosa, we did not expect you home so soon; Senor Mendoza is in the upstairs bedroom packing."

Rosa dared hope he was leaving shortly. It could mean only one thing; at the very least, he had secured the office of Governor as an interim position following Ramon's untimely death. He would be elated. Rosa hoped that might work in her favour. Her footsteps clattered on the marble floor, crossing the entrance hall. She glanced at the mirror covering the wall, shocked at her reflection, pale and fearful. Rosa couldn't help looking at her waistline. Was there a thickening? Or was it just her imagination? She sighed, resigning herself to the confrontation she knew was coming.

The mahogany staircase curved up to the second floor, each step taken more reluctant than the last. Rosa clawed her way to the top, holding onto the solid railing for support. On the landing stood three trunks, placed neatly side by side, awaiting one of the houseboys to collect and load them onto Carlos's carriage. It was a *Galeras*, drawn by four horses, able to transport up to ten people. Carlos was the sole occupant. He liked to travel in style. Carlos had it fitted out to accommodate his every need, even casual female company.

Rosa gripped the railing, feeling lightheaded after the exertion of climbing the stairs. She glanced back at Aida standing below, her face full of concern. Rosa often wondered why Carlos still employed the elderly housekeeper and her husband. Neither had been able to fulfil their original roles for some time. It was likely the only compassionate gesture he had shown his whole life.

The loud clang of a bell ringing echoed throughout the hacienda. Carlos's booming voice shouted instructions to his houseboy.

"Manuel, come and get my luggage. Handle them carefully, or I'll have your hide."

It was just like Carlos issuing a request along with a threat. He stepped out of the room they rarely shared, suddenly looming over Rosa's tiny form. She was dwarfed, not only by his physical presence but also by the power he exuded. She shuddered involuntarily.

"Rosa! You are home. Aida said you were not expected for some time. Perhaps you heard the good news of my appointment and hurried home to offer your congratulations?" There was a sarcastic smirk on Carlos's face. The last thing he expected was felicitations from Rosa.

Rosa noted the sarcasm. It struck her how much she hated his existence, a thought that came often.

"I'm pregnant." She blurted it out, the sound of her voice shocking even to Rosa. The statement was delivered in a loud voice, clear and concise.

Carlos looked as if he'd been struck, taking a step backwards, digesting the statement before he spoke, the smirk wiped from his face, replaced with a scowl of disbelief. His face suffused bright red, the rage building.

"You worthless whore, whose is it?" he spat at her.

Rosa was stunned. It didn't occur to her that he might suspect her of infidelity. For a brief moment, she was incensed.

"How dare you, Carlos? It is your child. I am not like you; I have only ever been with one man. I'm not surprised you don't recall impregnating me; I was unconscious, and you were drunk." Rosa delivered her words with venom, almost as effective as if she had slapped him.

Carlos exploded, unused to Rosa standing up to him. "I don't believe you. Barren for nine years, and now you want me to raise someone else's mistake? I don't think so!" With that, he lunged forward to leave.

Rosa, mistaking his action, hurriedly stepped backwards, bracing herself for the blow she believed was coming. She tried to get a hold, desperately grasping for the balustrade as she fell, tumbling down the staircase until she lay crumpled at the bottom, unmoving.

Carlos was stunned. He looked down into the terrified faces of Aida and Manuel, witnesses to it all. Other household staff were gathering to see what the commotion was.

"You saw her slip, Aida; it was an accident."

"Si Senor. The Mistress is bleeding badly, Senor; she must go to the hospital."

Although shaken, Carlos quickly gathered his wits, ordering the staff to carry Rosa to the carriage. While others attended Rosa, he had Manuel load his baggage, anxious to be away from there. Carlos was bound for Buenos Aires for his inauguration; nothing would interfere with that, not even if his wife were fighting for her life.

Sister Angelina was leaving the chapel after vespers as the Mendoza carriage pulled up in front of the infirmary, now closed. Carlos stepped out of the carriage. He didn't wish to engage with this nun, but he had to say something about his wife.

"I am sorry to trouble you at this hour, Sister, but my wife Rosa has had a terrible accident, and I fear she injured herself. I'm afraid I have no choice but to push on; I am required in Buenos Aires urgently. I am placing her in your capable hands. Rosa has spoken highly of the work you do here."

Sister Angelina felt her stomach lurch at Carlos's words. Rosa was injured; she didn't want to think about the circumstances but knew this man's display of concern lacked any sincerity whatsoever. Sister Angelina sent someone to fetch the Doctor while others assisted in carefully removing Rosa's still limp body from the coach. The household staff had done their best to stem the bleeding, but her pallor indicated she had lost a great deal of blood.

Before anyone could retrieve Rosa's belongings packed by the maid, the coach departed, leaving the small solitary case in the middle of the empty courtyard, the wheel tracks from the coach, the only sign Carlos had been there.

Sister Angelina's heart broke for Rosa; what a life she must have with this man. Now she was having his child. The baby! Sister Angelina strode to where Rosa lay unconscious; she could see the tell-tale bloodstain spreading across the lower half of Rosa's clothing. The future of Rosa and her baby was in God's hands.

By The Grace of God
☼

I moaned as another spasm of pain and gut-wrenching contractions gripped my body. Floating, weightless, as many hands lifted me. I kept drifting in and out of consciousness; voices filtered down to where I lay,

"Quickly, we must hurry; she is bleeding from inside."

Rushed along an endless corridor; lights swirled above my head. Hushed frantic voices competed with the sound of shuffling feet.

Did that cry come from me? My body wants to dispel this great weight from within, pushing, pushing...Through the blur, excruciating pain once more...then there was nothing.

Slowly sunlight peeped over the edge of the windowsill. Rosa opened her eyes. Still groggy. Throughout the night, the nurses had worked desperately to stem the bleeding threatening to take her life.

Sunlight illuminated the crucifix standing on the bare mantle above a fireplace. She studied the figurine of Christ, the light playing over the body's contours, giving it the illusion of life. The facial features of the Saviour were serene and filled with compassion. As her mind cleared, there was a dawning realisation of where she was; her memory came flooding back, recalling the horror of losing her footing at the top of the staircase. Rosa's hand flew to her stomach, finding it bound tightly. Experience told Rosa this could mean only one thing.

The door to her room opened, and a young nun in a white habit approached the bed, relieved to see Rosa was conscious. Gently she stroked Rosa's forehead and smiled, the gesture so kind. Rosa's eyes filled with tears.

"You must not distress yourself, Senora Mendoza; you are very weak," her lilting voice implored.

"I cannot rest until I know what has happened." Rosa could see the hesitation and sadness in the nun's eyes. She didn't need confirmed what she had already guessed, but it was essential to hear the words spoken aloud, accept their finality, and know it was the truth.

"Your little girl entered this life just after midnight Senora. When she arrived, she was already with the angels; I am so sorry." She added in a gentle voice, barely above a whisper, "She was beautiful but so tiny; it was much too soon. By the grace of God, she has found eternal peace in heaven. She was baptised at birth and laid to rest in the rose garden of the convent, where we pray each evening. We will pray for her soul and yours, Senora."

Rosa wept quietly, distraught. She had wished the child dead, and now she could not even ask forgiveness for such a wicked wish nor have a chance to say goodbye to the only child she would ever have.

"Am I being punished, Sister? Not being allowed to say farewell to the child?"

"No, Senora, that was not the reason; you have been hovering between life and death for three days; the burial was necessary."

Rosa was shocked. She had no recollection. She began sobbing, mentally berating herself for wishing an innocent child dead. When the sister attempted to comfort her, Rosa pushed her away.

"I don't deserve your sympathy, Sister; God took her because he knew I didn't want her, I didn't deserve her, and now he is punishing me for my sin."

The nun tried to pacify Rosa. "The Father does not take souls in spite, Senora, only in love and caring, and he has forgiven you any sin you feel is yours, I'm sure. I will leave you to rest now. Sister Angelina will be relieved you are awake; she's barely left your side since you came to us."

Alone, Rosa recalled how devastated she was learning she was pregnant. The tiny life conceived in anger and forced upon her body was no more. She would never have the chance to hold her, to tell her how sorry she was for not wanting her. Rosa wished the baby had survived in place of her own unworthy life.

Still weeping quietly, Rosa looked across at the crucifix and wondered when Jesus was taken from Mary what she must have felt. She implored, "Please, God, forgive me," thinking of verses from the bible, 'Blessed are those who mourn, for they shall be comforted'. She wondered if she even deserved God's mercy. 'The Lord gives, and The Lord takes away'. Rosa thought about how precious little control anyone had over their life. No one was the true master of their existence; so much was left to fate and the will of God.

Rosa's strength was poor due to the blood loss. Whenever she tried to stand, she became dizzy. Dr Perez cautioned her blood pressure was very low, but neither had he ruled out the possibility of a skull fracture. Rosa also sustained badly bruised ribs from the fall. Recovery would be slow.

She would have stayed at the convent indefinitely given a choice, but that would leave her family vulnerable and at Carlos's mercy. Eventually, she would have to go home. Sister Angelina had been incredibly supportive while she grieved, offering every solace. Also, the loving care shown to Rosa by the sisters would stay with her forever; it helped ease the ache in her heart.

Rosa was in a room customarily set aside for family when someone was actively dying. It was close to the chapel, away from the hustle and bustle of the clinic. She needed to heal emotionally and physically; she welcomed the solitude. After several days' rest, Rosa ventured out of her room; she had a mission to fulfil - to farewell her stillborn child.

Overwhelmed with so many mixed emotions, she needed to come to terms with her guilt and grief. Rosa finally summoned the courage to attend the rose garden where the Sisters had laid the baby to rest, bursting into tears as soon as she saw the small white cross, unembellished except for rosary beads.

The tiny grave nestled in a bed of salvia. The sight of the wildflower took Rosa back to their farm in Santa Rosa, where masses of the blue and purple flowers grew in drifts across the fields, its liquorice perfume filling the air. It felt almost like her father, Paulo, was also letting her know he was there.

Rosa knew everything happened by God's will. Asking for his blessing and forgiveness, she committed her baby to his loving care, believing they would reunite in heaven one day. She picked a small piece of salvia to wear, a habit she would continue in remembrance of this day.

Slowly improving, Rosa decided to explore the empty passages past the chapel. Rounding the bend, she was shocked to see two armed soldiers seated outside a room at the end of the corridor. Rosa strolled past them, averting her eyes, except for a glance towards the door. One soldier was sound asleep, his head falling forward onto his chest. The other sat, a bored look on his face as he fiddled with the barrel of his rifle. He didn't even bother to look up. Nurses scurried past Rosa and entered the room. Later full of curiosity, Rosa questioned them about who was behind the door. She learned the man was never left unguarded.

Rosa remembered seeing the arrival of a wagon and soldiers. It was the day she received the news she was pregnant. She recalled hurrying down the corridor to assist when she became dizzy and passed out. The nurses told her three captives were on the wagon that day, confirming only one survived.

The Fugitive
☼

It became a ritual of Rosa's to exercise up and down the corridor several times a day, hoping to catch a glimpse of the fugitive who had still not regained consciousness. The guards, convinced he would die, were less dedicated to their efforts. They started taking turns going outside to smoke. Every effort to catch a glimpse inside the room failed. Nurses were the exception, the only ones given free rein in providing care.

The sisters informed Rosa that the man's left leg had sustained a crush fracture when trampled by a horse before being dragged out onto the dirt road; his right leg had sustained deep lacerations. On arrival at the hospital, his whole body was covered in mud and other debris. She prayed passionately for his recovery as if somehow this would make amends for the life she had willed away.

One morning leaving her room earlier than usual, Rosa was surprised to see both chairs outside the usually guarded room empty. Drawing closer, the temptation to open the door too much. Her firm knock on the door went unanswered. Rosa's heart was pounding; perhaps he had died during the night. She slowly turned the handle on the door, quickly stepped inside the room, and closed the door behind her.

The poorly lit room was bare except for a small table at the side of the bed, and a cabinet fitted out with medical supplies. Rosa drew the curtain across the single-barred window. The noisy overhead fan did little to cool the room; instead, it just moved the hot air around. The smell of disinfectant permeated the room, mixed with a rancid odour.

Rosa's breath caught in her throat as she studied the man before her. He was much younger than she had anticipated, maybe

161

somewhere around twenty-five. His supine body lay unclad except for a swathe of bandages. The nuns had draped a small towel across the genital area for privacy. Minimal signs of life were present, only the slight rise and fall of his chest as he fought to take every breath. The bed was six and a half feet long; his frame extended almost its entire length.

As Rosa's eyes adjusted to the dim light, her next surprise was the realisation his skin was fairer than most and his hair colour brown. People of European ancestry born in Argentina, *Criolo* often had tawny-coloured skin. Still, their hair was always very dark, like *Mestizos,* descendants of early settlers integrating with indigenous natives. This man was neither of those? This only served to feed Rosa's curiosity even more. Why would a man not of this country be fighting the authorities?

Beads of moisture gathered on a furrowed brow, forming rivulets that crept down his weathered features; he most likely had a fever. The golden stubble on his jawline glistened; it wasn't easy to assess his looks; his face was severely swollen. A large dressing covered a sizable lump on his forehead. Lashes fluttered erratically. Rosa wondered what scene was playing behind those eyelids. His exposed skin though heavily tanned, had a sickly pallor, his sallow complexion a waxy hue.

It was fascinating for Rosa to observe the expressions playing across this rugged face, anger? Frustration? Fear? Rosa studied the pulse beating at the base of his neck; the rhythm was constant but very slow. She wondered if his life force was ebbing away—the sense of loss threatening to overwhelm her fragile state.

"Dear Lord, Rosa whispered aloud, please don't let this man die; grant him your heavenly grace, I beg you." The plea was almost absurd; this man was closer to dying than living. Rosa took the tiny sprig of salvia she was wearing and placed it on his pillow. Opening the door tentatively, she glanced outside. There was no sign of the guards as she slipped quietly out of the room.

Early one morning of the second week, gossip in the Convent Hospital was rife. Some wealthy Santa Fe rancher had come forward and vouched for the prisoner's innocence. The rancher stated he had been expecting this visitor from Cordoba to show him a prize bull he intended to sell. The man then informed them the person they were holding was Miguel Garcia, the son of Hidalgo Garcia of Garcia Holdings in southern Argentina. There would be an investigation to confirm the facts, but in light of the statement and the prisoner's poor physical state, he was no longer considered a possible threat. The guards were withdrawn, much to Sister Angelina's relief.

Several days later, Sister Anna hurried into Rosa's room, a look of consternation on her face, "Senora Mendoza, do you think you could assist me in dressing a patient's wounds? We are very short-handed today; I would be so grateful. Sister Angelina is aware and has given her approval if you agree. She doesn't wish to burden you if you are not well enough."

Rosa readily agreed. She was much improved, and boredom was becoming a problem. Helping with the laundry, folding sheets and towels, and wrapping bandages was no longer enough to keep her occupied. She was eager to help.

They stopped outside the room occupied by the man Rosa now knew as Miguel Garcia. It seemed he was an Argentinian, which only answered part of the mystery—having tried to access this room for almost two weeks, and now invited to enter. It was ironic!

The first thing confronting Rosa was the smell. Miguel's wounds were infected. Sister Anna whispered,

"It will not be a pretty sight."

Nothing prepared Rosa for what was about to come. They scrubbed their hands thoroughly, put on clean aprons, and sprinkled natural oils onto cloth masks to minimize the odour. Urns of smouldering sage outside the window helped reduce the smell and purify the air.

Sister Anna began soaking off the old dressings. As the putrid gauze lifted, so did the flesh. Miguel moaned. It was difficult watching someone suffering; Rosa was filled with pity. In his semi-conscious state, Miguel's face was a grimace of pain. Finally, the soiled dressings disposed of, red, raw patches, ugly and weeping, covered his right leg and part of his lower torso. His left leg remained splinted and heavily bandaged. As gently as possible, they debrided the remaining dead flesh, cleansing and redressing the wounds.

A tear traced an uneven path down Miguel's cheek; instinctively, Rosa brushed it away with her fingertips. A hoarse voice, little more than a whisper, took her by surprise, "Gracias, Sister." He thought she was one of the nuns. For an instant, their eyes locked in silent communication; maybe he sensed Rosa's empathy. His forehead creased into a deep frown, and his eyes clouded over as he slipped into unconsciousness once more.

Rosa brushed his cheek with her fingers, expecting his skin to be tough and resistant, but found it soft to her touch; she became aware Sister Anna was tugging her sleeve, looking at her intensely, a strange expression on her face.

"It would not be wise to get too involved emotionally with our patient Senora. Don't forget; If he survives his injuries, he may yet have to answer to the law."

Of course, Carlos's law. Rosa reminded herself she was the wife of his sworn enemy, and he would certainly not think of her as an angel of mercy if he knew that.

Rosa ignored the nun's final remarks; in her heart, she knew he would survive. She believed God would answer her prayers.

Over the next week, Rosa briefly visited Miguel's room each day. She prayed for his recovery and placed a small piece of Salvia on his pillow. It was as if she was leaving a little of herself to watch over him, willing him to survive.

On her last visit, Rosa noted the dramatic improvement in his colour. Most of the facial swelling had subsided. He was sleeping peacefully, his breathing regular. He was a handsome man.

Carlos was too busy with matters of State to visit Rosa during her recovery. He received daily reports on her condition; his main interest focused on visitors or outside contacts she might have, still not convinced the baby she lost was not his.

Having secured his position as Governor, Carlos embarked on a goodwill tour, visiting each province, trying to dissipate the growing unrest over land seizures and cattle rustling, the source of the earlier riots in Santa Fe. The promise to increase law and order and bring a halt to the unrest was achievable, considering he was the main perpetrator behind the attacks! Carlos had no intention of not cashing in on his position as Governor, but he decided to take things slowly for the time being until the unrest settled down.

Later that day, Sister Angelina informed her Carlos had returned to Solitario Lobo and would send a carriage in the morning for her return home. The word 'home' stuck in her throat, almost choking her. A building does not make a home, no matter how affluent. A home was a place defined by the love and warmth shared between the people inside—a place filled with laughter, not the empty cold structure where she lived.

The carriage arrived at midday as arranged by Carlos. One of his lackeys assisted Rosa onboard. Sister Angelina and several of the nuns came to bid her farewell. She clutched a medallion in her left hand that Sister Angelina had given her that morning, hoping she might draw strength from it when times were difficult. Made of silver, The Holy Father carved into the surface, his hands clasping those of a small child. Inscribed on the back were the words,

"Suffer the little children to come unto me."

A further inscription beneath said, 'Another little Angel – Isabella'. Rosa's eyes filled with tears as she accepted it, a memento of a little daughter she would never know, baptized to honour her mother far away. It would be a long time before her scars would heal.

The Homecoming
☼

As the carriage pulled up to the front entrance, Rosa noted Carlos's coach was absent; one small blessing, she was not up to confronting him just yet. Rosa's footsteps echoed across the entrance hall as Aida greeted her warmly, clucking like a broody hen protecting her chick, not quite knowing what to say, aware Rosa's pregnancy was no more.

The weariness was pressing down on Rosa's frame like a great weight. She wanted nothing more than to take refuge in her room, lay down, and embrace the solitude without any disturbances. Climbing the staircase was a mammoth effort; it seemed to go on forever. Rosa finally made it to the landing by leaning on Aida's arm.

Rosa was grateful for the housekeeper's presence; she had come to depend on Aida as her confidante, never having the opportunity to make friends outside the convent hospital. Rosa knew she could let down her guard with Aida; there was no need to keep up the pretence that her married life was anything but a disaster.

"Thank you, Aida, for all your kindness. I'm not sure I would have survived the last few years without your loving care. I will join you when I have rested."

"Si Senora. We have all missed you greatly; it is good to have you home." Aida hesitated as she was about to leave, adding with compassion and understanding, "We would not be here only for you, Senora Mendoza."

The words meant to console Rosa instead only added to her sadness. Yes, they had all been victims of Carlos's rage at one time or another. He made sure everyone was in fear of him. He was the master of his house.

166

Rosa sighed with resignation; she knew if things were to change, it must come from her. A short while ago, the idea of standing up to Carlos would have been unthinkable, knowing the repercussions, terrifying to contemplate. When Rosa hovered between life and death, something changed. Rosa experienced an uneasy calm knowing she could not go back to living the life she had before losing the baby; she would rather die. Sighing again, she drifted into a troubled sleep. Her heart was heavy with grief but filled with a new resolve.

The staccato voice of Carlos carried along the corridor, berating Aida for not waking Rosa to greet him properly, irritation in his voice. Rosa shook her head at his arrogance. Carlos strode into the room; he was the Governor and expected to be treated with importance.

"So, Rosa, you are home at last."

The smile was wide, showing perfect teeth. It reminded Rosa of a hungry piranha; the thought caused her to smile. Carlos relaxed at what he took to be a submissive response. Rosa reacted with indifference.

"Yes, it would seem I am home, Carlos."

The silence lengthened. Rosa watched Carlos squirm just a little. He couldn't just ignore the subject of her accident or its consequences, but it was apparent he would rather not deal with it. Carlos's expression became serious.

"I regret our quarrel compelling you to flee from me unnecessarily. But for that, the child you were carrying might have lived. I tried my best to catch you when you lost your footing, but in your agitated state, it wasn't possible."

Rosa was stunned. Carlos effectively transferred the blame squarely onto her shoulders in three short sentences. She opened her mouth to speak, but words failed her. Carlos was satisfied her silence indicated an end to the matter. He didn't directly address the assumption of Rosa's infidelity but was encouraged to add,

"Publicly, it would not do for it to appear all is not well between us, so I am prepared to forgive you for appearance's sake."

167

The words hung in the stillness. Rosa stared at the arrogant, unfeeling creature that he was, standing there puffed up with righteous indignation and self-importance as though he were the one wronged. He had not once enquired about her well-being; his only concern was his political standing in the community. Rosa was beyond disgust, loathing him even more.

Anger gave her a new impetus; slowly getting out of bed, she stood erect to face Carlos. Trying to control her emotions, she took time answering, choosing her words carefully, enunciating every syllable, her voice like ice. "Carlos, I will learn to accept and live with whatever part I had in losing our child, seeking God's forgiveness every day." Rosa took a deep breath steeling herself before continuing, "I want you to listen to me very carefully; I will tend to your home and entertain your guests when you wish. I will go to your political functions and stand at your side while you are campaigning, if necessary, but if you ever so much as touch me again, I will die by my own hand. I swear this by Almighty God, and I will do it publicly so that it leaves no doubt about where the blame lays, do you understand!"

Carlos's face had gone from scarlet to deathly white, a range of emotions distorting his features. He knew she meant every word. Memories of the past came flooding back. Carlos never really came to terms with the shame his mother's suicide caused him. He was always known as the kid whose mother killed herself.

Rosa could see he was trying to restrain the rage; she could also see his fear. No one, especially Rosa, had ever dared challenge Carlos before. Rosa's rejection of him was almost more than he could comprehend. Carlos's face was an ugly mask of fury; he sneered at her,

"That suits me fine; you were never worthy of me anyway, but don't think for one minute you can ever leave me; I will never let you go, not ever. You choose to embarrass me in any way, and your family will pay dearly!"

Carlos turned on his heel, slamming the door as he departed. Rosa could hear him raging as he stormed out of the house. She pitied anyone who crossed his path today. Suddenly weak in the legs, Rosa sat on the side of the bed, not believing she had finally found the courage to do what she had dreamed of doing almost from the day they were married.

For the first time in a very long while, Rosa felt a sense of peace. At first, fearing her courage would fail her, she was determined to hold to her convictions. She would rather die than allow Carlos to abuse her or submit to his cruelty and brutality ever again. Rosa experienced overwhelming relief. In those few minutes, she had taken back her life. Carlos's parting words reminded her it would come at a high price if she failed to uphold her role as the Governor's First Lady.

Carlos stayed away from the house for over a week. Where he went, Rosa didn't know and cared even less. Returning home from a visit to Sister Angelina, she found Carlos's belongings had been moved downstairs into a guest room at the far end of the mansion, alongside his office. They would see each other as little as possible, which suited her perfectly. Rosa also learned through the household grapevine that he intended to make the Governor's Lodge in Buenos Aires his permanent residence. Carlos had a lavish apartment there as well. Rosa was well aware he was never short of female company.

Conversation between them now took place only when necessary. Carlos addressed Rosa affectionately in the company of others as though nothing untoward had passed between them. An uneasy peace settled over the household. Occasionally, Rosa would glance up to see Carlos looking at her; the venom in his stare made the breath catch in her throat. The potential for violence, or worse, lay hidden just below the surface, biding its time.

Less than six weeks later, to her surprise, Carlos informed Rosa they would visit Hierro Castillo just outside Santa Rosa for a few months. She hadn't been south for years. Excited at the prospect of seeing her mother Isabella, sister Maria, and Aunt Luisa and family again, she could also assist Maria with her mother's care and renew her friendship with Fr Peter.

Rosa was careful not to show any signs of pleasure at the news, enough reason for Carlos to leave her behind. As it was, he left before her in the comfort of his *Galeras*; she would have to make do in the much smaller coach with the housekeeper and her husband. Rosa didn't care; it was hard to remember when she had been this happy.

Since Ramon's death, Carlos battled to find decent managers to care for their combined holdings and the *newly acquired* properties. Able to control the gauchos and soldiers doing his bidding in the north, things had gotten out of hand in the southern pampas. His plans were unravelling. The acquisition of land and cattle was less frequent; now, people were being brutalised and murdered for sport. Initially, Carlos gave a free hand to his hired thugs, a position they abused. There was a need to take back control, the reason he was heading south with a contingent of soldiers to address the problem. Carlos decided he would stay just long enough to achieve this. The sooner he could return to the Capital and his northern holdings, the better. Besides, he urgently needed to visit his eldest brother Philippe, the financial manager at Villa Maria south of Cordoba.

What happened to Rosa was of little consequence to Carlos; she could stay there as far as he was concerned. It was common knowledge Rosa had lost a child following a terrible accident. Carlos intimated a breakdown had followed, and she planned to rehabilitate in the care of her family. Carlos always managed to turn any situation to his advantage. The miscarriage was no exception.

Carlos was angry; the further south he went, he saw the destruction of countless properties vandalised and deserted. Livestock and domestic animals roamed unchecked. Reports of rapes, murders and disappearances were frequent.

Carlos lacked any conscience about most of it; his only concern, the trail might lead back to his doorstep and derail any chance of his becoming President of Argentina someday, and of course, the considerable loss of revenue.

Ten years earlier, it was expedient to remove Paulo Caron, who stood in the way of Carlos marrying his daughter Rosa, a mistake he now regretted. Carlos learned the half dozen Gauchos he'd employed back then had taken on more drifters to do their dirty work while they spent most of their time drunk and brawling, living the good life, answering to no one. They failed to discuss any such plans with Carlos.

Arriving at Hierro Castillo, Carlos and his men would rest overnight, hunt them down, and end it permanently!

Return to Santa Rosa
☼

Rosa contacted Fr Peter before her arrival, seeking permission to stay at the Lady of Rosary Church to spend time with her mother. He agreed readily; Rosa was always welcome there. It would be like old times. After dropping Rosa at the church, Aida and Alfredo would join the other household staff attending Carlos and his unruly mob.

When Rosa arrived, Fr Peter was standing near the bell tower discussing some change with the groundsman. Beaming, he helped her down from the carriage, embracing her warmly. Rosa was anxious to see her mother, concerned when Fr Peter cautioned her not to be unduly alarmed when she saw Isabella. He explained that physically she was in reasonably good health. Since the death of her beloved Paulo, her mental state has been a different matter, continuing to deteriorate slowly over time.

When Rosa approached, Isabella was sitting on her favourite garden bench overlooking the lake. She was unprepared to see her mother this way, fifty-one years of age, looking seventy. Her hair was more silver than black, and her eyes sunken and lifeless. Rosa sat beside her mother, enveloping her hands.

"Hello, mama, it's so good to see you; I have missed you so much." Rosa felt the sting of tears. "I've come to spend time with you and Maria."

At the mention of Maria's name, Isabella's face lit up as she smiled. "Maria is such a good girl. Do you know her?"

Rosa's heart was breaking as she replied, "Yes, mama, I know Maria. Together with Maria, you and I put flowers in the church each Sunday for Fr Peter, do you remember? It's Rosa Mama; I married and moved to Santa Fe."

172

Isabella frowned, trying hard to clear the fog getting in the way of her thoughts. She looked at the beautiful face with teary eyes…there was something very familiar; she could see Paulo's eyes, "Rosa, is that you?"

Rosa threw her arms around her mother, sobbing, grateful to have her 'back' even for a little while. They sat there clinging to each other. Fr Peter stood a good way off, saying a silent prayer, tears in his eyes.

It was Saturday just after midday when Maria came charging through the door of Isabella's rooms. Rosa was sitting beside her mother, holding her hand while she slept. Maria was squealing with excitement. Both of them talked at once, mostly about how each had changed. Maria was only eleven when Rosa married Carlos and fourteen when they moved to Santa Fe. They hadn't seen each other since then. Maria was no longer a young girl but a woman of twenty-one. Rosa wanted to know everything that had happened since she'd been gone. They talked non-stop until Isabella awoke. Rosa watched Isabella's face slowly change as recognition dawned. She had her daughters back together again; it was such a joyous reunion.

Maria picked up a large bunch of flowers she had brought for the altar the next day. The three set about preparing and arranging the flowers, reliving the past. It was like old times; the one lingering sadness was Delgado's absence, his whereabouts still unknown.

Once it became common knowledge that Rosa was home in Santa Rosa, the locals were keen to visit. Isabella's sister Luisa, her husband Nicolas, and their children Benito, Helena and Isolde arrived first. With Fr Peter's permission, Maria hurriedly arranged a celebration within the church grounds following Sunday mass.

Rosa was overcome with gratitude, rejoicing to see so many people attend and catch up with old friends, especially their neighbour. Juan Petto was visibly moved when he saw her. Fr Peter remarked he had not seen Isabella so spirited in a long time. It was as if she had a new lease on life.

During the homecoming celebrations, Maria shyly approached Rosa in the company of a tall young man. He shook her hand firmly,

173

politely excusing himself a short while later, unsure how to make small talk with the First Lady. Both Maria and Rosa chuckled to themselves. Rosa could see the love on Maria's face for this young man. How she envied never having had that experience.

Maria confided in Rosa that she and Cesar wished to marry. Initially, they planned to wait another year or so before marrying, but because Rosa was here, they decided to bring the marriage forward.

"Rosa, Delgado is not here, and mama is too unwell. Will you walk down the aisle with me in Papa's place? I would be honoured."

Rosa was thrilled to accept. Their hearts ached. They both knew the occasion would be tinged with sadness, knowing their father and brother would not be there to share the special day. They hugged for a long time, shedding tears of joy and sorrow. When given the news, Fr Peter was almost as excited as Rosa. He would post the Banns at the next mass.

After all the other guests departed, the sisters chatted until very late. It was such a beautiful night sitting out under the stars, reminiscing about what a wonderful childhood they shared growing up on the farm. How simple life was back then. Isabella turned in hours earlier, looking tired. She spent much of the afternoon smiling broadly at everyone. It didn't matter that she didn't recognise most of them, she was happy. The sisters agreed to leave the cleaning until morning, heading off to bed giggling like two naughty schoolgirls. It had been a wonderful day from beginning to end.

Saturday June 11th 1853, promised to be a glorious day. The church cottages were a hive of activity and buzzing with excitement. The church itself was resplendent with flowers. The community ladies excelled, preparing a beautiful wedding breakfast to follow the ceremony. Fr Peter strung dozens of coloured lights across the courtyard, the loaded tables abounded with treats, and the glasses sparkled. The atmosphere was electric with excitement.

Rosa resided in one of the church cottages adjoining Isabella's. She had not received one word from Carlos while she was there. Rumours circulated his men had been searching for a group of outlaws terrorising the countryside for years. Rosa considered sending a telegraphic message to Hierro Castillo about the wedding but chose not to. She knew Carlos would show no interest in her sister's wedding, except possibly to make an appearance and cause trouble. Should anyone ask about his absence, she would say he apologised, saddened at not being able to attend.

The day went perfectly, the ceremony especially touching. Fr Peter's blessing to the young couple was from the heart. Isabella was not always sure about what was happening, but everyone was smiling and happy, which meant something good was happening. The music and dancing took place on a starry night, as the young married couple joined the partygoers until midnight. As a wedding gift, Rosa had purchased a small cottage on the outskirts of Santa Rosa, a mile south, near the little school they both attended as children. Questioning Rosa's generosity, she was reassured it was little enough to repay her for the years she dedicated to caring for their mother.

There had to be some advantage to being married to a man as wealthy as Carlos. It was the only time she discovered anything positive about her marriage.

The cheering revellers farewelled the newly-wed couple as their carriage disappeared down the road towards their new home; Rosa prayed to Almighty God they would have a long and happy life.

Since Rosa's arrival she could see a vast improvement in her mother. By introducing familiar routines, Isabella had begun to do a few small things independently without assistance.

Rosa sat by the lake with her mother, watching heron wade in the shallows. She saw the swirl of dust in the distance long before the riders and coach came into view. It was Carlos, accompanied by a troupe of about ten soldiers. For a heart-stopping moment, Rosa feared he had come for her, overwhelmed with relief when his coach hurtled past on its way to Santa Rosa; later, Rosa learned they continued on their way to Buenos Aires.

After the execution of eight fugitives, word of Carlos's departure met with approval from the locals, relieved to hear the Governor and most of his soldiers had returned to the Capital. They proved to be no better than the ones they had hunted down. The townspeople prayed that when the last of his entourage was finally gone, the evil that plagued this peaceful community over the previous ten years would be at an end.

When Rosa first heard Carlos had left the district, she was overjoyed. Doubting, he would give her a second thought; with luck, she could stay here, take up her old role of helping look after the church and its surrounds, and permanently take care of her mother. She was fortunate, at least, to be financially secure.

Rosa decided to go to Hierro Castillo the next day, ensuring Aida and Alfredo got away safely. She wanted to collect a few personal items, having decided to make Santa Rosa her home. Rosa promised herself the luxury of one last bath before leaving. It would be the one thing she would miss, soaking in the substantial copper tub, hot soapy water up to her neck.

The Road to Recovery
☼

Miguel walked unaided for the first time in weeks, limping badly but upright. The nuns applauded. No one expected him to live. He defied the odds of having significant head trauma, blood loss, a crushed leg, broken ribs and multiple abrasions. He was tough and a fighter. Actively engaged in running the Garcia holdings had undoubtedly aided his fitness and stamina. Still, his will to never give up was the driving force of his survival. Although only twenty-two, his physique was impressive. Miguel had been in the Convent Santo Domingo Hospital for almost eight weeks. He had no recollection of the event leading to his injuries or what preceded them.

Dr Perez spoke to the soldiers sent to question Miguel about his possible involvement in the earlier riot, explaining his skull injury had resulted in Miguel suffering amnesia, which would most likely be permanent. There were no witnesses to Miguel taking an active part in the riot. Added to this was the sworn statement by Alberto Diaz, one of the largest stud breeders in Santa Fe, that Miguel was in the city that day to discuss the possible purchase of a bull he had for sale. Following discussions with Dr Perez, Miguel was no longer considered a suspect.

Miguel was grateful for the care he received in the hospital. He thanked Dr Perez and the Sisters, shaking hands with each of them as he said farewell, studying their faces. Someone was missing, but he didn't know who?

Alberto offered his home to Miguel for the remainder of his rehabilitation. The local officials were already conducting surveillance of his property. A further suspect about to become a house guest would surely lead to more intense scrutiny.

After witnessing Miguel being crushed in the riot, Alberto received a report from a trusted friend outlining his condition as soon as it was known. The trusted friend was Dr Perez, a man with no love for the Mendoza family. He treated victims daily who suffered under Ramon as their leader, and saw those same behaviours repeated in his son Carlos following his rise to power. The decimating impact on his country, the breakdown of law and order, and the continuing collapse of the judiciary and parliament were appalling.

Hidalgo and Elizabeth had been apprehensive, awaiting Miguel to report on the attack at the Silver Stallion Ranch and the condition of Orlando Valez and his family. As time elapsed without any further news, they became increasingly fearful. When contacted by Alberto Diaz detailing the events in Santa Fe, they were frantic. He assured them everything possible to aid Miguels's recovery was being done. He promised to keep them informed of any changes.

He offered them the opportunity to stay at his home but stressed the underlying danger should they decide to come to Santa Fe. While he understood their desire to be at Miguel's bedside, Alberto expressed his opinion that their presence would achieve little. Miguel was heavily sedated because of his injuries and guarded closely. No visitors were permitted. Hidalgo was grateful for everything Senor Diaz was doing, risking his safety by providing a sworn statement supporting Miguel's reason for being in Santa Fe.

Elizabeth and Hildago would have been happy leaving Theresa, their daughter, in charge of Ataliva Roca. She was more than capable of running the property in their absence. They would wait a couple of days and consider the wisdom of Senor Diaz's comments —the decision was taken out of their hands. In light of continuing riots throughout the countryside, Martial Law was declared. After the government instigated a curfew from 9 pm until 6 am, no one was permitted to leave their immediate vicinity. They would have to bide their time. Despite living twenty-eight miles from Santa Rosa, Fr Peter delivered mail and other supplies to surrounding properties on

178

his regular visits to parishioners. They would be fine. The hardest part would be waiting for Miguel to come home.

The sign emblazoned across the top of the timber headboard caused Miguel to smile *Toro Maestro* – bull master! Alberto was not shy about his ability as a cattleman. Over the next few weeks, Miguel came to appreciate and respect the rancher's skill, soon realising there was little about cattle Alberto didn't know. His knowledge was astounding. Miguel took every opportunity during his recovery to learn as much as possible from this man; it would stand him in good stead for the future.

Alberto enjoyed having an eager student like Miguel, who was willing to learn. He was already impressed someone as young as he knew so much about raising cattle. Alberto's expertise was recognising each animal's unique qualities and pairing them to sire the best offspring. Over twenty-five years, the reputation of Toro Maestro reigned supreme. The stud bulls produced were the finest in all of Argentina, arguably the world. One of Alberto's bulls helped Hidalgo achieve his earlier successes, winning the Cattleman's Association award.

Miguel would be forever indebted to the man who saved him from possibly being executed and then generously opened his home to this bent and somewhat broken stranger. Both men had much in common. They loved the land with equal passion, and both were committed to ridding Argentina of the forces leading to its destruction.

The best part of his stay there was the opportunity to send and receive regular telegraphic messages to and from his family. When Hidalgo and Elizabeth received the first message from Miguel confirming his improved condition and sending his love, they hugged each other and cried, thanking Almighty God.

Theresa took great delight in sending telegrams teasing Miguel about finding any excuse to have a holiday, leaving her to do all the dirty work around the ranch while he was away having a *good time*! Miguel missed his big sister more than words could express. He couldn't wait to go home and be present in their lives once more.

When he came so close to death, he realised, above all else, that family was everything.

Return to Ataliva Roca

1853

Miguel was almost fully recovered. He would always have a limp as a legacy of his time in Santa Fe, but he was alive. Besides, the limp was only noticeable when he overworked his body and was tired.

It wasn't a hard decision to abandon the idea of checking out their northern properties before heading back to Ataliva Roca. After witnessing the devastation of Orlando Velez and his family, and the chaos on his way from Villa Maria to Cordoba and then Santa Fe, Miguel was anxious to get home as soon as possible. The trip was close to six hundred and eighty miles. What troubled Miguel more than concern his body might not withstand the rigours of the journey, was the possible danger of encountering thugs doing the dirty work of those governing the country.

As the trip progressed, Miguel's concern grew. At each posada, the stories became increasingly alarming. He was used to hearing about poisoned wells, beatings and intimidation, or the coercion to sell properties cheaply. Initially, only one or two properties within the township boundary would be affected, just enough to unsettle the whole community and create the fear they may be next.

The closer Miguel got to Santa Rosa, the casualty rate grew. Told there was a group of six or eight thugs doing this dirty work; some said as many as *ten or more*. It became impossible to verify the extent of the problem and what was fact or fiction.

Miguel kept pushing himself as hard as he dared. Despite having two spare horses and his mount, the horses were exhausted when he reached the intended posada each night. After eight days of travel, it was only a day's ride from home. South of Catrilo, his final stop found the posada abandoned and the corral empty. He prayed the overnight rest would be enough to sustain the horses. He had to complete the journey.

There was plenty of firewood available, some tea and stale biscuits. It would have to do. Riders always carried salted beef to see them through. While the fire took hold, Miguel fed and watered the horses; they were a priority. After finishing his meagre meal, he pulled his bedroll closer to the fire and settled for the night. The intention was to leave before daylight. It was risky travelling in the dark, but he wanted to be at Ataliva by midday.

Miguel tied his horse to the hitching rail outside the general store in Santa Rosa. It was as though time had stood still since his previous visit. Nothing had changed. The decision to make a brief stop to rest his horses and restock his saddlebags was welcome. The store wasn't due to open for another two hours, but Miguel knocked anyway. After a few minutes, he could hear shuffling as a gruff voice responded.

Senor Torella opened the door, a little grumpy, until he recognised Miguel, greeting him with a firm handshake. It was a very different Miguel Garcia looking back at him, than the one he'd known only a few years earlier.

Senor Torella quickly relayed all the current gossip in the district. It seemed the Governor was in residence. He had arrived some weeks earlier with a small troupe of soldiers. The word was they had come to track down the thugs and drifters terrorising the southern countryside for years and suggested they were responsible for the death of Hidalgo's sharefarmer, Paulo Caron, ten years back. Miguel, very young at the time, only vaguely recalled the trouble. Since then, things had been reasonably quiet around Santa Rosa but escalated in other places. Over the last few years, it had been bad everywhere. Many people disappeared overnight, apparently abandoning their properties out of fear. Senor Torella's conversation confirmed everything Miguel heard elsewhere.

182

"Take care, Senor Garcia; the Governor's men are no better, it seems. A few days ago, they found the bodies of the eight suspected men shot and hanged near a property west of Santa Rosa. When the property owner investigated the sound of gunfire, they shot him, then raped and murdered his wife before leaving!"

Froth sprayed from the animal's mouth, its rib cage heaving as it sucked in great gulps of air. Spurs dug deep into the horse's flanks; Miguel was ashamed at treating such a fine animal this way. He had ridden his horse hard the last ten miles; the closer he came to Ataliva Roca, the more he felt a sense of doom.

Topping the rise above the Hacienda, he was relieved to see the maroon stucco walls intact. Now it seemed all the haste was unnecessary. He felt rather foolish. Catching his breath while resting his mount, Miguel let his eyes scan the property, suddenly aware that this very busy ranch showed no movement. Miguel's brow furrowed, his ears strained to catch any familiar sounds on the breeze, to give some sign, any sign, that all was well. Suddenly he felt chilled to the bone, spurring life back into the stallion; he raced down the hillside.

Despair is a word that needs no explanation. It conjures up visions of anguish associated with pain and loss. When you witness something beyond comprehension, so abhorrent to every part of your being, your mind shuts down, taking refuge in denial. In desperation, you pray what you are experiencing is some terrible nightmare from which you will awaken at any moment. Time stands still, but there is no awakening. With dread, Miguel realised the horror was all too real, the confronting vile images forever imprinted on his brain.

The life he'd known was no more. A day would never pass without the exquisite pain of loss drilling a hole in his heart, remembering the sight before him. Hidalgo, always such an elegant man, lay sprawled across a cane chair. Tall in stature, broad-shouldered, his naturally olive skin burnt caramel from many hours in the sun where he laboured with the vigour of a man half his sixty-four years. The once dark lustrous wavy hair, now silver, framed his kind, gentle face, a face contorted in shock and anger, expressions frozen on his ashen features.

Miguel looked at Hidalgo's lifeless body, imagining his father's final moments facing his attackers. Clearly, he had put up a tremendous fight; carnage lay everywhere. Copious blood on the ground spoke of others carrying significant wounds; Miguel prayed those wounds would be fatal. Despite Hidalgo's efforts to fight off the assailants, the swift action of a knife across his throat ended his courageous battle instantly.

Miguel began to weep silently, gently embracing his father, like a lost little boy suddenly discovering their parent. His grief was profound, but he feared worse was to come. The hope that his mother, Elizabeth and sister, Theresa, might have escaped while Hidalgo defended their household was a silent, desperate plea. Miguel, weakened from shock, his legs barely supporting him, held onto the handrail as he walked unsteadily along the veranda, his boots echoing in the silence. Every breath he took required a monumental effort.

His eyes adjusted slowly to the darkened interior as he entered the hacienda, the scene before him beyond revulsion. His mother and sister lay murdered, strewn on the floor like discarded broken dolls, limbs askew, their clothing ripped from their bodies before suffering the ultimate depravity of how many before their torture finally ended.

Almost in a stupor, Miguel aimlessly picked up the remnants of clothing and, with reverence, covered their nakedness. He could do no more now; he was no longer capable; The line between sanity and insanity was suddenly finite. For the first time in his life, Miguel realised how easy it would be to go insane, withdraw into the dark recesses of his mind and block out the ugliness in the world around him. The barbarians had destroyed his whole world in one tumultuous day. Miguel wondered if life was worth living.

Unsure how much time had elapsed, Miguel found himself back at the entrance to their property; he had no recollection of leaving the house. The numbness and shock cleared briefly. Someone must be accountable for this despicable crime. In that instant, Miguel knew what he must do with absolute clarity, not just to avenge Hidalgo, his mother, Elizabeth and Theresa. Many had suffered a similar fate. Miguel knew there would be more. Carlos Mendoza must be stopped

– permanently! Miguel headed for the Mendoza mansion by the lake, spurring his horse into a gallop.

They Will be Avenged

☼

There wasn't an area of ground in the southern pampas unfamiliar to Miguel. From when Theresa was eleven, and he was eight, they spent hours in the saddle each day weaving their way through stands of Tala wood or rainforests rich with cedar and laurel. They immersed themselves in fertile grasslands, wading through pampas grass, searching for stray cattle, and wandering far and wide on the open range.

Miguel knew every trail between Ataliva Roca and Hierro Castilo like the back of his hand. By the significant amount of blood on the ground, one or more men were severely injured. It was a safe bet the murdering swine would follow the main trail, which wound around several swampy areas leading to the large lake adjacent to the Governor's mansion. There was a much shorter route which cut across two small ridges. It was narrow and difficult to traverse for anyone unfamiliar with the area.

With luck on his side, he might get ahead of them before they reached the sanctuary of the mansion. Miguel intended to confront Carlos Mendoza face to face and stop him once and for all. He accepted killing Carlos would most likely result in his death, which was of little consequence. Everything he'd ever valued and lived for lay destroyed back at Ataliva Roca.

Fate intervened once more. He could hear voices approaching the one location where the two trails intersected in a clearing ahead. The one advantage he had was surprise. He was aware of them, but his presence was as yet unknown. He had the opportunity to get into position before they appeared. The group of men limped into the open, where Miguel lay in wait. He was surprised there were only five men; he expected at least a dozen. They were a rough-looking bunch. Two were slumped forward on their mounts, both disorderly and bloody. Miguel guessed that was Hidalgo's legacy. As the thought crossed his mind, one man slid to the ground, lifeless; the timing was perfect, creating the opportunity for surprise; their attention now focused on the fallen man.

Miguel stepped out into the clearing unnoticed and took aim, shooting one of the mounted riders. His second shot found its mark in the head of the soldier bending over his fallen colleague on the ground. The fourth soldier, already dismounted, was trying desperately to retrieve his rifle from the holster on his saddle. Abandoning the idea, he pulled a knife from his belt and charged Miguel, knocking him off balance, dislodging the gun from his hand as he fell. They exchanged several blows as they wrestled on the ground. Miguel lunged for his pistol, rolling over as his assailant came down on top of him. Miguel fired at point-blank range, killing his opponent instantly, but not before the man managed to plunge the knife into Miguel's abdomen. Miguel was aware he'd been stabbed but was more concerned about the fifth soldier in the group. He needn't have worried; this one was still slumped forward in the saddle, his horse covered in blood.

Miguel took the bandana from around his neck, rolled it into a ball, and forced it into the open wound. It was the only thing available to stem the bleeding. He was less than a mile from the mansion; there was no time to lose; the sound of gunshots would have carried to the estate indicating something was amiss.

Abandoning his horse as the mansion came into sight, he used the shelter of the trees for cover; approaching the side of the building, he gained entry through an open door leading onto the veranda. Miguel observed at least three soldiers standing at the front entrance and one standing on guard in the sentry post at the end of the tree-lined drive. There was a small carriage near the front steps.

Miguel could hear household staff chattering in a distant part of the house. He cautiously began his search of the ground floor rooms with his weapon at the ready, reasoning Carlos would be somewhere nearby in an office. Miguel approached the last room in this wing at the end of a corridor as a commotion erupted outside. Stepping back into the room he'd just exited, he glanced out the window to see the soldiers in an uproar, the horse of one of the men he'd dispatched now cantering towards them down the drive riderless, covered in blood. Miguel was running out of time. He was also beginning to feel the effect of the knife wound. Even though it was packed tight, blood from his wound was seeping slowly down his clothing. Soon he would leave a tell-tale trail.

The voices of the soldiers rang out as they began to search the house. Miguel bolted to the end room, throwing the door wide, his gun at the ready. He found himself standing in a bathhouse; the door slammed shut behind him. A large copper tub stood on a small platform near the far side of the room; a narrow wooden ledge ran parallel to the wall, intended to hold towels, robes and toiletries. A curtain designed to provide privacy hung wide open, each side restrained by a silken cord.

The shock for Miguel was seeing a young woman, naked, staring back at him from the tub. He could hear the soldiers running from room to room. Thinking quickly, he jumped onto the ledge behind the tub, freeing the sash on the curtain. In a menacing voice, he warned the woman,

"If you value your life, Senora, do not speak out, I warn you!"."

Rosa, her mouth agape, sat wide-eyed, not daring to move. Suddenly the door was flung open, and one of the soldiers stood there, about to enter.

Rosa found her voice, "How dare you invade my privacy; if the Governor were here, he would have your head."

Quickly turning around, the soldier apologised over his shoulder,

"I am sorry, Senora Mendoza, we are looking for a possible killer. There was gunfire a short while ago, and now one of the soldier's horses, covered in blood, has returned without a rider. We feared whoever disposed of the rider might have come here."

Rosa watched in fascination as blood began to drip off the tip of the boot protruding over the edge of the tub, creating tiny circles in the water as it dispersed. Terrified, she looked up into the face of the man flattened against the wall, shielded from view by the curtain, a pistol in his left hand, and his right hand clutching the left side of his abdomen. The man was the same one who once thought she was a nursing nun.

Rosa tried to keep the tremble out of her voice as she spoke. "How ridiculous; it's no secret the Governor left for Buenos Aires two days ago; why would someone come here? Close the door behind you and leave the house immediately!"

"Si Senora, I am most sorry to have disturbed you."

Miguel could hear the soldiers retreating; he needed to get out of there while they organised a search party to look for their missing men. He slid down the wall, resting on the narrow ledge. Rosa didn't dare move, still uncertain if he intended to harm her.

Carlos was no longer there; Miguel's plan to kill him was in vain. Ignoring Rosa, he searched nearby, finding a thick towelling robe on the bench. Rosa watched as he placed a wad of towelling over the weeping wound, tightly winding the robe's sash around his body and securing it.

Miguel hesitated, struck by a familiar scent – liquorice. A vase of salvia perched on a bench alongside a hand basin. He glanced in the direction of the terrified woman in the tub, was there something familiar about her?

Then Miguel saw the half door where the used bathwater was dispersed. Barely big enough for a man to squeeze through. He was gone as swiftly as he'd arrived.

The Turning Point
☼

Miguel knew when Carlos learned of the attack on his household, he would realise he was the intended target. There would be a sizable price on his head. Once, it was also common knowledge that Miguel had been in Santa Rosa on the way to his family and their subsequent deaths, so he would be implicated in killing the soldiers. If Miguel was to survive as a wanted man, he must flee the country.

Chile was the logical choice for escape, the closest border crossing, a long way to the northwest of Argentina. Travelling over the mountains presented challenges. It would be difficult, but not impossible. Puelche and Mapuche natives had crossed the Andes many times, forging trails across the Uspallata Pass to the Aconcagua Valley.

Usually, the local indigenous population remained close to their home territory, cultivating maize, potatoes, beans and squash, supplementing their diet further by fishing and hunting. Only when food became scarce during prolonged drought did they send hunting parties across the mountains to capture free-range cattle from the plains, driving them back to villages near the new city of Santiago. There was always the risk Miguel might encounter a hunting party. It was a risk he would have to take.

Miguel headed northwest towards Mendoza, almost 700 miles away, the closest town to the border crossing, and an estimated two-weeks journey. Wounded and weak from blood loss, the first consideration was to find a safe place to shelter until he regained some strength. It was a minor miracle the knife entering his left lower abdomen had not pierced a vital organ or major blood vessel.

After about an hour, Miguel came upon a small farmhouse. Staying hidden from view under cover of thick scrub, he remained out of sight, studying the surroundings. There were no apparent signs of life. He noted the property's unkempt appearance and the absence of animals in the holding pens, a further indication it was deserted. Waiting until it was almost dark, Miguel cautiously made his way around the building's perimeter to the rear, out of sight of the road. The house remained in darkness, confirming no one was in residence. He broke a window and entered one of two buildings joined by a sagging walkway.

The room Miguel entered appeared to be the dining room. The first thing that struck him was the smell. The musty odour of mould mixed with a sour stench. In the fading light, Miguel was shocked at the scene before him. Plates with the remnants of an unfinished meal in the final stages of decomposition littered the table. A half-filled jug of congealed milk accounted for the rancid smell. He tried to imagine what might prompt a family to leave in such haste. What emergency would force them to flee immediately?

Too tired to pursue the thought, Miguel desperately needed to rest but knew he must deal with his wound first. He urgently needed to remove the makeshift packing and clean and redress the injury; doing so would cause it to bleed again, but that was unavoidable. Searching the dwelling for dressing materials, it was disconcerting seeing the other rooms untouched, nothing out of place. When the people left, it was safe to say they fled in whatever clothes they were wearing, taking nothing else, well, almost nothing. A shrine on a side table, now empty, leaving only the faded shape of the cross once hanging there. Miguel prayed God guided those fleeing to safety.

After gathering some unidentifiable liquid from a cabinet containing herbal mixtures, Miguel cleaned the wound. Not daring to risk lighting a fire to heat some water, he rinsed the area well instead. As suspected, blood oozed from the newly exposed wound. Probably not a bad thing to flush out any foreign matter remaining. Applying the herbal concoction, Miguel thought he would pass out. The pain was severe, more than when first stabbed. The area was inflamed and

191

tender, with a swollen red perimeter around the injury. He was concerned.

Miguel recognised the scent of myrtle, known for its healing properties and analgesia. He took deep breaths, trying not to pass out; he completed the dressing, repacking the wound with small strips of material torn from a clean bed sheet. A compression bandage wrapped around his body held the dressing in place. Overcome with exhaustion, Miguel collapsed onto the nearest bed, drifting into deep slumber almost immediately.

Waking at daylight, he sat bolt upright, not sure for a second where he was, the wound in his left side a sudden, sharp reminder. He winced in pain. Rising quickly, he surveyed his surroundings, peering carefully through the windows, assuring himself he was in no immediate danger, a situation that could change at any time.

The silence was eerie. On any day, a farmyard was a symphony of sounds. Donkeys braying, dogs barking, the groan of farm machinery and constant chatter of farmhands in the fields. There were not even any birds singing. It was as if Mother Nature was holding her breath, waiting to see what would happen next.

Ravenous, Miguel tried to recall how long since he'd eaten solid food. Rummaging in the stores, he found a moderate supply of dried goods. Most farmers ate what they produced, pork, beef, poultry, fruit and vegetables, supplemented by grains such as barley, corn, lentils and maize. Grinding grain, they made flour for baking bread, tortillas and the like. It was a healthy lifestyle. Most households kept a milking cow. The womenfolk were skilled at churning butter, producing soft cheeses, and cooking the most delicious dessert, *dulce de leche*.

Miguel closed his eyes, recalling his mother making it, the sweet butterscotch smell filling the kitchen. A wave of nostalgia and sadness swept over him, remembering the loved ones he would never see again. Holding back the grief was almost impossible, but this was a time for survival. When he was safe, there would be time to grieve.

Miguel sighed; he would have to make do with whatever supplies were at hand. At least there was sufficient to keep him going

192

for a while. Fortunately, there was plenty of dry feed for his horse and fresh water; he was lucky; many farmers found their wells poisoned.

Miguel slept fitfully on and off over the next two days, gradually growing stronger. Finally driven by hunger, when almost dark, he risked lighting a small fire in a pit he dug in the soft earth inside the barn. The open thatched roof dispersed the smoke unevenly rather than creating a tell-tale plume. Making some dough with cornmeal and water, Miguel rolled small balls, flattening them to form tortillas. Cooked on a cleaned shovel blade, he devoured several of the flatbread, first bathing them in some honey found in a cupboard; it was like finding a treasure trove. Foraging in the abandoned vegetable garden, he'd also found several root vegetables and some squash. Miguel quickly cooked up a half-decent meal. Before extinguishing the fire, he made a brew of matte`. No home in Argentina was ever without a supply.

This small respite had done Miguel a world of good. For the first time, he dared to hope he might not only survive but live to fight another day.

Carefully, he ventured outside as the sun slowly disappeared over the horizon. Grey clouds shrouded the half-moon; a gentle breeze carried the sweet scent of jasmine. He could see the distant sparkle of the lights at Winifrena. Such a peaceful scene. The sense of serenity couldn't be more deceptive. Miguel had been here four days; leaving now felt right. It was an excellent time to go, travel throughout the night, avoid large townships, and hope to take advantage of more abandoned farms should the opportunity arise.

Over the next week, Miguel avoided confrontation, encountering only an occasional farmer. Most paid him little attention or ignored him completely. It wasn't a time to be too curious about anyone or anything. Many animals roamed free, clear evidence they were no longer attended to—a sad state but helpful for indicating where there might be a possible refuge.

As the journey progressed, Miguel experienced a change of mood. Out of immediate danger, he had time to reflect on the evil overtaking Argentina, seriously considering what he could do to help change that situation.

Taking shelter in a deserted farmhouse halfway to Mendoza, he led his horse to the barn, startled suddenly to realise he was not alone. Not expecting company either, an older man cowered in the corner, terror etched on his face. He raised his hands above his head as if to ward off blows.

Miguel reassured the man he was in no danger, "Do not fear; I mean you no harm, Senor." There were visible signs he'd received a severe beating. Slowly lowering his bruised arms, the man, overcome with relief, wept unashamedly. Miguel quickly provided some food and water. The man gulped down the water but surprisingly declined food. Meekly, he apologised,

"I am sorry for the odour, Senor; I have been unable to walk and attend to toileting."

Miguel could see his fouled clothing, noting his feet were swollen to twice their normal size, the bottoms blackened and covered in dried blood. The assailants had tortured him, leaving him for dead.

Miguel's revulsion was only slightly less intense than the fury inside him. He made the man as comfortable as possible and then tried to settle down for the night. Miguel was distressed, wondering what to do with this man. He didn't want to abandon him but knew he couldn't tag along. It was imperative to keep moving.

In the morning, Miguel was shocked to find the older man slumped forward, lifeless. He had passed silently sometime during the night. Tears stung Miguel's eyes, ashamed to realise he hadn't even inquired about the man's name. How quickly it was to become dehumanised. Sheltered from the road, he dug a hasty grave; it was the least he could do. He lowered his head and prayed for both of their souls.

Fleeing across the border to Chile was no longer an option. Suddenly the decision was easy; Miguel didn't have to think twice. Rumours persisted about a rebel force fighting for justice somewhere in the mountain region near Cordoba; mounting his horse, the animal turned and headed north as if by instinct.

Seeking Revenge

☼

Late afternoon, Miguel steered his horse along the main street of La Cumbrecita. The horse's hooves stirred up small puffs of dust, the usual summer rain long overdue. La Cumbrecita was only nineteen miles southwest of Cordoba. He knew he was exposed and the risk of entering town this way. Miguel decided it was way past time for caution. He needed to make contact with the rebels quickly.

The air was still, except for the dragonflies buzzing around his head. Hitching his horse to the rail outside the Cantina, Miguel pushed open the rickety swing doors. The rusty hinges groaned loudly as he stepped gingerly into the bar, every head turning in his direction, a dozen patrons eyeing him suspiciously.

The barman stood polishing glasses with a tattered cloth, his head inclined, studying Miguel as he entered. There was something commanding about this tall stranger with a fair complexion and sky-blue eyes. Maybe he was a government spy? The barman glanced at the rifle resting under the bar at the ready. This man walked with a certain dignity and pride, holding himself erect. It was easy to see he was a man of some position, despite his obvious youth. Miguel stepped up to the bar,

"Tequila, please?" The voice was firm, steady, unafraid – the request delivered with authority.

Unshaven and scruffy, the bartender filled a glass without a word, placing it on the bar. His eyes narrowed. Never losing eye contact with Miguel, he measured himself against this much younger man, then addressing the stranger with a mocking tone, he voiced the question on everyone's lips,

"And what brings you to these parts, Senor?"

Miguel hesitated before answering. He knew he had to choose his words carefully. One wrong word could put his life in great jeopardy. Miguel responded casually, as he studied his drink, "I am looking for a job. I believe there is work in the mountains for those willing. The sound of shuffling feet told Miguel his words hit a nerve.

The bartender, now with fire in his eyes, his surly expression gone, asked pointedly, "To what sort of work do you refer, senor?" He let his right-hand rest on the butt of the rifle.

"I will do anything asked of me," Miguel answered smoothly, staring straight into the eyes of the bartender.

"Who was it said work was available? You are not from around here. Perhaps you are not aware working in the mountains can be dangerous."

Miguel hesitated before answering, "No, I'm from well south of here. Our family property experienced some trouble – my father died as a result. I am looking for a fresh start."

The silence was profound; Miguel's words hung in the air. You could have heard a pin drop. The words were simple enough; the problem hinted at but not voiced, resonating with each man present. For the first time, the bartender noticed the bloodstains on Miguel's shirt.

"You seem to be wounded, Senor? Would this have anything to do with the trouble on your property?" It was a bold question.

"It has everything to do with the trouble and my father's death; I have a special debt to repay."

The bartender looked at Miguel, studied the set of his shoulders, and heard the determination in his voice. This one had suffered much. There was steel behind those blue eyes; his voice was cold as ice. Yes, someone was owed an outstanding *debt*, and the bartender would not have traded places with whomever it was for all the riches in the world.

"I will ask around Senor to see what is available. Are you staying in town?"

"Yes, until I get the work I seek," Miguel responded, leaving no doubt about his intentions. "Do you have rooms available?"

"There is accommodation upstairs," the bartender indicated, flicking his head to the side. He passed a key to Miguel, "At the top of the stairs, take the first door on your right; you can rest there until supper, Senor."

The journey had been long; Miguel was tired and dusty. After a quick wash, he lowered his weary body onto the bed, allowing the softness to envelop him, a welcome change from the usual stiff bedroll on hard ground. The room was sparsely furnished with a single bed, one dilapidated raffia chair, and a small circular table in the corner; the veneer surface was covered in scratches and burn marks from careless smokers. A faded lace curtain fluttered at the open window, flowing in and out as if the room were breathing.

In the stillness, a shot rang out. Miguel sat bolt upright; he had unwittingly drifted off to sleep; he reached out instinctively for the pistol he carried everywhere with him now, usually hidden in his pack. Raucous laughter drifted to him from the saloon below; he relaxed, realising it was only some drunk celebrating a little too enthusiastically. He lay back down on the pillow, his heart pounding – it took a long time to return to a normal rhythm.

Laying there watching the evening sky streaked with crimson, Miguel wondered if he should risk sharing more details with the bartender and compromise his safety further.

The shutters on the window rattled and clanged, heralding the arrival of the Pampero wind as it whistled through the almost deserted streets of La Cumbrecita. Miguel hoped it would not trigger a violent storm with dry lightning, frequently the cause of flash firestorms. Miguel pulled the covers around him, listening to the mournful howl of the wind, feeling unsettled.

Suddenly the door to his room was thrust open, and Miguel found himself looking down the barrel of a rifle held close to his face. Four men stood glaring at him, bandanas hiding their features. The bartender hovered close behind.

"Who are you, Senor? And what are you doing here in La Cumbrecita?" the deep voice spat the words menacingly.

It was now or never; Miguel had no choice but to be honest. They might be working for the government, which would spell certain death, or he could deny the reasons for his presence to these men and risk death regardless.

"My name is Miguel Garcia. I am from Ataliva Roca in the far south of Argentina. Criminals working for the government stole my family property, slaughtered my father, and defiled my mother and sister before murdering them. With my last breath, I have sworn to avenge their deaths. I wish to join the rebels in the mountains; if they reject me, I will fight alone. I am strong and not afraid to die. Everyone I cared for and worked for is gone, so I have nothing left to lose, but I have much to contribute."

The silence lengthened. You could feel the air, charged with electricity, like the raging storm outside.

The leader slowly lowered the rifle to the floor and stepped forward. "You are not much more than a boy, but I can see tragedy has turned you into a man. I understand your need to honour your family and seek revenge. We have a common goal, Senor; like you, we have all suffered at the hands of these government scum. Our mission is to rid ourselves of the evil that has infiltrated our government. I believe we can help each other."

The leader removed his bandana and leaned closer, staring into Miguel's face. "I warn you, be very sure of your commitment here, Senor, because there is no turning back. Make no mistake, anyone standing in our way will be considered a traitor and suffer the same fate as our enemies. Do you understand?"

"Yes, I understand and accept any terms you might set," Miguel said with feeling.

Smiling, the leader extended his right hand to the shaken Miguel. "Welcome, my name is Vincente; this is Emilio, Victor and Juan," he pointed to his companions. "We have no last names; they are not necessary. It is wise not to know too much about each other. If captured and tortured, there is less chance we might put our comrades or their families at risk. From now on, you will be just Miguel. There will be two others joining you on the journey to our camp. Like yourself, they came to us under similar circumstances.

Emilio will accompany you, Jamie and Mateo, back to camp. You will not be informed where it is until you arrive there. If there is an attack, Emilio will leave you. If he believes his capture is likely, he will take his own life; do you understand, Senor? Nothing must get in the way of our fight for the freedom of our people."

Miguel understood with absolute clarity; he wouldn't have it any other way. At last, his heart might have a chance to heal. If successful, he would have the opportunity to avenge his family and reclaim what was rightfully his.

Vincente indicated he must go, "Others are waiting for us to join them. We have some business to attend, but we sometimes call on old friends that support us." Vincente smiled at the bartender, who returned his broad grin like old friends sharing a joke. "Come, we must be gone from the area before the moon is up. Soldiers conduct regular patrols. There is no way of knowing where they might be next. They will shoot first and ask questions later."

Departing along the top floor veranda, the group descended quietly down the external staircase at the rear of the building, exiting into a narrow laneway. Miguel's horse was there, already saddled. The bartender handed him a pouch of food and water. With a bland expression and a voice lacking any emotion, he said,

"Your supper Senor, good luck," silently, he headed swiftly back up the staircase, soon swallowed by the shadows.

Miguel mounted his horse, and the group split in two, each heading in their designated directions. He was part of four riders heading north out of town, keeping to the perimeter of the tree line. Miguel glanced over his shoulder; Vincente and the dozen others accompanying him had already disappeared.

A Stroke of Genius

☼

Making Buenos Aires his headquarters was a stroke of genius. Preferable to his hacienda in Santa Fe, a city too far from the heart of the country, Buenos Aires.

Carlos had *friends* in high places, although friendship with Carlos was born of mutual need. No one did anything without some payoff. He was a master at knowing who could be manipulated or intimidated or whom he should pander to for information he required.

Tonight, Carlos was hosting a formal party for members of the Board of Representatives and local city councils. Women were excluded. A black-tie event, it was by invitation only. Carlos planned the evening carefully, down to the last detail. The most exclusive food and wine, accompanied by parlour music during the meal. It was touted as a thank-you for the support received during his first year in office. Afterwards, a select few would join Carlos to enjoy the company of several ladies, high-class call girls who had mingled with European Royalty and bedded quite a few.

When he became Governor, Carlos refurbished a whole floor of the multi-storey Governor's mansion, setting aside several rooms to accommodate *company*. Rooms with a well-stocked bar, comfortable bed and lavish furnishings, gilded mirrors and Venetian chandeliers.

The evening delivered everything promised; many happy colleagues headed home, while a group of ten men now indulged in every sexual fantasy they had ever imagined. Four remained in the private apartments. Carlos had the waiter serve brandy and cigars to the six men relaxing in the lounge after their pleasure; excusing himself, he headed down the corridor and entered the last room, locking the door behind him. He walked to a desk on the far side of the room, making himself comfortable in the easy chair, and poured himself a generous brandy. Turning off the light, he carefully positioned the small square box on the table in front of him, ensuring it was stable before pulling the sash on the curtain covering the glass.

A wide grin spread across Carlo's face as he watched Enrique Rubio, the Commissioner for Environment and Planning on the Buenos Aires Council, enjoying oral sex enthusiastically. With precision, he managed to take several photos of the whole event. This new medium was a blessing; it did away with having to engage witnesses, always a risk they might talk later and implicate him.

Enrique was a *happily married man,* but the way he was pounding the blonde with the ample breasts, Carlos wagered he never had someone like her at home. Each apartment had a similar viewing window behind one of the ornate mirrors, but only Enrique's captured Carlos's interest that night.

Noone turned up unannounced at the planning commissioner's office. Any visitor had to make an appointment to see the Commissioner, but who would refuse the Governor's *spontaneous* visit? Enrique greeted Carlos at the office door, more than a little surprised at this unexpected pleasure. They weren't close acquaintances. He was flattered being invited to the recent soiree hosted by the Governor, somewhat embarrassed at having drunk more than usual and finding himself joining a select few in somewhat of an orgy. He blushed at the memory; things such as this were totally out of character for him.

Carlos's smile was broad, like greeting a dear friend, his hand grasping Enriques firmly.

"I'm sure you are extremely busy, Enrique; I won't detain you too long." Carlos made himself comfortable in one of the oversized leather chairs.

Enrique was beginning to feel uncomfortable; something didn't feel right. Usually, one would address the governor as Your Excellency, unless part of his inner circle, then Governor was acceptable.

"How may I help you, Governor?"

Carlos hesitated before answering, choosing his words carefully. "There has been much discussion of late concerning the joint venture between the British and Argentina, introducing a rail network, am I correct?"

Enrique, unsettled, quickly put up his hand to halt the conversation. "I am sorry, Governor, you must understand that in my position, I am not at liberty to discuss such highly confidential matters, not even with you, Senor."

Carlos replied, his voice smooth, reassuring. "Of course, Enrique, I understand your situation. I simply want to know where the proposed rail link will be built?"

Enrique's mouth dropped open; he began to sweat. Speculation about the rail link was common gossip. Although it wasn't confirmed yet, no one knew where the first railway line would go; except him. Enrique was still formulating a response in his head when Carlos casually made a suggestion.

"Let me make it easy for you; I don't want you to tell me anything. I will give you a *present* and then I want you to write one word on a piece of paper. We need never speak of this meeting again. It will be for only you and me to know."

Enrique thought the governor had lost his mind. He watched as he pushed a brown envelope across the desk, sure it contained a bribe, Enrique, at first offended, decided to refuse, but curiosity got the better of him. How much did Carlos think his honour was worth? Indignantly, he lifted the envelope flap and emptied what he thought was money onto the desk in front of Carlos.

Neither man said a word. Carlos looked amused as the colour drained from Enrique's face. Instead of money, three black and white photos spilt across the table, any one of the graphic photos capable of ending his hard-fought career, his marriage, his whole way of life. The silence was deafening. Enrique could feel his heart racing. His hand shook as he picked up a pen, looking at the slip of paper Carlos slid in front of him like a venomous snake about to strike. Trembling, he scribbled a name, dropping the pen as he put his head in his hands.

Enrique didn't look up as Carlos arose; he only heard the governor's chair push back and saw his hand retrieve the slip of paper before heading to the door.

"Oh, by the way," Carlos's voice once more, silky smooth, "You may keep the photos; I have plenty of copies." The door closed without a sound.

From that day forward, life would never be the same for Enrique. The devil knew exactly how much his soul cost.

Carlos studied the piece of paper in his hand, 'Ramos Meja', six miles northwest of Buenos Aires. This sleepy little village was about to become the new focus of Carlos's attention. A rapid transport system would produce a bankroll for the asking. It wouldn't take a genius to work out the likely route exiting from Ramos Meja. It was time to visit Philippe and direct the transfer of substantial funds to where they would reap the most benefit.

A putrid smell filled Miguel's nostrils
    "What the hell is that?" Jamie's screwed-up features said it all

FINDING THE MASS GRAVE – Late Summer 1854

Rebel Camp – Arrival
☼

The conversation was sparse before finding the grave. Afterwards, it was non-existent. Each man struggled to process the horror of the discovery.

Miguel's head was spinning. He desperately tried to recall the last time he encountered individual friends, now wondering if their absence was self-imposed or whether they, too, were laying in the shallow grave back there or somewhere similar. The smell of the grave permeated his brain; it would stay with him forever.

The sun's heat was overpowering when the riders took shelter under the shadow of a rock ledge. The going was much slower in the lower reaches of the mountain range. The animals moved carefully over the loose, uneven surface. "We should be there soon." It was more of a statement than any attempt at conversation. Emilio had maintained his sullen silence throughout the whole trip. "You go on ahead, and I will join you soon. I will ensure we leave no signs of our presence behind." With that, he turned his horse around and was gone.

Under other circumstances, Miguel would have enjoyed spending time in this valley. The colours were spectacular, from every shade of burnt sienna to flashes of gold. Tiny flecks of iron pyrite, fools-gold, glistened everywhere. Looking along the jagged wall of the rock face, a person could trace the earth's history through the many layers laid down over aeons.

As they climbed the final ridge two hours later, the men realised Emilios' 'soon' had been a somewhat hasty assumption. There was no sign of him returning as yet. Miguel looked out over the countryside in every direction; the scenery was almost identical. It would be nearly impossible to find a specific location if unfamiliar with the area, and easy to get lost. Somehow, Miguel found that comforting, confident their whereabouts would be hard to track. The tension slowly eased from his body for the first time in weeks.

Miguel was light-headed; he desperately needed to rest; he hoped it wouldn't be much further. Several men appeared as if from nowhere, pointing their rifles menacingly at the three riders. Miguel and his companions raised their arms in surrender. Speaking for the trio, he recounted their acquaintance with Vincente and the others in La Cumbrecita and why they were there. Emilio's voice broke the silence,

"This gringo and the other two dogs are with me." There was some delight in his words. The shouting and laughter amongst the riders was bawdy. They lowered their rifles, warmly greeting Emilio. It was apparent he was held in high esteem. The rebel group indicated Miguel and his companions should ride in front of the group.

Beyond the ridge, another world existed. A plateau lush with grass stretched before Miguel's disbelieving eyes. Toward the far perimeter, a large encampment nestled along the tree line. They would learn later of the permanent water supply nearby, fed by a mountain spring, a handy quirk of nature.

What surprised Miguel was the number of men he could see, perhaps as many as fifty or sixty. Unexpectedly there were also women. The horsemen slowly trotted to the centre of the camp, attracting everyone's attention. The rebels came together in small groups, eyeing the strangers suspiciously, full of curiosity. Miguel heard someone say 'gringo'. The derogatory name always made him cringe. He never thought of himself as anything other than a native of Argentina. He understood his fair hair bleached further by the sun, and his blue eyes set him apart. He would have to prove himself. Now was not the time to take offence.

As they approached the far side of the large encampment, a middle-aged man with white hair raised himself from where he was sitting, standing erect as they dismounted from their horses. At the front of the trio, Emilio introduced Miguel, Jamie and Mateo, recounting how Vincente believed they could assist the rebels in their cause, sending him to guide them to the camp. Emilio then introduced

Pedro, the apparent leader of the base; only he had the authority to approve their joining the rebel group.

Miguel studied the man before him, surprised to see he could be no more than forty-five. His lean brown body spoke of many things. Lithe and fit, his eyes flicked over Miguel, summing him up instantly. Extending his hand, Miguel felt strong fingers clasp his. When he spoke, his voice was firm; those around stood to attention as Pedro welcomed Miguel and the others.

"I am sorry your entry here was under difficult circumstances, Senor, but we do not have a choice; the camp's security is paramount. I hope you understand. We welcome anyone sympathetic to our cause."

Carmelita

☼

Carmelita was only one of several single women in the camp; most were mature, either with partners or widowed. Just walking into the compound when she first arrived attracted the attention of every unattached male. A single woman with her looks and body always spelt trouble, even when it was not her intention.

Born and raised in a bordello, the relationship with her mother was tenuous at best. She never knew her father. Carmelita found herself mistress to a wealthy grazier, using her feminine wiles, the only skill acquired growing up. Following the grazier's assassination and those of his close associates, she fled, fearing she might be next. She joined a small group escaping the growing conflict, eventually ending up in the rebel camp, and once more found herself at the mercy of others.

Deep in thought, her mood sombre, Carmelita watched the breeze send showers of sparks into the darkening sky. She sat mesmerized by the pulsating coals, reflecting on her life, controlled by others or circumstances beyond her ability to predict.

Carmelita had to agree life in the rebel camp wasn't bad, apart from the fact she didn't like living so far away from the city or dealing with the cold. Still, those inconveniences were a small price to pay for her safety. Carmelita shuddered, thinking of what happened to her lover; she was lucky enough to keep her head on her shoulders. The one indisputable truth Carmelita knew with certainty, she was a survivor.

A good judge of men, Carmelita quickly decided which candidate to target as her protector. She knew all too well nothing was for free. In exchange for her physical favours, she would be safe.

To some, the idea might be shocking, but that was of little consequence, having used her body to get her way with men most of her adult life.

Ernesto was a brawny hunk, not the best-looking of the bunch or the smartest, but his size alone demanded respect. He was one of the team leaders sent out on regular forays to gather supplies or attack government raiding parties. His absences suited Carmelita perfectly; they gave her a break from his somewhat dull personality. He always celebrated with the others when they returned from a successful raid. Following a massive Asado feast, there would be drinking and dancing late into the night. Ernesto was often too drunk to bed her until the morning after, when he'd sobered up. Carmelita didn't share Ernesto's shelter permanently, only when it suited him. While sharing Ernesto's bed was a casual arrangement, everyone knew she was his woman. The other men left her alone.

Weeks rolled into months. It would be winter soon. They would have to relocate the camp. Even this low down on the mountain, snowdrifts made entry and exit to their valley impassable at times. Carmelita shivered, reminded again of how much she hated the cold. Pedro, the camp leader, sat down beside her making small talk. He missed a woman's company following the murder of his wife and the destruction of his farm several years earlier. He admired Carmelita, nothing more.

Pedro was the first to formulate the idea of a rebel gang to fight the thugs working for the government. For many years, he hunted foxes and wolves in this area. He knew where there was abundant food, shelter from the elements, and a permanent water supply. Carmelita enjoyed talking with Pedro. He was an intelligent man and funny. She was well aware his interest in her was purely social, which also put her at ease. Mostly she avoided male company, fearing they were likely to misinterpret her interest. Others came to join them around the fire and share Pedro's tales of adventures.

There were two groups absent from the camp at present. One group seeking supplies, the other sent to engage with Mendoza's men, based on information fed back to the centre. Camp supporters were brave locals who risked instant execution if caught helping the rebels or associating with them.

Carmelita awoke with a start; she had a bad dream. She was being pursued. It always seemed like she was running away from something or someone. She could hear the camp stirring around her. Stella's bed was already empty; no doubt she was busy building up the fire to cook breakfast. Arising, she set about helping the other women.

The smell of oatmeal cooking drifted over to where Carmelita was preparing thick slabs of bread for toasting; she was already thinking about the day's chores or what the ladies might cook for dinner. Carmelita sighed; another day like any other, her mood from the previous night descending once more.

It was mid-afternoon when the four horsemen appeared on the far side of the camp in the company of those standing guard, their entry adjacent to the cooking compound. Carmelita was chatting to one of the wives in the central area. Everyone stopped what they were doing instantly; the menfolk scattered throughout the encampment, gathering as the newcomers crossed open ground to where the leader was seated on a stump.

Carmelita recognised Emilio. He had flirted with her when she first arrived. Surly and arrogant, he conversed only with the menfolk. Emilio didn't take kindly to her dismissal of his advances, ignoring her ever since.

Carmelita's eyes flicked over the two Emilio introduced as Jamie and Mateo. An insignificant-looking pair with shifty eyes. She didn't trust either of them. They had every appearance of petty thieves. She had known plenty in her time and had been one herself when necessary. The last one…Miguel was something else. He sat tall in the saddle, broad shoulders straining against the leather of his jacket. His fine features accentuated his good looks.

Pedro extended his hand to greet the men, inviting them to join him for refreshments. Most of the conversation was lost on Carmelita as she studied the young man. Watching Miguel dismount, he grimaced, clutching his side. It was then she noticed the extensive bloodstain on his shirt. Miguel removed his hat, wiping his forearm across his brow. Carmelita's indrawn breath was not the only one. Dark brown curls spilt onto the collar of his vest, his hair bleached golden on the ends.

Some of the men murmured amongst themselves. To them, he was a foreigner. Carmelita entertained only one thought. It was a long time since she'd set eyes on anyone that attractive. As if Miguel had read her mind, he glanced in her direction, smiled briefly, nodded his head, and turned his attention back to Pedro. Carmelita was captivated by Miguel's piercing blue eyes.

Life and Death

☼

He could hear the screams; when he came upon them, people ran, frantic to escape, but there was nowhere to go. Everything was happening as if in slow motion. He put his hand out, trying to reach a small boy standing in front of him, silent, terror on his face, hands pressed firmly over his ears, his eyes shut tight. If Miguel could reach him, maybe he could save him...

Miguel sat bolt upright, drenched with sweat and his head throbbing. His body was on fire, none of it due to the nightmare. A jagged pain tore through his side. The memories attached to finding the mass grave were now part of him; he doubted he could ever erase them; this was something different; he was ill.

Miguel and the others had been in the camp for two days. He'd tried to ignore the increasing tenderness in his side and the constant throbbing.

Managing to stand on shaky legs struggling to carry his weight, he stepped outside his tent. The freezing night air failed to register in his brain. A group of eight remained huddled close to the roaring fire, well rugged up against the chill, chatting to Pedro quietly, trying not to disturb the others. They looked up as Miguel staggered forward, dropping slowly to his knees.

Carmelita dipped the cloth into fresh warm water and sponged Miguel once more, as she had done for the last twenty-four hours. He was delirious. Pedro stood quietly, discussing Miguel's condition with Arturo. He had been a blacksmith in San Luis and knew a great deal about animals. He reasoned attending to humans wasn't that much different. If sickly, a person purged the gut; open wounds were stitched; anything bleeding cauterised; and if something was infected, you drained or amputated it if need be.

Arturo didn't hold out much hope when he saw the wound on Miguel's side. He didn't doubt the source of a raging infection; the wound was severely swollen, red, and sealed over. Arturo knew the poison had already spread through the body, and death was the likely outcome. After a discussion with Pedro, they decided on a course of action. Taking a long narrow knife, Pedro cleaned it and then heated it in the fire. Arturo gathered a pitcher of raw alcohol brewed in the camp and powdered sulphur he kept handy for preventing spiny grass cuts on the horse's flanks from becoming infected. Pedro rounded up four of his strongest men to pin Miguel down while Arturo worked on his wound. In his delirium, Miguel thrashed repeatedly.

The single scream was blood-curdling. More than one of the men holding Miguel wanted to puke as Arturo opened the wound; puss spilt from his abdomen. Placing him on his side to expel as much as possible, Arturo washed the wound out with the alcohol until the bloody ooze looked *normal*. Still unconscious, Miguel didn't react when Arturo inserted the red-hot knife, cauterising small blood vessels to stop the bleeding. The smell of burning flesh was too much for one of the men, who gagged and hastily departed. Finally, Pedro instilled the sulphur; and the dressing was complete. The rest was now between Miguel and his maker.

For the first two days, Miguel hovered between life and death. On the third day, his fever broke. Petro and Arturo stood studying him; finally, in agreement, he would live. They left Carmelita to continue with tepid sponges and wound care. When she volunteered to assist, it was more out of curiosity about this handsome stranger than any noble gesture on her part.

She tried to make sense of his garbled speech as he drifted in and out of consciousness. Often his face twisted into a grimace; was it grief? Agony? Without being told, Carmelita knew this man had suffered. She wondered about *Theresa,* the name he often spoke, a lost love? On the morning of the fourth day, he called out "Theresa", followed by anguished cries, *"No, no, no"*. Something shifted inside Carmelita. She had never seen any man show this much emotion over any woman. No one had ever cared for her this way. Carmelita was both jealous and sad. It was unlikely she would ever know such love.

It was dusk when Miguel opened his eyes. A beautiful young woman, her head tilted to one side, sat on a stool, her eyes closed. He vaguely remembered seeing her when he first arrived, unsure when that was. Touching his side, he could feel the thick dressing. It was still painful when he moved, but nothing like it had been.

"Buenos Dios, Senorita."

Having dozed off, Carmelita lifted her weary head at the sound of Miguel's voice. She was still holding the wet sponge cloth. Carmelita smiled, "Welcome back. You must be on good terms with our Saviour Senor."

"Please, call me Miguel. It seems I owe the camp my life. Thank you, Senorita, for taking care of me; I am most grateful." Miguel smiled; Carmelita felt her pulse jump.

"Please, Senor…Miguel, call me Carmelita. It was my pleasure to assist. I normally spend all my days in the cooking section. Being involved with your care was a welcome change. Pedro, our leader, and Arturo, our blacksmith, must take the credit for your recovery."

"How long have I been like this? I remember waking from a bad dream, burning up, and that's the last I remember."

"It's been four days. You had only been with us two days when you took ill. There is a water pitcher next to your bed. Senor, you are dehydrated from the fever; you would be wise to drink as much as possible. There are also some nuts and fruit should your appetite return. I was about to turn in for the night. I will let Pedro know you are awake. You should rest now."

Carmelita stood up to go; Miguel reached out and took her hand.

"I can never thank you enough for your kindness; I hope I can repay it one day."

Carmelita smiled, not wanting the moment to end. It was a long time since any man had put his hand on her without expecting anything. She was moved. Finally, he released her.

Picking up her things, Carmelita turned to say goodnight. Miguel's eyes were already closed. She smiled, keen to take some rest as well; it had been a long four days. She had much to think about, not the least of which was the woman named Theresa.

Life In the Camp

☼

Miguel's recovery was gradual, nearly three months. He used this time to learn as much as possible about how the camp functioned. Pedro was in no hurry to assign Miguel to one of the raiding parties. He enjoyed his company and found his intelligent input into improving the running of the camp of great value. Miguel was proving to be an asset.

Any misapprehension Miguel's arrival in camp generated soon evaporated. He proved likeable, showing great interest in everyone's role, was amenable to taking advice, and was respectful of the men who had been with Pedro from the beginning. Pedro recognised, despite his youth, Miguel had all the attributes of a leader. The decision to groom him to take over should anything happen to him was already made. First, Miguel would have to earn everyone's respect and trust if they were to follow his lead. Pedro recognised a potential problem, Ernesto, captain of one of the raiding parties and Carmelita's lover.

Miguel was grateful for Carmelita's excellent care. She began seeking his company regularly. Flattered, he responded eagerly, though he was embarrassed to admit up to this point in his life; he had no experience with women whatsoever. The commitment to work on Ataliva Roca took up the best part of twenty-four hours a day, seven days a week. Only a few special Holy days, like Christmas and Easter, were set aside to give thanks or celebrate. The other relevant factor was most cattlemen spent the majority of their time in the company of other men. Girls like his sister Theresa were rare; Miguel couldn't think of any others.

Carmelita was not shy in letting her attraction to Miguel be known from the outset. When she brushed past him, as she often did, Miguel could smell her woman scent. It was growing more difficult to control the bulge inside his trousers. She took every opportunity to spend as much time with him as possible. At first, she had a legitimate reason to attend to his wound dressings, letting her hands linger across his chest or muscular arms a little longer than necessary. Carmelita was a voluptuous woman and very aware of her effect on men; she knew Miguel was responding.

It was only a matter of time before he invited her into his bed, something she would have already accomplished, except for Miguel's extreme shyness and his trying to treat her like a lady. Carmelita found it charming but was becoming impatient. She wanted to bed Miguel. He was a virgin, she was sure, making the idea of sex with him even more enticing. The thought of teaching him erotic things he couldn't even imagine was exciting. Carmelita smiled to herself, feeling the pulse in her groin, anticipating the pleasure of getting to know his body from the waist down. Throughout the camp, everyone knew Carmelita was Ernesto's woman…except Miguel. The way Carmelita was flirting with him, it appeared she had forgotten also!

Pedro was the leader in the camp, and his word was law, but when it came to personal issues, he believed in minding his own business. He also understood very clearly that the one thing capable of causing disharmony was the interaction between the men and the women, especially when two men were interested in the same woman. He needed to speak to Miguel.

It was a clear night. By mid-Autumn, the temperatures were dropping. Most of the camp dwellers had turned in for the night. Miguel sat on a log, drawing warmth from the open fire. Across the compound, he could hear the clatter from the cook's camp clearing up after the evening meal and preparing for their early morning start.

Without any breeze, the wood smoke spiralled upwards as Pedro appeared at Miguel's side, nodded without speaking, and then sat beside him. Both men were comfortable with the silence. There

217

wasn't a need for conversation. The rest of the group had already discussed plans for the next day. Pedro was the first to speak.

"It will be good having all the working parties home. We need to think about relocating soon before Winter strikes. We risk being trapped in the valley if we have early snow." Pedro knew the lower Andes like no other. He'd hunted here as a boy with his father and grandfather. He sometimes wondered if life would have been different had he stayed here; his family might still be alive.

"I must speak with you, Miguel. It is a personal matter, one normally I would consider none of my business. When men and women spend time in each other's company, attractions happen, such as between Carmelita and yourself," Pedro raised his hand as Miguel attempted to respond. "I am not seeking any explanation, nor do you need me to sanction your behaviour, but you must know that Carmelita is considered the partner of Ernesto, one of my team captains. The morning he left, it was from her bed, and there was nothing to suggest they were no longer together. Whatever you choose to do beyond this conversation is entirely up to you."

Pedro stood, patted Miguel sympathetically on the shoulder and walked off towards his shelter without looking back. Miguel wondered why life had to be so complicated; he also felt stupid. Carmelita was very desirable. He was in a camp with at least forty or more single men. The fact she wasn't with anyone hadn't crossed his mind. He should have known better.

Miguel could hear her soft footfalls before she reached his side, casually holding onto his shoulder to steady herself as she sat down. Miguel flinched as if he'd touched a hot poker. Carmelita withdrew her hand; she immediately knew something had changed. Very casually, she asked Miguel a simple question,

"Do you think it will snow before June?"

Just as casually, Miguel answered, "I'm not the best one to answer that; Pedro will surely know."

Miguel never once raised his face to look at her. His voice was polite but devoid of emotion or feeling when he spoke. Carmelita was overwhelmed with a rush of emotions, anger, betrayal, desperation, and abandonment. She knew she was being ridiculous; whatever connection they shared remained unspoken. She'd been *dumped* many times, usually when a wife or girlfriend turned up unexpectedly, and though this was even more innocent, it somehow hurt more.

Carmelita couldn't understand why she was so upset, finally admitting genuine feelings for Miguel, something she hadn't anticipated.

Miguel stood, feeling awkward. Carmelita had been the one to make all the advances, although he knew she was aware of his receptive behaviour. He wasn't entirely innocent either, blushing at the thought, recalling how often he'd imagined making love to her.

"I'll be saying goodnight then, Carmelita; see you tomorrow," Miguel said over his shoulder, and then he was gone.

Carmelita sat alone, curled forward, hugging her knees, staring deep into the smouldering coals. She felt tears on her cheeks, another surprise. It had been a long time since she shed tears over anyone.

Ernesto had been absent from the camp for some time, seeking to set up outside contacts in the surrounding community, a hazardous venture for both parties involved. The people he approached were simple farmers, not used to dealing with dangerous situations threatening their existence. Though sympathetic to the cause, many declined out of fear. Fortunately, there were those willing to help, recognising the only way their lives would get back to normal and their country set free, was to destroy those leading the corruption. It had been a long-few-months. Ernesto and his men were ready to go home.

Visitor In the Night
☼

Lifting the tent flap noiselessly, he slipped quietly inside. Watching Carmelita sleeping peacefully, feeling himself harden. She smelled like a summer breeze, her breathing shallow, even. He had been dreaming of this. Lowering himself over her, he placed his mouth over her exposed breast. Her nipple hardened as she roused, moaning, slipping her arms around his neck. Carmelita whispered,

"Miguel"

Pushing away from her abruptly, he stood, fury quickly replacing his passion. Carmelita came fully awake. In the darkness, she could smell the tobacco breath on her chest. It was Ernesto.

Speaking through gritted teeth, with a tremor in his voice, he asked menacingly, "So tell me, lover, how does Miguel caress your breast?"

She was desperate to diffuse Ernesto's anger. If he chose to, he could snap her neck. Verbally attacking Ernesto threw him off balance, giving her time to think of something plausible. Damn Miguel.

Carmelita defended herself like a cornered tigress, "You are the only one who shares my bed, you fool! You wake me in the middle of the night while I'm dreaming, speaking nonsense, and you attack me. How dare you! Please tell me why I would look at another man when I have you. You look after me. You are strong, handsome, and best of all, no one ever made love to me as you do."

Carmelita had never spoken like this to Ernesto, but she sensed her life might depend on it. He wasn't bright, and like most men, he had a big ego. She was praying it was enough.

220

Ernesto hesitated, wanting to believe her. What she said was reasonable; she was deeply asleep when he touched her, which made sense.

Carmelita took advantage of Ernesto's hesitation, quickly rising to her knees; she reached out to him in the dark and began caressing his genital area; Ernesto's passion promptly returned. Carmelita exposed his flesh and took him into her mouth, working the head of his penis with her tongue. Ernesto groaned loudly, pulling her head towards him, enjoying every sensation. Every flick of her tongue sent electric shocks through him as Carmelita worked her magic. Ernesto was pounding her mouth, finally climaxing with a roar. He had never been this forceful with her; she was still afraid.

Lying as convincingly as she could, she crooned to him, "At last, you are home again, my love; I am complete."

Ernesto was very quiet, still enjoying the aftermath of his release. Carmelita felt for his hand, drawing him down to her bed, holding him in a warm embrace, finding his mouth and returning his passion. He began caressing her between the legs, his fingers seeking her warmth. Ernesto was hard again, and then he was inside her, unleashing his pent-up desire. The release when it came leaving Ernesto spent.

This was not the night she had dreamed of only a few short hours ago. Ernesto was asleep, his mouth agape, snoring, his arms wrapped tightly around Carmelita. She wasn't going anywhere in a hurry. Carmelita had said all the right things, all the things she knew he wanted to hear. No one could see the pain in her heart or the tears in her eyes.

There was jubilation in the camp as daylight broke. Two teams captained by Vincente and Ernesto had returned overnight. Many men were still asleep, but others arose early, eager to catch up with the camp news.

Pedro greeted them all warmly. There was a commotion in the cook's camp as everyone was preparing a breakfast feast. The carry-on outside woke Ernesto. Carmelita was already gone, helping the others. He lay there for a long time, thinking about last night, convincing himself his suspicions about Carmelita were unfounded.

221

When he disturbed her, it was from some silly dream. Even if she was dreaming about an old lover, she was his woman and here with him now. He didn't fear memories of old lovers from the past. He wasn't going to lose any sleep over such rubbish.

The camp was in full swing when Ernesto emerged from Carmelita's tent. After a brief nod and smile at her, he headed across the compound, making straight for Pedro, wrapping him in a hug. The two engaged in a mock wrestle until finally parting, each grinning broadly.

Pedro clasped Ernesto's hand firmly. "Welcome home; it's good to see you, my friend. Congratulations on a job well done. Your men have been filling me in on all the details. Come and sit with me, and I'll fill you in on what's been happening here."

Vincente joined them, now replenished after a good rest in a safe environment. Away from their haven, no one knew when they might be ambushed, caught in a trap or unexpectedly come across a troop of soldiers. Addressing himself to Ernesto, he asked innocently,

"Did you sleep well, my friend? I hope you are well-rested?"

Ernesto grinned; he knew Vincente was teasing him. Both teams arrived at the camp together, Ernesto heading directly for Carmelita's tent. All three men laughed knowingly.

Vincente turned to Pedro, "What about the men I sent back with Emilio? I saw him just now; they arrived safely, it seems."

Pedro hesitated for a second, considering his response. "They had a bad experience on their journey. They came across a mass grave; it wasn't possible to estimate the number of people who died there. An evil the government will hopefully pay for one day."

The men, drinking matte`, were suddenly silent, thinking about finding such a terrible thing. Pedro continued,

"The two, Mateo and Jamie, probably escaped a noose somewhere, I suspect, but they are proving to be good fighting men and have been keeping out of trouble. The other man you sent me is a different kettle of fish. Miguel is proving to be a potential leader."

222

Ernesto froze as he heard the name 'Miguel'. Pedro watched his face turn scarlet. He didn't utter a word, just paid close attention to everything Pedro was saying.

"We nearly lost Miguel; he arrived with a badly infected wound, *removing* some of the governor's men." Pedro took a sip of his tea, casually looking over the top of his mug at Ernesto's face. His expression was like thunder.

Ernesto asked Pedro, his usually booming voice quiet, "So, who performed the miracle cure?"

Pedro wondered what had happened in Carmelita's tent; Ernesto was keen to know about Miguel. Pedro had no reason to avoid the question; he just stated the facts.

"Our resident *doctor*, the blacksmith Arturo, literally saved his life. It was touch and go for a while, but between Arturo and Carmelita, they nursed him back to life."

Ernesto didn't wait for any further conversation. Putting his mug down, he walked off toward his campsite. Vincente looked at Pedro, puzzled,

"What's wrong with Ernesto, I wonder?" Pedro looked back and just shrugged.

"I'm guessing lack of sleep is catching up with him," he laughed, changing the subject.

Vincente laughed, getting his meaning, and started chatting again, Pedro appeared to be listening intently, but his mind was elsewhere. He sensed things were about to change, suspecting it would not be for the better.

Following Vincente's gaze, Pedro turned to see Miguel approaching, smiling; Vincente arose, extending his hand.

"I hear you are already becoming indispensable in the camp, Miguel?"

Miguel laughed awkwardly, shook his head and looked at Pedro quizzically. Pedro invited Miguel to join them as breakfast began to appear. Large platters of roasted meat, eggs, and bread arrived as a crowd gathered.

Pedro sat watching Carmelita carrying a tray, offering food to men and women as they arrived. She avoided Miguel like the plague, not even looking in his direction, confirming to Pedro something had taken place between them following his warning the previous evening. Pedro was also just as sure something had happened between Carmelita and Ernesto. Miguel's behaviour was no different than usual; he was oblivious to any undercurrent.

One Big Happy Family
☼

The whole camp was in a jubilant mood. One of the supply teams arrived mid-morning loaded with produce. They managed a side trip to the hotel in La Cumbecita. The owner, a good friend, parted with a barrel of beer and a case of tequila. A party was in order.

Carmelita was apprehensive as she cleaned up after breakfast. She spotted Ernesto leaving her tent; he nodded and smiled, heading across the compound. She hadn't seen him since. As the morning wore on, her tense mood grew. By now, he would be aware that one of the new arrivals in the camp was named Miguel.

Carmelita had no idea what to do next. She had not sighted Ernesto since around 7 a.m. Some women headed for the stream to wash clothes; they would be gone until around lunchtime. Carmelita decided to join them; it might be her best option.

The one saving grace for Carmelita was that nothing had happened between her and Miguel; thank God! Hindsight was a wonderful thing. If Ernesto believed Carmelita had been with somebody else, he would probably kill them both. Now it was up to her to convince him of her fidelity, but how to explain her calling out Miguel's name?

Just after midday, Ernesto returned to the group of men gathered around the campfire. The conversation was relaxed and happy. Miguel, accompanied by Pedro, had already been introduced to most of the returning rebels when Ernesto sauntered over to where Pedro and Miguel were standing. Miguel knew straight away who he was. Stepping forward, he extended his hand to Ernesto in greeting, looking him straight in the eye, a smile on his face.

"A pleasure to meet you, Ernesto; Pedro tells me you are one of his best men." Miguel shook his hand warmly. Ernesto responded, gripping Miguel's hand a little more tightly than necessary.

Ernesto studied Miguel closely. He had faced many enemies in his day, always alert to any potential threat they might pose, ready to do battle without a second thought. His unique ability to judge his opposition accurately had saved his life more than once. Ernesto decided this young stud hadn't even lived yet; he wasn't much more than a boy and would never be his match. He relaxed. He couldn't be sure what was in Carmelita's head, but this was a small camp, and if Carmelita had stepped out of line with Miguel, someone would have happily shared the news by now.

Carmelita carrying a basket of clean linen with the returning womenfolk, heard Ernesto's booming laughter; she would recognise it anywhere. That was not the sound of an angry man. Risking a glance at the group of men, she was surprised to see Ernesto, Pedro, Miguel and Vincente deep in conversation, relaxed, convivial. Carmelita felt weak with relief. Her legs were shaking when she arrived at her tent.

The ladies changed quickly, gathered up the food they had prepared earlier, and headed across the compound to join the celebrations. Trestle tables groaned under the weight of food and drink. The aroma of empanadas and roasting beef smothered with chilli and other tempting spices brought the camp to a standstill. Everyone stopped what they were doing and headed to where Guido was pouring generous amounts of tequila or helped themselves to an assortment of roasted meat, rice, salad, enchiladas…and more tequila.

Carmelita took a deep breath, sidled up to Ernesto and slipped her arm through his, flashing him her most provocative smile. Ernesto didn't respond for a few seconds. His eyes bored into Carmelita's; then, his mouth was crushing hers, laying claim. When he lifted his head, he was laughing, casually slapping her on the rump,

"Get me something to eat, woman; I'm starving. If I don't have something soon, I'll have to eat you."

226

It was a clear display of possession and whose partner she was, a reminder also to Carmelita! Everyone laughed a little uncomfortably. Ernesto glanced at Miguel, studying his tequila, his face expressionless. Carmelita laughed nervously, departing quickly, obedient to Ernesto's command.

The evening passed harmoniously. Everyone had a good time singing, dancing, having a quiet drink and listening to several men strumming guitars. Pedro missed nothing. Miguel was the soul of discretion. When Ernesto raised the subject of his life-threatening wounds, Miguel casually replied,

"Without the excellent care of Arturo and your woman, I would have surely died. I am eternally grateful."

Carmelita stayed by Ernesto's side throughout the evening, touching his arm often, her eyes never once looking in Miguels's direction. Occasionally Ernesto put his arm around Carmelita. She relaxed. The night was over; everyone slowly drifted away to their shelters.

Ernesto entered his tent with Carmelita close behind. There was still a knot in the pit of her stomach. She was not naive enough to think Ernesto would forget her earlier slip of the tongue. He was standing inside waiting for her. Carmelita smiled, walking towards him sensuously; she slipped her arms around his neck, inviting his mouth. Ernesto didn't move. Carmelita tensed, watching the expression on his face change. Slowly he removed her arms, twisting his fingers tightly through her hair; he pulled her face close to his,

"If you ever look at another man with lust in your eyes or entertain the idea of being with anyone in my absence, I will kill you. Do you understand? You belong to me until I decide otherwise."

Carmelita was afraid Ernesto would rip the hair out of her scalp; he was holding it so tightly. She could barely nod her head.

He pushed her backwards onto the bedding without another word, letting his trousers drop to his ankles. He was on top of Carmelita before she had time to catch her breath, ripping her undergarment away, pushing himself inside her forcibly, riding her until he came. There was no foreplay or sweet words, no attempt to satisfy her. He had barely finished when he straddled her once more, grunting like some rutting animal. When he finished, he fell to one side, his arm resting across his forehead. He didn't even bother looking at her,

"Now get out whore."

Carmelita knew better than to say anything, gathered her torn underwear, and left, shaken. Whatever hold she had over Ernesto was gone, now just his whore to do with whatever he liked. At that moment, Carmelita hated all men. She'd only ever met one decent one; look where that got her.

The Raiding Parties
☼

In late Autumn of 1855, Miguel, now sufficiently recovered from his wounds, joined one of the five raiding parties. Teams alternated between gathering supplies or being assigned to attack Mendoza's men at every opportunity. Some were absent from the camp for about a week, others for up to three months. The timing and strength of raids also depended on the number of casualties or deaths they sustained.

A shortage of supplies in all the provinces began to occur. Many farms were still in operation, but with the expectation the soldiers would eventually target them, they secretly started stockpiling caches of dry goods. While frightened engaging directly with the rebels would cause reprisals, the farmers were still committed to sharing whatever produce they could spare.

The indiscriminate killings and intimidation eased when Carlos Mendoza became Governor. Continuing to annexe prime properties for personal gain, the astute businessman also recognised the need for an active farming community to keep the country running. The significant loss of tax revenue with so many properties abandoned also affected funding for his far-reaching plans. The hardships and lack of supplies to larger towns and cities caused increasing hostility amongst the population. There was a groundswell of anger and frustration building.

The rebels were no force against an army of soldiers. Their strength lay in way-laying small contingencies of soldiers or the government's hired thugs. One of the things working in their favour was the growing unrest amongst the general population. The increasing number of protest marches forced Carlos to retain a significant number of troops close at hand to protect him and control the masses. He didn't perceive ranchers scattered over the countryside as any real threat to his raiding parties. That was until Pedro's well-organised groups started to have an impact.

Initially, they would organise a few teams targeting a different area. The idea was to initiate an insignificant raid that required the soldiers' attention, and strike with their main force elsewhere. Many of the men they were fighting were displaced gauchos. They were tough men, not easily fooled, and excellent trackers, but they were lazy and lacked discipline. Gauchos were born to work cattle; this was not the work they lived for; instead, often, they found a town or village with a bar, filling in the day drinking.

The best horsemen in Pedro's camp acted as runners, swift riders who gathered information about the movement of Carlos's troops and returned to camp as quickly as possible. Pedro had an uncanny ability to estimate where the targeted area might be. The plan was to have his men waiting to *greet* the raiders, showing them no mercy. The only way to eliminate the threat was to ensure it no longer existed.

The battles were not without cost; there were casualties and occasional deaths. Due to Pedro's meticulous planning, fortunately, the losses were few. Whenever they did lose someone, everyone in the camp was affected. They had become like family.

Once in a while, they were too late; the raiders had taken whatever they were after and fled. If the landowner showed any resistance, the odds were they would burn down his hacienda. Pedro's men did their best to assist, relocating them temporarily with someone willing to help. Often the menfolk, so enraged by the brutal treatment, would send their wife and children to shelter with other family members, while they joined Pedro's team in the fight against the corruption. Miguel recognised the need to establish safe houses in as many areas as possible. He raised the suggestion with Pedro, who was impressed with the idea and proposed it at the next camp council. All the team captains agreed.

Pedro placed Miguel in charge of setting up the groundwork, having a considerable advantage in possessing an intimate knowledge of the most prominent ranches throughout Argentina and familiarity with smaller share farmers. He had a reasonable idea of who might help, even knowing it would be at considerable risk. Miguel was well known throughout the cattle industry and greatly respected like his father before him.

Miguel and Pedro shared many hours around the campfire. They forged a close bond, having lost loved ones in similar circumstances. It was complicated forming close friendships knowing they too may be taken from you at any time. They were in the fight of their lives.

Pedro once expressed to Miguel how much he wished he could join him and the others with the raiding parties. Nothing specific was ever said, but Miguel suspected he was not as physically well as he once imagined, one of the reasons he abstained. Pedro was vital to the organisation; if killed in a raid, it could mean the end of the rebel camp. He would continue in the role best suited to their needs. Miguel was becoming his right-hand man, quickly learning the finer details of what was required, and showing the same ability as Pedro in anticipating what they needed to do next.

The camp had long since ceased thinking of Miguel as a *gringo*. He was one of them. All admired his sharp mind, courage, and fighting spirit when engaged with the enemy. He was fearless. His skill on horseback was second to none. Everyone showed him complete respect, with one exception, Ernesto. He continued to consider Miguel a potential rival for Carmelita's affections.

A Chance Meeting
☼

Miguel and his men could see the column of smoke rising from the property where they were heading. They were too late; the soldiers, having lost recent battles engaging the rebels, started to give out false leads in the hope of trapping them or evading them altogether. Over the previous two years, Pedro's men had earned a fearsome reputation. The soldiers were more inclined to avoid them rather than confront them.

A dozen rebels dismounted, encircling the property's perimeter, remaining out of sight. There were six horses tethered to the corral railing. No one was standing guard, and there were no sentries. They were confident of not being disturbed. Miguel cautiously approached the side of the house; he could hear raised voices. Risking a glance, he could see all the soldier's attention was focused on two male figures kneeling in the centre of the yard, a man in his early thirties and a much older man. They both showed signs of having been beaten.

The man in charge screamed at the farmer, "Don't lie to me, dog. I know you have produce hidden somewhere. We came this way only a few weeks ago, and the corn was ripe for harvesting." With that, he swung a cattle whip across the man's back. Blood oozed through the remnants of his shirt as the farmer cried out in pain.

"No more, no more, I beg you. I have nothing hidden, I swear. The rebels came and took whatever we had a week ago."

"You lie, dog. If that were true, why was it not reported? I've had enough." With that, he pulled out his pistol and pointed it at the younger man. "You have five seconds to tell me where the supplies

232

are, or I'll kill your son." Placing his pistol against the man's lowered head, he began counting. "One, two…"

Before he got to three, Miguel's bullet shattered the back of the soldier's skull; he dropped like a stone. Miguel's men swarmed the yard, shooting until all six soldiers lay on the ground, then quickly turned their attention to aiding the badly beaten men. The younger man was already trying to help his companion, who was not faring as well.

"Praise God, Senor; we had almost given up hope your men would get here in time; the soldiers came sooner than expected." The younger man stood up, grasping Miguel's hand shaking it vigorously, full of gratitude for their rescue. "My name is Delgado; I am not Manolo Clement's son, just his friend."

Without warning, he shoved Miguel forcefully to one side. A shot rang out. With a final effort, one of the soldiers on the ground near Miguel discharged his pistol, hoping to take the rebel leader with him to the grave. Several shots rang out, ensuring there would be no more such attempts.

Miguel was shocked; regaining his feet, he turned to thank Delgado for saving his life. The other man hadn't moved; he was standing to one side. He turned slowly towards Miguel, a stunned look on his face. It was only then Miguel saw the bullet hole penetrating the man's chest. As Miguel put out his hand, Delgado crumpled to the ground.

Manolo's anguished cry rang out, "No, Delgado, my friend!" Then he began to weep. "He deserved so much more. His father was murdered eleven years ago by thugs working for the Government. He fled to Buenos Aires and struggled to make a living, finally deciding he could do more good by joining those fighting for Argentina. My wife and I found him in our barn, almost starving. We fed and sheltered him until he was well. I had a serious accident last year and was barely managing with help from my wife. As thanks, Delgado offered to stay and assist until my recovery was complete. Unfortunately, the damage I suffered was permanent. Shortly after, my wife died unexpectedly, and Delgado just stayed. He chose not to leave me. He was like a son to me. I have no other family; I intended to leave the farm to him when I was gone."

Miguel listened to Manolo's sad story, shattered that Delgado had sacrificed his own life to save Miguel's and left this poor man devastated. He would offer him sanctuary with Pedro's men. It was the least he could do. It was apparent Manolo could not manage here alone.

Still weeping, Manolo said, "I do not even know who might contact his family so far away in Santa Rosa, or even if he still has family there."

Miguel gasped in disbelief, recalling his father's distress at having one of his share farmers beaten to death - Paulo Caron. Miguel could not recall ever meeting the Caron family, but he would certainly never forget Delgado Caron.

A Change of Plans
☼

Pedro realised the size of the rebel camp had outgrown its capacity to function effectively. As the trouble spread far and wide, the rebel's interventions became less effective; they needed to be where the action was likely to happen. Frequently they were too far away, coming to the aid of a farmer too late. Small groups were the answer; a few men could be almost invisible.

Pedro called a council meeting; there was much to discuss. Miguel had done his job well. His knowledge of substantial ranches throughout the Pampas and most of Argentina proved invaluable. He was persuasive in convincing the owners that the only way to rid Argentina of the corruption overrunning the country was to band together to enforce a change. He agreed it involved risk, but pointed out to the owners that they were at risk of government raids anyway. Miguel convinced them working together as allies could bring this to an end.

Unrest was escalating in all the major cities. Cordoba, Santa Fe, Rosario and Buenos Aires required more and more troops to keep the angry crowds in check, leaving the government raiding parties undermanned; this continued to work in the rebel's favour.

Small groups of Pedro's men, two or three in number, would become farmhands on appointed properties, all within range of each other. They would provide free labour to the owner, on the understanding they might be required to leave at a minute's notice to join an attack on a raiding party, afterwards dispersing, becoming farmhands once more, blending into the surroundings, until called upon to assemble again.

The larger ranches had telegraphic communication. It was easy to send a coded message with precise details identifying the targeted area. Not only were the rebels more effective, the ranch owners quickly realised the advantage of having free labour where there had been a desperate shortage of farmhands. They also recognised the value of having highly experienced fighting men ready to defend their property without regard to their own lives. An increasing number of ranchers willingly joined in.

Pedro targeted a range of significant locations, with a growing number of supporters to access. A core group remained in the mountain camp. Many were property owners, injured or displaced by the government forces, physically unable to join those fighting, but of great value in taking up other necessary roles to maintain the camp. There were horses and livestock requiring care and a need for general maintenance in the absence of their fighting colleagues.

The rebels were thriving, now numbering over a hundred. Surprisingly, for such a diverse group, the atmosphere was harmonious. They resolved disputes amicably with discussion or by taking a vote. Those dispatched as farmhands rotated regularly with replacements, allowing them to rest and maintain their social connection within the group.

Pedro was careful to ensure Miguel and Ernesto were rarely in camp simultaneously. As two leaders, their particular roles saw them delivering different services. Ernesto's suspicion about Miguel's involvement with Carmelita never resolved; he remained wary of his company. Miguel was vigilant in avoiding any unnecessary contact with Carmelita, always polite when receiving food from her in her role as a kitchen hand, but ensuring he was never alone in her company.

Carmelita still wondered what had changed Miguel's attitude towards her, although in hindsight, if he'd embraced her advances, they would probably both be dead by now, killed by Ernesto!

Leaving The Mountain Lair
☼

Cosquin was only twenty miles northwest of Cordoba, placing Pedro's group within striking distance. However, thanks to a quirk of nature, the winter camp wasn't exposed; a naturally occurring fold in the mountain range formed long ago by volcanic action hid them from view.

Pedro hunted here with his father when the only visitors to the area were a few natives. His father was tracking a wounded cougar to finish the kill and harvest its pelt, surprised to find that the animal had vanished when he climbed a nearby ridge. Following its tracks, they found a rift leading into the fold. Dismounting, they led their horses through the narrow gap, stunned to find a small circular valley hidden on the other side. They were more excited by that discovery than finding their missing cougar, dead, forty feet away. The valley was lush with grass; a wide sandy strip ran along the far side, a good indication there was artesian water below.

Over the years, Pedro returned to the valley often, especially when hunting in the winter. The climate inside was less harsh than out on the open plain.

It was unlikely anyone would stumble on them this far from Cordoba unless they were deliberately searching for those that didn't wish to be found. Pedro stationed two guards above the entrance to the valley. They had a clear view for miles, allowing the camp time to take evasive action if needed. Pedro knew from a distance the fold was undetectable. He was confident they were safe. As an added precaution, they only lit the campfires at night for warmth and food preparation, carefully extinguishing them before daylight to avoid any tell-tale signs of smoke.

The weeks flew by. Dispersing teams was more difficult from this location. It was necessary to head west and skirt around Cordoba before turning south towards Mercedes. Added to this, Winter made the trek to home base more arduous. After a particularly heavy snowstorm, Pedro suspended sending out the teams. Most of the groups were in the camp; it would lift everyone's spirits to have a decent break.

Pedro decided a party was in order. While racks of beef roasted, he produced a small barrel of rum, to the delight and hearty cheers from the men. As the evening wore on, raucous laughter grew; some danced and sang, serenaded by guitar. The remainder sat contentedly watching those foolish enough to overindulge.

Since arriving in the camp with Miguel, Jamie and Mateo kept to themselves. Pedro, a good judge of character, placed them under close surveillance, suspecting they had the potential to cause trouble. He was adept at identifying those who lived outside the law more frequently than abiding by it. Until now, Pedro happily conceded; they had not given him any reason to complain. Tonight, he was concerned. Jamie was very drunk. At first, he played the fool, making everyone laugh, but his behaviour got out of hand; he began flirting outrageously with all the ladies. Most ignored or laughed at him until Carmelita arrived with a jug to top up empty mugs. Swaying, Jamie held out his mug; as Carmelita approached to fill it, he grabbed her around the waist, pulling her close to his body, kissing her full on the mouth.

For a big man, Ernesto was light on his feet; he moved like lightning, jerking Carmelita out of Jamie's grasp with his right hand and smashing his left fist into Jamie's face. Falling backwards, Jamie squealed in pain as the fire singed the back of his head. Outraged, he staggered to his feet, charging at Ernesto with his whole body, knocking him off his feet.

The camp was now in an uproar. Pedro moved quickly to intervene, hoping to stop an all-out brawl. Stepping between the two men with his arms raised, he hoped to encourage an amicable

238

solution. He didn't see the knife in Ernesto's hand as he lunged at Jamie.

Everyone was standing yelling one moment and suddenly struck silent the next. The knife was buried up to the hilt in Pedro's abdomen. A look of disbelief spread across his face. Miguel raced to his side as Pedro slowly turned his head, scanning the sea of faces, closed his eyes for the last time and fell.

Everyone started screaming and shouting at both Jamie and Ernesto. Mateo dragged Jamie away before things escalated, making themselves scarce. They wanted no part in whatever might follow.

Gutted, Ernesto stood fixed on the spot, roaring like a wounded bull, trying to control his grief. He respected Pedro like no other; he thought of him as a brother.

"Please, forgive me, Pedro," he implored. "It was an accident."

A space cleared around Ernesto; nobody quite knew what to say or do. Finally, Miguel stepped forward towards Ernesto, not intending any action. Ernesto jumped back, drew his pistol, pointed it at Miguel,

"Do not come near me Gringo, or you will join my amigo Pedro," Ernesto's voice broke as he spoke Pedro's name. "It was self-defence; Pedro's death was an accident."

"Ernesto, there is no need for this; let us talk about what happened."

Ignoring Miguel's words, he spat at his feet, "I will not serve under you! I will settle my score with you another time."

Ernesto backed away from the campfire, his pistol still drawn, heading towards where the horses sheltered. "Anyone who tries to stop me or follow me, I will put in the ground." No one moved, and then he was gone.

Some of the women began wailing. The men who had been with Pedro since the beginning gathered to console each other for their terrible loss. Even Miguel, who had only been with Pedro for a couple of years, was devastated by his death. The others stood waiting for him to say what they should do next. It was now up to Miguel to lead the rebel camp

Filling The Void

☼

The transition to being the camp leader wasn't going to be easy. Miguel had big shoes to fill. Much changed with Pedro's death; the camp's stability was now threatened. Additionally, Ernesto, one of the most valuable team leaders, was gone. Whatever flaws existed in his personality or habits were far outweighed by his reliability and the cohesion he generated amongst his men. Ernesto's departure was a huge loss.

Shortly after, Jamie and Mateo decided to leave the camp, also. Jamie acknowledged his drunken behaviour sparked the whole event leading to Pedro's death. There were no direct reprisals, but the atmosphere became so uncomfortable they chose to leave. No one encouraged them to stay.

Farewelling their leader was hard. The only consolation was knowing how much Pedro loved this place. He was now the eternal guardian of the hidden valley. Miguel was glad they would relocate to the mountains soon. The Winter of 1855 was coming to an explosive and unexpected end.

The hiatus left by Pedro's death still hadn't been breached, and the mood throughout the camp remained sombre. The only one whose spirit lifted was Carmelita. Ever resourceful, she now saw her way clear in pursuing Miguel, who had other ideas. Miguel hadn't forgotten her flagrant attempts to seduce him while still very much partnered with someone else. He decided Carmelita was someone to be admired from a distance. Besides, as the new camp leader, it was up to him to lead by example. Many remained loyal to Ernesto, still considering Carmelita Ernesto's woman, even in his absence. Miguel didn't intend to damage the fragile trust shown to him at present.

240

Miguel called a council of team leaders. They needed to choose a replacement for Ernesto and start formalising plans for future operations. Miguel stood to address the men, looking each one carefully in the eye.

"I ask for your patience, amigos. This role is not one I sought nor am fully comfortable with fulfilling. Those seated around this table are far more experienced and have been in this camp much longer. I invite you, without malice, to step forward if you wish to assume the position of leader."

There was silence; most showed surprise at Miguel's words. They all turned towards Thomas, one of Pedro's closest associates. He had been with him since the beginning and was a man of great wisdom.

"Miguel, it is with a heavy heart that we sit here without Pedro, but we are all aware of his confidence in your ability to lead the camp. We are mostly farmers, forced to become fighters. We have strength and courage but lack direction. I could teach you to plant crops but not how to plan for battle." Everyone laughed at the lighter moment. "You lead, and we will follow."

Miguel found it difficult to speak. He was incredibly humbled. He was also aware that Thomas's nod of approval meant the rest of them would follow him without dissent.

"You honour me. I swear to fight with my last breath until Argentina is free, and we can all go home. I swear this in Pedro's memory."

The room erupted with cheers. It was decided. Miguel would lead them to victory.

Over the following months, Thomas and Miguel formed a close bond, deliberating on many issues. Miguel respected his opinion. The older man would challenge any idea Miguel had if he didn't believe it could succeed. They became an effective team, not unlike the relationship he'd had with Pedro.

Miguel was sure Thomas was more than capable of filling Pedro's shoes but also realised he didn't wish to be the one to send those he knew like brothers; into situations where there was every chance they might not return. He was happy for Miguel to carry that burden of responsibility.

One balmy night two runners rode into the camp from Santa Fe. They reported the city was in an uproar. Protests were becoming more prevalent, despite the increasing brutality of the soldiers. The troop numbers continually decreased as the Governor filtered off more to protect his position in Buenos Aires.

The news was welcome. It allowed Miguel to place men strategically to follow the troop's movements, allowing them to estimate where and when to attack, and achieve the best outcome. Another morsel of news made Miguel prick up his ears. It seemed the Governor's wife was returning north to Santa Fe, intending to stay at the Convent Hospital until she could join her husband. The convent was safe from attack, and it would be better to reside there for the present rather than in the Governor's Santa Fe mansion Solitario Lobo.

An idea began to form in Miguel's mind. What leverage might have a bearing on forcing the Governor to end his corrupt ways? Take away something he valued more than wealth and power – his wife! In that instant, Miguel knew what he must do. They would kidnap Senora Mendoza, the First Lady, and hold her hostage as a bargaining tool until the Governor agreed to step down.

As the leader, most of Miguel's time was spent at base camp managing the finer details of multiple operations. He couldn't be absent for any extended period. There was only one person to trust with this mission, Vincente. He knew the area like the back of his hand, and Miguel knew Vincente could be trusted to follow instructions to the letter.

There was only one road from Rosario to Santa Fe. A couple of hours north of Rosario, the road forked east, a perfect spot to intercept a coach. The information indicated the First Lady would travel under an assumed name without an escort.

Vincente would take a group of a dozen men. Although they didn't anticipate any resistance, it was better to be prepared just in case. Miguel estimated they could be gone for up to two weeks, not

242

knowing when to expect her coach. Miguel had business south of Cordoba of greater importance to their long-term plans. He wouldn't be present when Vincente returned, but Miguel left strict instructions for taking care of their hostage. Two women would be assigned to guard her, sharing accommodation to achieve this and keep her under surveillance at all times. They would use Carmelita's tent, more sizeable than most, already shared with one of the widows in the camp, Stella. Together, they would perform guard duty.

Santa Rosa

☼

1856

Good Friday, April 18th. Rosa had risen early to give thanks. Sitting alone in the Chapel, she reflected on her life's path in this church, from a young, innocent girl arranging flowers for the altar, to the present day. Where did the time go? It seemed impossible that it was over two years since her return to Santa Rosa to help with her mother's care. Isabella would never regain her former self, but she was content spending time in her daughters' company and sitting at the lake watching the wildlife.

News from the north suggested the political turmoil continued. While it had diminished, lately, there was a renewed escalation. Following Carlos's departure from Hierro Castillo, a major landholder and his family were found brutally murdered. It was never made clear by whom. Within a few days, five soldiers were also found dead. The speculation was they were all killed by the same person or persons. Rosa knew better. When she heard of the Garcia family murders, the unexpected visit by Miguel Garcia to her bathing room at the mansion made sense. He was looking for Carlos, undoubtedly the instigator of the Garcia murders.

According to Fr Peter, the storekeeper reported seeing Miguel early one morning heading to his home at Ataliva Roca; he'd been unsighted since then. No one dared to suggest he was the murderer, speculating that he was also a likely victim whose body was yet to be discovered. Rosa recalled he was bleeding badly; it was indeed a possibility. In her mind, there was no doubt how Carlos's men met their end.

Fr Peter had an unspoken agreement not to discuss Carlos. It was a subject too painful for either of them. Rosa knew the priest kept

244

abreast of what was happening in the north; he received regular dispatches from his Brother Philippe, a Franciscan Brother managing the finances for the Church and several properties operated by the Brothers at Villa Maria. Large tracts of fertile land were annexed initially by the Jesuit Order until they fell out of favour with the Crown. Since then, the Franciscan order had control of the properties.

Rosa had not heard from Carlos since his return to Buenos Aires; the only correspondence was a brief note from Aida with the sad news her elderly husband Alfredo had passed. The household staff, following instructions, told anyone enquiring after Senora Mendoza that she had a nervous breakdown following the loss of their much-wanted child and remained in the care of her family. Rosa was furious at the lie, but it was worth it if it kept Carlos away from her. She didn't dare contact Aida to pass on her condolences, fearing it might jeopardise the housekeeper. She was sure Aida knew the truth of the matter and would understand.

Rosa did speculate Carlos might punish her by cutting off her financial support at some stage. He possibly hadn't thought of it or decided it was worth the cost to ensure she stayed out of his way.

Something was troubling Fr Peter of late. He surprised Rosa one morning with the news he was taking an extended trip to see his brother Philippe.

"Is your brother unwell, Father?" Rosa was puzzled by the priest's response. He hesitated before answering.

"Not in the conventional sense Rosa, but he is afflicted and needs my council. I cannot deny him."

Rosa was more than capable of looking after the church proper and the cottages. She would open the church daily; those wishing to attend in his absence could do so. In the priest's absence, a parish member was available to fill the position of Deacon should the need arise. There was much speculation about why he was going, but everyone agreed a break might be a good thing; he had worked tirelessly for the community since he first set foot in Santa Rosa, and no one begrudged him for taking some leave.

Three weeks after Fr Peter's departure, Maria paid Rosa an unexpected visit one morning. She was excited to tell Maria and her mother about a surprise trip to the city her husband, Cesar, had planned for her birthday. While Rosa completed her chores, Maria prepared morning tea; they would have it at the lakeside with Isabella.

It was a fine day, with not a cloud in the sky. The sisters chattered happily, balancing trays loaded with tea and cakes. When they reached Isabella, she was smiling, her eyes closed.

Rosa spoke gently, not to startle her, "Mama, look who's come to visit us, Maria, she's brought us some delicious cake… mama?"

Maria dropped the tray, crying out, "Mama, no!"

Rosa was desolate that Fr Peter would not be there to officiate and give his final blessing for Isabella's burial. Rosa let him know of her passing, sending word to Brother Philippe. He would be heartbroken by her death; their friendship started long ago when he first arrived in Santa Rosa.

The funeral, despite Fr Peter's absence, was beautiful. Isabella was well-known in the community and loved by all. Everyone agreed; her passing at just fifty-four was far too young. The wake was held in the church courtyard to accommodate the many visitors who came to pay their respects. Fr Peter sent a beautiful tribute to be read at the eulogy, expressing his significant loss at her passing.

When everyone had gone home, Rosa and Maria returned to the gravesite on the hill, the newly turned soil covered with countless floral tributes, the two white crosses marking the final resting place of their parents, side by side. Holding each other, they grieved openly, aware no amount of tears would ease the pain of their loss. Life without her would never be the same. The only consolation was the certainty their wonderful parents were together once more.

Brother's United
☼

Peter was relieved the end of his journey was in sight; he was both amazed and saddened by the experience. He hadn't been in the city for some years, not since the state funeral for his father, Ramon. In Buenos Aires, the expansion was astounding. The city limits stretched for twenty miles. The population growth was primarily due to the influx of immigrants from five continents. Conversely, seeing the poverty in some quarters was disheartening.

People displaced from their land with no place to go headed for the city, hoping to find work of any description. The number affected far outweighed employment opportunities. Many were left sleeping on the streets, depending on the charity of others, or reduced to begging. Some, once proudly independent, couldn't contemplate the humiliating experience of begging and so took their own lives. In desperation, others turned to petty crime.

Peter was happy to say farewell to Buenos Aires, only to find Rosario and Santa Fe not much better. He couldn't bear the thought that the city of Cordoba where he grew up, had descended into the same lawlessness, deciding instead to head directly to Villa Maria to see his eldest brother. Philippe had requested Peter visit him urgently, choosing not to elaborate on the circumstances. Leaving his parish in the care of others went against Peter's sense of responsibility. However, he knew his brother would never make such a request unless it were an emergency.

Peter was shocked to see Philippe. He was a changed man, his colour poor; he'd lost weight. He could feel a noticeable tremor when he put his arms around Philippe in greeting.

"Philippe, I am alarmed; you look terrible dear brother. Are you sick?"

Indicating no with a forlorn shake of his head, Philippe responded, "Let me show you to your room. After you have rested a little and had some refreshment, we'll take a walk in the garden and talk."

Frowning, Peter was more alarmed than ever. Whatever Philippe intended to discuss wasn't for the ears of others. At that moment, Brother Bernado, the Mission General at Villa Maria, joined them on the front veranda. Smiling warmly, he shook Peter's hand.

"Welcome to Villa Maria Fr Peter; Brother Phillipe informed us you were to visit the area and had requested permission to spend a few days with us. Like Senor Mendoza, it is our pleasure to welcome you here anytime."

Peter's sharply indrawn breath was audible, so Carlos has been here, and often it seems. Peter stole a glance at Phillipe, whose total attention remained focused on Brother Bernado, who continued,

"This is a highly productive property; we regret there is little time to socialise. I'm sure you understand?"

"Most certainly, Brother Bernado, I do not wish to disrupt the important work here; I am very self-sufficient."

Brother Bernado smiled and nodded, "Brother Philippe has been granted three days' leave to show you around and ensure you make the most of your stay." With that, he nodded once more and excused himself.

Peter turned to look at Phillipe, paler than before, his hands visibly trembling. For a moment, Peter thought he was going to cry.

"Come, I'll show you to your room." He made no other comment.

Following Philippe along a narrow corridor, they entered a small, sparsely furnished room. There were two hooks on the wall to hang an overshirt and robe, a bed, and a small chest of drawers on which a Crucifix rested.

"Have a little break, and I'll join you shortly." Without waiting for a reply, Philippe retired.

Peter rested on the bed, vacantly staring at the ceiling, wondering what on earth was going on. What interest did Carlos have in visiting

248

Villa Maria? It certainly had nothing to do with his religious affiliation. Something was terribly wrong; he was filled with dread.

It was mid-afternoon as they strolled through the vineyards that stretched as far as the eye could see. It was impressive, as was the remainder of the property. Peter had only been there once, many years ago. He had forgotten how beautiful it was. Of course, it had grown tremenously since then, now a diverse operation on a grand scale. It was still run mainly by the Brothers, with added help.

"What's going on, Philippe? Why has Carlos been visiting here, and how often?"

They stopped at one of several irrigation ponds. A work shed stood nearby, where farm tools and the like were stored. Under a small stand of trees was a rough wooden table and bench seat. Philippe sat down, putting his head in his hands.

"I don't know where to begin, Peter," his voice shook, and he began to cry. "God forgive me; I unwittingly helped Carlos. I turned a blind eye to what I knew to be unlawful practices. In doing so, I provided the means for him to continue his corrupt behaviour."

Peter knew he shouldn't be surprised by anything Carlos might do, but he was shocked and outraged that Philippe had been dragged into whatever evil schemes Carlos was up to.

"It started a long while ago with father. I was always intimidated by his overpowering demands; Carlos is no different. It's no excuse, Peter, I know. After our father died, the Franciscan Brothers welcomed Carlos just as willingly. He initiated sanctions on others that allowed Villa Maria to flourish—made large donations, giving them advantages over their competitors and control of the markets. Of course, this was all done in the church's name, so it was acceptable. Anything for the greater good and Mother Church. Since then, Carlos has been money laundering using his ill-gotten gains to fund illegal projects under the guise of Villa Maria."

Peter didn't know what to say. He never quite understood why his father Ramon took such interest and went to such pains to see Philippe established in the Brotherhood at Villa Maria. Initially, he was bitterly opposed to either of his two older sons following the church's doctrines. Suddenly there was an about-face. He demanded that if Philippe intended to pursue his theological studies, he must simultaneously obtain a degree in accountancy and business management. Now it was all beginning to make sense.

Villa Maria was close to Cordoba, only ninety-three miles away. How convenient to foster a strong bond with the Franciscan Brothers and have them accept his son into their order. Then he manipulated Philippe to disperse money gained from cattle rustling and goods sold on the black market and regulate the produce market. Worst of all blackmailed those he needed to control—culminating in money Laundering on a grand scale.

Being so close to their father, Carlos quickly became aware of Ramon's shrewd business plans and how they worked. Conducted under the shield of respectability afforded by the Franciscan Order, no one would ever question them. Peter was appalled. He couldn't help but feel empathy for Philippe; he was always a gentle soul, believing there was good in everyone. Somehow his Naivetivity had been corrupted.

"Philippe, have you shared the burden of your pain and guilt in confession? Discussed how to address the problem?"

Philippe nodded, looking perplexed, "It is complicated, Peter; much of Carlos's business transactions are intertwined with Villa Maria's. Should there be an expose, the scandal would be far-reaching, all the way back to Spain; it would embarrass the Crown and damage the Catholic Church irreparably. I was not given direct advice, only told, 'you will find the answer, my son!"

"My God, Philippe, did you think this was just about money? The evil overrunning our country has cost lives, the destruction of families, people disappearing, rape, torture!"

"I pray God forgives me; Peter, what do I do? They will continue turning a blind eye here. The Brotherhood has left it up to me to fix."

"Philippe, this can't go on. We have to stop Carlos; he is out of control. The money only feeds his need for greater power. I believe he is no longer satisfied as Governor; there is talk he is preparing to stand for President of Argentina at the next election."

"Thank you, Peter, for answering my call for help. Sharing my shameful part in this has lifted a weight off my shoulders and is truly a blessing. I see now my penance must be to remedy this, no matter the consequences."

Peter put his arms around Philippe, "Bless you, brother. May God give you the strength and the wisdom to deal with this."

Following a visit to the chapel to pray for God's guidance, the brothers talked long into the night, formulating a way forward, aware of the far-reaching consequences. Once set in motion, there would be no turning back.

Rebuilding The Future

☼

Peter's carriage pulled up at the rear of Our Lady of The Rosary. He sat for a long time. He was absent for only three weeks, but much had happened following his departure.

Peter glanced down to the bench at the lake; his heart ached. His dear friend Isabella had died in his absence. Peter was heartbroken at not being here to farewell her and lend support to Rosa, Maria and the rest of Isabella's family. He sighed. He was a pious man, accepting God's will in all things, but sometimes life didn't seem fair. Then there was his visit with brother Philippe where they discussed ways to control their younger brother Carlos, whose political ambitions were out of control. He had to be stopped.

Rosa came out of the cottage, throwing herself into the open arms of the priest. Together they stood locked in grief, sharing the pain of Isabella's loss, the only consolation knowing she was finally with her beloved Paulo.

"Rosa, my child, I am so sorry I was not here when your mother left us. I will say a special mass for her on Sunday. God's will is beyond question, but my heart will always be heavy in her absence."

Rosa nodded as Fr Peter wiped away her tears. Life must go on. She sighed, thinking about the conversation she was about to have with the priest as they went inside. Seated with a warming cup of tea in her hand, Rosa broached the subject on her mind.

"Fr Peter, I have made a decision. I mean to return to Santa Fe."

Peter looked almost stricken at the words, but they weren't unexpected. Rosa was a young woman and needed to engage in life once more. He respected and applauded her decision to dedicate her life to the care of her mother. Still, now that Isabella was gone, it would be wrong to encourage her to stay, a fleeting thought, selfish but understandable. Peter realised long ago that Rosa and Maria were the closest he would ever come to having children; he cared for them as if they were. He must put Rosa's wishes before his own. Maria would again take over the care of the church in Rosa's absence and keep them all connected.

Rosa could see her news had affected him deeply, but she could see he was also burdened by whatever had taken place with his elder brother Philippe. Rosa did not wish to pry but felt compelled to say something.

"Fr Peter, would it help to talk about whatever is troubling you?"

Shaking his head, he replied, "Thank you, Rosa, for your thoughtfulness, but no, you, of all people, would be the last person I'd burden my troubles with!"

Rosa frowned; such an odd response? Rosa's gut feeling said it had something to do with Carlos; she didn't know why.

They never discussed Carlos, but for one fleeting moment, Peter prayed she was not returning to their marital home. Following his visit with Philippe, he knew their plans would significantly affect Carlos's life and, therefore, his behaviour. Carlos was at his ugliest when things didn't go his way. Peter wanted Rosa as far away from Carlos as possible when the consequences of their actions came into force.

"Rosa, I support any choice that will make your life happy. Where will you go?"

"I want to return to the hospital at the Convent Santo Domingo. I know I will be made welcome, they are always so busy, and I must admit I have missed them and the satisfaction of being useful to others."

Peter smiled; this was typical of Rosa, always thinking of others. With thinly-veiled concern, he asked, "Where will you stay?" Peter held his breath.

Rosa knew the question he was really asking. "I will seek sanctuary in the convent. I pray Sr Angelina will permit me to reside there."

Peter breathed a sigh of relief. Rosa would be safe at the convent. Although he was sad Rosa would no longer be present for their many chats, he was happy for her. He smiled, taking hold of her hand, "Bless you, my child. May God watch over you every step of the way."

Maria was less happy with Rosa's decision. She understood her reasoning but had enjoyed her sister's company for the last couple of years. As well as being sisters, they were the best of friends. She would miss Rosa terribly.

Rosa tried to reassure Maria, "I promise I will make regular visits. I want to come back and watch my nieces and nephews grow," Rosa laughed as Maria blushed.

"There is no hurry, Cesar and I want to enjoy some time together first."

Rosa said no more. She suspected they had been trying for a child for some time without luck.

Saying farewell to her Aunt Luisa and family was almost as hard.

Rosa was surprised at how quickly she put her belongings together. Since returning to Santa Rosa, she had no desire to visit Hierro Castillo following Carlos's departure to Buenos Aires.

While sad to say farewell to Maria and Fr Peter, Rosa was excited to return to Santa Fe and the convent.

Sr Angelina was overjoyed, enthusiastically welcoming the news of Rosa's return and more than happy to arrange a permanent place for her to stay. Sr Angelina knew Rosa well, recognising her needs were simple. Sparse accommodation would not phase her one bit.

Return To Santa Fe

☼

From Santa Rosa to Santa Fe via Buenos Aires was six hundred miles. Rosa did not relish the thought. Although the road had improved dramatically, it was still arduous. No longer troubled by potential attacks of natives, the number of displaced persons was of more significant concern. Since the ruling party plunged Argentina into hardship with all the political upheaval, supplies dwindled dramatically. Many barely made a living, scavenging anything they could to survive. Criminal behaviour was rife.

Going was slow. If there were no fresh horses to access at abandoned posadas, their animals required another twenty-four-hour rest. Rosa didn't mind; it was a welcome respite. The coach was roomy, and the remaining four passengers were amiable, but the conversation was stilted. No one seemed inclined to make small talk. Everyone knew Rosa was married to the Governor but had resided in the church cottage, caring for her mother until her death. None of the passengers knew Rosa personally; conversation was awkward under the circumstances.

The coach was bound for Buenos Aires. Rosa would disembark at Lujan before it headed southeast to the Capital. It might mean staying overnight in Lujan waiting for a connecting coach heading north, but Rosa didn't mind, anything to avoid having her presence noted in Buenos Aires. The last thing she wanted to do was risk any contact with Carlos. It was still a long way to go to Pergamino, Rosario and Santa Fe. The fewer people who knew she was in the area, the better. Rosa had chosen to travel as Rosa Caron. No one on the coach had questioned why; some thought it was out of respect for her recently deceased mother.

Two hours north of Rosario, the coach was making good time. If there was a change of horses available at the next stop, with any luck, they should make Santa Fe before nightfall. It had been a long tiring journey; she was exhausted. Santa Fe would be a whole new beginning.

Suddenly the coach swayed violently as several rifle shots rang out. Rosa shook her head in disbelief, being this close to the end of a safe passage, only to be waylaid by bandits. Stealing a glance out the open window, Rosa counted at least a dozen men on horseback surrounding the coach; bandanas covered their features. The driver and his guard immediately dropped their weapons before being instructed to do so. The driver spoke up as the leader of the group approached, waving his pistol at the driver menacingly,

"Senor, I beg you, do not shoot; we carry no bullion or goods of any value. We are a passenger coach, I swear; see for yourself!"

The group leader took his time guiding his horse to the open window. Everyone inside recoiled in fear, unsure if their lives were about to end. He scrutinised the passengers, a middle-aged couple, two gentlemen travelling independently and a young woman.

To her utter shock, the leader pointed the pistol in her direction and, in a gruff voice, said, "You, get out of the coach."

Rosa didn't react… "There must be some mistake", she said loudly, "I have nothing of any value, Senor." Rosa was trying to sound brave but felt anything but that.

"Only yourself, Senora." The leader replied in a soft voice, letting his words sink in.

Rosa felt her heart lurch. This was no band of robbers. They were the rebel fighters the whole country was talking about, and they had got precisely what they came for – her! Someone at the convent in Santa Fe must have discussed her planned return, another listener paying attention to such information and passing it on. Perhaps there was speculation the Governor was also returning, and it was him they were seeking.

"I am of no use to you, Senor," Rosa spoke the words confidently, a tremor in her voice betraying her bravado, her heart

256

beating crazily, wondering if she was facing execution for Carlos's misdeeds. Rosa didn't have long to consider the thought.

The leader leant down, almost wrenching the coach door off its hinges,

"I beg to differ, Senora; get out of the coach now! Unless you would have me shoot the others and drag you off?"

Rosa hurriedly climbed down from the coach, her carry-on baggage already on the ground, quickly dispensed by the driver.

The leader instructed the driver to continue his journey with the added warning, "Should you consider using your weapons in retaliation, the wife of the Governor will be the first victim."

The driver and his sidekick looked at each other, then quickly spurred the horses into a gallop. Rosa looked on in despair as the coach disappeared down the road. The only positive outcome was they wanted her alive. Had they planned to execute her, she would already be dead.

Rosa – Rebel Camp
☼

Unceremoniously, bound and gagged, Rosa was kept that way until well clear of any settlements. She remained blindfolded for the remainder of the journey.

The rebels arrived jubilant at the camp; the kidnapping had been successful, achieved without injury. It was cause for celebration. Vincente was a hero. Rosa learned the leader was away with another raiding party but due to return. He would be the one to decide her fate.

Handed over to a group of women, she was to be strictly supervised. Placed under the watchful eye of a young woman named Carmelita, whose sullen expression indicated her displeasure at being assigned the role.

The camp had three sections—the most extensive, the living quarters with fifty-odd timber shelters covered with animal hides and some basic lodgings, no more than makeshift lean-tos'. A central fireplace was piled waist-high with timber, ready for the approaching night. A short distance away was a timber dwelling, followed by an open compound two hundred feet wide. A few tents were erected close to an enormous fire pit on the far side. Iron pots of varying sizes lay alongside other cooking implements, identifying where the food preparation took place. It was here Carmelita led Rosa.

Carmelita described how the camp functioned. Rosa would help cook the food and later assist in clearing up. Supplying and preparing food for such a large camp would require appreciable organisation.

Rosa noted a trail beyond the main camp converging with the tree line. Informed this led to two secluded areas, one for bathing, and further on one set aside for toileting. A spring-fed lagoon with crystal water served the camp and livestock well. The timber structure to the right of the living quarters had a dual purpose. It held perishable stores, doubling as a meeting place for the men's counsel. Carmelita did not elaborate. Nearby, a fenced enclosure housed two cows and several goats. Countless chickens roamed freely. There were sounds indicating horses were somewhere beyond the forest's edge, no doubt protected from the elements.

Rosa was grateful to be away from the main camp. As she walked through the compound on arrival, those nearby spat on the ground in her direction, indicating their unspoken animosity. She was a political prisoner caught up in local warfare. The knowledge they were holding the wife of their main protagonist fuelled their loathing.

No one spoke to Rosa throughout the remainder of the evening. She was to share a dwelling with Carmelita and one other woman, Stella, the two assigned to take turns watching her. The accommodation looked like an Indian tepee, constructed of long timber poles covered with cowhide. It was surprisingly warm inside. Cowhide also covered the floor. Several bundles of animal hides, possibly fox, were neatly stacked inside the opening flap. Most of the camp dwellers turned in early to avoid the cold. Although the camp was only in the lower reaches of the mountain range, night temperatures regularly dropped below zero.

Rosa closed her eyes, listening to the sounds around her. Somewhere in the forest, a night owl called to its mate. Idly, she wondered what it might be saying; the thought made her smile. It was strange being a captive in a hostile environment, yet unafraid. Anywhere other than where Carlos might appear was perfect. Rosa couldn't remember when she had felt this free. The sound of someone gently strumming a guitar, accompanied by female laughter, carried on the night breeze. Rosa relaxed, breathing in harmony with the music, surrendering her body to sleep.

"It's time to get up!" Carmelita's belligerent voice intoned.

Startled, it took a few minutes for Rosa to get her bearings. Carmelita hovered over her, prodding with her foot, repeating the same command.

"It's time to get up. We start early here, everyone shares the duties, and you are no exception." This was not a request.

The circumstances of her kidnapping, the long journey to the mountain campsite, and sleeping on the ground had all taken their toll; Rosa's body ached. She followed Carmelita to the secluded area where the women bathed and toileted. There appeared to be about eight women like Carmelita and herself on their own. Other women were visible in the central part of the camp, with partners or husbands. There were no children.

The chatter amongst the women was friendly. They had arrived here fleeing difficult circumstances and quickly developed a common bond; an easy camaraderie existed. Their very survival depended on each other. No one spoke to Rosa; she was not one of them. On the contrary, she was the enemy. Rosa wondered how they would react if they knew the reality of her circumstances. Ironically, she was probably more of a victim of Carlos's cruelty than anyone. She had more in common with them than they could ever imagine.

Heading back into camp, Carmelita barked instructions to Rosa, "You will gather firewood and ensure the fire never goes out. You will top up the barrels of drinking water throughout the camp, roll up the bedding each morning, see to the cleaning of pots and other utensils, dispose of the rubbish…"

The litany of orders continued; Rosa mentally switched off, intending to do whatever Carmelita ordered her to do. Regardless, she suspected nothing she did would be to Carmelita's satisfaction; not pleased at being saddled with this hostage also meant sharing her tent with one more person. Previously, she had only been burdened with Stella unless Ernesto visited her.

As the sun crept over the treetops, Rosa had her first real chance to look around. On the far side of the camp, most men huddled around the embers of the previous night's campfire, drinking tea. One of the men threw a sizable log onto the smouldering ashes, sending an explosion of sparks into the gentle morning breeze. Breathing deeply, Rosa recognised the smell of burning alder, not the usual acrid smell of smoke, but sweet-smelling like honey; it reminded her of growing up on the farm and camping out.

There was a buzz of anticipation. Serving the breakfast, Rosa gleaned enough from the conversation to understand the remainder of the camp inhabitants were overdue. The men didn't appear concerned; raids were well-planned and executed precisely.

Back in the cooking area, the sound of men's raised voices reached Rosa before she heard the gallop of horse hoofs entering the compound. About a dozen riders appeared. They dismounted, quickly surrounded by their comrades. A few minutes later, several mules appeared, pulling a loaded wagon. A cheer went up; congratulations on another successful mission. Several men unloaded the wagon and attended to the mules and horses, weary after their journey.

A path in the group opened up, making way for the leader, already informed the kidnapping of the governor's wife had been successful. Rosa stood transfixed, her shocked expression sending alarm bells through Carmelita, who immediately turned her gaze to Miguel, only to see the same expression mirrored on his face. Miguel recognised Rosa instantly; instinctively, he touched his left abdomen. Memories came flooding back, balancing on the ledge behind the bath, bracing a stab wound, watching the blood trickle down his leg into the bathwater of the woman standing before him.

Discovering Carlos had already left the mansion, his focus was to escape when he was distracted by a familiar perfume. He remembered looking at the woman, for a fleeting moment, feeling as though he knew her, then hearing the soldiers shouting as they searched room by room, and his menacing threat to her,

"If you value your life, Senora, do not speak out, I warn you."

Miguel's only intent at the time was to escape Carlos's men. He had given little thought to whom she might be since.

In hindsight, he realised, in his weakened state, this woman could easily have betrayed him to the soldier who broke into the bathroom. Only her protest made the soldier withdraw, allowing Miguel the opportunity to escape. He wondered why he'd never thought about it until now? Recovering his composure, he addressed her briefly,

261

"Senora, consider yourself a guest of this camp until your husband, the Governor, restores order to Argentina. He and his corrupt ruling party must step down. It is unfortunate, but it seems you are the one to pay the consequences for his criminal behaviour."

Unwittingly, Rosa laughed. The thought of Carlos doing anything to preserve her safety was so ludicrous.

Miguel's face turned scarlet; he was livid. Stepping up to within inches of Rosa's face, he spat the words at her,

"Do you think this is funny, Senora? I assure you, there is nothing humorous in your situation. Many in this camp would hang you without a second thought. Your only value to us is as a bargaining tool. Think about that, Senora, if you wish to be amused." Still furious, he turned on his heel, intending to ignore Rosa for the remainder of her imprisonment. She was still alive; whatever debt he owed her for his earlier escape was now paid in full!

Rosa was wretched, realising her inappropriate laughter had created a misunderstanding. She knew beyond doubt Carlos would give up nothing for her. On the contrary, the thought of her death would probably delight him. He would be free to do whatever he liked and have one less burden.

Rosa considered what might happen when her value as a hostage proved to be worthless. She doubted letting her go would be an option.

True Colours

☼

Ernesto had been gone from the camp for two weeks. The mood was sombre; he had been with Pedro almost from the beginning. Whatever he lacked in strategic thinking, he made up for with reliability and determination, and he was a fierce fighter. Losing both men was a tragedy. The only one who failed to miss him was Carmelita, although she did well feigning melancholy in his absence.

Nothing was the same between her and Ernesto following his suspicion she had been with Miguel or lusted after him at the very least. Miguel hadn't given Carmelita a second thought once he walked out; she was trouble. Pedro had been canny enough to send out both men simultaneously on missions, easing Ernesto's doubts about Miguel being back in camp with Carmelita in his absence. Miguel tried several times to bridge the rift with Ernesto, finally giving up, realising Ernesto would never get over his suspicion he and Carmelita had been together.

Since Ernesto threatened her, Carmelita avoided being anywhere near Miguel. Now there was no need for caution; Ernesto was gone. She was also sick of playing the victim. Besides, her desire for Miguel had never lessened. She needed a man, and she wanted him.

Carmelita recalled when the rebels presented Rosa to Miguel for the first time, she was alarmed at their reaction. It was apparent they shared an earlier connection. After witnessing Rosa laugh in Miguel's face and his furious response, any concerns Carmelita had that Rosa might be a potential rival vanished. Angry at being designated to guard her, Carmelita secretly hoped Rosa might try to escape and maybe get taken by a wolf pack or a puma. She didn't care.

Supper finished early; there was an uneasy atmosphere, and the sporadic chatter was tense. Replacement groups of men had been assigned and would leave the next day. Everyone headed to their shelters to spend the last evening with their women folk, unsure when, or if, they would see them again. There was always the chance one or more men might not return. The danger was ever present. The single men huddled in small groups for a final drink before turning in, aware they needed to be up before dawn.

Carmelita chose to guard Rosa most of that day. Stella thought it odd, knowing her initial reluctance at being saddled with the task at all. Settling for the evening, Carmelita casually suggested she might sit by the fire for a while, now leaving Stella on guard. Looking in Stella's direction, Rosa watched as she raised her eyebrows, frowned a little, pursed her lips, and nodded without replying. Carmelita quickly changed her blouse before leaving the tent, choosing a silken garment with a low-cut neckline. Stella shook her head slowly but didn't comment. Rosa tried not to think too hard about what might be happening; too weary of thinking about anything much, she fell asleep almost instantly.

The compound was deserted as Carmelita skirted around the perimeter of tents and lean twos. A few muffled voices broke the silence, the words indistinguishable; someone was laughing, another shedding tears. There was a dim glow coming from the meeting hall. Overhearing Miguel's plans to one of the men earlier in the day, Carmelita knew precisely where he would be this evening. Miguel was taking an inventory of what the returning men needed to acquire through La Cumbrecita. She decided it presented the perfect opportunity to seek out his company away from prying eyes.

Miguel looked up, startled, as Carmelita appeared. Unguarded, his eyes quickly took in her shapely body and full breasts straining against the thin material of her blouse. Carmelita missed nothing, seeing all she needed to know. He still wanted her.

"Miguel, I am sorry if I've disturbed you?" she said innocently.

His voice was emotionless but polite; Miguel asked, "What can I do for you, Carmelita? As you can see, I am busy. Can it not wait

264

until tomorrow?" If he were candid, Miguel wanted to avoid spending any time alone with Carmelita. He didn't trust her but trusted himself even less. It was not easy to forget the touch of her hands on his body bathing him, nor her scent when she bent over him. Back then, he thought of little else except finding the courage to take her to bed.

Carmelita, amused, watched the changing expressions on Miguel's face, knowing he was struggling to maintain his composure. "I know the men are leaving early, and I just wanted to be sure you were aware our supplies of fresh vegetables are critically low?". Carmelita was banking on Miguel having scant knowledge of the quantity remaining, seeing they were stored in the cooking area. She was sure someone would have conveyed something about the dwindling supply, but the question gave her a valid reason to be there.

Still gathering his wits at Carmelita's presence, Miguel was caught off guard by the genuine concern expressed. He wondered if he had misjudged her motives for being there. Miguel stood up from his crouched position, answering politely, "Anita has kept me informed, thank you for your concern, Carmelita."

With three quick steps, she was in front of him, placing her right hand on his abdomen over the healed stab wound. "Does your side still give you trouble, Miguel?"

Her touch was unexpected; Miguel flushed, battling to quell the throbbing in his groin.

The material rough to her touch, Carmelita slid her hand down the front of his trousers. Miguel clamped his hand over her wrist, swiftly pulling her hand away, but not before she felt the stirring of an erection.

"It's fine; thank you, Carmelita, you were an excellent nurse, but I have no further need of your skills."

Carmelita stepped back abruptly as if Miguel had slapped her, his response clear. He had no intention of filling Ernesto's role as her lover. "I will say good night then." Without another word, she turned and left. Carmelita was furious and humiliated. Other men had fought bitterly to share her favours.

Rosa awoke alarmed, a stabbing pain in her back. The tent was in complete darkness. She could hear Carmelita cursing under her breath as she settled into her bedding. If she didn't know better, she might have suspected Carmelita deliberately kicked her in the back as she stepped over her.

Survival

☼

Rosa was desolate; she understood her situation only too clearly. She was expendable. The only solution was to find a way to make herself of value to the camp. Assisting with meal preparation and daily chores would not be enough reason to spare her life.

An opportunity presented itself unexpectedly. Five camp members developed a high fever, their condition slowly deteriorating. Several men in the group reported similar experiences elsewhere. They spoke of many deaths, those who survived remained unwell for months.

Working with the Sisters at the convent hospital, Rosa studied natural remedies, their source primarily of native origin. Thousands of years before the Spanish arrived, the indigenous natives devised medicines for most of their ailments. When the Jesuit Fathers arrived in northwest Argentina, they befriended the native Huarpe and Guarani people, quickly adopting their methods for treating unfamiliar illnesses.

At certain times of the year, migrating birds settled on the swampy areas of the open plains to breed. The nomadic tribes hunted them for their flesh, feathers and eggs. They believed the fever came from the many insects that inhabited the swamp.

Rosa knew of a tree the natives called Quina Quina. They brewed a bitter liquid from the bark, which proved effective for treating fever. Someone had given this *tea* the name *quinine*. Rosa requested a meeting with the camp leader. Miguel had ignored her since their fiery first meeting, even when she was serving him food or in the general vicinity collecting plates and utensils from the eating area.

Carmelita stood alongside Rosa outside the large tent, annoyed at being dragged away from work to guard this stupid woman. Rosa could hear the voices of several men inside, concluding their business. They filed out one by one, not bothering to acknowledge either woman's presence. The insult further annoyed Carmelita. She liked to be noticed!

Miguel invited Rosa to enter, his voice loud, the tone less than friendly. Seated behind a rough table, he studied a pile of drawings, not bothering to look up as she entered.

"What do you want, Senora Mendoza?" he said indifferently.

"Senor, it is not widely known, but I spent a good deal of time working with the Sisters at the Convent de Santo Hospital in Santa Fe. I learned many remedies, and I believe I know how to cure the fever affecting some of your men."

At the mention of the hospital in Santa Fe, Miguel's head shot up. He knew he would have died without the care he received there. Many questions about his stay remained unanswered. Miguel had no intention of discussing them with this woman.

"Speak up, Senora; I am interested in anything that might aid my men. That's not to say I will believe what you say without proof."

Rosa's voice was firm, imploring, her conviction strong. "There is a certain tree well known to the Indians that grows in the lower Andes mountains, Senor Garcia; I have seen them growing here, near the stream. I recognise them from the pictures I studied. You harvest the bark and boil it to extract the juice. I believe it will cure the fever."

At first, Miguel considered it might be some trick in an attempt to escape but decided she sounded sincere; besides, there was nothing to lose in testing the information.

"You will go with two of my men, Senora. When you identify the trees, one will collect whatever you need from them, while the other man ensures you do not disappear into the bush."

Rosa nodded, turning to leave, anxious to get started. She didn't intend to waste time trying to explain escape was the furthest thing from her mind; she would rather be here in the camp than anywhere else. He wouldn't have believed her anyway!

Three Quina-Quina trees, covered in cream and pink blossoms, stood near the far end of the clearing beside the stream. Rosa had no idea about the best time for harvesting the bark. Manolo, one of Miguel's men, cut a swathe around the trunk and a further lower down. Carefully peeling off a large strip of bark, he cut it into smaller pieces and placed them into a pouch.

Rosa returned to camp and began brewing the tea in a large pot. She remembered the nuns adding some wild honey to lessen the bitter taste. There was a buzz around the campsite. Quite an audience gathered to watch the spectacle of Rosa preparing her brew. The dark liquid, strained through some cloth and cooled, was as close as Rosa remembered it, only ever seeing it prepared once.

Standing up from the fireplace with a jug of the liquid, Rosa found Miguel front and centre of the crowd, curiosity on his face. He held out a drinking vessel. Without a word, Rosa poured enough liquid to fill about one-third of the mug.

"Senora Mendoza, I think you should be the first to do the honours," Miguel took the jug from Rosa's hand, swapping it for the mug of liquid. He was taking no chances. If this were poison, she would be the first to die.

Even with the honey added, it was ghastly, so bitter that her mouth felt dry immediately after swallowing it. She did her best not to gag. Miguel looked at her quizzically, and Rosa responded.

"I never promised it would be pleasant, Senor, only that I believed it would cure the fever."

Satisfied there was no trick to Rosa's brew, Miguel quickly had a portion dispensed to each of the afflicted men, commencing with the most seriously ill, Julio. There were now seven men affected. Rosa also suggested their bodies be sponged frequently with warm water and lay where there was a breeze. Rosa volunteered to assist. Miguel nodded his head and departed. Everyone else went about their business. There was much speculation about the 'Governor's woman' having such knowledge. Some were sceptical, believing it was a ploy to gain favour.

For the majority, their fever broke within twenty-four hours; Julio was the only one slow to recover. He had been at death's door. The remainder improved at a rapid rate. By the third day, they were over the worst of it. Rosa encouraged them to drink plenty of water, replacing that lost with the fever. She also added, with some amusement,

"Make sure you drink plenty of lime with your Tequila!"

Although it was not recommended they drink alcohol in their condition, she knew how they would celebrate; the lime would aid their recovery. Rosa also stressed the need for rest. Experience taught her fatigue was the usual legacy of the illness.

There was a subtle change of mood around the camp following the recovery of their comrades. Rosa was happy at no longer being treated like a leper; a few even smiled at her. A few days later, Rosa sitting on her haunches, stirring a cauldron of stew, watched Miguel saunter across the compound headed in her direction. He was a fine-looking man. She remembered admiring his physique when helping dress his putrid wounds. She also remembered constantly praying to the Holy Mother to bless and keep him alive. How ironic her life was now in his hands.

"Senora," Rosa jumped, startled to find Miguel standing beside her. "It seems the camp owes you a debt of gratitude. All of my people are either fully recovered or well on the way. It's a powerful thing to possess such valuable knowledge. The Sisters taught you well."

Miguel started to walk away and then paused. Turning slowly, he looked closely at Rosa before speaking. "Four years ago, I was a patient in Santo Domingo Hospital for an extended period. Might you have been there then, Senora?"

Rosa looked at Miguel, his face expressionless, his startling blue eyes studying her.

"I, too, was a patient there, Senor Garcia, following which I continued helping the Sisters who were always short-handed." Rosa felt the sting of tears, recalling the terrible sadness associated with her miscarriage.

Miguel frowned; the face of the woman before him filled with unimaginable pain. He felt empathy for her; perhaps she had suffered as much as he, although he couldn't imagine how – she was the governor's wife. Miguel couldn't help but remark,

"I'm surprised Governor Mendoza allowed you to soil your hands, Senora?"

A look of absolute loathing passed across Rosa's face at the mention of the governor. Miguel was taken aback. Rosa didn't answer. Instead, she turned swiftly on her heel, disappearing into her tent, pulling the flap closed behind her.

Miguel was trying to fathom what had just happened; he'd only spoken a few words. Somehow, regretfully, he had unintentionally wounded this complicated woman.

Disaster Strikes
☼

It would be a welcome return to camp for the men, away many weeks; they were exhausted. In their absence, so much had changed. Pedro was dead, and Ernesto, one of their foremost team leaders, had fled under tragic circumstances. Miguel was now in charge of the camp. During their duty of service, they had lost five courageous men. Their homecoming would not be without sadness. Fighting in the area had escalated dramatically over the last two months. While the rebels were rewarded with increasing victories, such success had come at a high price.

Thomas sent a runner back to the camp to inform Miguel of their location and departure time. They would meet at La Cumbrecita with the men replacing them. Thomas's men would rest briefly, exchange relevant information, and load needed supplies before heading north to the rebel camp near Cosquin, some forty miles away, under cover of darkness.

La Cumbrecita was considered a sanctuary. The whole town supported the rebels in their efforts to unseat the Government. Carlos's thugs had raided the surrounding villages many times, robbing them of liquor from the Cantina, any valuables they could steal, or sometimes harassing the local women, or all three. The townspeople hated them with a vengeance.

It was a small town, and nothing went unnoticed. Any stranger was closely scrutinised. If suspected of being a government agent, quickly and silently dispensed with.

Carlos realised if he had any chance of gaining control, he needed to release most of his troupes from the Capital. He would disperse them over several central locations near Mendoza, Cordoba, and San Luis, where most of the rebel reprisals against his men took place; this would allow them to regroup faster and replace men lost in battle. There must be a concerted effort to locate and destroy the rebel headquarters. There was a lot of territory to cover.

Carlos had suspected for some time La Cumbrecita played a significant role in either supporting the rebels or, at the very least, turning a blind eye to their activities and providing cover for them. He planned to stake out the area, dispatching a contingent of men based in Cordoba.

Thomas was completely relaxed. Like his men, he was excited to be heading home. They were only a few miles southwest of La Cumbrecita. Four groups had joined together; there were still three more to come. So far, their trip had been without incident. Thomas usually sent a scout ahead to assess any risk and signal the all-clear. A single rider would not attract undue attention if anyone were on the lookout.

They were so close to town; he didn't bother this time, sure had there been any sign of possible trouble or increased activity in the surrounding area, he would have received word from his many informants in town. Soldiers and other thugs working for the Government made their presence known long before they appeared in the next village, leaving a trail of destruction or despair in their wake. Such news always travelled fast.

A dozen men entered the outskirts of town, talking cheerfully about their great thirst,

"I'll race anyone of you to the bottom of a barrel," Paco boasted.

Everyone laughed; they were all looking forward to their first cold beer. Thomas, about to respond, stopped mid-sentence, suddenly aware they were on the edge of town, but there was not a single thing moving. His instinct for danger came too late; the first shot rang out, taking the life of the man beside him.

All hell broke loose as fifteen riders firing their pistols at his men came charging towards them with sabres drawn. Thomas's men responded instinctively; these seasoned fighting men knew their lives depended on it.

They were in close quarters, man and beast, fighting hand to hand; Thomas engaged the soldier leading the charge, taking him out, but not before the sabre he was wielding sliced through Thomas's side.

The fighting was fierce, and the outcome hung in the balance until the remaining rebel troupes hearing rifle shots ahead, raced to their aid. It was a bloody scene. When it ended, three more of Thomas's men lay dead. He was bleeding badly.

The fighting had barely ceased when townspeople started appearing. Unable to warn of the soldier's presence beforehand, they descended on the battle scene to help dispose of bodies and restore the area to disguise any sign of activity. One of the locals, aware the soldiers had set a trap, rode north to warn the rebels heading to town to be alert to the possibility of an attack.

Sergio, leading the relief team, arrived in town. He was dismayed to see the number of friends and colleagues killed. Sergio decided to abandon their planned operation. They would all return to camp and regroup as quickly as possible.

The townspeople would dispose of the soldier's horses by taking them several miles away and setting them free. They would likely join the wild horses roaming the plains. It was a pity; they were fine animals, but anyone caught with a horse bearing the brand of the Cavalry meant instant death, no questions asked.

Sergio's men collected the two wagons loaded with supplies for the camp as they passed through town. The now unconscious Thomas was on a third wagon with the remaining wounded. Desperate to return to the rebel camp as quickly as possible, they abandoned their usual practice of laying a false trail. There was no time for such caution today. Thomas's life hung in the balance.

A Time to Live or a Time to Die

☼

Well into the night, Miguel heard the distant rifle shot ring out. He and the rest of the men were on their feet immediately, grabbing their weapons while the women went to seek shelter. A sentry would only fire a shot to warn of danger or other serious situations.

The men sent out early that morning were the first to arrive back. The camp gathered around to hear the dire news of the ambush, reporting that at least seven of their men were dead. The women looked on anxiously, wondering if their man might be amongst the fallen. There was no time to grieve the loss.

Miguel sprang into action; casualties were coming, some with severe wounds. Several men stoked up the fires and gathered more wood while the women started boiling cauldrons of water to sterilize their makeshift surgical tools. Other women gathered clean cloth to use as dressings or to tear into strips to fashion bandages.

The largest tent was Carmelita's; quickly cleared of bedding, it was turned into a makeshift operating theatre and lit with as many lamps as possible. Alongside would be a smaller tent to treat minor casualties. Arturo, the blacksmith, gathered up all his medicants and utensils in readiness.

Rosa appeared at Miguel's side, her face anxious, "What can I do to help?"

Miguel wasn't sure what to expect, although quietly, so as not to alarm the others; Guido, one of his men, spoke to him earlier, saying Thomas was severely wounded and not likely to survive.

"Thank you, Senora. For the present, can you assist Arturo until we see what is needed?"

Rosa immediately set about steeping a cloth in boiling water, laying it on a waist-high bench. Arturo watched as she placed the

275

makeshift instruments, freshly sterilized, in a systematic order onto the cloth. It was apparent she knew what she was doing.

When the others arrived at the camp, they were ready for them. Everyone assumed their assigned roles, some assisting the injured, others taking care of the horses or unloading the wagons. The greatest concern for everyone was Thomas. They carried his inert body as gently as possible, placing it on the makeshift operating table while Arturo and Miguel began assessing his wounds.

Miguel directed everyone to leave the tent except those assisting or fetching supplies. Arturo gasped when they exposed Thomas's flesh. Unconscious, he was oblivious to the deep gash running diagonally from just above his right groin to the middle of his chest. It was a miracle no major artery or vein was severed. Regardless, his blood loss was still extreme.

Arturo had never dealt with any wound of this magnitude. He looked at Miguel helplessly, "Miguel, I can only do my best, but this is a wound requiring the skills of a doctor, not a blacksmith." He said despairingly.

Rosa spoke up, "I am not a doctor, but I spent many hours in surgery assisting Dr Perez with such wounds. Would you trust me to try?"

Miguel looked at Arturo and saw the relief on his face, understanding how hard it must be to help someone severely injured, knowing it was a friend whose life now depended on your skill to save them.

Miguel nodded to Rosa, who had already tied her hair back, donned a clean apron, and was now scrubbing her hands in sterilized water. Arturo stood at her side, ready to assist, taking in every step of the procedure, amazed at her ability with the makeshift instruments. He must talk to her later and ask how he could improve them. He had fashioned them from any piece of scrap metal he could find. They were primitive.

The first thing Rosa did was cauterize the damaged blood vessels, which were still oozing. His men had done their best to stem the bleeding, but by his pallor, it was apparent Thomas had lost a great deal of blood.

Two hours had passed, and Rosa began to feel light-headed. Lost in concentration, she was unaware of anyone else but Arturo. People came and went, soundlessly removing soiled material, bringing fresh supplies, and replenishing the boiled water. Finally, the surgery was complete. Rosa could relax.

Swaying a little as she stepped back from the table, Rosa felt Miguel's strong arms grip her waist to steady her. "Thank you; I am more tired than I expected."

Miguel nodded, his emotions raw, finding it difficult to form words. Whether Thomas survived or not, Miguel believed he had just witnessed a miracle. The irony of his captive saving the life of his most crucial team leader did not escape him.

Rosa washed her hands as the others tidied up around her. Before she turned to go, surprising everyone, she stood over Thomas's still form, making the sign of the cross, and praying,

"Holy Father, I ask your blessing for this man, Thomas, a servant of the Lord, prepared to lay down his life for his country. I pray you Grace him with your love and spare his life; amen."

When Rosa looked up, Miguel's eyes filled with tears of gratitude. Everyone made the sign of the cross. Rosa became aware of Carmelita's raised voice outside the tent; she and Stella had been helping Arturo.

"He lives," she shouted.

The two words brought a crescendo of cries. When Rosa stepped outside the tent, she was astounded to see the whole camp celebrating around a blazing fire. Despite being close to midnight, every camp member had kept a vigil, praying for Thomas.

Once hostile faces now looked at Rosa through new eyes. Some faces were teary others just nodded their thanks. There was no need for words.

Rosa suddenly realized she didn't have a tent to go to and desperately needed to lay down. Miguel took her by the elbow and guided her towards his tent without a word.

"I cannot thank you enough, Senora, get some well-earned rest; I will bunk in with the men later. First, I will sit with Thomas for a while."

Rosa nodded, too exhausted to make small talk, "Call me if I am needed." She collapsed onto the bed and was almost asleep before her head hit the pillow.

The sun was well up when Rosa opened her eyes; laying there, she wondered if Thomas made it through the night. She tried to recall the order of events from last night. It was as though her hands were guided by divine power. Rosa doubted her skills were as advanced as demonstrated while attending Thomas. Wherever it came from, she was eternally grateful.

Carmelita had obviously been instructed not to wake her. Rosa smiled to herself. She almost missed the usual surly greeting. Rubbing the sleep from her eyes, she decided it was time to get up.

A New Dawn

☼

Rosa walked out into blazing sunshine. The camp was surprisingly quiet. Usually, the majority were up by daybreak, although it had been a very late night for most, anxious to see if Thomas would survive. Thomas! Rosa headed across the compound to Carmelita's tent, unsure where she and Stella had spent the night.

Hesitating before stepping inside the tent, Rosa prayed she would not find Thomas had died. The first thing she saw was Miguel huddled on the ground, wrapped in deer skins. He had kept a bedside vigil overnight in case Thomas awakened. Not wanting to disturb him, she stood there quietly, observing Thomas. His breathing was shallow but steady. So far, so good. He was an awful colour, which was not surprising. His blood loss was not the only challenge to overcome; there was always the risk of infection. Rosa tried everything possible during the surgery to maintain a sterile environment, using alcohol, the only thing available. She would have to depend on Arturo's supply of yarrow and sulphur poultices to do the rest and, of course, Thomas's will to survive.

Rosa turned her attention back to Miguel. He stirred, stretching his body full length. Once more, Rosa had to admit Miguel was a handsome man. Opening his eyes, he was suddenly embarrassed seeing Rosa standing there. She smiled; she thought he looked fetching, his shyness not something she had seen before.

Quickly standing, Miguel ran his fingers through his wavy locks, at the moment, a tangled mess. Rosa's scrutiny made him feel uncomfortable. He quickly changed the focus of their encounter back to Thomas.

"How is he doing, Senora? Will he live?"

Rosa really couldn't say. That Thomas was still alive was a good sign. By all accounts, he should have already been dead.

"He is a fighter Senor Garcia, or he would not be still with us; God is merciful."

Not for the first time, Miguel wondered how this woman came to be with Carlos Mendoza.

Carmelita came sweeping into the tent, none too pleased at finding Rosa in conversation with Miguel. She interrupted them tersely, "There is food available in the main camp. The women have been preparing it since early morning," she shot an indignant look in Rosa's direction.

Rosa smiled at Carmelita, ignoring the intended sarcasm, "Thank you, Carmelita."

Carmelita chose not to look at either of them, turned on her heel and left.

Rosa smiled at Miguel, raising her eyebrows as she shrugged her shoulders as if to say, 'we better go then'. Quickly following Carmelita's lead, she headed across the compound to the area set aside for meals. She failed to see the broad smile spread across Miguel's face.

Gradually Thomas's condition improved. By the end of the first week, it was safe to consider he would live. He was now taking regular sips of water and a little thin broth with assistance. That effort was enough to drain whatever energy he could muster for the time being.

Miguel was overjoyed. Losing Thomas shortly after Pedro's death would have been devastating. In quiet reflection, he acknowledged it was all thanks to Rosa's skill.

Initially, Miguel feared reprisals for the missing troops, expecting it would come sooner rather than later. He didn't know Carlos was dealing with widespread rioting and vigilante attacks by disgruntled citizens. For the time being, a dozen or so missing soldiers were the least of the Governor's worries.

The shift in the atmosphere throughout the camp towards Rosa was noticeable, almost a complete turnaround. Her presence once ignored, now Rosa was invited to join in conversations, even receiving friendly nods from those who wouldn't have opposed her execution not so long ago. Rosa could only hope the events of the last couple of weeks would be enough to secure her freedom.

A Change of Heart

☼

Just before dawn, all was still. Soon the cook's camp would be abuzz with activity. Rosa lay quietly, enjoying the tranquillity. She became aware of Stella's breathing; there was a distinct wheeze she'd never noticed.

Carmelita headed out of the tent as soon as she awoke, not bothering to greet either woman. Raising her eyebrows, Stella shrugged, and Rosa smiled in acknowledgement. Carmelita struggled to be civil these days. It was evident she resented Rosa bitterly. Stella suspected it had more to do with Miguel than her.

Miguel's visits to the cook's camp increased in frequency. Usually, there was a valid reason, checking on supplies or shortages of fresh produce or the need for minor repairs to any dwellings.

Carmelita was no fool; she didn't buy it for a minute; he was there hoping to bump into Rosa, who continued to do her chores, seemingly oblivious to Miguel's presence. At times he looked flustered. With tasks sorted, he would depart in haste, not having any valid reason to delay his departure.

Stella was amused at Carmelita's reaction but curious about Rosa's lack of insight. The two women were clearing up after breakfast when Stella made a statement to Rosa, "You do realise Miguel visits the cooking camp area to see you don't you?"

Rosa hadn't given his visits much thought; she was shocked at Stella's suggestion as Stella's grin grew into a smile.

Finished with their chores, the two sat for a cup of tea. Rosa looked down at Stella's ankles, frowning; they were swollen.

"Are you having trouble breathing, Stella?"

282

Surprised by the question, she nodded, "Yes. I don't know why." Stella was a large lady, around fifty-five.

Rosa was concerned, "I think there is a problem affecting your heart, Stella, it can be dangerous, but I think I can help; let me speak to Miguel first."

Rosa approached Miguel's tent feeling self-conscious after her earlier conversation with Stella. Miguel's face lit up, surprised by Rosa's unexpected visit. Rosa's heart jumped a little.

"Senor Garcia, may I speak with you, please? I am concerned about Stella."

Miguel motioned for Rosa to sit down, "Please call me Miguel. How can I help you?"

Rosa looked into Miguel's eyes, forgetting for a second why she came, suddenly flustered. "I'm sorry to bother you; I think Stella needs medicine to draw fluid away from her heart and lungs. I know of plants in the field that can help with this problem. May I have your permission to go and gather them?"

Miguel looked hard at Rosa before speaking, knowing it was not a ploy to escape. He'd come to realise Rosa saw the camp as home. He nodded, "Take someone with you to help; choose whomever you like."

Rosa smiled at this declaration of trust. "Thank you, Miguel." She blushed, calling him by name for the first time. "I have one other suggestion; if I may, I can show others what medicinal plants grow in the area, how to prepare them, and what ailments they'll treat."

Miguel smiled, "Sharing your knowledge will be invaluable; thank you, Rosa, it's appreciated."

Excusing herself, Rosa was anxious to help ease Stella's discomfort. She was elated to find an Acacia Caven tree called *Churqui* by the Indians, easily identified by its nasty thorns and distinct yellow flowers. Each part of the plant was beneficial for different ailments. The leaves, brewed as tea, acted as a diuretic, able to draw fluid from the body. Apart from the inconvenience of Stella having to frequent the toilet more often, there were no adverse side effects. The result was rapid, Stella was breathing freely, and her swollen ankles were gone. She was full of gratitude. Word circulated in the camp. People began approaching Rosa, requesting they join in learning about the medicinal plants. The greater the camaraderie between Rosa and those in the camp, the moodier Carmelita became.

A few days later, one of the men gathering logs fell, breaking his arm. It was a nasty fracture. Arturo immediately sought Rosa's help to address the injury.

She was becoming invaluable to the camp.

Wearing The Crown
☼

At times the burden of leadership weighed heavily on Miguel. He had the respect of his men despite his youth, but in his heart, he knew he could never measure up to Pedro. He missed his friend and mentor terribly. Miguel sighed, stirring the ashes with a stick; he threw another log on the fire. He was the last to turn in for the night.

At times like this, alone, he couldn't help but recall his happy childhood, he and Theresa running around the ranch. How simple life was back then. They loved sitting huddled together around an open fireplace, logs crackling, listening enthralled as their father talked about the 'good old days' when he, not much more than a boy, went hunting wolves on the prairie with his father. Their mother sat nearby, smiling contentedly, fashioning some garment, eventually ushering them off to bed after making them hot chocolate, finally tucking them in with hugs and kisses. He missed them all more than words could say.

"Am I intruding?"

Miguel was startled by Rosa's unexpected appearance, suddenly uncomfortable in her presence. He shrugged, feigning indifference. "No, Senora Mendoza, not at all; I was just reminiscing about another time and place before all this madness began." Realising the source of all the 'madness' was this woman's husband. Miguel stopped short of elaborating, falling silent.

Rosa sat down a short distance away. Without looking at Miguel, and in a voice just above a whisper, her voice shaky as she spoke, "Senor Garcia…Miguel, may I ask a favour? Call me Rosa or anything else, but please don't call me Senora Mendoza again."

Miguel lifted his head so they were at eye level. He studied Rosa's face and saw the pain in her eyes. The question on his mind for some time was now on his lips, then spoken aloud before he could halt it. "Why did you ever marry a monster like Carlos Mendoza?"

Rosa struggled to find words in reply. There were so many terrible memories from that time. Starting with the circumstances of her father's death and the fear her family would be destitute. She was gullible to Carlos's lies and unprepared for the utter degradation of her wedding night. How could she make anyone understand when she barely understood herself?

Miguel sat watching Rosa's changing expressions. He saw the unspoken suffering, guessing she had paid a high price to become the First Lady. Now remorseful and embarrassed by Rosa's discomfort, he apologised. "I am sorry, Senora, it is none of my business."

Rosa closed her eyes. She was back in Our Lady of The Rosary church with Maria when the shouting started. Speaking softly, almost to herself, "We were so young and innocent, we knew nothing about the evil that could exist inside someone." Once she started, Rosa couldn't stop. The words spilt out, each filled with a lifetime of pain and regret.

"I was a simple country girl, my brother, sister and I, raised on a farm with two loving parents. We knew nothing about the likes of Carlos. When my father died suddenly, my mother collapsed, unable to cope. My older brother disappeared to the city, and my younger sister depended on me to look after her. Our wonderful priest and friend, Fr Peter, supported us, but I was afraid for our future. Carlos swept in, offering to take care of my family…if I married him. He was Fr Peter's brother; I had no reason to believe he was anything other than a decent man."

Miguel listened, appalled and mortally ashamed of how harshly he'd judged her.

Tears spilt down Rosa's cheeks, "If only my father Paulo had not died. Worse still is knowing it was most likely Carlos who ordered the beating that ultimately killed him."

Rosa's words exploded in Miguel's head. "Rosa, where was this? Where do you come from?"

Without looking up, Rosa responded, still lost in painful memories. "Santa Rosa in the pampa of southern Argentina."

Miguel was dumb-struck. He didn't know what to say, fearful of the answer to his next question. "Rosa, was your brother's name Delgado Caron?"

Rosa lifted her face, her expression shocked. "How could you know that? Where did you hear that name?" Rosa was desperate to know more.

Miguel put his head in his hands. Surely this couldn't be possible! The woman sitting in front of him, whom he took hostage, was the sister of the man who saved his life. If it weren't for Delgado Caron, he would not be sitting here now.

"I don't know what to say, Rosa; I am so sorry. Your brother saved my life and, in doing so, forfeited his own."

Miguel's words were like a knife slicing through Rosa's heart. Since arriving in the camp, she had quickly found peace, feeling as though she belonged, and even disregarded the potential danger of soldiers attacking their base at any time. With Miguel's few words, her happiness disintegrated once more. Rosa stood, shaking uncontrollably, sobbing.

Instinctively Miguel stepped forward to comfort her, wrapping his arms around her; he held her close, afraid she might fall. Rosa's breaking heart was the only sound disturbing the night.

The two stood locked in grief—Miguel, grateful and despairing of the life lost. Rosa was desolate at the thought of never seeing Delgado again.

No longer enemies, the pair were joined irrevocably by a quirk of fate.

Bridging The Gap

☼

Awakened by a commotion outside, Rosa wondered what was happening. The chickens were under siege by the rooster. It was easy to shut her eyes and imagine she was back on the farm in Santa Rosa, the untold promise of the day ahead. She recalled playing in the swirling mist each morning, marvelling at the glistening spider webs clinging to the trees like lace doilies.

"You're late; get up!" Carmelita's belligerent voice broke the spell.

Rosa sighed, quickly rising to help the other women prepare breakfast. Those present greeted Rosa with a smile. Others were yet to attend, but Carmelita ignored their absence, taking every opportunity to harass her instead. Rosa chose to ignore the barbs, doing her best to keep out of Carmelita's way.

Since the late-night encounter with Miguel, there was a distinct change in his behaviour. Whenever they were near, he would nod and smile. Carmelita was the first to notice the difference.

During the day, no real interaction occurred between the men and the women, each concentrating on their assigned roles. Only in the evening, when gathered around the campfire, did any actual socialising occur.

Sitting on the opposite side of the compound, Rosa was deep in conversation with Stella. She had become good friends with the older woman. From the outset, Stella judged Rosa to be somehow just unlucky enough to have been caught up with the likes of Carlos Mendoza.

Carmelita stationed herself close to the men. She always preferred male company, never having enjoyed the small talk of women. Men were much more fascinating, and Carmelita liked the attention. She understood men, learning long ago that getting what you wanted from a man was an art she prided herself on possessing - until she met Miguel. Carmelita sat brooding, eyeing Rosa with disdain. It had been a while since Ernesto fled the camp. Until recently, no one paid her attention, but of late, a few of the single men had made it clear her company would be welcome. Carmelita smiled graciously, flattered, hoping it might make Miguel sit up and take notice. Instead, he just appeared oblivious.

Someone started strumming a guitar; the gentle strains drifted across the camp, soothing strained nerves. Most stopped talking to listen. One of the men began singing, his deep voice hauntingly beautiful. Rosa sat entranced, listening to the words, admiring the performance of both men,

"Run, Gypsy, run, flee as fast as you can,
your lover pursues you; feel the warmth of his hand.
The taste of your lips is like honey and wine,
tarry no longer, or you will be mine."

While most eyes focused on the performers, Carmelita sat studying Miguel. His eyes never left Rosa unless she happened to look in his direction; only then did he look away. Carmelita was mortified. She had been reading men's body language as far back as she could remember.

Miguel was no longer looking at Rosa like a hostage, but like a victim he wanted to protect. Carmelita knew with absolute certainty while Rosa remained in the camp, her chances of becoming Miguel's lover were futile.

Stella and Rosa stopped talking abruptly, surprised at seeing Carmelita storm off across the compound. Rosa sighed; whatever had upset Carmelita, Rosa was sure she would be in line for more of her vitriol.

Rosa Tricked by Carmelita

☼

From the beginning, Carmelita made it clear she only tolerated Rosa's presence on the orders of the camp commander. Since saving Thomas's life, Rosa attained a kind of hero status. Keeping her under surveillance was no longer deemed necessary. Over eight weeks, Rosa had gone from a captive to being accepted by the entire camp. Carmelita was furious.

Bitterly jealous, she took every opportunity to be near Miguel. He never openly rejected her presence, was polite in conversation and grateful for any assistance she offered...but he avoided any personal contact. Carmelita refused to accept he wasn't interested in her; convinced instead, it was the bitch Rosa getting in the way

While he rarely spoke to Rosa, his body language betrayed him, studying her when she was unaware of his scrutiny. Each day Carmelita felt her hold on Miguel slipping away. The relationship she imagined with him was now a distant hope while Rosa remained. She had to go!

Rosa could smell liquorice before she saw it – salvia! Unusual finding this plant growing in such a cool climate. She was delighted, picking a posy to return to camp and entwining a sprig in her hair. The scent evoked so many memories, her father, the baby she lost... Miguel.

Heading back from the lagoon, Rosa was still deep in thought as she passed Miguel's tent, suddenly hearing her name called,

"Rosa, might I speak with you for a moment?" Miguel retreated. He had his back to her as she followed him into his tent.

"How may I help Miguel? Is there a problem?"

In the confined space, the heady perfume of the herb was pervasive. Miguel froze, turning slowly to stare at Rosa, first seeing the blossom in her hair and then the posy she was holding. He was back in Santo Domingo Hospital, drifting in and out of consciousness. The one thing he remembered through the blur of pain was that perfume.

Miguel struggled to find the words, "You once said you were a patient at Santa Fe hospital and assisted the nuns. Were you ever among those looking after me?"

Rosa hesitated before answering, considering whether to lie. She wasn't sure she was ready to bring up such painful memories... finally deciding it was just easier, to be honest. "I was; I helped dress your wounds often, but mostly I sat by your bed willing you to live, praying for God to spare you."

Miguel was shocked, "I was unknown to you; why?"

Rosa lowered her head, ashamed. "I willed my unborn child to die; somehow, in my mind, I felt praying for God to spare you might help negate my sin."

Miguel was speechless. When he found his voice, his response was as much a question as a statement. "It was you who left the purple flowers?"

Miguel intended to discuss the possibility of Rosa leaving the camp forgotten for the present; both stood looking at each other, not knowing what to say next.

Emilio burst into the tent, unaware of Rosa's presence, feeling awkward, finding them both looking somewhat stunned.

Rosa was the first to recover her wits, "I'll leave you gentlemen to discuss business; we can talk later, Miguel."

Miguel nodded, still too dumbfounded by the revelation Rosa was involved in the care that saved his life.

The discussion Miguel had with Rosa days earlier weighed heavily on his mind, along with the realisation holding Rosa as a means of bringing the Governor to heel was futile. He finally grasped she was a victim just like them. Miguel called for a council among the group leaders. He proposed they release Rosa. Most could see what he was saying made sense, except two men bitterly opposed the idea. Felix and Omar never wavered in their quest for revenge. Someone had to pay for the deeds of Carlos Mendoza. Who better than his wife? They rejected the idea of releasing her, believing she would betray them and lead troops back to their lair. Angrily, they suggested executing her would be the wisest course of action. The idea caused an uproar amongst the other leaders, especially Miguel.

"Would you have us stoop to the same level of depravity as the people we are trying to remove from power? If we become animals like them, what have we achieved? We will not do as you suggest." The other leaders agreed. The meeting was finally over, and the group dispersed. Council decisions were kept private, but angry voices had carried; there was much speculation throughout the campsite.

Felix and Omar's lust for revenge would not be appeased. They were angry at the denial of their request. The reaction of the council members towards them also caused great offence. Some showed open disgust at the suggestion of an execution, deliberately avoiding the company of the two men. As word of the meeting's outcome filtered out to the general members of the camp, they too distanced themselves from the pair, especially those who had experienced Rosa's kindness. The majority sprang to her defence, choosing to side against two of their own.

The whole situation was galling to Felix and Omar, who were furious over the camp supporting Rosa. They decided, given half a chance, they would take matters into their own hands, no longer abiding by the decisions made by the command and at odds with the entire encampment. They retired to their tent, consoling themselves by drinking copious amounts of alcohol, critical of the fools taken in by the Governor's whore.

Carmelita smiled to herself; maybe there was an easy answer to her dilemma. Using her feminine wiles to get her way with men was nothing new. Being raised in a brothel, Carmelita witnessed how easily women could manipulate men to do anything they wanted, promising to reward them with favours. Her mother, Inez, was the daughter of a housekeeper working for a wealthy rancher in Santa Fe.

The Lopez family had a good life until the rancher impregnated Inez when she was barely sixteen. Despite her pleas of innocence, her parents, more concerned about the prospect of jeopardising their employment, abandoned Inez.

Desperate, Inez had little alternative but to survive by any means available. The local brothel owner agreed to take her in, allowing her to keep her child in exchange for joining the other working girls in trading their favours. Carmelita grew up admiring and hating her mother at the same time. She admired her for keeping her baby girl. Still, she hated her for raising Carmelita amongst the seedy dregs of society, one of her mother's sleazy boyfriends destroying her innocence when she was nine.

Carmelita escaped when she was eighteen, becoming the mistress of a wealthy grazier—kept in relevant comfort for several years until the grazier and his entire family were murdered, along with anyone close to him who might have some claim to his estate. In fear for her life, Carmelita fled, joining others seeking safety, their eventual destination, the mountain sanctuary of the rebels.

Men were such fools. Felix and Omar were no different. Carmelita was sure she could convince them Rosa would compromise their safety by betraying them if set free. She would find a way to help them achieve their goal.

Day of Reckoning
☼

Just before daylight, Carmelita returned to her tent without drawing undue attention. She was carrying a basket of wet clothes. After hanging them out to dry, Carmelita joined the others in preparing breakfast, casually chatting about plans for the day ahead. No one inquired where Rosa was, and she certainly had no intention of drawing attention to her absence.

There were now around seventy men and women in the camp; the remaining farm workers were in groups of three or four, dispersed among a dozen ranches in the central Pampas region, all within a few miles of each other.

Miguel was on one of his infrequent goodwill visits; it allowed him to thank the property owners in person for their participation. There was a need to gauge if they remained committed to helping the rebels, and it also presented a perfect opportunity to identify any problems that might have arisen. There was no direct link with the rebel camp like the properties enjoyed, so the three team leaders in charge of the men carried a lot of responsibility. Satisfied all was well, Miguel headed home, intending to spend his first night well north of San Luis, his second night short of Cordoba, and return to camp the following evening.

Immediately Miguel entered the camp; he knew something was wrong. The air was thick with tension. Vincente quickly approached him as he dismounted, speaking in a subdued voice, anxious, offering no formal greeting.

"The group leaders are in the meeting-house; we need to talk urgently; let one of the men tend to your horse." Without another word, they headed towards the building.

Miguel had a sense of foreboding, "What's happened? What has you so alarmed?"

Vincente wasn't sure where to begin. He started nervously, "We knew you were due to return soon. I didn't wish to commit our men to a potentially dangerous search without your direction." Vincente shifted uncomfortably before continuing awkwardly, "Felix and Omar fled the camp sometime before daylight yesterday morning."

Miguel was puzzled why they looked so distressed by this. Lately, Felix and Omar had been at odds with their comrades, drinking more heavily than usual and argumentative, they were good fighting men, but their leaving was no great drama. No one spoke, and the silence lengthened. The room had an icy chill. Miguel's heart began to race. He didn't want to ask the question, already knowing the answer. "Did they take anyone with them?"

Vincente was pale and shaken, nodding his head slowly, replying with one word, "Rosa."

Miguel felt ill; both Felix and Omar had wanted her executed. She might be dead already. "Vincente, I leave you in charge; carry on with the plans we decided. I must go; I have no idea for how long."

Vincente knew where he was going, "Do you wish to take some men with you, Miguel?"

"No, I will travel light. One rider will not attract attention. Have two horses and saddle bags ready in the next half hour. I wish to speak with Carmelita before I go. They shared a tent; she may have seen or heard something."

Miguel charged out of the shack, striding across the compound towards the cook's camp, thunder on his face. "Where is Carmelita? I wish to speak with her."

Stella spoke up, visibly upset, "She is at the creek, Miguel. Is this about Rosa?"

In a harsh voice, Miguel asked abruptly, "What do you know?"

"No one realised Rosa was missing until she failed to appear at breakfast. Carmelita had been to do some washing, helping with breakfast when she returned. It was only then someone inquired about Rosa. Since she was no longer under guard, there was no need to keep track of her whereabouts. We are sorry, Miguel; she had become one of us." Stella began to cry.

Miguel tried to stay calm and comfort Stella. "It is no one's fault, Stella; I don't hold anyone responsible. When was the last time anyone saw Felix and Omar? Does anyone have any idea which direction they might have taken?"

Everyone shook their heads. There were no obvious leads to follow.

Miguel headed for the creek to speak with Carmelita. Crossing the compound, he saw the horses he requested ready and waiting. Hurrying, he made his way through the bush track to the stream.

Carmelita was daydreaming as she dawdled back from the bathing area. Miguel's sudden appearance startled her. With her guard down, her face contorted with fear. Miguel covered the space between them, grabbing Carmelita roughly by the wrist.

"Your face tells me everything I needed to know. Where have they taken her?" Miguel screamed at Carmelita.

Carmelita cowered, afraid Miguel would strike her, realising he wasn't about to believe her innocence. Instead, she decided to lie, hoping Miguel might show some compassion. Crying uncontrollably, Carmelita begged Miguel's forgiveness, "Felix and Omar forced me to help them trap Rosa. They threatened my life if I refused."

Miguel studied Carmelita

"Please tell me, Carmelita, why would either of these two men, who you barely knew, choose you to help them take Rosa? And if that were true, you had plenty of time after they left to alert the others when you knew you were no longer in danger? Unless you indicated a willingness to help them. Perhaps it was even your suggestion?"

Carmelita stood frantically shaking her head in denial, terrified by the look on Miguel's face.

In a scathing voice, he demanded, "Which way did they go?"

Head lowered, Carmelita raised a shaking hand pointing south, the opposite direction to where Omar and Felix had departed.

Unprepared for Miguel's appearance, she hadn't taken the time to think it through. He knew she was lying. Miguel returned to camp from the south; their paths would have surely crossed if the trio had gone that way.

Miguel grasped Carmelita's jaw in his right hand, forcing her head up. His face, filled with loathing, came within a hair's breadth of hers.

"You helped save my life when I first arrived here. It is the only thing stopping me from ending yours right now!" Miguel spat the words at Carmelita, who was whimpering. Releasing her, he turned on his heel, yelling back at her, "Do not be in the camp when I return; I warn you!"

Miguel took the reins from Vincente but did not mount his horse straight away; instead stood looking at the other man. Vincente began to wonder if he was supposed to say something?

Miguel finally spoke, his voice devoid of any emotion, enunciating every word, so there was no mistaking his meaning,

"Carmelita will be leaving in the morning; ensure she takes everything she owns with her and leaves nothing behind; I want there to be no trace of her when I return." Miguel continued, "The camp must relocate as quickly as possible to where we discussed. I will meet you there."

Vincente was shocked. He opened his mouth to say something but thought better of it. Miguel was not initiating something for discussion; he was giving commands. There was only one reason Miguel would expel Carmelita from the camp. Somehow, she was involved in Rosa's disappearance.

Needle in a Haystack

☼

Miguel knew it was dangerous travelling at night. He chose one of three trails leading away from the camp, limiting how far he should go. If he chose the wrong trail, he would have to backtrack and waste time he couldn't spare. Felix and Omar already had two days' head start. At first light, he would search for any signs. Three people travelling on horseback shouldn't be too hard to track.

Finding a makeshift spot to shelter, Miguel forced himself to remain awake, listening for any disturbances from the horses, a sure sign a puma was in the vicinity looking for an easy meal; in a defensive gesture, he grasped his rifle closer to his body.

He and Pedro discussed possible places of refuge in their spare time should they have to relocate at short notice. They considered anywhere within a hundred-mile radius. As Miguel lay in the dark, he drew on that shared knowledge. It would be somewhere isolated, off the beaten track, with access to food and water for the animals and good shelter for the rebels. One place in the San Marco Sierras kept coming to mind. The Punilla Valley on the Mina Clavira River.

Rousing from a deep sleep, Miguel sat up, startled. Despite every effort, fatigue had beaten his will to stay awake. Nevertheless, it was what he needed to bolster his stamina for the task ahead. The crisp air burnt his lungs with every breath; the temperature was probably not much above freezing. As an easterly breeze lifted, the first rays of the rising sun turned the skyline pink. Shaking his head to clear his thoughts, he looked at his surroundings. A hazy mist swirled about his feet; It would be impossible to pick up any tracks until this cleared.

298

Miguel tried to force himself not to think about Rosa. Doing so was almost impossible; contemplating what she might be going through served no purpose but make him almost physically ill. He couldn't help but think how utterly wrong he'd been from the beginning about nearly everything. He reviled the woman because she was the spouse of someone evil, Carlos Mendoza, assuming she enjoyed sharing his spoils.

At first, Miguel congratulated himself on hatching the idea of taking Rosa hostage, intending to rein in the Governor. What a fool he'd been to believe Carlos had consideration for anyone but himself. Over the following weeks observing Rosa cure his men dying from fever, he started to see her for the person she was, and then she saved Thomas's life. The latter would have indeed died without Rosa's medical skills.

No one can fake kindness and compassion that convincingly. Miguel realised Rosa was a genuinely caring person. He'd wondered how she became entangled with Carlos, believing there was more to the story. After Rosa broke down, he finally learned the truth. She never elaborated on what Carlos did to her, but Rosa's hatred of the man was unmistakable. That same night he found out Delgado Caron, the man who saved his life, was Rosa's brother. Only later, the final realisation, Rosa helped care for him when his life hung in the balance in Santo Domingo Convent Hospital.

Because of his stupidity, Rosa was in the hands of two men who wanted her dead. They had nothing to lose. He was in no doubt they would kill Rosa, but not before they vented their anger and frustration at the Governor by punishing his wife. Miguel knew precisely what that meant.

He tried desperately not to conjure up the images imprinted on his brain; his mother, Elizabeth, and sister, Theresa, brutally raped and murdered.

For the first time in a long while, Miguel prayed. Over the last few years, he had little faith in anything, having seen too much cruelty and criminal behaviour. In desperation, he hoped he was wrong, praying God would heed his pleas and keep Rosa alive.

Abused by Felix and Omar

☼

The scorching sun caused rivulets of sweat to trickle down Rosa's parched skin. Leather bindings on her wrists bit deeply into the flesh. Time lost meaning as the horses' hooves beat an endless rhythm on the hard, dry earth. They entered a long valley alongside a river bed. Clear pools shimmered invitingly. Cliff walls on either side loomed overhead as slivers of sunlight danced over the valley walls, casting eerie shadows.

The trio had travelled almost non-stop after fleeing the rebel camp, fearful stopping too close to the rebel camp would compromise their escape. Rosa knew they must stop soon and find shelter before dark. Carmelita aided them well, providing a good supply of alcohol for their journey, agreeing if Miguel organised a search party, she would lie about which direction they had taken. Omar and Felix didn't know why Carmelita helped them; they didn't care; It suited them perfectly. Both men were still intoxicated; neither had stopped drinking since the kidnapping.

Carmelita had Rosa accompany her to the river early on the pretext of helping her gather water. She briefly saw Carmelita's smiling face, and then Omar appeared at her side before she was knocked unconscious from behind.

Her head still ached from that initial blow, as did the rest of her body. Rosa's hands were numb from being tied to the saddle horn for so long. In no doubt of her fate, she only prayed her death would be swift—the uncertainty of what might happen before she died terrified her.

Realising the horses had stopped, she raised her weary head to see what the men were doing. The fierce sunlight caused her to squint; her head spun, and she felt nauseous. She had not eaten all day, surviving with a few infrequent stops taking some water. They moved into the shade of an overhanging rock ledge; the men dismounted and removed their saddlebags, leaving the horses free to seek water, knowing they would not go far. A short distance away, Rosa could see an opening in the cliff face, a small cave, one of many.

Rough hands undid Rosa's bindings. Felix dragged her from her mount, dumping her on the ground in a crumpled heap. Her wrists stung with the sudden return of circulation. There had been only a little conversation between the two men during the journey, but now they were animated, fantasizing about what they planned to do with Rosa. She stared up into the leering stony faces of Omar and Felix, overcome with fear.

"Please, I beg you, do not do this," she pleaded. Rosa began to whimper, begging for mercy. If anything, this only served to excite the men even more. Omar stood over her, unsteady, swaying, already unbuttoning his trousers, his intentions clear, a sickening smile spread across his face. Rosa had never been more terrified in her life. It was like being with Carlos all over again…only worse. Rosa fleetingly thought how death would be preferable than being defiled by these vile creatures.

Felix bent down his calloused hands, trying to rip off her clothing to no avail, finally, in a fit of frustration, splitting them from top to bottom with his hunting knife.

"True, Senora, you will die, but it would be a pity to waste the opportunity to sample your body, no chance for such rewards in the rebel camp," his laughter sickening.

Felix instructed Omar to pin her shoulders, his face contorted like something wild let loose. Rosa closed her eyes, trying to block out what was happening. Felix descended over her. The smell of his sweaty body and alcohol breath invaded her senses. Searing pain caused her to yell loudly as Felix bit her breast and then her stomach. He was like a rabid animal.

"Senora, it's a long time since I've eaten this well. How sweet you taste."

Rosa thought she would vomit with the stench of Omar leaning over her, encouraging Felix.

"Leave some for me, amigo," he laughed.

Rosa was crying silently, praying to die.

Felix sat up wearing a lurid grin, climbing on top of Rosa and pushing Omar out of the way in one swift movement. Omar toppled over, laughing drunkenly.

Rosa let out a piercing scream as Felix forced his penis into her like a thrusting dagger. Agonised screams bounced off the canyon walls, a chilling echo of despair.

When finished, Felix sat back, gloating. Now it was Omar's turn. He loved caressing women's breasts; he started slobbering all over Rosa. He cursed in disgust, too drunk to get an erection, adding to Felix's amusement. Roughly forcing fingers into Rosa, he masturbated with his free hand, finally coming.

Rosa drifted in and out of consciousness. It was dark, the air not as cold as expected, the sun's heat trapped in the canyon walls, emanating warmth long after the sun had disappeared. Too sore to move, Rosa rolled her head to one side. She could see the glow of a fire at the cave's entrance. Smoke drifted across the valley, carrying the remnant scent of food—the low hum of Omar and Felix's conversation broken up by the breeze.

Rosa lay in the sandy dirt, her soul and spirit destroyed, shamed with their filth.

Before abandoning Rosa for the last time, they casually discussed how they might dispose of her, eventually deciding to let nature take its course. Punilla Valley in the San Marcos Sierras was a long way from any township and not on any regular travel route. Both men were satisfied Rosa was incapable of walking any distance. They doubted she could survive another day, two at the most. Puma inhabited the area, as did foxes, wolves and bush dogs. The cliffs were home to eagles, vultures and crows, all eager to feed off any carrion.

With the disposal of Rosa's body agreed upon, the men headed off to shelter for the night, casually discussing their plans to relocate first to San Luis and eventually cross over into Chile, head for Santiago and lay low for a while. Their only concern was a possible encounter with native Mapuche or Quechua hunting parties. They would need to remain alert. Rosa could hear the crunch of their boots on the river stones as they departed, their voices drifting away as she lapsed into unconsciousness, her brain slowly shutting down.

During the night, she awakened sluggishly, her vision blurred. Rosa could make out the shape of five horses some distance off at the water's edge. She decided her brain must be playing tricks; there were only three horses from the start. Rosa had no idea how much time had elapsed. Clawing the ground with her hands, she retrieved some of her ripped clothing, gathering it around her, trying to cover her nakedness, loathe to look down at her body still bearing the remnants of Felix and Omar's lust. Such thoughts were fleeting as she slipped into the darkness once more.

Loud snoring reverberated throughout the long narrow cave. Omar and Felix lay slumped against the rock wall where each had fallen into drunken slumber; neither heard the tall stranger enter the cave, each step precise, unhurried. The pistol shot was like a thousand whips cracking. Felix and Omar, awake suddenly, reached for their rifles – but it was too late; they lay at Miguel's feet. The enormity of the situation was instantly apparent to both men. Like simpering fools, they begged Miguel for mercy, blaming their folly on too much alcohol.

"Please, Miguel, you must believe us; we meant no disrespect to you. It was just a bit of fun," Felix cried. "See, she is alive; no harm done. We are satisfied she has paid *Mendoza's* dues."

A wide grin spread across Miguel's face. Both men looked relieved, taking this as a sign of his understanding. It failed to register with either man; the smile never reached Miguel's eyes. He raised the pistol slowly until it was level with Omar's head. The cold steel gleamed in the half-light. Omar opened his mouth to protest, but the words died on his lips as a bullet smashed through his skull, splattering brain tissue on Felix sitting alongside him. White with terror, Felix screamed an agonised wail that filled the air, cut short as another pistol shot rang out, finding its mark.

The three men had fought many battles together, like brothers side by side. Miguel also remembered a time when his mother and sister were at the mercy of scum like these. He felt no remorse for his action whatsoever.

The first rays of sunlight crept over the valley wall as Rosa opened her eyes again. A large shadow loomed above. Rosa tensed with horror, afraid the abuse would begin again, but the deathly pale face looking down at her was Miguels. Rosa's heart almost burst at the sight of him, and then remembering her state, she cringed in shame.

Miguel, with infinite gentleness, scooped her up in his arms, carrying her to the protection and warmth of the cave. Rosa glimpsed the rage on Miguel's features in the flickering firelight. She noted dispassionately the trail of blood leading further back into the cave. Rosa was unclear about what had happened but felt certain Omar and Felix would never abuse anyone again. She had always loathed violence in any form but couldn't help but rejoice at the prospect of their deaths. Nothing could ever replace what they had destroyed in her, but somehow, knowing they were dead gave her a measure of peace. She prayed their souls suffered eternal damnation. Rosa felt detached from her surroundings, her thoughts disjointed. She supposed she was in shock.

Miguel fetched water from a rockpool, gently bathing Rosa without physical contact or exposing her body. Trembling the whole time, she wept silently, unable to look at Miguel's face.

Later in the morning, after managing a little food and drink, Miguel helped Rosa mount her horse. She wore Miguel's shirt and had a saddle blanket wrapped around her waist. Numb with everything that had occurred over the previous two days, Rosa believed her life no longer held any meaning.

As they left the valley behind, the full sun casting a magnificent orange glow over the Sierras gave the scene a sense of serenity and peace. What a mockery nature could be, Rosa thought. How could life seem normal again after the devastation she had experienced only a few short hours ago?

Miguel was silent, dealing with his own demons, knowing he would never get over the guilt he felt for his part in Rosa's abuse. He was so ashamed. He didn't even know how to begin a conversation with her. Rosa embraced the silence, welcomed it; she had nothing to say.

Neither glanced back at where so much evil had taken place; their thoughts similar; both prayed they would never set foot here again.

The Devil You Know

☼

In her young life, Carmelita had faced many challenges; this was just one more. She was bitter at being ejected from the camp, all because of Rosa, someone she considered insignificant. In hindsight, Carmelita realised her stupid mistake in helping Felix and Omar. If she'd supported the idea of releasing Rosa and waiting a while, Rosa would have been out of Carmelita's way, giving her free reign to pursue Miguel. Still, Carmelita's jealousy drove her need to see Rosa suffer and pay back Miguel for rejecting her.

Making the outskirts of Cordoba on the first day, Carmelita sought shelter in an abandoned farmhouse. There was no fresh food there; all she had was the small amount she brought with her; it would have to do. A few oranges hung on a tree alongside the house; They would supplement her meagre supplies. Hunger was the least of her problems. There was plenty of firewood for the stove; at least she would be warm. It was good to be out of the mountains.

Carmelita could not go far without funds; she had already decided the best place to make money was Santa Fe, a river port. Plenty of sailors or fishermen were always eager to part with their cash, drinking, or being *entertained* by some woman, their usual pastime. Carmelita knew she was beautiful. It would not be hard to persuade any cantina owner; hiring her would be good for business. She would head into Cordoba tomorrow and sell her horse to pay for passage on the first available coach to Santa Fe.

After five days of travelling, Carmelita was weary and disgruntled. Unable to arrange direct passage to Santa Fe, she accepted the first coach headed in that direction, which meant a detour via Rosario. Out of boredom, Carmelita started flirting with the two male passengers sharing the coach, a situation not appreciated by either of their wives.

The coach slowed. Carmelita looked out the window and saw they were pulling into a Posada for a rest stop. They were perhaps twenty miles from Rosario. One of the coachmen climbed down to tether the horses. Carmelita jumped, startled as a rifle discharged.

"Do not move, Senor or the next bullet will be yours." A deep male voice warned.

The driver, still holding the horse's reins, froze in his tracks, "Please, Senor, we have no bullion, I swear, only passengers and a few goods."

"Tell your passengers to get out of the coach and empty their pockets, now!" The bandit demanded.

Carmelita sat frozen on the spot; she would know that menacing voice anywhere; it was Ernesto.

Stepping from the coach, the men emptied their pockets of cash and other valuables—no one intended to challenge this fierce-looking bandit, a bandana covering his face. Looking over the passengers as they assembled, he hesitated only slightly. In a voice full of disgust, he admonished them for the paltry offerings.

"What miserable pickings. You are fortunate I don't just shoot the lot of you out of spite. At the very least, you have brought me some female company to enjoy for a little while."

Carmelita had no doubt where this was heading; feigning fear, she was amused at the terror on the faces of the two other women, horrified they might be the chosen one.

Ernesto pointed the rifle in her direction, "You, stand aside. The rest of you, get back on the coach and leave now. You have one minute before I start shooting."

No one had to be told twice. The words were barely out of Ernesto's mouth before the coachman scrambled back aboard. The passengers were fighting each other, trying to do the same. In a matter of minutes, the only sign a coach had been there was the tell-tale column of dust following it down the road heading towards Rosario.

The bandana slid from Ernesto's face. He was wearing a wide-toothed grin. Paying no attention to the bounty on the road, he only had eyes for one prize.

"Carmelita, we are destined to be together, it seems!"

Her heart sinking, Carmelita knew there was no escaping her fate. She would concoct some story about how life in the camp wasn't the same without him. Ernesto's ego would love that. Nothing mattered; reduced to being petty thieves robbing passing coaches, they were likely to end up hanged anyway.

Carmelita launched herself at Ernesto, throwing her arms around his neck and wrapping her legs around his body.

"Carmelita, my love, I've missed you," his mouth came crushing down on hers.

Double Jeopardy
☼

They were just short of Santa Fe when the troupe of soldiers came into view. Carmelita's heart sank. She could feel a noose around her neck already. Looking at Ernesto with dismay, she was surprised by his calmness.

"Let me do the talking, *Carina*. You cry on cue and cover up your breasts -for the time being," He said, grinning luridly.

The Sargeant at Arms raised his rifle, halting their progress. Still pointing it at them menacingly, he indicated to both, "Get off your horse. Who are you, and what business brings you here?"

Carmelita was amazed to see Ernesto assume the manner of a peasant. He removed his hat in deference, lowering his head and paying homage.

"Senor, we have been searching for help. We were captives of rebels in the mountains beyond Cordoba. Stealing two horses, we managed to escape. Reaching Cordoba, we sought help from the soldiers stationed there, but they were gone! Please help us."

Carmelita cried on cue, grasping the soldier's foot, kissing his boot, and looking up with a tear-stained face while leaning forward, allowing a clear view down the front of her blouse.

Flustered, the soldier quickly ordered his men to render assistance; this was Carmelita's cue to faint.

"Carmelita, we are saved; it is okay." Ernesto's voice implored, and he bent over her, feigning concern.

The Sargeant quickly had his men clear a space on the back of their supply wagon while he assisted Carmelita aboard. "We must return to Santa Fe immediately; the Governor will want to speak with you and find out what information you have to share." With that, he commanded his men about-face and set off at a rapid pace for Santa Fe.

Ernesto glanced at Carmelita as they swung through the iron gates into the sweeping drive of a magnificent Hacienda. There were guards everywhere. The foot soldier in charge stepped forward as the Sargeant approached.

"I must see the Governor at once. I have vital information regarding the rebel stronghold in the mountains." The remainder of his men were directed to the rear of the estate.

The Sargeant, Carmelita and Ernesto were guided across the courtyard, through a vestibule, into an opulent office.

The foot soldier in charge barked an order, "Wait here; remain standing. I will inform the Governor!"

The Sargeant came to attention, looking uncomfortable. He had not been in the presence of the Governor before but was keenly aware of his reputation. Ernesto, usually confident in any situation, looked quite the opposite. He kept shifting his weight from foot to food. He was on edge. Carmelita just stood silently, looking terrified. They were in deep trouble.

The silence was broken by a man shouting obscenities at some household member.

"Manuel, you imbecile, why are my things not already in the coach? I should have been on the road to Buenos Aires an hour ago." Someone interrupted the tirade to inform the Governor of their presence.

Carlos strode into the room, a furious look on his face, ready to vent his anger on whoever it was delaying his departure even further. His eyes flicked over the soldier and the brawny-looking peon, alighting on the young woman visibly shaking. Her fear was enough to arouse Carlos's interest; his demeanour changed instantly.

"My dear, I can see you are distressed; why has no one offered you a seat? Please, be seated." With a cursory glance at Ernesto, he waved his hand, signalling he should also sit.

"Sargeant, have my housekeeper bring refreshments for my guests." The soldier hurried from the room, relieved to be out of the firing line.

"Now tell me quickly of your time in the rebel camp; and any news of my wife, Rosa."

Carmelita became nervous when the governor mentioned Rosa, but curiously, his manner lacked concern.

When first told of his wife's kidnapping, Carlos flew into a wild rage. Those observing this behaviour mistakenly assumed his outrage expressed fear she was in mortal danger. He was infuriated by her capture; it made him look vulnerable to a bunch of petty thugs. Worse still was discovering Miguel Garcia was the camp leader. Carlos had Miguel's family murdered. When his attempt to avenge their deaths failed, Carlos knew Miguel would never give up hunting for him, immediately putting a 250,000 pesos bounty on his head…no doubt his current *guests* were well aware of that!

"Enough; I will have you share the finer details with my troops. I have urgent business in Buenos Aires that will change the face of Argentina." Carlos beamed as he made the last statement. The 'business' he was crowing about must be of paramount importance.

Astutely aware of Carlos's reaction to her, Carmelita could see an opportunity to escape the hangman's noose. Whatever else he might be, first and foremost, he was a man.

A housemaid arrived and offered refreshments to Carmelita and Ernesto. Carlos barely controlled his impatience. The housemaid informed him his carriage was ready.

Carlos snapped into action. Pointing at Ernesto, he commanded, "You will go with my men and give them every detail possible to assist them in locating this criminal rabble. I will see them destroyed once and for all. You will then travel with the men escorting me to Buenos Aires while the remainder head to Cordoba. All the necessary instructions will be telegraphed to my headquarters in Cordoba, ready for when they arrive." Turning on the charm, Carlos shifted his attention to Carmelita.

"You, my dear, have been through a terrible ordeal; you must travel comfortably to Buenos Aires. You will share my coach."

311

Looking closely at Ernesto, Carlos's eyes narrowed. "You have no objection, Senor?"

Carmelita watched Ernesto weigh up the situation. He knew, without a doubt, that any objection would likely see him have a nasty accident. His hold on Carmelita was at an end.

"Your Excellency, I am most grateful for your help, especially knowing Senorita Lopez is in your care." Ernesto addressing Carmelita this way, confirmed her single status and indicated he relinquished any claims on her person.

Carlos relaxed, even smiling at Ernesto. "Good, then it is all settled. I will see you again when we all arrive in Buenos Aires. You will travel with my men, Senor. They will see to your comfort when they set up camp." It was not a request but a statement.

Carlos addressed Carmelita, "Do not fear, Senorita; I will ensure you have comfortable quarters wherever we stop."

Carmelita smiled sweetly, "Your kindness is humbling, Your Excellency; I thank you." She didn't dare look at Ernesto.

Carmelita doubted they would be barely out of the grounds of Solitario Lobo before the Governor's hands would be all over her.

Out of The Frying Pan
☼

It was mid-morning when Carlos's coach entered the back streets of Recoleta, pulling up outside a small elegant building. The entrance was through a side gate, discretely shielding those arriving or leaving. Carmelita climbed down from the coach; she was aching, less from the rough journey than from Carlos's treatment of her body.

In his mid-forties, Carlos was a physically powerful man who enjoyed dominating his sexual partners. Originally intending to dispense with her company on reaching the Capital, he decided to install Carmelita in his private residence instead...for the present. Carlos lived in the Governor's mansion in the City, his Recoleta property purely for indulging his sexual appetite away from prying eyes.

The housekeeper, an austere middle-aged woman, greeted Carmelita cordially, maintaining a bland expression. She had seen many house guests come and go. There was a rapid turnover of the women he bedded. Carlos was easily bored. His physical demands saw others leave of their own accord.

Shown to her room, Carmelita was entranced, exposed to such luxury for the first time. Crystal chandeliers glistened, reflected again in the gilded mirrors. One wall hosted a giant mural, a country landscape. Tentatively, she opened one of the doors on the mirrored robe, gasping at the beautiful gowns inside. At the very least, Carlos was generous with his women.

The dresser top was littered with bottles of expensive perfumes, lip colours, face powders and pomades. Jewelled hair clips and an assortment of feminine paraphernalia filled a crystal bowl. The dresser itself contained more silk undergarments than Carmelita had ever seen before. Walking past the enormous bed, she let her fingers trail across the soft brocade quilt; she was in awe of her surroundings.

A door led off from the bedroom; Carmelita investigating, found herself in a magnificent bathing room. Pale blue ceramic tiles graced the walls. On the floor, a mosaic mermaid swam in a sea of blue. The domed skylight spilt shafts of sunlight over the entire room, giving the illusion the *water* was moving.

A large porcelain tub with gold taps stood on a platform. Smiling, Carmelita pictured herself luxuriating in steaming perfumed water. She was going to make the most of her stay, daring to dream this could be the beginning of a new future.

Marching into the Capital building in high spirits, Carlos was eager to get on with the carefully orchestrated plans initiated over a year ago. There were barriers to the proposed rail network for Argentina, discussed many times during the previous fifteen years. The scale and costs of such a project were challenging. Political reservations also played a part. The British were once in control of Argentina for a brief period. A great deal of mistrust remained. The idea of undertaking a joint venture with a potential enemy was risky.

Carlos realised the use of British technology and financial input was essential. Without it, the proposal would be shelved once more. Despite all his human failings, his instinct for making lucrative investments with the potential to amass great wealth was finely honed, second to none. The applications for transporting goods, people and other services by linking the major towns with a network of railroad coaches would revolutionise Argentina and make it one of the wealthiest countries in the world.

In the next few months, he would sell enough assets to finance a deal with the British independently. In his position as Governor, he had the power to manipulate any other factors standing in the way of a successful outcome. His hidden agenda was to usurp British input, leaving him totally in control eventually.

From their inception, Carlos's business transactions with his British counterparts were handled in the strictest confidence. He only trusted one person to help complete his plans: his brother Philippe, a trusted Franciscan Brother. No one would question his actions.

Carlos looked up as one of his men appeared at his door, standing to attention and saluting, hesitant to enter. He had left orders not to be disturbed. He snapped at the soldier, "What is it that can't wait? Can nobody think for themselves around here?"

It was a ludicrous statement. Everyone knew the consequences of failing to gain the Governor's permission before proceeding with anything.

"I'm sorry, Your Excellency, the Garrison Guard has just delivered a message to say the informant, Ernesto Rojas, who returned with them from Santa Fe, has disappeared."

Carlos shook his head in disgust. Still in a relatively good mood, he only offered a mild rebuke.

"He's probably whoring somewhere in a back street brothel by now. I believe he passed on all the information he possessed about the rebel camp; forget him. Tell the guard to get on and do something useful for a change!" With that, Carlos waved the soldier away.

The Decision to Leave

☼

Rosa lay watching the rise and fall of Miguel's chest, the rhythmical intake of air, followed by whispers as he exhaled. Fine honey-coloured stubble covered his chin, strangely at odds with his sun-ripened skin. The surrounding silence contrasted with the questions screaming inside Rosa's head. 'What just happened?' And more importantly, 'what do I do now?' So often, life didn't seem to make any sense.

Rosa closed her eyes, the memory of the last few hours engulfing her. Laying there replete from the aftermath of lovemaking, she wanted to recall every second in exquisite detail. Stolen moments between two mismatched lovers separated by insurmountable barriers. One a felon with a price on his head, the other the wife of his sworn enemy.

It started with an argument, Rosa insisting Miguel allow her to return home. Not yet fully recovered from her ordeal in the desert, Rosa knew the constabulary were fiercely hunting for Miguel and his troupe, including her. Miguel vehemently fought her suggestion, having the final say as the leader. Rosa also acknowledged she was afraid of the growing bond between them. Following the brutal assault and rape, Rosa withdrew into her soul, barely meeting others' eyes, shamed, beaten, and destroyed. She came to depend on Miguel for everything. He was the only one who understood what she had survived.

Following the assault on Rosa, Miguel's whole attitude changed; his mood swings were frequent, and he lived somewhere in a state between rage and stunned silence. He didn't know how to deal with his internal turmoil and remorse. If he hadn't orchestrated Rosa's kidnapping, he wouldn't now be looking at this damaged woman, broken, possibly beyond repair. Killing the two perpetrators did little to assuage his guilt nor help him find a way to bring Rosa's spirit back to life. Over the last few weeks, the tension between them continued to build.

It was late; the camp settled for the night. The lookouts and guards were already in position. The only other night sounds the odd snorting or foot stamping of the horses and the occasional bird call. She had gone to Miguel's tent to argue her case. Rosa's voice broke into Miguel's reverie, insisting on her release. Something snapped in Miguel's brain; he whirled around, standing toe to toe with Rosa; he grasped her arms roughly. "You will do as I say and when I say it."

Just as his anger dissipated, Miguel shuddered at the look sweeping over Rosa's face, the memory of other violent hands still too raw. Rosa stood stricken, her face pale.

Horrified, Miguel took a half step back, shaken to the core by the look on Rosa's face, "I am so, so sorry; I didn't mean to frighten you, I swear."

Rosa nodded weakly. She whispered, "I know you are considering what you believe best."

Miguel let Rosa's words hang in the air. Was it that? Or was it something else? Miguel acknowledged the source of the knot in his gut for the first time. Every time Rosa discussed her release, the vice in his stomach tightened. Miguel didn't want Rosa to go. The silence stretched between them. Miguel felt his muscles tense; all the power drained from his voice. When he spoke, it was barely audible, invoking Rosa's name, almost like a prayer, his voice breaking on his final words, "Rosa, I don't want you to go."

The space between them evaporated, their faces almost touching. Bright blue eyes stared into Rosa's face seeking permission to touch her, hold her, love her. He dared not move; he knew he had no right to expect anything but rejection. Rosa's hand tentatively reached up and brushed Miguel's cheek tenderly before leaning forward, putting her head against his chest. She could feel the rapid beat of his heart beneath the thin fabric of his shirt. Strong arms enveloped her as Miguel bent down, his mouth hungrily seeking hers.

317

Rosa tensed. Miguel struggled to restrain his desire; he relaxed his arms.

"It's okay, I understand, don't be afraid. If it's too soon, that's all right," Miguel reassured her.

Rosa was confused by the depth of conflicting emotions sweeping over her. She knew she would be safe in Miguels's hands, and despite her recent ordeal, she wanted Miguel. The thought made her blush, especially the realisation she had never really desired a man before, except the dream lover of her youth, the Knight on horseback coming to take her to the fabulous hacienda she envisaged. Any such dreams shattered with her marriage and the brutality of her wedding night. Rosa shuddered.

Miguel felt the shudder and let his hands drop to his side, interpreting this as his need to step away. Something came alive in Rosa. For the first time, there was a need to know what it was like to be loved by a man, give herself completely, feel gentle hands on her body, and feel this man inside her.

Rosa reached out and took Miguel's hand, placing it on her breast. Miguel sucked in his breath, feeling Rosa's nipple respond to his gently caressing hand.

"Miguel, hold me, love me."

Like two magnets irresistibly drawn together, he pulled her body against his. He was so hard but knew he must take things slowly. Miguel let his lips slide down Rosa's neck, gently nuzzling her ear, the pulse beating crazily at the nape of her neck. Lowering his head further, he placed his mouth over her breast through her clothing, teasing the hardened nipple with his tongue. Rosa groaned, feeling desire rise inside her for the first time.

Miguel whispered tender loving words, slowly removing Rosa's clothing gently. Her trust humbled him. She was beautiful, the fading marks from her earlier ordeal still visible. Suddenly nervous, Miguel had no experience to draw on. Years of conflict had stolen his youth. He was a full-grown man desiring this woman so badly it hurt. He wanted to make their union special.

Rosa's lips opened as Miguel's mouth found hers, the sweetness beyond anything she had imagined, their tongues gently seeking and exploring. He lowered Rosa onto the mattress and felt her body arch to meet him. Whatever hesitation he felt evaporated. Miguel was like a starving man; he couldn't get enough of her, wanting to protect her and consume her all at the same time.

Rosa was whimpering now, but this was no woman in pain, but one reaching the pinnacle of desire, grasping Miguel to her, hungry to feel the full force of him inside her. They moved in unison, creating waves of magic with each thrust; Miguel climaxed first, as spasms wracked Rosa's body, with one final explosive release and loud moans escaping her lips. She never dreamed it could be like this, that such feelings existed deep inside, just waiting to be set free.

Rosa stirred from sleep, shivering. She pulled the covers up around them. Miguel, beside her, slept peacefully. How beautiful he looked lying there, as though he didn't have a care in the world. They made love several times throughout the night, rejoicing in new discoveries and sharing the joy of complete abandon. They were so at ease with each other; it was as if they had been together for a long time.

Rosa knew these few hours had changed her life forever. She must leave; she knew this now more than ever. A married woman, six years Miguel's senior, his whole life was still ahead of him. When the political nightmare was over, and Carlos was finally deposed, Miguel had a chance to reclaim his life, move forward, marry someone and build a future. The best Rosa could hope for was to leave Carlos, return to Santa Fe, and seek sanctuary within the church. Divorce was out of the question; the church would never sanction such a thing. Besides, she knew Carlos would never set her free. At least there would be the memory of these last few hours, hopefully enough to sustain Rosa for a lifetime.

As the first rays of dawn seeped under the tent flap, Rosa knew she must go now. Delaying her departure any longer meant risking Miguel waking up. If he tried to stop her, she may give in to the overwhelming urge to abandon the idea of leaving altogether and take a chance they could share a life despite the insurmountable barriers.

Taking one last look at Miguel's sleeping form, a sob caught in Rosa's throat as she memorised every nuance about him, knowing it had to last a lifetime, and then she was gone, slipping into the shadows. The early morning mist aided her escape. Rosa's knew where the sentry posts were and how best to avoid them. Stealthily untethering a bay mare from the pack, Rosa silently led the horse down the trail to the rift, not mounting her horse until well clear of the camp, leaving the only man who had ever made her feel loved. Tears spilt down her cheeks. The time would come when grief would consume her. There was no time for that now.

Coming Full Circle

☼

Rosa knew it was only a good day's ride to Cordoba. Surprisingly, though isolated in the wilderness, she wasn't afraid. She no longer doubted her resilience to survive almost anything.

The pain of leaving Miguel was raw. Their time together was brief, but once she recognised her deep love for him, nothing could diminish or erase its effect. For the first time in her life, she knew what it was like to give and receive love. The feeling of being joined with him was seared into her memory forever. The caresses, exploring each other's bodies, coming to know it as no other would. The gentleness of tender kisses, arousal of every fibre of her being, until the passion took command, both lost in giving everything to each other until Miguel and Rosa were physically spent.

There was no solution to her inner conflict. Rosa believed marriage vows were sacred, taken before God. It was a lifetime commitment, even to a monster like Carlos. Perhaps it was a union in name only, but she was still the wife of Carlos Mendoza.

Few night sounds could be heard across the open plain, the hum of insects, the howl of a lone wolf somewhere far away, and the sobbing of a young woman with a broken heart.

It was late morning. The mountain ridge was just a distant blur; Rosa had ridden hard, stopping under a shady tree to rest briefly and refresh her horse. The day was hot; the heat haze shimmered in the distance. A cool breeze was more than welcome. Rosa leant against the tree; she was emotionally exhausted. Tired and dirty, she imagined soaking in her old copper tub. Suddenly alert, she sat bolt upright, hearing the sound of horses approaching. Around the bend in the road, about thirty heavily armed soldiers came into view. A wagon at the rear carried what looked like a small cannon. Rosa stood as the captain in charge rode up quickly, dismounting beside her. Rosa promptly adopted the role of the victim, grasping his arm desperately and dissolving into tears.

"Thank God you found me, Senor; I feared I would die at the hands of the rebels. I escaped and have been wandering for several days. I've had little to eat, and my water has gone." Rosa added to the drama by pretending to faint; the soldier took hold of her, breaking Rosa's fall.

"What is your name Senora, and from which direction did you come?"

"My name is Rosa; my husband is Carlos Mendoza, the Governor. I was on the way to Santa Fe weeks ago but was kidnapped by the rebels and held for ransom. My husband must be frantic by now."

At the mention of Carlos's name, the soldier almost saluted Rosa. Shouting orders to his men to bring food and water, he helped Rosa sit back against the tree. He could see she was dishevelled and genuinely distraught.

"Senora Mendoza, I am in somewhat of a dilemma. We are on a mission to destroy the rebel camp. We believe there could be a hundred men there. Can you confirm this, Senora?"

Rosa was desperate, trying to think how she could distract them from their course. Feigning surprise, she replied, "I saw no more than thirty or less, although I was restrained and kept under guard. May I ask who provided such information, Captain?"

He replied hesitantly, "We received word from Sant Fe Senora. Like yourself, two hostages, a man and a woman who escaped the rebels, were picked up near Santa Fe and later transported to Buenos Aires for further questioning."

Rosa suspected it might be Carmelita and Ernesto; Rosa's heart almost stopped. They would sell their souls and those of the rebels if it meant a reward. "Thank God they are safe. I knew there were more hostages, but I was isolated from the others. Captain, I know my husband will have posted a large reward for my safe return. I must get to him as quickly as possible. I trust only you to accomplish this!"

Rosa watched as the captain struggled with what he should do. On the one hand, he had his orders, but the thought of a large reward and the glory of saving the Governor's beloved wife was too great a temptation.

"You are safe now, Senora; I will ensure you are returned safely to His Excellency."

"Thank you, Captain; Carlos will be personally indebted to you. Sending half of your men to escort me and ensure my safety will not go unrewarded and will show Carlos you understand and respect how highly valued I am to him."

Rosa watched as the captain's face changed from uncertainty to acceptance of the proposal. If he delivered the First Lady safely to her distraught husband, he could see the possibility of promotion and a financial reward.

Barking out orders, he directed the second in charge to proceed with half the men while he escorted the First Lady to safety with the rest of the troupe. He could already envisage the promotion to major and imagine the gold braid on his uniform.

The stopover in Cordoba was brief; Rosa wanted to keep moving before Carlos received word of her 'rescue' and countermanded any actions already taken.

The captain, initially surprised by Rosa's reluctance to take a few days to rest, was more than impressed by how keen she was to reunite with her husband. The plan was to head for Rosario, change horses, and then continue to Buenos Aires. Rosa was now in the relative comfort of a carriage, contemplating what her next move should be.

North of Rosario, Rosa became 'ill', insisting they detour to the convent hospital in Santa Fe, where she was well known and would receive the best care.

"Captain, I am more than happy to be escorted to the hospital by your men while you continue to Buenos Aires to be received by the Governor. As soon as I reach Santa Fe, I will telegraph the Governor of my safe arrival. Carlos will be beside himself." Rosa could barely keep a straight face. She would have given anything to see Carlos's face when he received the news.

The Last Laugh
☼

Carlos was relaxing in his office, having dispatched the final coded message to his Bank in Buenos Aires, his brother Philippe at Villa Maria, and the British envoy. He was congratulating himself, anticipating what was to follow.

There was a knock on his door; a very nervous soldier stood to attention, a strained look on his face.

"What is it, man? Spit it out; I am busy!"

"Your Excellency, I have an urgent message from your headquarters in Santa Fe, relayed from Cordoba. Unfortunately, you had already departed for the Capital, and so the information is only now reaching here." He took a deep breath, his expression one of trepidation, sensing the news he was about to share would not be to the Governor's liking. "Captain Asguard leading the troupe from Cordoba in search of the rebel camp, came upon the First Lady, who managed to escape the rebels. He sends his assurances she is safe and receiving the best care possible."

Carlos's face turned scarlet; he didn't speak; he could tell there was more.

"On the strength of the information provided by Senora Mendoza, he ordered half his men to continue the search while he and the remainder of his troupe are escorting Senora Mendoza safely to Buenos Aires."

Carlos exploded; picking up the writing set off his desk, he hurled it across the room at the soldier, who fortunately ducked. It shattered against the far wall, splattering ink everywhere. He was beyond livid. Carlos ordered an urgent message sent to recall his men. He cursed Rosa vehemently, unclear what trickery she was up to but

325

certain she would deliberately mislead his men if possible. He was just as sure she would not be arriving in Buenos Aires.

When first informed rebels had kidnapped Rosa, he was hopeful they might rid him of her once and for all.

In response to attempting a recall of his soldiers, he received a further report from Cordoba confirming the troupe had unexpectedly chanced upon the entire rebel camp relocating. Expecting no more than thirty men, they found themselves hopelessly outnumbered. Left with no choice but to engage the enemy, they were systematically slaughtered, with only one severely wounded man, making it back to Cordoba to report what had happened.

Carlos went raging through the Capital building, berating everyone he encountered. The same unfortunate soldier appeared again with more news; he was visibly shaking.

"Your Excellency, Captain Asguard has arrived and is now under escort on the way to your office."

The soldier hastily departed while Carlos charged down the corridor to his office to find the captain standing at attention, an escort on either side. Seated behind his desk, Carlos glared up at the captain, barely able to restrain his fury.

"Captain, please, share the information that persuaded you to be derelict in your duty?"

The captain expecting to be rewarded and possibly receive a citation, quickly realised something had gone wrong. He began to tremble.

Carlos continued, spitting out the venom he'd been holding in. "Perhaps you might explain your strategy whereby you sacrificed your troupe's lives, dispatching half of the men at your disposal when a hundred-odd rebels outnumbered them?"

Captain Asguard, white with shock, stammered, "But your Excellency, the First Lady assured us the rebels in the camp were fewer than thirty."

"You fool, you stupid, vain fool…so where is my illustrious wife? Pray tell!"

The captain realised too late that he had been a pawn in Senora Mendoza's hands, completely taken in by her lies about the rebel camp and her overwhelming desire to join her loving husband. Nothing he said would save the day.

Dropping to one knee, he begged for Carlos's mercy. "Your excellency, I was honouring the First Lady's wishes to join you as quickly as possible. In fear of travelling unescorted on the way here, I acceded to her request that half of my troupe attend her." He was nearly choking on his words, desperate to say anything that might keep him from a hangman's noose. "Unfortunately, on the way to Rosario, Senora Mendoza became ill, insisting she be taken to the convent hospital in Santa Fe instead."

Carlos screamed at him, "You simpering fool, since when does a woman command my troops!" Turning to the escort team, he snarled his orders. "Strip him of his rank and uniform, and throw him into solitary confinement." The captain was still pleading for mercy as the two escorts dragged him down the corridor.

Carlos sat behind his desk brooding, wishing he could lay his hands on Rosa this very minute and break her neck, but not before making her suffer in every way possible. Realising his plans for the day were ruined, he started drinking Tequila. He needed to work off his mood. Perhaps a night at Recoleta might help.

It would seem the information gained from the two informants Carmelita and her friend, didn't align with where the rebels intercepted his men, far from it, nor was the number of insurgents stated anywhere near the actual number present. Carlos was sure extracting the truth of the matter from Carmelita was just the medicine he needed. Anticipating her pain was enough to make him hard. Carlos rang a bell for his manservant. "Have my coach ready in half an hour; I intend to spend the night at Recoleta; I will be back tomorrow."

The hot water released the aroma of the scented oils; the heady perfume was tantalising. Carmelita lowered herself slowly into the tub, sliding down the smooth porcelain. It fitted the shape of her body perfectly. The housekeeper had left some time ago to shop in town.

Never having spent much time on her own, Carmelita was enjoying the solitude…only she wasn't alone. The doors onto the outdoor patio swung freely as the tall visitor stepped inside the room, his movement through the house silenced by the soft covering on the floor. Carmelita didn't hear the bath room door open.

Sliding below the water, Carmelita rinsed the suds from her hair while thinking about spending the afternoon in the sun, laying on one of the long cane chairs outside.

Carmelita stiffened as she felt the strong hands on her shoulders, then relaxed, thinking it was Carlos returning to play, until she tried to surface, feeling the resistance. Surprise quickly turned to panic. The solid hands held firm. She struggled, thrashing about in the water, desperate for air, to no avail. Carmelita's final conscious thought…realizing the arms holding her underwater belonged to Ernesto.

House of Cards
☼

Today was the day it all came together. If Carlos could pull off this deal, it would be a clear run to the Presidency. A fine figure of a man still, he surveyed his image in the mirror, perhaps a bit portly around the middle, smiling to himself; too much good food and wine. He almost preened like a peacock. Carlos's rise to the top was swift. Of course, in his mind, all due to his business prowess rather than shady business dealings or outright corruption.

Carlos checked the clock; it was 8.50 a.m. Just a fifteen-minute ride to the bank where he would collect the bank draft for the extraordinary sum of almost ninety-eight million pesos. As half-owner of the burgeoning Argentine Rail, he would control the transport of not only commerce but the rapid transport of people all over Argentina and, eventually, the continent. The concept was extraordinary. Granted, he would share the honour with the British; for the time being. Ultimately, he would *acquire* the shares needed for complete control.

As Governor of the Province of Buenos Aires, he was already a powerful man. Many attempted to estimate his wealth, much to his amusement. They weren't even close. Those who knew him intimately doubted it was luck when Carlos purchased large tracts of land where the newly proposed rail link was to go. Many of his opponents were determined to investigate such a *coincidence*. Every search initiated came to a dead end. Carlos welcomed the transparency, knowing it would add to his legitimacy, confident no connection could be established.

Over the previous few years, Carlos tried to create an air of respectability. He still had his whores, but no longer frequented the back street brothels. Now entertaining much more discreetly, high-class women with looks and poise. Not that he treated them any differently, his sexual appetite still depended on his debasing them in some way or causing them discomfort.

Carlos hadn't seen Rosa for several years. Her absence had worked in his favour. Everyone felt sympathy for the Governor, whose wife had never recovered from her mental breakdown following the loss of their child. Out of sight, out of mind. Carlos's last word of Rosa was from his brother Peter, informing him Rosa's mother, Isabella, had died. Belatedly, he sent a significant floral tribute, more out of admiration for the woman than for Rosa's loss. He smiled, recalling their first meeting when he set eyes on Rosa. Isabella was the only person who ever sensed the *real* Carlos from the instant they met.

Then the stupid woman got herself kidnapped! Carlos, ever hopeful it might be the end of Rosa, furious when he recalled the stupidity of his soldiers. The captain in charge sent half his men to escort her back to the *safety* of her beloved husband. He was expecting a reward for his diligence in saving Rosa, thrown instead into the stockade, unlikely to see freedom again. The final ugly chapter was finding the whore Carmelita drowned in the bath. Carlos refused to think about such things on this auspicious day.

Looking out the window below, a contingent of soldiers in red and black finery controlled restless horses, anxious to be away. The signing of the Bi-Lateral Agreement would take place in two hours in Carlos's office. One final look in the mirror, a last check of the clock, and he was ready.

Carlos sat fidgeting, waiting impatiently for the Bank Manager to return with the necessary papers to sign and release the funds. He acknowledged, in all likelihood, it was probably the most significant transaction the bank would ever conduct, but where the hell was he?

Senor Mendia entered the office, a stricken expression on his face, his brow furrowed. He lifted both hands in the air, expressing his disbelief and inability to explain the situation.

330

"Your Excellency - Governor, I am at a total loss. I apologise, but I am unable to accommodate the transaction as planned."

Carlos was instantly livid, this transaction had been meticulously planned, and measures put in place to complete the necessary paperwork today!

"What do you mean, you fool? What is the hold-up?"

"I am sorry, Governor, the funds to be transferred, established yesterday, are no longer in your account. I thought there may have been a misunderstanding, and the funds mistakenly sent to the wrong institution. I know you have a line of credit with other banks. When I spoke to each manager, they confirmed any existing funds they held had been transferred late yesterday to the Franciscan Brotherhood - in Spain."

Carlos leapt out of the chair, grabbing the Bank Manager by the throat, "That's not possible; no one has that authority. By whose order was this done?" Carlos screamed at him.

Almost choking, Estaban Mendia replied in a whisper, "Brother Philippe Mendoza."

Carlos's face turned scarlet and then deathly pale. Nothing like this could be happening to someone as powerful as him. Why? And by his own brother. What did he have to gain, a Franciscan Brother who pledged a vow of poverty? With a cold heart, Carlos realised this ultimate betrayal would effectively destroy him, something that could not have escaped Philippe. His political ambition, and effectively his life, were dismantled in one fell swoop. This was no mistake; this was deliberate.

Carlos let the relieved Bank Manager go and turned, charging down the stairs and out of the building. Filled with vengeance, he wanted as many people to suffer as possible. Before dismissing his men, Carlos ordered the execution of the soldier fooled by Rosa's lies. They quickly moved aside as he charged through them, seeing his wrath and the first sign Carlos was becoming unhinged. He leapt into his carriage and headed north, only one thing on his mind now, a debt he must repay in person

331

ROMANS: 13:4

☼

Carlos had little recollection of the previous four days. He slept fitfully, haunted by nightmares from his childhood, the retribution of his enemies, the recent death of his elderly housekeeper, Aida, who was like a surrogate mother to him, and the unexpected death of his father Ramon years earlier.

The only thing Carlos was proud of in his life was the empire he had created – and now that was gone. It never occurred to him to consider the fragility of his life - that it rested in the hands of a simple man of God.

During the journey to Villa Maria, Carlos took whatever he needed. None opposed this well-dressed man who spoke with authority, commanding others to see his horses fed and watered and bring food to his room. Several people recognised him as the Governor. His behaviour was odd; they suspected he had some mental breakdown. Carlos could barely sit still, and it was only briefly when he did. He continually fidgeted, occasionally slamming his fist on the table, repeatedly mumbling, "My own brother!" Those he encountered speculated a tragedy had driven him to despair, believing it may be the loss of a family member. The assumption was not far from the truth, but it had nothing to do with the death of a loved one.

Brother Bernado answered the resounding knock echoing throughout the empty halls of the Priory. It was 4 a.m., not yet daylight. Brother Bernado raised the lamp to see who was making such a racket at this time of the morning, shocked to see Carlos Mendoza, the Governor, standing before him unshaven, dishevelled, his clothing soiled. He looked dreadful.

"Your Excellency, please come in. What has happened? Are you unwell? What brings you here at this early hour and in such a state?"

Word of the Governor's downfall, while common knowledge in many parts of Argentina, had not yet reached this secluded community. Almost one hundred miles from Cordoba, the Franciscan order was out of touch with the outside world; their only regular contact was when taking produce to markets in the city.

Carlos was shaking. The air was bitterly cold, accounting only partly for some of his discomfort. Forgoing a courteous greeting, instead, he issued a demand,

"It is urgent I see my brother Philippe," Carlos's rasping voice was harsh. It was not a request; it was a command.

Brother Bernado hesitated. It was apparent the Governor was not himself. He appeared to be suffering some sort of collapse. It was most unusual to allow entry to any visitor out of hours. Still, Brother Bernado hoped allowing him to visit his brother might be the solution to his obvious distress. On that premise, he allowed Carlos to continue through the monastery to Philippe's room while he returned to his quarters. It was only a couple of hours to the early prayer period, Mattins. He would try for a little more sleep.

Carlos stood outside Philippe's door, lungs sucking in the cold night air, preparing himself for the confrontation. His fury spent for the moment; he wanted to know why? There was no resistance when turning the door handle. Always a light sleeper, the sound was enough to awaken Philippe.

Still half asleep, Philippe couldn't make out the form standing in the doorway; it was too tall to be Brother Bernado. He couldn't imagine who else it might be at this early hour. Striking a taper, he lit the lamp alongside the Crucifix on his side table, sitting up abruptly as Carlos entered the room and closed the door quietly behind him.

"Carlos!" Philippe exclaimed. His visit wasn't unexpected in light of the recent relocation of Carlos's funds, although he was surprised at the swiftness of his arrival. Usually, Philippe was almost as frightened of Carlos as he had been of their father, Ramon. Today instead, there was calmness. The mammoth step he'd taken to negate the wrongs of the previous six years was like absolution. He was at peace with his action of restitution. He could do no more.

Carlos looked at his brother with absolute loathing. This pious, insignificant Franciscan monk had singlehandedly destroyed an empire. "Why Philippe? Why? What possessed you to do such evil and wipe out everything I've worked so hard to achieve?" Carlos screamed at him.

Phillipe remained calm, his voice steady. "Carlos, we both know you built your empire on lies and treachery. God knows how many lives you destroyed while you filled your coffers, and brother, I do not negate my part in this. Without my help, none of it would have been possible.

Carlos turned his back to Philippe, barely able to look at him. He snarled, "You still haven't said why? And for what? It's quite clearly not for personal gain. You have always been satisfied living like a pauper!" He looked around at what he considered miserable living conditions.

Philippe stood, "You wouldn't understand, Carlos; you were different. Nothing was ever good enough for you. You always had to have more. We could see it was never going to end."

"We?" Carlos shouted, spinning around to face Philippe.

"Peter and I discussed how we might get you to see reason but realised you would never negotiate. The only way was to force you to see how wrong it was to destroy anyone standing in your way. The one way to accomplish that was to remove the means. You still have clear title to your property Solitario in Santa Fe and Hierro Castillo in Santa Rosa, both valuable and successfully functioning ranches that generate a lot of money."

Carlos punched Philippe as hard as possible, sending blood spurting from his brother's nose. "How dare you and Peter decide my life for me. I was one of the wealthiest men in the country and going to be the next President of Argentina. You self-righteous little nothing, doing me the *favour* of letting me keep two miserable properties!"

Philippe staggered to his feet, still trying to stem the blood dripping onto his nightshirt.

Carlos, beyond words, picked up the Crucifix smashing it onto the side table, violently dislodging the base, sending it flying across the room. "To hell with you, Peter, and your useless God." With that, he stepped up to Philippe plunging the exposed shaft of the Crucifix deep into his brother's chest. The shocked look on Philippe's face lasted only seconds before the metal sliced through his heart.

Carlos watched Philippe slide to the floor, not feeling one ounce of remorse. All he could think of in his crazed state was 'an eye for an eye'. There was no turning back now. There was just one more eye that needed to be ripped out.

When one seeks revenge, they should first dig two graves

CONFUCIUS

☼

Carlos lay staring at the ceiling, strangely calm following the previous few days. He'd mainly travelled at night, resting through the day in abandoned shelters or farms. Sleep was fitful; his mind obsessed with one thing: paying a final visit to his brother Peter in Santa Rosa.

Even in his manic state, the logistics of such a journey from Villa Maria to Santa Rosa had not escaped him. There was far too much open space devoid of resources to head directly there. He needed to plan the trip carefully. He headed southeast to the Mendoza property at Perjamino, then Lujan, intending to skirt Buenos Aires and restock supplies at Riachuelo. He was well known there, often frequenting a brothel in his early days of campaigning. They would know better than to refuse him entry. He would wait until dark before leaving for Santa Rosa. One thing was working in Carlos's favour. The seasonal rain had started, a deluge, keeping most people indoors; he managed to pass unnoticed.

The collapse of the Mendoza empire was now widely known, a source of joy for some and trepidation for others. Carlos had a lot of enemies, but even those he considered friends were as tainted by corruption as he. They would not protect him, hoping he might be hunted and killed, relieved, knowing the secrets they shared would die with him.

336

News reporting the murder of the Governor's brother was spreading. Carlos was the prime suspect. Most of his troupe of soldiers and gaucho thugs would be on the lookout for him. Despite their corrupt behaviour under his direction, he knew they would not turn a blind eye in this instance. Carlos had not only murdered his brother but a servant of the Holy Church, a mortal sin that could not go unpunished.

Carlos tossed and turned, his sleep filled with nightmares of his mother's abandonment and his father's death. He awoke in a lather of sweat, reflecting on his forty-five years, trying to remember when he was truly happy. Philippe's words kept ringing in his head, *"Nothing was ever good enough for you; you always wanted bigger and better."* There were moments of pleasure, but none gave him lasting happiness. His marriage to Rosa for political expedience had been a disaster. His many luxurious mansions never enjoyed; they merely gave him status. He was always away scheming for bigger and better things. Carlos could only ever recall two people in his life for whom he held anything resembling affection. Aida, his housekeeper, and his beloved father. Carlos started weeping at the thought of them both deceased; it was the only time he shed a tear in his life.

A cold wind whistled through the heart of Santa Rosa. Peter, not yet risen for early morning prayers, was jolted awake. He was filled with a sense of foreboding. He lay there disoriented at first; sure, he heard someone calling his name. Surmising it was the wind howling through the shutters, he berated himself for being so foolish; getting out of bed, he made his way to the kitchen to light up the wood stove and warm his chilled bones.

Throughout the morning, the sense of unease remained. Following lunch, Peter chattered with the groundsman about a few minor repairs before the storm season hit with full force. Peter looked up, hearing the sound of a wagon approaching the church's front entrance, surprised to see it was Senor Torella, the storekeeper. Not expecting a delivery of supplies, Peter wondered what on earth brought him to Our Lady of The Rosary; he was not known for his piety. Peter smiled at the thought as he walked outside to greet him.

One look at Paco Torella stopped Peter in his tracks; the man's face was ashen and full of sorrow.

"Fr Peter, I am the bearer of terrible news, I'm afraid; perhaps you should sit down?"

Peter didn't move; in his heart, he knew the burden of feeling he'd carried all morning was for a reason, "Please, just tell me the news, Senor Torella."

Lowering his head, the poor man couldn't bear to witness the look on the priest's face when he shared the message on the telegraph,

"I am sorry to inform you, Fr Peter, your brother Philippe has been murdered, allegedly by the Governor, Carlos Mendoza."

Peter grasped Paco's arm to steady himself, almost collapsing. Lowering himself onto the church's steps, he made the sign of the cross and began to weep.

"I don't know what to say, Fr Peter, such a terrible thing to happen. Is there anyone I can contact for you?"

Peter sat shaking his head, tears running down his face. He knew there would be retribution for the plan he and Philippe put together to bring Carlos to heel, but never in his wildest imagination did he envisage it would cost Philippe his life. Peter knew Carlos would be livid and most likely end any association with his brothers, but never this.

Peter believed Carlos had lost his sanity to do something so heinous. Carlos defined his position in life by his wealth; without it, he considered himself nothing. Philippe had paid the ultimate price. Peter knew what came next. He didn't even have to ask where Carlos was. Beyond any doubt, he was on his way to Santa Rosa.

Riachuelo – Rio La Plata

☼

1858

The whole of the country was in turmoil. The Governor had disappeared, a bounty on his head, implicated in several murders. The economy of Argentina was on the brink of collapse. There was a great deal of conjecture the two were somehow linked.

Overnight, all the enterprises connected to Mendoza Holdings were under siege. At the first hint of trouble, the vultures gathered, eager to grab their share of the spoils before the Government Liquidators stepped in.

Many were shocked at the enormous portfolio of properties Carlos had compiled. He was asset-rich but cash poor. Over the previous twelve months, he had been quietly selling off large portions of his holdings and some other investments, amassing a small fortune in funds—his sole aim was to be one of the founding fathers of Argentine Rail. Despite sharing ownership with the British, Carlos realised it was akin to having a license to print money.

Carlos stirred from a troubled sleep, pulling the bedclothes up around him; he was shivering but covered in a lather of sweat. His throat was dry, and his head ached. He had a fever. Sitting up, he looked around, confused. Huddled in the corner was a woman, naked except for a woven blanket wrapped tightly around her bruised body. Her hair was dishevelled, her face fearful. The most noticeable detail, she was tethered to a solid oak robe by a thick leather strap like some domestic animal.

Carlos's head cleared momentarily; even feeling unwell, he managed to smirk, remembering his arrival, and becoming reacquainted with the Madam of the house. There was a reason

Carlos chose her. Vera wasn't the most buxom or desirable, but she owned the brothel and was his insurance.

Carlos didn't delude himself for one minute. Any one of the whores working there would hand him over to the authorities at a minute's notice. A bounty on his head made the prospect even more enticing. However, their only means of employment rested on the survival of their Madam – Vera.

Carlos turned up late afternoon the previous day in the middle of a severe thunderstorm, drenched to the bone. There were no other callers; one of the girls welcomed him in before Vera realised it was her old client, Carlos. She was only too aware of the recent catastrophic circumstances he'd left in his wake. Any thought of refusing him entry was gone; it was too late.

"Vera, I have missed your company and that of your companions. I haven't been this way for a while. I thought it was time we caught up."

Vera tried to stay calm, but she was terrified. She had no idea why Carlos was south of Buenos Aires, but she would do whatever she could to accommodate his wishes. He was a dangerous man, not one to be crossed. He always paid well for the services of her girls, but he was a cruel man and enjoyed inflicting pain. Vera desperately tried to decide which of her girls could cope with his often-perverse pleasures.

As if reading her mind, Carlos smiled, "Let me set your mind at rest, Vera; on this occasion, no one can satisfy my desires other than you, my dear. The weather changed my plans, but I'll be gone first light; never fear."

Vera felt ill; she began to shake, now happy to offer up anyone in her place. "Carlos, look around; many girls are more beautiful than I. Take your pick; I expect no fee. It is my treat, for old times' sake."

Carlos smiled at the suggestion. Vera was in no position to bargain, and she knew it. With a sinking heart, she realised Carlos choosing her was no accident.

Carlos addressed the room full of scantily clad young women, all sitting bolt upright, too scared to speak or move.

"Ladies, Vera will have the pleasure of entertaining me overnight. I suggest you close the establishment and enjoy the night off. It would also be unwise to answer the door to strangers for security reasons." There was an ominous tone in Carlos's voice. "It's been a tiresome journey, be so good as to bring food and dry clothing to Vera's room."

With that, he propelled Vera ahead of him up the stairs without looking back, calling over his shoulder in a booming voice, "If anyone entertains the idea of sending for help, I'll slit Vera's throat... so that you understand."

By the time Vera entered her room, she was weeping silently, scared out of her wits, more frightened than ever before. By all accounts, Carlos had killed three people so far, including his brother; she had no doubt, given any reason, he would happily make her his fourth.

Carlos was already stepping out of his wet clothes as the door closed behind him, his manhood erect, an evil smirk on his face, excited by her abject fear.

"Take your clothes off now."

The fever was playing tricks with his mind. Vera's face looked distorted, or was that just where he'd hit her? Carlos dragged his body out of bed; it must be time to be on his way. Vera cowered as he made his way to the window. The pounding rain showed no signs of abating. Looking down below, what was once a muddy quagmire, had disappeared under a foot of water. In the distance, he could see the swollen river. Carlos was suddenly dismayed; if he was to cross the Puente de Galvez bridge safely, he had to go now. It was the only way to Santa Rosa. He didn't have a choice.

Quickly donning dry clothes, he gathered his things, swallowed the last mouthful of tequila in the glass by the bed, and headed out the door and down the steps. His carriage was standing where he had left it. The horses were unsettled, left hitched to the carriage overnight; they were not going to move without persuasion. Carlos raised his whip, slashing it across the horse's rump. Rearing up, it almost fell, barely gaining footing before galloping forward.

341

Men grouped around the entrance road to the bridge were halting all foot traffic. The water was lapping over the edge of the bridge with a torrent of water coming from upstream, joining the main river.

Carlos worked his carriage between the onlookers. Someone was shouting up to him over the howling rain,

"You'd be a fool to try and cross Senor; it's too dangerous." Carlos ignored the warning. Thinking Carlos hadn't heard him, the man grasped the horse's bridle to lead it to one side.

Carlos lashed out with the whip striking the man across the face, spurring his horses forward onto the bridge. There was no turning back. Carlos could see there was only a little water on the bridge itself at present. He thought the others were fools.

The horses, already skittish, trod warily across the timber planks, unable to see their footing for the water. They moved gingerly at first, slowly gaining confidence as they worked their way forward. They were about halfway across when Carlos felt the bridge shudder. He never saw the wall of water. The storm silenced the sound of the rushing water as it took out the first two wooden columns of the bridge and then the bridge itself; Carlos, the carriage and the horses were lost in the foaming Riachuelo River.

Carlos's sins were washed away by the hand of God.

Restitution

Since the massacre of the government troops, Miguel remained uneasy. Such an assault was bound to bring retribution. That unexpected encounter clearly showed their mountain camp's location had been breached. Not once did he suspect it was Rosa, but he knew Carmelita or Ernesto would likely betray the rebel camp if it meant saving their own necks. The fort at Cordoba increased the search parties hunting the rebels; finding the right trail was challenging but not impossible. It was only a matter of time.

When he went searching for Rosa, he left Vincente in charge. They both agreed the winter camp would do for the time being. It was fortunate they came upon the soldiers far to the north of their intended location, leaving no indication of where they were heading.

Regardless, Miguel's uneasiness continued. Both Carmelita and Ernesto knew where the winter camp was also. In all likelihood, that information was in the hands of the army by now. If their search of the mountains proved fruitless, it would only be a matter of time before they investigated this area.

Miguel tried not to think about Rosa. The memories were bittersweet. Their time together was so brief. Finding her gone after their night together, he was so angry. Deep inside, he understood why she left, but anger was easier to deal with than longing.

Shots echoed across the valley; they came from the sentries on guard. The whole camp scrambled to their defence positions, rifles at the ready. Miguel had his men build a barricade as a precaution. Where the rift opened into the valley was a bottleneck, no wider than two men. There was every chance they could defend their position if there were a charge.

They could hear men shouting… "Don't shoot, don't shoot, it's all over!"

One of their scouts from La Cumbrecita, Emilio, burst into the clearing, his arms raised, his face beaming. "The government has fallen; the whole of Argentina is in chaos."

Miguel was shocked, like everyone else, eager to know what had happened.

"They are saying the governor went insane, killing his brother, a Franciscan Monk and several others during his rampage. He was in hiding for a while in Riachuelo. His intention, it seems, was to escape inland, but he drowned when the Puente de Galvez bridge collapsed."

The camp erupted, the noise deafening. In an instant, the fear of attack was gone, and a celebration took place instead. Miguel gave up a silent prayer; it would end the years of corrupt government. What a strange time; he was desperate to see their struggle end but hadn't contemplated what would come next. He had been fighting this battle now for over five years. Accepting the conflict was over felt surreal.

The camp took less than a week to dismantle. Many abandoned what they couldn't carry with them. Everyone was eager to head home; most had no idea what they might find.

Miguel and several others cautiously headed into Cordoba. The place was a shambles. People had rioted, smashing or looting anything remotely connected to the government. There was a lot of public anger. The clean-up was just beginning. Miguel headed for the telegraph office to get the latest reports. Similar things were happening all over the country. The Capital had been under siege. Most of the soldiers and other government thugs fled in fear of reprisals, those choosing to remain were quickly overcome and thrown in jail.

The political hierarchy unravelled with Carlos's untimely death. Sweeping changes took place almost at once, as influential community leaders seized the opportunity to regain control of the parliament and the department of justice, bringing the country into some semblance of order. Many of the corrupt perpetrators fled, avoiding imprisonment.

Miguel hadn't anticipated how hard it would be to say farewell to his men at arms. They had become like brothers, defending each other, sharing the hardships, and easing the loneliness. Their lives could begin again. Miguel wasn't sure what that meant for him.

A few others joined Miguel in heading to the Capital. They needed to petition whoever was in charge for the return of their land and titles. The political situation would take time to amend, but at last, there was the hope of a free Argentina.

Ataliva Roca

☼

1858

Before Miguel crossed the boundary into Ataliva Roca, the tears were falling. What should have been a time of grand celebration was overshadowed by sadness. Landholdings finally returned to rightful owners; Argentina was free from the tyranny of corrupt officials for the first time in nearly twenty years. Rich fields had lain barren for so long, ranching and mining in disarray. At last, there was a chance for the country to heal and restore its shattered economy bled dry by greedy politicians and their followers.

Miguel stood on the threshold of Garcia property, incredulous to think his departure was a mere five years earlier—the things experienced during his absence seemed like another lifetime; his heart was desolate. The hideous memories of that last day imprinted on his brain forever, a recurring nightmare that disturbed his sleep many times. Justice had finally prevailed, but it was an empty victory for Miguel.

The journey to the hacienda was slow; there was no need to hurry. There would be no Theresa rushing to greet her big brother as she squealed with delight. No mother's loving arms encircling him, her head pressed against his chest. Closing his eyes, he could smell the lavender she often pinned to her golden locks. Hidalgo would be standing one pace behind Elizabeth, smiling proudly. Although Miguel never doubted Hidalgo's boundless love for him, a firm handshake and pat on the back were the only display of affection his father ever expressed, how his heart ached for them all.

Approaching the familiar hacienda, Miguel was surprised at how orderly everything looked, even seeing cattle and horses in the distant holding pens. Had somebody tended the grounds recently? Dismounting, tethering his horse to the hitching rail, Miguel's heart was pounding, anxiety building in his throat. He was finding it hard to breathe. Unexpectedly the heavy oak doors swung open. Much to Miguel's shock and disbelief, Elena and her husband, Jose` emerged. Elena, weeping, threw herself into Miguel's arms, relieved he was still alive.

They all tried to speak at once, Miguel questioning where they had been during the upheaval. He wondered many times whether they had survived the raiding party. Elena wanted to know every detail of Miguel's journey and how he'd managed to stay alive. A cloud passed over Elena's face noting Miguel's tear-stained face. Someone had to start the conversation about Hidalgo, Elizabeth and Theresa.

Miguel listened in silence as Elena explained how the ranch hands fled with their families, fearing death when the raid started, returning after the soldiers had gone, and finding the horrific scene Miguel left behind. Elena recounted the care taken in laying his father, mother and sister to rest under the weeping Mayten trees at the side of the family chapel. Miguel sobbed openly, a broken man all over again.

When he left four years earlier, Miguel's one regret was abandoning his family. So filled with rage, his only thought was to avenge their deaths. They were beyond help, but now he felt great shame having left them. Elena's arms encircled him, just as his mothers would have. Instead, they comforted each other in their shared grief. While Ataliva Roca would never be the same as before, it would always be home.

Springtime was always such a beautiful time at Ataliva Roca; Miguel sat quietly on one of the ornately carved benches his mother loved so much. It once graced the veranda of the hacienda. He had it placed under the trees sheltering the three white crosses, his family's final resting place. The afternoon breeze was soothing. He watched tiny pale green flowers dispelled from the branches above settle on the ground, blanketing the graves. It was somehow comforting.

Miguel developed the habit of sitting there at dusk until nightfall claimed the last of the light. He often contemplated how different life might have been if his family were still alive. An air of melancholy settled over him, his ability to function at times overwhelmed.

Slowly Ataliva Roca was returning to its former glory. During the soldier's attack, the ranch hands had driven the cattle and horses far west into the hills and beyond, where they could free range undisturbed, away from the reaches of the criminals who murdered the Garcia family. They rounded up the extensive herd in anticipation of taking them to market. Production in the fields was in full swing. Great stretches of maize spread across vast tracts of pasture, the crowning golden tassels weaving in the wind, ready for harvesting.

Miguel lay stretched across his bed, exhausted after a long day's toil, a gentle breeze playing across his naked body. He acknowledged the growing emptiness he felt inside. The absence of his family hit him hard. Almost a year after his return, the pain remained intense. Although their deaths occurred years before, it wasn't until he came back to Ataliva Roca did he genuinely begin to mourn their loss. The grieving process was not something anyone could control.

Progress throughout Argentina was massive; every province was flourishing. Farmers and sharecroppers returned to their abandoned properties to start anew, just as many would never return. Miguel felt revulsion sweep over him briefly, recalling the mass grave he and his travelling companions stumbled on heading to the rebel camp. Other sites were found later. They might never know the accurate tally of those ruthlessly murdered.

Miguel tried not to let his thoughts wander there, but his mind eventually turned to his time spent in the mountain camp. Rarely did he think about the hardships experienced, the men who became comrades, or even the ever-present danger. Some things were tinged with sadness, others with regret, even shame, but mostly his thoughts were about Rosa. Eventually, they all culminated in Miguel remembering their night of passion. He smiled in the darkness.

How bitterly they had argued about Rosa leaving. Somewhere in that fury, it had turned to desire. At that moment, he wanted her more than he had ever wanted anything else in his life. Miguel rarely embraced such memories, the agony and the ecstasy of that night too much to bear. He could still recall the feel of her mouth on his, the sensation on his lips as they caressed her body, feel her arch beneath him as he entered her, hear her soft moans of pleasure…

When Miguel searched for Rosa in Santa Fe after the conflict ended, he found the Governor's mansion had been burnt to the ground. Enquiries at the Convent Hospital proved fruitless. All searches came to a dead end; it was as if she had disappeared from the face of the earth.

Since then, Miguel had not seriously considered Rosa's whereabouts before this moment. He had wondered about her returning to Carlos when she fled the camp. While the only sensible course of action, Rosa's leaving did little to ease the ache in his heart. Back then, there was no possibility they could be together. There were no barriers any longer…only Rosa herself.

There was one person who would most likely know where she might be. In times of trouble, Rosa always turned to him, Father Peter, the priest at Our Lady of the Rosary Church in Santa Rosa, merely twenty-eight miles away. The solution was suddenly so simple. Miguel wondered why he'd not considered the idea before now.

When Miguel set off to find Rosa, he wasn't sure she would be receptive to seeing him. He'd risked her life when he went to the Governor's mansion to kill Carlos, later dragging her off a coach and holding her for ransom. Realising her kidnapping was a mistake, Miguel failed to protect her, leading to her defilement, finally taking advantage of her when she was most vulnerable. God, why would she want to see him?

Rosa might dismiss him without a second glance, but he would never know until he saw her again.

Finding Rosa
☼

Miguel entered the village church for the first time in many years; he had been baptised here long ago. Approaching the Priest in the chancel, he was shocked at Fr Peter's appearance; he was stooped over like an old man; time had not been kind to the priest. In light of the terrible things that affected their lives, he was sure the priest would have chosen to go as far away from Santa Rosa as possible.

They greeted each other warmly, exchanging small pleasantries. It had been so long since they had spent any time together. Miguel was fully aware of the part Fr Peter played in the tragic death of his older brother Philippe and, indirectly, the death of his other brother Carlos. It was apparent how much this affected him, weighing heavily on his soul.

Miguel enquired about Rosa's whereabouts as casually as possible, "I know how close you were to the Caron family, Father; I thought you may know where Senora Mendoza is living?"

The priest stood stock still, suddenly unsteady on his feet; he staggered as though he might fall. His face bore the strangest look, as though he had sustained a hard blow and was resisting the impact to avoid collapse. Miguel noted Fr Peter's pallor as the priest grasped desperately for the pew and sat down, putting his head in both hands...the prolonged silence was unbearable; Miguel could stand it no longer,

"Answer me, please, Father; surely there is no longer a need for secrecy; Rosa is finally safe."

The priest could barely raise his eyes to meet Miguel's pleading stare. Miguel gasped at the pain he could see etched on the priest's face, tears welling up and spilling down the older man's cheeks. Fr

Peter crossed himself as if the words forced from his lips were causing him physical pain; they tumbled out in a rush, each driving a knife through Miguel's heart. "Praise be to God, may she rest in peace," he continued, blessing himself, his words barely above a whisper. "I cannot talk of it; it's not mine to tell." There were no more words to be spoken, the silence all-encompassing as if they were in a vacuum.

Miguel felt dizzy and realised he was holding his breath. This was incredulous. Life couldn't be that cruel, surely, not after what they had been through, to have it snatched away. Feeling as though he was in some surreal nightmare, he heard his words, harsh, desolate, "Where is she?" he asked, his face now ashen, his voice full of despair.

The priest pointed towards the stained-glass window on the church's upper side without rising.

Miguel recalled the monotonous rhythm of his horses' hooves on the road. He was weary, relieved his quest was almost complete. Rounding the bend, the church came into view at the bottom of the hill. He remembered admiring the beautiful jacarandas in full bloom. He barely noticed the considerable number of white crosses and headstones scattered along the hillside; they held no real significance...until now.

Slowly, Miguel made his way toward the entrance, his leaden footsteps echoing on the uneven flagstone blocks; the only other sound a dove fluttering somewhere high above in the rafters. Briefly startled, Miguel looked up, his eyes glancing momentarily on the alabaster statue of the Holy Mother, her arms outstretched as if expressing her helplessness, a look of benevolence on her face.

Miguel stepped out into the blinding sunlight. It all felt so wrong. How could life go on as usual when it felt like his whole world had disintegrated once more?

Miguel wiped the back of his riding glove across his brow, sweeping away the sweat and grime, suddenly chilled inside despite the blazing sun overhead. Glancing from each wooden cross to the next, feeling greater despair with each fruitless step, finally, there it was, a short distance from the others – stark, white, solitary, bearing her name in bold letters... 'ROSALINDA CARON.' She had reverted to her maiden name, one final attempt to erase Carlos from her life forever.

Miguel's knee's buckled, the tranquillity shattered by guttural sobs wracking his body. Only now, when it was too late, did he allow himself to acknowledge the depth of his love for Rosa. Miguel had never felt so lost and alone. Rosa was his first love, his only love. Unbidden, born of mutual pain inflicted by the same evil, they were drawn together as enemies and parted as lovers. His heart ached at what might have been.

When Miguel experienced his family's terrible loss, he thought it impossible to feel such agonising pain again; he was wrong. How long he sat there grieving, staring at Rosa's grave, he couldn't say, but giving more thought to her death, he became increasingly puzzled about the circumstances. Why? How? What was it about Rosa's death Fr Peter wasn't saying?

The smell of sweet lavender drifted into his consciousness, and for the first time, Miguel took notice of the small posy of flowers below the cross, touching them gently, letting his fingers trail through the soft petals, almost with reverence. Miguel's brow furrowed; who brought the flowers, he wondered. Fr Peter? He didn't think so. They were fresh, placed earlier that day, no doubt. Miguel looked around, noting there was no one nearby, only two scrawny dogs chasing each other in circles and an old man with a donkey and cart laden with hay in the distance. Instinctively Miguel knew fresh flowers would come again – and he would be waiting!

Mid-morning the next day, Miguel saw her in the distance, a relatively young, attractive woman carrying a bunch of flowers in her left hand, a child perched on her right hip, his tiny arms hooked around her neck. He could hear her melodic voice as she chatted happily with the child. Miguel kept out of sight in the tree line as she approached the graveyard.

Placing the child on the ground to run off and play, she made the sign of the cross before kneeling in front of Rosa's grave, lovingly laying the tiny bouquet on the grave and removing the spent flowers from yesterday. Her hands clasped together; she began praying quietly, her voice just above a whisper. Miguel could see the sadness on her face. Before he stepped out to her side, he allowed her time to complete her prayers.

Speaking softly, he asked, "Who are you? What was Rosa to you?"

Startled, the girl cried, "Please, Senor, don't hurt me, I beg you."

Miguel raised his hand quickly to reassure her he meant no harm. "I'm sorry, I didn't mean to frighten you; I only ask because… Rosa was special to me." The words caught in Miguel's throat, threatening to choke him.

The young woman relaxed, eyeing Miguel closely before replying, "My name is Maria; Rosa was my sister."

With that, she started to weep softly, as much out of relief, knowing Miguel posed no threat, as with the sadness that overwhelmed her whenever she came here. Again, Miguel apologised for startling her. While he was trying to comfort her, they both became aware of the tiny infant tugging at the sleeve of Maria's blouse. Maria blessed herself once more before standing, quickly gathering up the restless child into her arms, slowly turning as she did so towards Miguel, noting his sadness and studying his face closely. Suddenly a look of joy illuminated her face, her eyes wide, staring incredulously.

"You are Miguel?" she asked tentatively, a hint of excitement and desperation in her voice.

Miguel nodded, frowning, wondering what Rosa had shared about their time together.

Maria's voice caught in her throat; fighting back the tears, she held out the small wriggling boy towards Miguel.

"I knew you would come to receive Rosa's final gift of love, Senor – the one she created, despite knowing it would cost her life."

Miguel, now totally bewildered, received the child into his arms, his heart skipping a beat. He looked down into a tiny face, the image of Rosa's - but for one exception, the brightest blue eyes imaginable!

Maria smiled, "His name is Delgado…Delgardo Miguel Garcia."

Suddenly life had a whole new meaning.

The Author
☼

When her marriage ended in 1992, Bev Young's passion for writing was put on hold, superseded by the need for a steady income. A qualified Registered Nurse, she moved to Sydney to specialise in Palliative Care until relocating to Queensland in 2004. She continued nursing in aged care, retiring in 2018 to pursue writing full-time.

Spare time away from writing, Bev indulged her love for travel and regular visits with her only son Anthony and daughter-in-law, Wendy. Their fantastic property near Baffle Creek in Queensland is always enticing, with freshly caught fish, prawns and mud crabs.

Glossary

ALCADESA	Mayor
ALGARROBO	A native tree belonging to the carob family, with medicinal qualities
ALMACEN	General Store
ASADA	Bar-B-Cue
BOLAS	Weighted cords used to 'bring down' an animal by wrapping around their legs
BOMBACHES	Full pleated breeches (pants), part of distinctive clothing worn by Gauchos
CABALLO	Horse
CABALLERIA	Cavalry
CARINA	Term of endearment – 'sweet', 'honey'
CARRETAS	Huge goods wagon up to three metres high, drawn by three pairs of oxen
CASA	House
CAUDILLOS	Band of armed men
CEIBO	The national tree of Argentina. Profuse flowers of red.
CHICHA	Alcohol brewed from maize
CHIRIPA	A waistband with multiple purposes (for a weapon, money) worn by Gauchos
CIMARRON	Introduced animals, wild, belonging to anyone (horses, cattle)
COMISERIA	Police station
CRIOLES	People of European ancestry
DIABLO	Devil
ESPINAL	Thorny Grasslands found in parts of Argentina
ESTANCIA	Ranch

FALCONE	Long curved knife with a silver handle, usually elaborately engraved
GALERAS	A type of stage coach pulled by four horses, able to hold up to ten people
GAUCHO	A cowboy of the South American Pampas (Usually Spanish and Native origin)
GUANACO	Native animal closely related to Llamas
GUARANI	An indigenous tribe, along with Quechua, Querandi and many more.
HIERRO CASTILLO	Iron Castle
HACIENDA	A large estate or plantation, with a dwelling.
MALONE	Indian raid
MESTIZOS	People of mixed Spanish and Indigenous native heritage
OMBU TREES	Predominant native tree resistant to fire
PAMPA	Land mass in Argentina named by Quechua natives - meaning 'flat plain'
PEON	Unskilled Labourer
POSADA	Rest stop for travellers, and for exchange of horses or oxen
PULPERIA	A place where alcohol is served
QUINA-QUINA	Native tree, the bark used to produce Quinine, anti-malarial medicine
RHEA	Large native (flightless) bird, similar to the African Ostrich and Australian Emu
SANGRE	Blood
SEMENTAL	Stallion
SERAPE	The specific gait (horse) employed by gaucho riders
SOLDADO	Soldiers
SOLITARIO LOBO	Lone wolf
TOLDERIAS	Indian camps
TORO	Bull
TORTILLA	Pancake like flat bread made from maize flour

Annoted Bibliography
☼

Blondich, A.S.(et al)(2016). *Coca:* the history and medical significance of an ancient Andean tradition. Emergency Medical International. PMC free article, PMID: 27144028.

Borchers, Andrea. T,(et al)(Aug 2000). *Inflammation and Native American medicine:* the role of botanicals. The American Journal of Clinical Nutrition, Vol.72, Issue 2, 339-347.

Britannica, The Editors of the Encyclopedia. *Cinchona.* Encyclopaedia Britannica(2018, 9th Nov). https://www.britannica.com/plant/cinchona. Accessed 26th April, 2022.

Bandoni, A.J., Chekherdemian, M.F., Cruz.(1978). Farmacopea Nacional Argentina. 6th Edition. Editorial Codea.S.A. Buenos Aires.

Malar, J.(et al)(2011). *Quinine, an old anti-malarial drug in a modern world:* role in the Treatment of malaria. PMC free article Google Scholar. Published Online, 2011, May 24th doi:10:1186/1475-2875-10-144.

Meade. Teresa, A.(2016). History of Modern Latin America: 1800 to the present. Pub: Wiley Blackwell; 2nd Edition(8th Jan 2016).

Molares, S.(et al)(2009). *Ethnobotanical review of the Mapuche medicinal flora:* use patterns on a regional scale. Ethnopharmacol 2009. Mar 18; 122(2):251-60 doi:10.1016/j.jep.

2009.01.003. Epub 2009, Jan 8th.

Priestly, Joseph. (1733-1804). Wood Library Museum: The History of Anesthesiology. Reprint Series: Part 11-Nitrous Oxide. wlmrep_11_11pdf.pdf.

Hoss de le Comte, Monica Goria. (2009). The Pampa. Publisher:Maizal, Buenos Aires, Argentina.

Scuchman,Mark.D.(1990). Childhood Education and Politics in Nineteenth Century Argentina: The case of Buenos Aires. The Hispanic American Historical Review. Vol.70, No.1(Feb 1990). Pp109-138. Pub: Duke university Press.

Szuchman, Mark.D.(1988). Order, Family and Community in Buenos Aires 1810-1860, Stanford University Press, 1988. Xiii, 307pp.

Wikepedia Foundation: Cathedrals in Argentina. http://en.wikipedia.org/wiki/List_of_Cathedrals_in_Argentina. Last edited 11th Mar, 2022.

Secondary Source: www.gcatholic.org

Wikepedia Foundation, citing: Falkner, Thomas.(1774). *Puelches:*A description of Patagonia and the adjoining part of South America. P.99. Publisher, C.Pugh.

Wikepedia Foundation: Mendoza, Argentina. https://en.wikipedia.org/wiki/Mendoza_Argentina. Last Updated 9th Dec 2020, ppm1-8.

Wikepedia Foundation, citing: Nicholson, G.Edward.(1960).*Chicha maize types and chicha Manufacture in Peru:* Economic Botany.14(4):290-299. Doi.10.1007/BF02908039. S2ID 36357387.

www.ingramcontent.com/pod-product-compliance
Lightning Source LLC
Chambersburg PA
CBHW030513120726
47904CB00005B/1449